P9-APC-257

JOHN REED

TEN DAYS THAT SHOOK THE WORLD

JOHN REED

TEN DAYS THAT SHOOK THE WORLD

TEN DAYS THAT SHOOK THE WORLD

BY

JOHN REED

CONTENTS

PREFACE

THIS book is a slice of intensified history—history as I saw it. It does not pretend to be anything but a detailed account of the November Revolution, when the Bolsheviki, at the head of the workers and soldiers, seized the state power of Russia and placed it in the hands of the Soviets.

Naturally most of it deals with "Red Petrograd," the capital and heart of the insurrection. But the reader must realize that what took place in Petrograd was almost exactly duplicated, with greater or lesser intensity, at different intervals of time, all over Russia.

In this book, the first of several which I am writing, I must confine myself to a chronicle of those events which I myself observed and experienced, and those supported by reliable evidence; preceded by two chapters briefly outlining the background and causes of the November Revolution. I am aware that these two chapters make difficult reading, but they are essential to an understanding of what follows.

Many questions will suggest themselves to the mind of the reader. What is Bolshevism? What kind of a governmental structure did the Bolsheviki set up? If the Bolsheviki championed the Constituent Assembly before the November Revolution, why did they disperse it by force of arms afterward? And if the bourgeoisie opposed the Constituent Assembly until the danger of Bolshevism became apparent, why did they champion it afterward?

These and many other questions cannot be answered here. In another volume, "Kornilov to Brest-Litovsk," I trace the course of the Revolution up to and including the German peace. There I explain the origin and functions of the Revolutionary organisations, the evolution of popular sentiment, the dissolution of the Constituent Assembly, the structure of the Soviet state, and the course and outcome of the Brest- Litovsk negotiations....

In considering the rise of the Bolsheviki it is necessary to understand that Russian economic life and the Russian army were not disorganised on November 7th, 1917, but many months before, as the logical result of a process which began as far back as 1915. The corrupt reactionaries in control of the Tsar's Court deliberately undertook to wreck Russia in order to make a separate peace with Germany. The lack of arms on the front, which had caused the great retreat of the summer of 1915, the lack of food in the army and in the great cities, the break-down of manufactures and transportation in 1916—all these we know now were part of a gigantic campaign of sabotage. This was halted just in time by the March Revolution.

For the first few months of the new régime, in spite of the confusion incident upon a great Revolution, when one hundred and sixty millions of the world's most oppressed peoples suddenly achieved liberty, both the internal situation and the combative power of the army actually improved.

But the "honeymoon" was short. The propertied classes wanted merely a political revolution, which would take the power from the Tsar and give it to them. They wanted Russia to be a constitutional Republic, like France or the United States; or a constitutional Monarchy, like England. On the other hand, the masses of the people wanted real industrial and agrarian democracy.

William English Walling, in his book, "Russia's Message," an account of the Revolution of 1905, describes very well the state of mind of the Russian workers, who were later to support Bolshevism almost unanimously:

They (the working people) saw it was possible that even under a free Government, if it fell into the hands of other social classes, they might still continue to starve....

The Russian workman is revolutionary, but he is neither violent, dogmatic, nor unintelligent. He is ready for barricades, but he has studied them, and alone of the workers of the world he has learned about them from actual experience. He is ready and willing to fight his oppressor, the capitalist class, to a finish. But he does not ignore the existence of other classes. He merely asks that the other classes take one side or the other in the bitter conflict that draws near....

They (the workers) were all agreed that our (American) political institutions were preferable to their own, but they were not very anxious to exchange one despot for another (i.e., the capitalist class)....

The workingmen of Russia did not have themselves shot down, executed by hundreds in Moscow, Riga and Odessa, imprisoned by thousands in every Russian jail, and exiled to the deserts and the arctic regions, in exchange for the doubtful privileges of the workingmen of Goldfields and Cripple Creek....

And so developed in Russia, in the midst of a foreign war, the Social Revolution on top of the Political Revolution, culminating in the triumph of Bolshevism.

Mr. A. J. Sack, director in this country of the Russian Information Bureau, which opposes the Soviet Government, has this to say in his book, "The Birth of the Russian Democracy": The Bolsheviks organised their own cabinet, with Nicholas Lenine as Premier and Leon Trotsky— Minister of Foreign Affairs. The inevitability of their coming into power became evident almost immediately after the March Revolution. The history of the Bolsheviki, after the Revolution, is a history of their steady growth....

Foreigners, and Americans especially, frequently emphasise the "ignorance" of the Russian workers. It is true they lacked the political experience of the peoples of the West, but they were very well trained in voluntary organisation. In 1917 there were more than twelve million members of the Russian consumers' Cooperative societies; and the Soviets themselves are a wonderful demonstration of their organising genius. Moreover, there is probably not a people in the world so well educated in Socialist theory and its practical application.

William English Walling thus characterises them:

The Russian working people are for the most part able to read and write. For many years the country has been in such a disturbed condition that they have had the advantage of leadership not only of intelligent individuals in their midst, but of a large part of the equally revolutionary educated class, who have turned to the working people with their ideas for the political and social regeneration of Russia....

Many writers explain their hostility to the Soviet Government by arguing that the last phase of the Russian Revolution was simply a struggle of the "respectable" elements against the brutal attacks of Bolshevism. However, it was the propertied classes, who, when they realised the growth in power of the popular revolutionary organisations, undertook to destroy them and to halt the Revolution. To this end the propertied classes finally resorted to desperate measures. In order to wreck the Kerensky Ministry and the Soviets, transportation was disorganised and internal troubles provoked; to crush the Factory- Shop Committees, plants were shut down, and fuel and raw materials diverted; to break the Army Committees at the front, capital punishment was restored and military defeat connived at.

This was all excellent fuel for the Bolshevik fire. The Bolsheviki retorted by preaching the class war, and by asserting the supremacy of the Soviets.

Between these two extremes, with the other factions which whole- heartedly or half-heartedly supported them, were the so-called "moderate" Socialists, the Mensheviki and Socialist Revolutionaries, and several smaller parties. These groups were also attacked by the propertied classes, but their power of resistance was crippled by their theories.

Roughly, the Mensheviki and Socialist Revolutionaries believed that Russia was not economically ripe for a social revolution—that only a *political* revolution was possible. According to their interpretation, the Russian masses were not educated enough to take over the power; any attempt to do so would inevitably bring on a reaction, by means of which some ruthless opportunist might restore the old régime. And so it followed that when the "moderate" Socialists were forced to assume the power, they were afraid to use it.

They believed that Russia must pass through the stages of political and economic development known to Western Europe, and emerge at last, with the rest of the world, into full-fledged Socialism. Naturally, therefore, they agreed with the propertied classes that Russia must first be a parliamentary state—though with some improvements on the Western democracies. As a consequence, they insisted upon the collaboration of the propertied classes in the Government.

From this it was an easy step to supporting them. The "moderate" Socialists needed the bourgeoisie. But the bourgeoisie did not need the "moderate" Socialists. So it resulted in the

Socialist Ministers being obliged to give way, little by little, on their entire program, while the propertied classes grew more and more insistent.

And at the end, when the Bolsheviki upset the whole hollow compromise, the Mensheviki and Socialist Revolutionaries found themselves fighting on the side of the propertied classes…. In almost every country in the world to-day the same phenomenon is visible.

Instead of being a destructive force, it seems to me that the Bolsheviki were the only party in Russia with a constructive program and the power to impose it on the country. If they had not succeeded to the Government when they did, there is little doubt in my mind that the armies of Imperial Germany would have been in Petrograd and Moscow in December, and Russia would again be ridden by a Tsar….

It is still fashionable, after a whole year of the Soviet Government, to speak of the Bolshevik insurrection as an "adventure." Adventure it was, and one of the most marvellous mankind ever embarked upon, sweeping into history at the head of the toiling masses, and staking everything on their vast and simple desires. Already the machinery had been set up by which the land of the great estates could be distributed among the peasants. The Factory-Shop Committees and the Trade Unions were there to put into operation workers' control of industry. In every village, town, city, district and province there were Soviets of Workers', Soldiers' and Peasants' Deputies, prepared to assume the task of local administration.

No matter what one thinks of Bolshevism, it is undeniable that the Russian Revolution is one of the great events of human history, and the rise of the Bolsheviki a phenomenon of world-wide importance. Just as historians search the records for the minutest details of the story of the Paris Commune, so they will want to know what happened in Petrograd in November, 1917, the spirit which animated the people, and how the leaders looked, talked and acted. It is with this in view that I have written this book.

In the struggle my sympathies were not neutral. But in telling the story of those great days I have tried to see events with the eye of a conscientious reporter, interested in setting down the truth. J. R. New York, January 1st 1919.

Notes and Explanations

To the average reader the multiplicity of Russian organisations-political groups, Committees and Central Committees, Soviets, Dumas and Unions-will prove extremely confusing. For this reason I am giving here a few brief definitions and explanations.

Political Parties

In the elections to the Constituent Assembly, there were seventeen tickets in Petrograd, and in some of the provincial towns as many as forty; but the following summary of the aims and composition of political parties is limited to the groups and factions mentioned in this book. Only the essence of their programmes and the general character of their constituencies can be noticed....

1. *Monarchists,* of various shades, *Octobrists,* etc. These once-powerful factions no longer existed openly; they either worked underground, or their members joined the *Cadets,* as the *Cadets* came by degrees to stand for their political programme. Representatives in this book, Rodzianko, Shulgin.

2. *Cadets.* So-called from the initials of its name, Constitutional Democrats. Its official name is "Party of the People's Freedom." Under the Tsar composed of Liberals from the propertied classes, the *Cadets* were the great party of *political* reform, roughly corresponding to the Progressive Party in America. When the Revolution broke out in March, 1917, the *Cadets* formed the first Provisional Government. The *Cadet* Ministry was overthrown in April because it declared itself in favour of Allied imperialistic aims, including the imperialistic aims of the Tsar's Government. As the Revolution became more and more a *social economic* Revolution, the *Cadets* grew more and more conservative. Its representatives in this book are: Miliukov, Vinaver, Shatsky.

2a. *Group of Public Men*. After the *Cadets* had become unpopular through their relations with the Kornilov counter-revolution, the *Group of Public Men* was formed in Moscow. Delegates from the *Group of Public Men* were given portfolios in the last Kerensky Cabinet. The *Group* declared itself non-partisan, although its intellectual leaders were men like Rodzianko and Shulgin. It was composed of the more "modern" bankers, merchants and manufacturers, who were intelligent enough to realise that the Soviets must be fought by their own weapon-economic organisation. Typical of the *Group:* Lianozov, Konovalov.

3. *Populist Socialists,* or *Trudoviki* (Labour Group). Numerically a small party, composed of cautious intellectuals, the leaders of the Cooperative societies, and conservative peasants. Professing to be Socialists, the *Populists* really supported the interests of the petty bourgeoisie-clerks, shopkeepers, etc. By direct descent, inheritors of the compromising tradition of the Labour Group in the Fourth Imperial Duma, which was composed largely of peasant representatives. Kerensky was the leader of the *Trudoviki* in the Imperial Duma when the Revolution of March, 1917, broke out. The *Populist Socialists* are a nationalistic party. Their representatives in this book are: Peshekhanov, Tchaikovsky.

4. *Russian Social Democratic Labour Party.* Originally Marxian Socialists. At a party congress held in 1903, the party split, on the question of tactics, into two factions-the Majority (Bolshinstvo), and the Minority (Menshinstvo). From this sprang the names "Bolsheviki" and "Mensheviki"-"members of the majority" and "members of the minority." These two wings became two separate parties, both calling themselves "Russian Social Democratic Labour Party," and both professing to be Marxians. Since the Revolution of 1905 the Bolsheviki were really the minority, becoming again the majority in September, 1917.

a. *Mensheviki.* This party includes all shades of Socialists who believe that society must progress by natural evolution toward Socialism, and that the working-class must conquer political power first. Also a nationalistic party. This was the party of the Socialist intellectuals, which means: all the means of education having been in the hands of the propertied classes, the intellectuals instinctively reacted to their training, and took the side of the propertied classes. Among their representatives in this book are: Dan, Lieber, Tseretelli.

b. *Mensheviki Internationalists.* The radical wing of the *Mensheviki,* internationalists and opposed to all coalition with the propertied classes; yet unwilling to break loose from the conservative Mensheviki, and opposed to the dictatorship of the working-class advocated by the Bolsheviki. Trotzky was long a member of this group. Among their leaders: Martov, Martinov.

c. *Bolsheviki.* Now call themselves the *Communist Party,* in order to emphasise their complete separation from the tradition of "moderate" or "parliamentary" Socialism, which dominates the Mensheviki and the so-called Majority Socialists in all countries. The *Bolsheviki* proposed immediate proletarian insurrection, and seizure of the reins of Government, in order to hasten the coming of Socialism by forcibly taking over industry, land, natural resources and financial institutions. This party expresses the desires chiefly of the factory workers, but also of a large section of the poor peasants. The name "Bolshevik" can *not* be translated by "Maximalist." The Maximalists are a separate group. Among the leaders: Lenin, Trotzky, Lunatcharsky.

d. *United Social Democrats Internationalists.* Also called the *Novaya Zhizn* (New Life) group, from the name of the very influential newspaper which was its organ. A little group of intellectuals with a very small following among the working-class, except the personal following of Maxim Gorky, its leader. Intellectuals, with almost the same programme as the *Mensheviki Internationalists,* except that the *Novaya Zhizn* group refused to be tied to either of the two great factions. Opposed the Bolshevik tactics, but remained in the Soviet Government. Other representatives in this book: Avilov, Kramarov.

e. *Yedinstvo.* A very small and dwindling group, composed almost entirely of the personal following of Plekhanov, one of the pioneers of the Russian Social Democratic movement in the 80's, and its greatest theoretician. Now an old man, Plekhanov was extremely patriotic, too conservative even for the Mensheviki. After the Bolshevik *coup d'etat, Yedinstvo* disappeared.

5. *Socialist Revolutionary party.* Called *Essaires* from the initials of their name. Originally the revolutionary party of the peasants, the party of the Fighting Organisations-the Terrorists. After the March Revolution, it was joined by many who had never been Socialists. At that time it stood for the abolition of private property in land only, the owners to be compensated in some fashion. Finally the increasing revolutionary feeling of peasants forced the *Essaires* to abandon the "compensation" clause, and led to the younger and more fiery intellectuals breaking off from the main party in the fall of 1917 and forming a new party, the *Left Socialist Revolutionary party*. The *Essaires,* who were afterward always called by the radical groups *"Right Socialist Revolutionaries,"* adopted the political attitude of the Mensheviki, and worked together with them. They finally came to represent the wealthier peasants, the intellectuals, and the politically uneducated populations of remote rural districts. Among them there was, however, a wider difference of shades of political and economic opinion than among the Mensheviki. Among their leaders mentioned in these pages: Avksentiev, Gotz, Kerensky, Tchernov, "Babuschka" Breshkovskaya.

a. *Left Socialist Revolutionaries.* Although theoretically sharing the Bolshevik programme of dictatorship of the working-class, at first were reluctant to follow the ruthless Bolshevik tactics. However, the *Left Socialist Revolutionaries* remained in the Soviet Government, sharing the Cabinet portfolios, especially that of Agriculture. They withdrew from the Government several times, but always returned. As the peasants left the ranks of the *Essaires* in increasing numbers, they joined the *Left Socialist Revolutionary party,* which became the great peasant party supporting the Soviet Government, standing for confiscation without compensation of the great landed estates, and their disposition by the peasants themselves. Among the leaders: Spiridonova, Karelin, Kamkov, Kalagayev.

b. *Maximalists.* An off-shoot of the *Socialist Revolutionary party* in the Revolution of 1905, when it was a powerful peasant movement, demanding the immediate application of the maximum Socialist programme. Now an insignificant group of peasant anarchists.

Parliamentary Procedure

Russian meetings and conventions are organised after the continental model rather than our own. The first action is usually the election of officers and the *presidium.*

The *presidium* is a presiding committee, composed of representatives of the groups and political factions represented in the assembly, in proportion to their numbers. The *presidium* arranges the Order of Business, and its members can be called upon by the President to take the chair *pro tem.*

Each question (*vopros*) is stated in a general way and then debated, and at the close of the debate resolutions are submitted by the different factions, and each one voted on separately. The Order of Business can be, and usually is, smashed to pieces in the first half hour. On the plea of "emergency," which the crowd almost always grants, anybody from the floor can get up and say anything on any subject. The crowd controls the meeting, practically the only functions of the speaker being to keep order by ringing a little bell, and to recognise speakers. Almost all the real work of the session is done in caucuses of the different groups and political factions, which almost always cast their votes in a body and are represented by floor-leaders. The result is, however, that at every important new point, or vote, the session takes a recess to enable the different groups and political factions to hold a caucus.

The crowd is extremely noisy, cheering or heckling speakers, over-riding the plans of the *presidium*. Among the customary cries are: *"Prosim!* Please! Go on!" *"Pravilno!"* or *"Eto vierno!* That's true! Right!" *"Do volno!* Enough!" *"Doloi!* Down with him!" *"Posor!* Shame!" and *"Teesche!* Silence! Not so noisy!"

Popular Organisations

1. Soviet. The word *soviet* means "council." Under the Tsar the Imperial Council of State was called *Gosudarstvennyi Soviet.* Since the Revolution, however, the term *Soviet* has come to be associated with a certain type of parliament elected by members of working-class economic organisations-the Soviet of Workers', of Soldiers', or of Peasants' Deputies. I have therefore limited the word to these bodies, and wherever else it occurs I have translated it "Council."

Besides the local *Soviets,* elected in every city, town and village of Russia-and in large cities, also Ward *(Raionny) Soviets*-there are also the *oblastne* or *gubiernsky* (district or provincial) *Soviets,* and the Central Executive Committee of the All-Russian *Soviets* in the capital, called from its initials *Tsay-ee-kah.* (See below, "Central Committees").

Almost everywhere the *Soviets* of Workers' and of Soldiers' Deputies combined very soon after the March Revolution. In special matters concerning their peculiar interests, however, the Workers' and the Soldiers' Sections continued to meet separately. The *Soviets* of Peasants' Deputies did not join the other two until after the Bolshevik *coup d'etat.* They, too, were organised like the workers and soldiers, with an Executive Committee of the All-Russian Peasants' *Soviets* in the capital.

2. *Trade Unions*. Although mostly industrial in form, the Russian labour unions were still called Trade Unions, and at the time of the Bolshevik Revolution had from three to four million members. These Unions were also organised in an All-Russian body, a sort of Russian Federation of Labour, which had its Central Executive Committee in the capital.

3. *Factory-Shop Committees*. These were spontaneous organisations created in the factories by the workers in their attempt to control industry, taking advantage of the administrative break-down incident upon the Revolution. Their function was by revolutionary action to take over and run the factories. The *Factory-Shop Committees* also had their All-Russian organisation, with a Central Committee at Petrograd, which co-operated with the Trade Unions.

4. *Dumas*. The word *duma* means roughly "deliberative body." The old Imperial Duma, which persisted six months after the Revolution, in a democratised form, died a natural death in September, 1917. The *City Duma* referred to in this book was the reorganised Municipal Council, often called "Municipal Self-Government." It was elected by direct and secret ballot, and its only reason for failure to hold the masses during the Bolshevik

Revolution was the general decline in influence of all purely *political* representation in the fact of the growing power of organisations based on *economic* groups.

5. *Zemstvos*. May be roughly translated "county councils." Under the Tsar semi-political, semi-social bodies with very little administrative power, developed and controlled largely by intellectual Liberals among the land-owning classes. Their most important function was education and social service among the peasants. During the war the *Zemstvos* gradually took over the entire feeding and clothing of the Russian Army, as well as the buying from foreign countries, and work among the soldiers generally corresponding to the work of the American Y. M. C. A. at the Front. After the March Revolution the *Zemstvos* were democratized, with a view to making them the organs of local government in the rural districts. But like the *City Dumas,* they could not compete with the *Soviets.*

6. *Cooperatives*. These were the workers' and peasants' Consumers' Cooperative societies, which had several million members all over Russia before the Revolution. Founded by Liberals and "moderate" Socialists, the Cooperative movement was not supported by the revolutionary Socialist groups, because it was a substitute for the complete transference of means of production and distribution into the hands of the workers. After the March Revolution the *Cooperatives* spread rapidly, and were dominated by Populist Socialists, Mensheviki and Socialist Revolutionaries, and acted as a conservative political force until the Bolshevik Revolution. However, it was the *Cooperatives* which fed Russia when the old structure of commerce and transportation collapsed.

7. *Army Committees*. The *Army Committees* were formed by the soldiers at the front to combat the reactionary influence of the old regime officers. Every company, regiment, brigade, division and corps had its committee, over all of which was elected the *Army Committee.* The *Central Army Committee* cooperated with the General Staff. The administrative break-down in the army incident upon the Revolution threw upon the shoulders of the *Army Committees* most of the work of the Quartermaster's Department, and in some cases, even the command of troops.

8. *Fleet Committees*. The corresponding organisations in the Navy.

Central Committees

In the spring and summer of 1917, All-Russian conventions of every sort of organisation were held at Petrograd. There were national congresses of Workers', Soldiers' and Peasants' Soviets, Trade Unions, Factory-Shop Committees, Army and Fleet Committees-besides every branch of the military and naval service, Cooperatives, Nationalities, etc. Each of these conventions elected a Central Committee, or a Central Executive Committee, to guard its particular interests at the seat of Government. As the Provisional Government grew weaker, these Central Committees were forced to assume more and more administrative powers.

The most important Central Committees mentioned in this book are:

Union of Unions. During the Revolution of 1905, Professor Miliukov and other Liberals established unions of professional men-doctors, lawyers, physicians, etc. These were united under one central organisation, the *Union of Unions.* In 1905 the *Union of Unions* acted with the revolutionary democracy; in 1917, however, the *Union of Unions* opposed the Bolshevik uprising, and united the Government employees who went on strike against the authority of the Soviets.

Tsay-ee-kah. All-Russian Central Executive Committee of the Soviets of Workers' and Soldiers' Deputies. So called from the initials of its name.

Tsentroflot. "Centre-Fleet"-the Central Fleet Committee.

Vikzhel. All-Russian Central Committee of the Railway Workers' Union. So called from the initials of its name.

Other Organisations

Red Guards. The armed factory workers of Russia. The *Red Guards* were first formed during the Revolution of 1905, and sprang into existence again in the days of March, 1917, when a force was needed to keep order in the city. At that time they were armed, and all efforts of the Provisional Government to disarm them were more or less unsuccessful. At every great crisis in the Revolution the *Red Guards* appeared on the streets, untrained and undisciplined, but full of Revolutionary zeal.

White Guards. Bourgeois volunteers, who emerged in the last stages of the Revolution, to defend private property from the Bolshevik attempt to abolish it. A great many of them were University students.

Tekhintsi. The so-called "Savage Division" in the army, made up of Mohametan tribesmen from Central Asia, and personally devoted to General Kornilov. The *Tekhintsi* were noted for their blind obedience and their savage cruelty in warfare.

Death Battalions. Or *Shock Battalions.* The Women's Battalion is known to the world as the *Death Battalion,* but there were many *Death Battalions* composed of men. These were formed in the summer of 1917 by Kerensky, for the purpose of strengthening the discipline and combative fire of the army by heroic example. The *Death Battalions* were composed mostly of intense young patriots. These came for the most part from among the sons of the propertied classes.

Union of Officers. An organisation formed among the reactionary officers in the army to combat politically the growing power of the Army Committees.

Knights of St. George. The Cross of St. George was awarded for distinguished action in battle. Its holder automatically became a *"Knight of St. George."* The predominant influence in the organisation was that of the supporters of the military idea.

Peasants' Union. In 1905, the *Peasants' Union* was a revolutionary peasants' organisation. In 1917, however, it had become the political expression of the more prosperous peasants, to fight the growing power and revolutionary aims of the Soviets of Peasants' Deputies.

Chronology and Spelling

I have adopted in this book our Calendar throughout, instead of the former Russian Calendar, which was thirteen days earlier.

In the spelling of Russian names and words, I have made no attempt to follow any scientific rules for transliteration, but have tried to give the spelling which would lead the English-speaking reader to the simplest approximation of their pronunciation.

Sources

Much of the material in this book is from my own notes. I have also relied, however, upon a heterogeneous file of several hundred assorted Russian newspapers, covering almost every day of the time described, of files of the English paper, the *Russian Daily News,* and of the two French papers, *Journal de Russie* and *Entente.* But far more valuable than these is the *Bulletin de la Presse* issued daily by the French Information Bureau in Petrograd, which reports all important happenings, speeches and the comment of the Russian press. Of this I have an almost complete file from the spring of 1917 to the end of January, 1918.

Besides the foregoing, I have in my possession almost every proclamation, decree and announcement posted on the walls of Petrograd from the middle of September, 1917, to the end of January, 1918. Also the official publication of all Government decrees and orders, and the official Government publication of the secret treaties and other documents discovered in the Ministry of Foreign Affairs when the Bolsheviki took it over.

Ten Days That Shook The World

TEN DAYS THAT SHOOK THE WORLD

By

JOHN REED

CHAPTER I

Background

TOWARD the end of September, 1917, an alien Professor of Sociology visiting Russia came to see me in Petrograd. He had been informed by business men and intellectuals that the Revolution was slowing down. The Professor wrote an article about it, and then travelled around the country, visiting factory towns and peasant communities-where, to his astonishment, the Revolution seemed to be speeding up. Among the wage-earners and the land-working people it was common to hear talk of "all land to the peasants, all factories to the workers." If the Professor had visited the front, he would have heard the whole Army talking Peace....

The Professor was puzzled, but he need not have been; both observations were correct. The property-owning classes were becoming more conservative, the masses of the people more radical.

There was a feeling among business men and the *intelligentzia* generally that the Revolution had gone quite far enough, and lasted too long; that things should settle down. This sentiment was shared by the dominant "moderate" Socialist groups, the *oborontsi* Mensheviki and Socialist Revolutionaries, who supported the Provisional Government of Kerensky.

On October 14th the official organ of the "moderate" Socialists said:

The drama of Revolution has two acts; the destruction of the old régime and the creation of the new one. The first act has lasted long enough. Now it is time to go on to the second, and to play it as rapidly as possible. As a great revolutionist put it, "Let us hasten, friends, to terminate the Revolution. He who makes it last too long will not gather the fruits...."

Among the worker, soldier and peasant masses, however, there was a stubborn feeling that the "first act" was not yet played out. On the front the Army Committees were always running foul of officers who could not get used to treating their men like human beings; in the rear the Land Committees elected by the peasants were being jailed for trying to carry out Government regulations concerning the land; and the workmen in the factories were fighting black-lists and lockouts. Nay, furthermore, returning political exiles were being excluded from the country as "undesirable" citizens; and in some cases, men who returned from abroad to their villages were prosecuted and imprisoned for revolutionary acts committed in 1905.

To the multiform discontent of the people the "moderate" Socialists had one answer: Wait for the Constituent Assembly, which is to meet in December. But the masses were not satisfied with that. The Constituent Assembly was all well and good; but there were certain definite things for which the Russian Revolution had been made, and for which the revolutionary martyrs rotted in their stark Brotherhood Grave on Mars Field, that must be achieved Constituent Assembly or no Constituent Assembly: Peace, Land, and Workers' Control of Industry. The Constituent Assembly had been postponed and postponed-would probably be postponed again, until the people were calm enough-perhaps to modify their demands! At any rate, here were eight months of the Revolution gone, and little enough to show for it....

Meanwhile the soldiers began to solve the peace question by simply deserting, the peasants burned manor-houses and took over the great estates, the workers sabotaged and struck.... Of course, as was natural, the manufacturers, land-owners and army officers exerted all their influence against any democratic compromise....

The policy of the Provisional Government alternated between ineffective reforms and stern repressive measures. An edict from the Socialist Minister of Labour ordered all the Workers' Committees henceforth to meet only after working hours. Among the troops at the front, "agitators" of opposition political parties were arrested, radical newspapers closed down, and capital punishment applied-to revolutionary propagandists. Attempts were made to disarm the Red Guard. Cossacks were sent to keep order in the provinces....

These measures were supported by the "moderate" Socialists and their leaders in the Ministry, who considered it necessary to cooperate with the propertied classes. The people rapidly deserted them, and went over to the Bolsheviki, who stood for Peace, Land, and Workers' Control of Industry, and a Government of the working-class. In September, 1917, matters reached a crisis. Against the overwhelming sentiment of the country, Kerensky and the "moderate" Socialists succeeded in establishing a Government of Coalition with the propertied classes; and as a result, the Mensheviki and Socialist Revolutionaries lost the confidence of the people forever.

An article in *Rabotchi Put* (Workers' Way) about the middle of October, entitled "The Socialist Ministers," expressed the feeling of the masses of the people against the "moderate" Socialists:

Here is a list of their services.

Tseretelli: disarmed the workmen with the assistance of General Polovtsev, checkmated the revolutionary soldiers, and approved of capital punishment in the army.

Skobeliev: commenced by trying to tax the capitalists 100% of their profits, and finished- and finished by an attempt to dissolve the Workers' Committees in the shops and factories.

Avksentiev: put several hundred peasants in prison, members of the Land Committees, and suppressed dozens of workers' and soldiers' newspapers.

Tchernov: signed the "Imperial" manifest, ordering the dissolution of the Finnish Diet.

Savinkov: concluded an open alliance with General Kornilov. If this saviour of the country was not able to betray Petrograd, it was due to reasons over which he had no control.

Zarudny: with the sanction of Alexinsky and Kerensky, put some of the best workers of the Revolution, soldiers and sailors, in prison.

Nikitin: acted as a vulgar policeman against the Railway Workers.

Kerensky: it is better not to say anything about him. The list of his services is too long....

A Congress of delegates of the Baltic Fleet, at Helsingfors, passed a resolution which began as follows:

We demand the immediate removal from the ranks of the Provisional Government of the "Socialist," the political adventurer-Kerensky, as one who is scandalising and ruining the great Revolution, and with it the revolutionary masses, by his shameless political blackmail on behalf of the bourgeoisie....

The direct result of all this was the rise of the Bolsheviki....

Since March, 1917, when the roaring torrents of workmen and soldiers beating upon the Tauride Palace compelled the reluctant Imperial Duma to assume the supreme power in Russia, it was the masses of the people, workers, soldiers and peasants, which forced every change in the course of the Revolution. They hurled the Miliukov Ministry down; it was their Soviet which proclaimed to the world the Russian peace terms-"No annexations, no indemnities, and the right of self-determination of peoples"; and again, in July, it was the spontaneous rising of the unorganised proletariat which once more stormed the Tauride Palace, to demand that the Soviets take over the Government of Russia.

The Bolsheviki, then a small political sect, put themselves at the head of the movement. As a result of the disastrous failure of the rising, public opinion turned against them, and their leaderless hordes slunk back into the Viborg Quarter, which is Petrograd's *St. Antoine.* Then followed a savage hunt of the Bolsheviki; hundreds were imprisoned, among them Trotzky, Madame Kollontai and Kameniev; Lenin and Zinoviev went into hiding, fugitives from justice; the Bolshevik papers were suppressed. Provocators and reactionaries raised the cry that the Bolsheviki were German agents, until people all over the world believed it.

But the Provisional Government found itself unable to substantiate its accusations; the documents proving pro-German conspiracy were discovered to be forgeries; [*] and one by one the Bolsheviki were [*Part of the famous "Sisson Documents"] released from prison without trial, on nominal or no bail-until only six remained. The impotence and indecision of the ever-changing Provisional Government was an argument nobody could refute. The Bolsheviki raised again the slogan so dear to the masses, "All Power to the Soviets!"-and they were not merely self-seeking, for at that time the majority of the Soviets was "moderate" Socialist, their bitter enemy.

But more potent still, they took the crude, simple desires of the workers, soldiers and peasants, and from them built their immediate programme. And so, while the *oborontsi* Mensheviki and Socialist Revolutionaries involved themselves in compromise with the bourgeoisie, the Bolsheviki rapidly captured the Russian masses. In July they were hunted and despised; by September the metropolitan workmen, the sailors of the Baltic Fleet, and the soldiers, had been won almost entirely to their cause. The September municipal elections in the large cities were significant; only 18 per cent of the returns were Menshevik and Socialist Revolutionary, against more than 70 per cent in June....

There remains a phenomenon which puzzled foreign observers: the fact that the Central Executive Committees of the Soviets, the Central Army and Fleet Committees, [*] and the Central Committees of some of [*See Notes and Explanations.] the Unions-notably, the Post and Telegraph Workers and the Railway Workers-opposed the Bolsheviki with the utmost violence. These Central Committees had all been elected in the middle of the summer, or even before, when the Mensheviki and Socialist Revolutionaries had an enormous following; and they delayed or prevented any new elections. Thus, according to the constitution of the Soviets of Workers' and Soldiers' Deputies, the All-Russian Congress *should have been called in September;* but the *Tsay-ee-kah* [*] would not [*See Notes and Explanations.] call the meeting, on the ground that the Constituent Assembly was only two months away, at which time, they hinted, the Soviets would abdicate. Meanwhile, one by one, the Bolsheviki were winning in the local Soviets all over the country, in the Union branches and the ranks of the soldiers and sailors. The Peasants' Soviets remained still conservative, because in the sluggish rural districts political consciousness developed slowly, and the Socialist Revolutionary party had been for a generation the party which had agitated among the peasants.... But even among the peasants a revolutionary wing was forming. It showed itself clearly in October, when the left wing of the Socialist Revolutionaries split off, and formed a new political faction, the Left Socialist Revolutionaries.

4

At the same time there were signs everywhere that the forces of reaction were gaining confidence. At the Troitsky Farce theatre in Petrograd, for example, a burlesque called *Sins of the Tsar* was interrupted by a group of Monarchists, who threatened to lynch the actors for "insulting the Emperor." Certain newspapers began to sigh for a "Russian Napoleon." It was the usual thing among bourgeois *intelligentzia* to refer to the Soviets of Workers' Deputies (Rabotchikh Deputatov) as *Sabatchikh* Deputatov-Dogs' Deputies.

On October 15th I had a conversation with a great Russian capitalist, Stepan Georgevitch Lianozov, known as the "Russian Rockefeller"-a Cadet by political faith.

"Revolution," he said, "is a sickness. Sooner or later the foreign powers must intervene here-as one would intervene to cure a sick child, and teach it how to walk. Of course it would be more or less improper, but the nations must realise the danger of Bolshevism in their own countries-such contagious ideas as 'proletarian dictatorship,' and 'world social revolution'... There is a chance that this intervention may not be necessary. Transportation is demoralised, the factories are closing down, and the Germans are advancing. Starvation and defeat may bring the Russian people to their senses...."

Mr. Lianozov was emphatic in his opinion that whatever happened, it would be impossible for merchants and manufacturers to permit the existence of the workers' Shop Committees, or to allow the workers any share in the management of industry.

"As for the Bolsheviki, they will be done away with by one of two methods. The Government can evacuate Petrograd, then a state of siege declared, and the military commander of the district can deal with these gentlemen without legal formalities.... *Or if, for example, the Constituent Assembly manifests any Utopian tendencies, it can be dispersed by force of arms....*"

Winter was coming on-the terrible Russian winter. I heard business men speak of it so: "Winter was always Russia's best friend. Perhaps now it will rid us of Revolution." On the freezing front miserable armies continued to starve and die, without enthusiasm. The railways were breaking down, food lessening, factories closing. The desperate masses cried out that the bourgeoisie was sabotaging the life of the people, causing defeat on the Front. Riga had been surrendered just after General Kornilov said publicly, "Must we pay with Riga the price of bringing the country to a sense of its duty?" [*] [* See "Kornilov to Brest-Litvosk" by John Reed. Boni and Liveright N.Y., 1919]

To Americans it is incredible that the class war should develop to such a pitch. But I have personally met officers on the Northern Front who frankly preferred military disaster to cooperation with the Soldiers' Committees. The secretary of the Petrograd branch of the Cadet party told me that the break-down of the country's economic life was part of a campaign to discredit the Revolution. An Allied diplomat, whose name I promised not to mention, confirmed this from his own knowledge. I know of certain coal-mines near Kharkov which were fired and flooded by their owners, of textile factories at Moscow whose engineers put the machinery out of order when they left, of railroad officials caught by the workers in the act of crippling locomotives....

A large section of the propertied classes preferred the Germans to the Revolution-even to the Provisional Government-and didn't hesitate to say so. In the Russian household where I lived, the subject of conversation at the dinner table was almost invariably the coming of the Germans, bringing "law and order."... One evening I spent at the house of a Moscow merchant; during tea we asked the eleven people at the table whether they preferred "Wilhelm or the Bolsheviki." The vote was ten to one for Wilhelm...

The speculators took advantage of the universal disorganisation to pile up fortunes, and to spend them in fantastic revelry or the corruption of Government officials. Foodstuffs and fuel were hoarded, or secretly sent out of the country to Sweden. In the first four months of the Revolution, for example, the reserve food-supplies were almost openly looted from the great Municipal warehouses of Petrograd, until the two-years' provision of grain had fallen to less than enough to feed the city for one month.... According to the official report of the last Minister of Supplies in the Provisional Government, coffee was bought wholesale in Vladivostok for two rubles a pound, and the consumer in Petrograd paid thirteen. In all the stores of the large cities were tons of food and clothing; but only the rich could buy them.

In a provincial town I knew a merchant family turned speculator_-maradior_ (bandit, ghoul) the Russians call it. The three sons had bribed their way out of military service. One gambled in foodstuffs. Another sold illegal gold from the Lena mines to mysterious parties in Finland. The third owned a controlling interest in a chocolate factory, which supplied the local Cooperative societies-on condition that the Cooperatives furnished him everything he needed. And so, while the masses of the people got a quarter pound of black bread on their bread cards, he had an abundance of white bread, sugar, tea, candy, cake and butter.... Yet when the soldiers at the front could no longer fight from cold, hunger and exhaustion, how indignantly did this family scream "Cowards!"-how "ashamed" they were "to be Russians"... When finally the Bolsheviki found and requisitioned vast hoarded stores of provisions, what "Robbers" they were.

Beneath all this external rottenness moved the old-time Dark Forces, unchanged since the fall of Nicholas the Second, secret still and very active. The agents of the notorious *Okhrana* still functioned, for and against the Tsar, for and against Kerensky-whoever would pay.... In the darkness, underground organisations of all sorts, such as the Black Hundreds, were busy attempting to restore reaction in some form or other.

In this atmosphere of corruption, of monstrous half-truths, one clear note sounded day after day, the deepening chorus of the Bolsheviki, "All Power to the Soviets! All power to the direct representatives of millions on millions of common workers, soldiers, peasants. Land, bread, an end to the senseless war, an end to secret diplomacy, speculation, treachery.... The Revolution is in danger, and with it the cause of the people all over the world!"

The struggle between the proletariat and the middle class, between the Soviets and the Government, which had begun in the first March days, was about to culminate. Having at one bound leaped from the Middle Ages into the twentieth century, Russia showed the startled world two systems of Revolution-the political and the social-in mortal combat.

What a revelation of the vitality of the Russian Revolution, after all these months of starvation and disillusionment! The bourgeoisie should have better known its Russia. Not for a long time in Russia will the "sickness" of Revolution have run its course....

Looking back, Russia before the November insurrection seems of another age, almost incredibly conservative. So quickly did we adapt ourselves to the newer, swifter life; just as Russian politics swung bodily to the Left-until the Cadets were outlawed as "enemies of the people," Kerensky became a "counter-revolutionist," the "middle" Socialist leaders, Tseretelli, Dan, Lieber, Gotz and Avksentiev, were too reactionary for their following, and men like Victor Tchernov, and even Maxim Gorky, belonged to the Right Wing....

About the middle of December, 1917, a group of Socialist Revolutionary leaders paid a private visit to Sir George Buchanan, the British Ambassador, and implored him not to mention the fact that they had been there, because they were "considered too far Right."

"And to think," said Sir George. "One year ago my Government instructed me not to receive Miliukov, because he was so dangerously Left!"

September and October are the worst months of the Russian year-especially the Petrograd year. Under dull grey skies, in the shortening days, the rain fell drenching, incessant. The mud underfoot was deep, slippery and clinging, tracked everywhere by heavy boots, and worse than usual because of the complete break-down of the Municipal administration. Bitter damp winds rushed in from the Gulf of Finland, and the chill fog rolled through the streets. At night, for motives of economy as well as fear of Zeppelins, the street-lights were few and far between; in private dwellings and apartment-houses the electricity was turned on from six o'clock until midnight, with candles forty cents apiece and little kerosene to be had. It was dark from three in the afternoon to ten in the morning. Robberies and housebreakings increased. In apartment houses the men took turns at all-night guard duty, armed with loaded rifles. This was under the Provisional Government.

Week by week food became scarcer. The daily allowance of bread fell from a pound and a half to a pound, then three quarters, half, and a quarter-pound. Toward the end there was a week without any bread at all. Sugar one was entitled to at the rate of two pounds a month- if one could get it at all, which was seldom. A bar of chocolate or a pound of tasteless candy cost anywhere from seven to ten rubles-at least a dollar. There was milk for about half the babies in the city; most hotels and private houses never saw it for months. In the fruit season apples and pears sold for a little less than a ruble apiece on the street-corner....

For milk and bread and sugar and tobacco one had to stand in *queue* long hours in the chill rain. Coming home from an all-night meeting I have seen the *kvost* (tail) beginning to form before dawn, mostly women, some with babies in their arms.... Carlyle, in his *French Revolution*, has described the French people as distinguished above all others by their faculty of standing in *queue*. Russia had accustomed herself to the practice, begun in the reign of Nicholas the Blessed as long ago as 1915, and from then continued intermittently until the summer of 1917, when it settled down as the regular order of things. Think of the poorly-clad people standing on the iron-white streets of Petrograd whole days in the Russian winter! I have listened in the bread-lines, hearing the bitter, acrid note of discontent which from time to time burst up through the miraculous goodnature of the Russian crowd....

Of course all the theatres were going every night, including Sundays. Karsavina appeared in a new Ballet at the Marinsky, all dance-loving Russia coming to see her. Shaliapin was singing. At the Alexandrinsky they were reviving Meyerhold's production of Tolstoy's "Death of Ivan the Terrible"; and at that performance I remember noticing a student of the Imperial School of Pages, in his dress uniform, who stood up correctly between the acts and faced the empty Imperial box, with its eagles all erased.... The *Krivoye Zerkalo* staged a sumptuous version of Schnitzler's "Reigen."

Although the Hermitage and other picture galleries had been evacuated to Moscow, there were weekly exhibitions of paintings. Hordes of the female *intelligentzia* went to hear lectures on Art, Literature and the Easy Philosophies. It was a particularly active season for Theosophists. And the Salvation Army, admitted to Russia for the first time in history, plastered the walls with announcements of gospel meetings, which amused and astounded Russian audiences....

As in all such times, the petty conventional life of the city went on, ignoring the Revolution as much as possible. The poets made verses-but not about the Revolution. The realistic painters painted scenes from mediæval Russian history-anything but the Revolution. Young ladies from the provinces came up to the capital to learn French and cultivate their voices, and the gay young beautiful officers wore their gold-trimmed crimson *bashliki* and their elaborate Caucasian swords around the hotel lobbies. The ladies of the minor bureaucratic set took tea with each other in the afternoon, carrying each her little gold or silver or jewelled sugar-box, and half a loaf of bread in her muff, and wished that the Tsar were back, or that the Germans would come, or anything that would solve the servant problem.... The daughter of a friend of mine came home one afternoon in hysterics because the woman street-car conductor had called her "Comrade!"

All around them great Russia was in travail, bearing a new world. The servants one used to treat like animals and pay next to nothing, were getting independent. A pair of shoes cost more than a hundred rubles, and as wages averaged about thirty-five rubles a month the servants refused to stand in *queue* and wear out their shoes. But more than that. In the new Russia every man and woman could vote; there were working-class newspapers, saying new and startling things; there were the Soviets; and there were the Unions. The *izvoshtchiki* (cab-drivers) had a Union; they were also represented in the Petrograd Soviet. The waiters and hotel servants were organised, and refused tips. On the walls of restaurants they put up signs which read, "No tips taken here-" or, "Just because a man has to make his living waiting on table is no reason to insult him by offering him a tip!"

At the Front the soldiers fought out their fight with the officers, and learned self-government through their committees. In the factories those unique Russian organisations, the Factory-Shop Committees, [*] gained experience and strength and a realisation of [* See Notes and Explanations] their historical mission by combat with the old order. All Russia was learning to read, and _reading-_politics, economics, history-because the people wanted to *know*.... In every city, in most towns, along the Front, each political faction had its newspaper-sometimes several. Hundreds of thousands of pamphlets were distributed by thousands of organisations, and poured into the armies, the villages, the factories, the streets. The thirst for education, so long thwarted, burst with the Revolution into a frenzy of expression. From Smolny Institute alone, the first six months, went out every day tons, car-loads, train-loads of literature, saturating the land. Russia absorbed reading matter like hot sand drinks water, insatiable. And it was not fables, falsified history, diluted religion, and the cheap fiction that corrupts-but social and economic theories, philosophy, the works of Tolstoy, Gogol, and Gorky....

Then the Talk, beside which Carlyle's "flood of French speech" was a mere trickle. Lectures, debates, speeches-in theatres, circuses, school-houses, clubs, Soviet meeting-rooms, Union headquarters, barracks.... Meetings in the trenches at the Front, in village squares, factories.... What a marvellous sight to see Putilovsky Zavod (the Putilov factory) pour out its forty thousand to listen to Social Democrats, Socialist Revolutionaries, Anarchists, anybody, whatever they had to say, as long as they would talk! For months in Petrograd, and all over Russia, every street-corner was a public tribune. In railway trains, street-cars, always the spurting up of impromptu debate, everywhere....

And the All-Russian Conferences and Congresses, drawing together the men of two continents-conventions of Soviets, of Cooperatives, Zemstvos, [*] nationalities, priests, peasants, political parties; the [* See Notes and Explanations] Democratic Conference, the Moscow Conference, the Council of the Russian Republic. There were always three or four conventions going on in Petrograd. At every meeting, attempts to limit the time of speakers voted down, and every man free to express the thought that was in him....

We came down to the front of the Twelfth Army, back of Riga, where gaunt and bootless men sickened in the mud of desperate trenches; and when they saw us they started up, with their pinched faces and the flesh showing blue through their torn clothing, demanding eagerly, "Did you bring anything to *read?*"

What though the outward and visible signs of change were many, what though the statue of Catharine the Great before the Alexandrinsky Theatre bore a little red flag in its hand, and others-somewhat faded-floated from all public buildings; and the Imperial monograms and eagles were either torn down or covered up; and in place of the fierce *gorodovoye* (city police) a mild-mannered and unarmed citizen militia patrolled the streets-still, there were many quaint anachronisms.

For example, Peter the Great's _Tabel o Rangov-_Table of Ranks-which he rivetted upon Russia with an iron hand, still held sway. Almost everybody from the school-boy up wore his prescribed uniform, with the insignia of the Emperor on button and shoulder-strap. Along about five o'clock in the afternoon the streets were full of subdued old gentlemen in uniform, with portfolios, going home from work in the huge, barrack-like Ministries or Government institutions, calculating perhaps how great a mortality among their superiors would advance them to the coveted *tchin* (rank) of Collegiate Assessor, or Privy Councillor, with the prospect of retirement on a comfortable pension, and possibly the Cross of St. Anne....

There is the story of Senator Sokolov, who in full tide of Revolution came to a meeting of the Senate one day in civilian clothes, and was not admitted because he did not wear the prescribed livery of the Tsar's service!

It was against this background of a whole nation in ferment and disintegration that the pageant of the Rising of the Russian Masses unrolled....

CHAPTER II

The Coming Storm

IN September General Kornilov marched on Petrograd to make himself military dictator of Russia. Behind him was suddenly revealed the mailed fist of the bourgeoisie, boldly attempting to crush the Revolution. Some of the Socialist Ministers were implicated; even Kerensky was under suspicion. Savinkov, summoned to explain to the Central Committee of his party, the Socialist Revolutionaries, refused and was expelled. Kornilov was arrested by the Soldiers' Committees. Generals were dismissed, Ministers suspended from their functions, and the Cabinet fell.

Kerensky tried to form a new Government, including the Cadets, party of the bourgeoisie. His party, the Socialist Revolutionaries, ordered him to exclude the Cadets. Kerensky declined to obey, and threatened to resign from the Cabinet if the Socialists insisted. However, popular feeling ran so high that for the moment he did not dare oppose it, and a temporary Directorate of Five of the old Ministers, with Kerensky at the head, assumed the power until the question should be settled.

The Kornilov affair drew together all the Socialist groups-"moderates" as well as revolutionists-in a passionate impulse of self-defence. There must be no more Kornilovs. A new Government must be created, responsible to the elements supporting the Revolution. So the *Tsay-ee-kah* invited the popular organisations to send delegates to a Democratic Conference, which should meet at Petrograd in September.

In the *Tsay-ee-kah* three factions immediately appeared. The Bolsheviki demanded that the All-Russian Congress of Soviets be summoned, and that they take over the power. The "centre" Socialist Revolutionaries, led by Tchernov, joined with the Left Socialist Revolutionaries, led by Kamkov and Spiridonova, the Mensheviki Internationalists under Martov, and the "centre" Mensheviki, [*] [* See Notes and Explanations.] represented by Bogdanov and Skobeliev, in demanding a purely Socialist Government. Tseretelli, Dan and Lieber, at the head of the right wing Mensheviki, and the right Socialist Revolutionaries under Avksentiev and Gotz, insisted that the propertied classes must be represented in the new Government.

Almost immediately the Bolsheviki won a majority in the Petrograd Soviet, and the Soviets of Moscow, Kiev, Odessa and other cities followed suit.

Alarmed, the Mensheviki and Socialist Revolutionaries in control of the *Tsay-ee-kah* decided that after all they feared the danger of Kornilov less than the danger of Lenin. They revised the plan of representation in the Democratic Conference, admitting more delegates from the Cooperative Societies and other conservative bodies. Even this packed assembly at first voted for a *Coalition Government without the Cadets.* Only Kerensky's open threat of resignation, and the alarming cries of the "moderate" Socialists that "the Republic is in danger" persuaded the Conference, by a small majority, to declare in favour of the principle of coalition with the bourgeoisie, and to sanction the establishment of a sort of consultative Parliament, without any legislative power, called the Provisional Council of the Russian Republic. In the new Ministry the propertied classes practically controlled, and in the Council of the Russian Republic they occupied a disproportionate number of seats.

The fact is that the *Tsay-ee-kah* no longer represented the rank and file of the Soviets, and had illegally refused to call another All-Russian Congress of Soviets, due in September. It had no intention of calling this Congress or of allowing it to be called. Its official organ, *Izviestia* (News), began to hint that the function of the Soviets was nearly at an end, and that they might soon be dissolved... At this time, too, the new Government announced as part of its policy the liquidation of "irresponsible organisations"-i.e. the Soviets.

The Bolsheviki responded by summoning the All-Russian Soviets to meet at Petrograd on November 2, and take over the Government of Russia. At the same time they withdrew from the Council of the Russian Republic, stating that they would not participate in a "Government of Treason to the People."

The withdrawal of the Bolsheviki, however, did not bring tranquillity to the ill-fated Council. The propertied classes, now in a position of power, became arrogant. The Cadets declared that the Government had no legal right to declare Russia a republic. They demanded stern measures in the Army and Navy to destroy the Soldiers' and Sailors' Committees, and denounced the Soviets. On the other side of the chamber the Mensheviki Internationalists and the Left Socialist Revolutionaries advocated immediate peace, land to the peasants, and workers' control of industry-practically the Bolshevik programme.

I heard Martov's speech in answer to the Cadets. Stooped over the desk of the tribune like the mortally sick man he was, and speaking in a voice so hoarse it could hardly be heard, he shook his finger toward the right benches:

"You call us defeatists; but the real defeatists are those who wait for a more propitious moment to conclude peace, insist upon postponing peace until later, until nothing is left of the Russian army, until Russia becomes the subject of bargaining between the different imperialist groups.... You are trying to impose upon the Russian people a policy dictated by the interests of the bourgeoisie. The question of peace should be raised without delay.... You will see then that not in vain has been the work of those whom you call German agents, of those Zimmerwaldists [*] who in all the [* Members of the revoloutionary internationalist wing of the Socialists of Europe, so-called because of their participation in the International Conference held at Zimmerwald, Switzerland, in 1915] lands have prepared the awakening of the conscience of the democratic masses...."

Between these two groups the Mensheviki and Socialist Revolutionaries wavered, irresistibly forced to the left by the pressure of the rising dissatisfaction of the masses. Deep hostility divided the chamber into irreconcilable groups.

This was the situation when the long-awaited announcement of the Allied Conference in Paris brought up the burning question of foreign policy....

Theoretically all Socialist parties in Russia were in favour of the earliest possible peace on democratic terms. As long ago as May, 1917, the Petrograd Soviet, then under control of the Mensheviki and Socialist Revolutionaries,had proclaimed the famous Russian peace-conditions. They had demanded that the Allies hold a conference to discuss war-aims. This conference had been promised for August; then postponed until September; then until October; and now it was fixed for November 10th.

The Provisional Government suggested two representatives-General Alexeyev, reactionary military man, and Terestchenko, Minister of Foreign Affairs. The Soviets chose Skobeliev to speak for them and drew up a manifesto, the famous *nakaz*- instructions. The Provisional Government objected to Skobeliev and his *nakaz;* the Allied ambassadors protested and finally Bonar Law in the British House of Commons, in answer to a question, responded coldly, "As far as I know the Paris Conference will not discuss the aims of the war at all, but only the methods of conducting it...."

At this the conservative Russian press was jubilant, and the Bolsheviki cried, "See where the compromising tactics of the Mensheviki and Socialist Revolutionaries have led them!"

Along a thousand miles of front the millions of men in Russia's armies stirred like the sea rising, pouring into the capital their hundreds upon hundreds of delegations, crying "Peace! Peace!"

I went across the river to the Cirque Moderne, to one of the great popular meetings which occurred all over the city, more numerous night after night. The bare, gloomy amphitheatre, lit by five tiny lights hanging from a thin wire, was packed from the ring up the steep sweep of grimy benches to the very roof-soldiers, sailors, workmen, women, all listening as if their lives depended upon it. A soldier was speaking-from the Five Hundred and Forty-eight Division, wherever and whatever that was:

"Comrades," he cried, and there was real anguish in his drawn face and despairing gestures. "The people at the top are always calling upon us to sacrifice more, sacrifice more, while those who have everything are left unmolested.

"We are at war with Germany. Would we invite German generals to serve on our Staff? Well we're at war with the capitalists too, and yet we invite them into our Government....

"The soldier says, 'Show me what I am fighting for. Is it Constantinople, or is it free Russia? Is it the democracy, or is it the capitalist plunderers? If you can prove to me that I am defending the Revolution then I'll go out and fight without capital punishment to force me.'

"When the land belongs to the peasants, and the factories to the workers, and the power to the Soviets, then we'll know we have something to fight for, and we'll fight for it!"

In the barracks, the factories, on the street-corners, end less soldier speakers, all clamouring for an end to the war, declaring that if the Government did not make an energetic effort to get peace, the army would leave the trenches and go home.

The spokesman for the Eighth Army:

"We are weak, we have only a few men left in each company. They must give us food and boots and reinforcements, or soon there will be left only empty trenches. Peace or supplies... either let the Government end the war or support the Army...."

For the Forty-sixth Siberian Artillery:

"The officers will not work with our Committees, they betray us to the enemy, they apply the death penalty to our agitators; and the counter-revolutionary Government supports them. We thought that the Revolution would bring peace. But now the Government forbids us even to talk of such things, and at the same time doesn't give us enough food to live on, or enough ammunition to fight with...."

From Europe came rumours of peace at the expense of Russia. ...

News of the treatment of Russian troops in France added to the discontent. The First Brigade had tried to replace its officers with Soldiers' Committees, like their comrades at home, and had refused an order to go to Salonika, demanding to be sent to Russia. They had been surrounded and starved, and then fired on by artillery, and many killed.

On October 29th I went to the white-marble and crimson hall of the Marinsky palace, where the Council of the Republic sat, to hear Terestchenko's declaration of the Government's foreign policy, awaited with such terrible anxiety by all the peace-thirsty and exhausted land.

A tall, impeccably-dressed young man with a smooth face and high cheek-bones, suavely reading his careful, non-committal speech. Nothing.... Only the same platitudes about crushing German militarism with the help of the Allies-about the "state interests" of Russia, about the "embarrassment" caused by Skobeliev's *nakaz*. He ended with the key-note:

"Russia is a great power. Russia will remain a great power, whatever happens. We must all defend her, we must show that we are defenders of a great ideal, and children of a great power."

Nobody was satisfied. The reactionaries wanted a "strong" imperialist policy; the democratic parties wanted an assurance that the Government would press for peace.... I reproduce an editorial in *Rabotchi i Soldat* (Worker and Soldier), organ of the Bolshevik Petrograd Soviet:

THE GOVERNMENT'S ANSWER TO THE TRENCHES

The most taciturn of our Ministers, Mr. Terestchenko, has actually told the trenches the following:

1. We are closely united with our Allies. (Not with the peoples, but with the Governments.)

2. There is no use for the democracy to discuss the possibility or impossibility of a winter campaign. That will be decided by the Governments of our Allies.

3. The 1st of July offensive was beneficial and a very happy affair. (He did not mention the consequences.)

4. It is not true that our Allies do not care about us. The Minister has in his possession very important declarations. (Declarations? What about deeds? What about the behaviour of the British fleet? The parleying of the British king with exiled counter-revolutionary General Gurko? The Minister did not mention all this.)

5. The *nakaz* to Skobeliev is bad; the Allies don't like it and the Russian diplomats don't like it. In the Allied Conference we must all 'speak one language.'

And is that all? That is all. What is the way out? The solution is, faith in the Allies and in Terestchenko. When will peace come? When the Allies permit.

That is how the Government replied to the trenches about peace!

Now in the background of Russian politics began to form the vague outlines of a sinister power-the Cossacks. *Novaya Zhizn* (New Life), Gorky's paper, called attention to their activities:

At the beginning of the Revolution the Cossacks refused to shoot down the people. When Kornilov marched on Petrograd they refused to follow him. From passive loyalty to the Revolution the Cossacks have passed to an active political offensive (against it). From the back-ground of the Revolution they have suddenly advanced to the front of the stage....

Kaledin, *ataman* of the Don Cossacks, had been dismissed by the Provisional Government for his complicity in the Kornilov affair. He flatly refused to resign, and surrounded by three immense Cossack armies lay at Novotcherkask, plotting and menacing. So great was his power that the Government was forced to ignore his insubordination. More than that, it was compelled formally to recognise the Council of the Union of Cossack Armies, and to declare illegal the newly-formed Cossack Section of the Soviets....

In the first part of October a Cossack delegation called upon Kerensky, arrogantly insisting that the charges against Kaledin be dropped, and reproaching the Minister-President for yielding to the Soviets. Kerensky agreed to let Kaledin alone, and then is reported to have said, "In the eyes of the Soviet leaders I am a despot and a tyrant.... As for the Provisional Government, not only does it not depend upon the Soviets, but it considers it regrettable that they exist at all."

At the same time another Cossack mission called upon the British ambassador, treating with him boldly as representatives of "the free Cossack people."

In the Don something very like a Cossack Republic had been established. The Kuban declared itself an independent Cossack State. The Soviets of Rostov-on-Don and Yekaterinburg were dispersed by armed Cossacks, and the headquarters of the Coal Miners' Union at Kharkov raided. In all its manifestations the Cossack movement was anti-Socialist and militaristic. Its leaders were nobles and great land-owners, like Kaledin, Kornilov, Generals Dutov, Karaulov and Bardizhe, and it was backed by the powerful merchants and bankers of Moscow....

Old Russia was rapidly breaking up. In Ukraine, in Finland, Poland, White Russia, the nationalist movements gathered strength and became bolder. The local Governments, controlled by the propertied classes, claimed autonomy, refusing to obey orders from Petrograd. At Helsingfors the Finnish Senate declined to loan money to the Provisional Government, declared Finland autonomous, and demanded the withdrawal of Russian troops. The bourgeois Rada at Kiev extended the boundaries of Ukraine until they included all the richest agricultural lands of South Russia, as far east as the Urals, and began the formation of a national army. Premier Vinnitchenko hinted at a separate peace with Germany-and the Provisional Government was helpless. Siberia, the Caucasus, demanded separate Constituent Assemblies. And in all these countries there was the beginning of a bitter struggle between the authorities and the local Soviets of Workers' and Soldiers' Deputies....

Conditions were daily more chaotic. Hundreds of thousands of soldiers were deserting the front and beginning to move in vast, aimless tides over the face of the land. The peasants of Tambov and Tver Governments, tired of waiting for the land, exasperated by the repressive measures of the Government, were burning manor-houses and massacring land-owners. Immense strikes and lock-outs convulsed Moscow, Odessa and the coal-mines of the Don. Transportation was paralysed; the army was starving and in the big cities there was no bread.

The Government, torn between the democratic and reactionary factions, could do nothing: when forced to act it always supported the interests of the propertied classes. Cossacks were sent to restore order among the peasants, to break the strikes. In Tashkent, Government authorities suppressed the Soviet. In Petrograd the Economic Council, established to rebuild the shattered economic life of the country, came to a deadlock between the opposing forces of capital and labour, and was dissolved by Kerensky. The old régime military men, backed by Cadets, demanded that harsh measures be adopted to restore discipline in the Army and the Navy. In vain Admiral Verderevsky, the venerable Minister of Marine, and General Verkhovsky, Minister of War, insisted that only a new, voluntary, democratic discipline, based on cooperation with the soldiers' and sailors' Committees, could save the army and navy. Their recommendations were ignored.

The reactionaries seemed determined to provoke popular anger. The trial of Kornilov was coming on. More and more openly the bourgeois press defended him, speaking of him as "the great Russian patriot." Burtzev's paper, *Obshtchee Dielo* (Common Cause), called for a dictatorship of Kornilov, Kaledin and Kerensky!

I had a talk with Burtzev one day in the press gallery of the Council of the Republic. A small, stooped figure with a wrinkled face, eyes near-sighted behind thick glasses, untidy hair and beard streaked with grey.

"Mark my words, young man! What Russia needs is a Strong Man. We should get our minds off the Revolution now and concentrate on the Germans. Bunglers, bunglers, to defeat Kornilov; and back of the bunglers are the German agents. Kornilov should have won...."

On the extreme right the organs of the scarcely-veiled Monarchists, Purishkevitch's *Narodny Tribun* (People's Tribune), *Novaya Rus* (New Russia), and *Zhivoye Slovo* (Living Word), openly advocated the extermination of the revolutionary democracy....

On the 23rd of October occurred the naval battle with a German squadron in the Gulf of Riga. On the pretext that Petrograd was in danger, the Provisional Government drew up plans for evacuating the capital. First the great munitions works were to go, distributed widely throughout Russia; and then the Government itself was to move to Moscow. Instantly the Bolsheviki began to cry out that the Government was abandoning the Red

Capital in order to weaken the Revolution. Riga had been sold to the Germans; now Petrograd was being betrayed!

The bourgeois press was joyful. "At Moscow," said the Cadet paper *Ryetch* (Speech), "the Government can pursue its work in a tranquil atmosphere, without being interfered with by anarchists." Rodzianko, leader of the right wing of the Cadet party, declared in *Utro Rossii* (The Morning of Russia) that the taking of Petrograd by the Germans would be a blessing, because it would destroy the Soviets and get rid of the revolutionary Baltic Fleet:

Petrograd is in danger (he wrote). I say to myself, "Let God take care of Petrograd." They fear that if Petrograd is lost the central revolutionary organisations will be destroyed. To that I answer that I rejoice if all these organisations are destroyed; for they will bring nothing but disaster upon Russia....

With the taking of Petrograd the Baltic Fleet will also be destroyed.... But there will be nothing to regret; most of the battleships are completely demoralised....

In the face of a storm of popular disapproval the plan of evacuation was repudiated.

Meanwhile the Congress of Soviets loomed over Russia like a thunder-cloud, shot through with lightnings. It was opposed, not only by the Government but by all the "moderate" Socialists. The Central Army and Fleet Committees, the Central Committees of some of the Trade Unions, the Peasants' Soviets, but most of all the *Tsay-ee-kah* itself, spared no pains to prevent the meeting. *Izviestia* and *Golos Soldata* (Voice of the Soldier), newspapers founded by the Petrograd Soviet but now in the hands of the *Tsay-ee-kah*, fiercely assailed it, as did the entire artillery of the Socialist Revolutionary party press, *Dielo Naroda* (People's Cause) and *Volia Naroda* (People's Will).

Delegates were sent through the country, messages flashed by wire to committees in charge of local Soviets, to Army Committees, instructing them to halt or delay elections to the Congress. Solemn public resolutions against the Congress, declarations that the democracy was opposed to the meeting so near the date of the Constituent Assembly, representatives from the Front, from the Union of Zemstvos, the Peasants' Union, Union of Cossack Armies, Union of Officers, Knights of St. George, Death Battalions, [*] protesting.... [*See Notes and Explanations.] The Council of the Russian Republic was one chorus of disapproval. The entire machinery set up by the Russian Revolution of March functioned to block the Congress of Soviets....

On the other hand was the shapeless will of the proletariat-the workmen, common soldiers and poor peasants. Many local Soviets were already Bolshevik; then there were the organisations of the industrial workers, the *Fabritchno-Zavodskiye Comitieti*- Factory-Shop Committees; and the insurgent Army and Fleet organisations. In some places the people, prevented from electing their regular Soviet delegates, held rump meetings and chose one of their number to go to Petrograd. In others they smashed the old obstructionist committees and formed new ones. A ground-swell of revolt heaved and cracked the crust which had been slowly hardening on the surface of revolutionary fires dormant all those months. Only an spontaneous mass-movement could bring about the All-Russian Congress of Soviets....

Day after day the Bolshevik orators toured the barracks and factories, violently denouncing "this Government of civil war." One Sunday we went, on a top-heavy steam tram that lumbered through oceans of mud, between stark factories and immense churches, to *Obukhovsky Zavod,* a Government munitions-plant out on the Schlüsselburg Prospekt.

The meeting took place between the gaunt brick walls of a huge unfinished building, ten thousand black-clothed men and women packed around a scaffolding draped in red, people heaped on piles of lumber and bricks, perched high upon shadowy girders, intent and thunder-voiced. Through the dull, heavy sky now and again burst the sun, flooding reddish light through the skeleton windows upon the mass of simple faces upturned to us.

Lunatcharsky, a slight, student-like figure with the sensitive face of an artist, was telling why the power must be taken by the Soviets. Nothing else could guarantee the Revolution against its enemies, who were deliberately ruining the country, ruining the army, creating opportunities for a new Konilov.

A soldier from the Rumanian front, thin, tragical and fierce, cried, "Comrades! We are starving at the front, we are stiff with cold. We are dying for no reason. I ask the American comrades to carry word to America, that the Russians will never give up their Revolution until they die. We will hold the fort with all our strength until the peoples of the world rise and help us! Tell the American workers to rise and fight for the Social Revolution!"

Then came Petrovsky, slight, slow-voiced, implacable: "Now is the time for deeds, not words. The economic situation is bad, but we must get used to it. They are trying to starve us and freeze us. They are trying to provoke us. But let them know that they can go too far- that if they dare to lay their hands upon the organisations of the proletariat we will sweep them away like scum from the face of the earth!"

The Bolshevik press suddenly expanded. Besides the two party papers, *Rabotchi Put* and *Soldat* (Soldier), there appeared a new paper for the peasants, *Derevenskaya Byednota* (Village Poorest), poured out in a daily half-million edition; and on October 17th, *Rabotchi i Soldat.* Its leading article summed up the Bolshevik point of view:

The fourth year's campaign will mean the annihilation of the army and the country.... There is danger for the safety of Petrograd.... Counter-revolutionists rejoice in the people's misfortunes.... The peasants brought to desperation come out in open rebellion; the landlords and Government authorities massacre them with punitive expeditions; factories and mines are closing down, workmen are threatened with starvation.... The bourgeoisie and its Generals want to restore a blind discipline in the army.... Supported by the bourgeoisie, the Kornilovtsi are openly getting ready to break up the meeting of the Constituent Assembly....

The Kerensky Government is against the people. He will destroy the country.... This paper stands for the people and by the people-the poor classes, workers, soldiers and peasants. The people can only be saved by the completion of the Revolution... and for this purpose the full power must be in the hands of the Soviets....

This paper advocates the following: All power to the Soviets-both in the capital and in the provinces.

Immediate truce on all fronts. An honest peace between peoples.

Landlord estates-without compensation-to the peasants.

Workers' control over industrial production.

A faithfully and honestly elected Constituent Assembly.

It is interesting to reproduce here a passage from that same paper-the organ of those Bolsheviki so well known to the world as German agents:

The German kaiser, covered with the blood of millions of dead people, wants to push his army against Petrograd. Let us call to the German workmen, soldiers and peasants, who want peace not less than we do, to... stand up against this damned war!

This can be done only by a revolutionary Government, which would speak really for the workmen, soldiers and peasants of Russia, and would appeal over the heads of the diplomats directly to the German troops, fill the German trenches with proclamations in the German language.... Our airmen would spread these proclamations all over Germany....

In the Council of the Republic the gulf between the two sides of the chamber deepened day by day.

"The propertied classes," cried Karelin, for the Left Socialist Revolutionaries, "want to exploit the revolutionary machine of the State to bind Russia to the war-chariot of the Allies! The revolutionary parties are absolutely against this policy...."

Old Nicholas Tchaikovsky, representing the Populist Socialists, spoke against giving the land to the peasants, and took the side of the Cadets: "We must have immediately strong discipline in the army.... Since the beginning of the war I have not ceased to insist that it is a crime to undertake social and economic reforms in war-time. We are committing that crime, and yet I am not the enemy of these reforms, because I am a Socialist."

Cries from the Left, "We don't believe you!" Mighty applause from the Right....

Adzhemov, for the Cadets, declared that there was no necessity to tell the army what it was fighting for, since every soldier ought to realise that the first task was to drive the enemy from Russian territory.

Kerensky himself came twice, to plead passionately for national unity, once bursting into tears at the end. The assembly heard him coldly, interrupting with ironical remarks.

Smolny Institute, headquarters of the *Tsay-ee-kah* and of the Petrograd Soviet, lay miles out on the edge of the city, beside the wide Neva. I went there on a street-car, moving snail-like with a groaning noise through the cobbled, muddy streets, and jammed with people. At the end of the line rose the graceful smoke-blue cupolas of Smolny Convent outlined in dull gold, beautiful; and beside it the great barracks like façade of Smolny Institute, two hundred yards long and three lofty stories high, the Imperial arms carved hugely in stone still insolent over the entrance....

Under the old régime a famous convent-school for the daughters of the Russian nobility, patronised by the Tsarina herself, the Institute had been taken over by the revolutionary organisations of workers and soldiers. Within were more than a hundred huge rooms, white and bare, on their doors enamelled plaques still informing the passerby that within was "Ladies' Class-room Number 4" or "Teachers' Bureau"; but over these hung crudely-lettered signs, evidence of the vitality of the new order: "Central Committee of the Petrograd Soviet" and *"Tsay-ee-kah"* and "Bureau of Foreign Affairs"; "Union of Socialist Soldiers," "Central Committee of the All-Russian Trade Unions," "Factory-Shop Committees," "Central Army Committee"; and the central offices and caucus-rooms of the political parties....

The long, vaulted corridors, lit by rare electric lights, were thronged with hurrying shapes of soldiers and workmen, some bent under the weight of huge bundles of newspapers, proclamations, printed propaganda of all sorts. The sound of their heavy boots made a deep and incessant thunder on the wooden floor.... Signs were posted up everywhere: "Comrades! For the sake of your health, preserve cleanliness!" Long tables stood at the head of the stairs on every floor, and on the landings, heaped with pamphlets and the literature of the different political parties, for sale....

The spacious, low-ceilinged refectory downstairs was still a dining-room. For two rubles I bought a ticket entitling me to dinner, and stood in line with a thousand others, waiting to get to the long serving-tables, where twenty men and women were ladling from immense cauldrons cabbage soup, hunks of meat and piles of *kasha,* slabs of black bread. Five kopeks paid for tea in a tin cup. From a basket one grabbed a greasy wooden spoon.... The benches along the wooden tables were packed with hungry proletarians, wolfing their food, plotting, shouting rough jokes across the room....

[Graphic page-33 — text of placard in russian, translation follows]

COMRADES FOR THE SAKE OF YOUR HEALTH, PRESERVE CLEANLINESS.

Upstairs was another eating-place, reserved for the *Tsay-ee-kah-* though every one went there. Here could be had bread thickly buttered and endless glasses of tea....

In the south wing on the second floor was the great hall of meetings, the former ball-room of the Institute. A lofty white room lighted by glazed-white chandeliers holding hundreds of ornate electric bulbs, and divided by two rows of massive columns; at one end a dais, flanked with two tall many-branched light standards, and a gold frame behind, from which the Imperial portrait had been cut. Here on festal occasions had been banked brilliant military and ecclesiastical uniforms, a setting for Grand Duchesses....

Just across the hall outside was the office of the Credentials Committee for the Congress of Soviets. I stood there watching the new delegates come in-burly, bearded soldiers, workmen in black blouses, a few long-haired peasants. The girl in charge-a member of Plekhanov's *Yedinstvo* [*] group-smiled contemptuously. "These are [* See Notes and Explanations] very different people from the delegates to the first *Siezd* (Congress)," she remarked. "See how rough and ignorant they look! The Dark People...." It was true; the depths of Russia had been stirred, and it was the bottom which came uppermost now. The Credentials Committee, appointed by the old *Tsay-ee-kah,* was challenging delegate after delegate, on the ground that they had been illegally elected. Karakhan, member of the Bolshevik Central Committee, simply grinned. "Never mind," he said, "When the time comes we'll see that you get your seats...."

Rabotchi i Soldat said:

The attention of delegates to the new All-Russian Congress is called to attempts of certain members of the Organising Committee to break up the Congress, by asserting that it will not take place, and that delegates had better leave Petrograd.... Pay no attention to these lies.... Great days are coming....

It was evident that a quorum would not come together by November 2, so the opening of the Congress was postponed to the 7th. But the whole country was now aroused; and the

Mensheviki and Socialist Revolutionaries, realising that they were defeated, suddenly changed their tactics and began to wire frantically to their provincial organisations to elect as many "moderate" Socialist delegates as possible. At the same time the Executive Committee of the Peasants' Soviets issued an emergency call for a Peasants' Congress, to meet December 13th and offset whatever action the workers and soldiers might take...

What would the Bolsheviki do? Rumours ran through the city that there would be an armed "demonstration," a *vystuplennie*-"coming out" of the workers and soldiers. The bourgeois and reactionary press prophesied insurrection, and urged the Government to arrest the Petrograd Soviet, or at least to prevent the meeting of the Congress. Such sheets as *Novaya Rus* advocated a general Bolshevik massacre.

Gorky's paper, *Novaya Zhizn*, agreed with the Bolsheviki that the reactionaries were attempting to destroy the Revolution, and that if necessary they must be resisted by force of arms; but all the parties of the revolutionary democracy must present a united front.

As long as the democracy has not organised its principal forces, so long as the resistance to its influence is still strong, there is no advantage in passing to the attack. But if the hostile elements appeal to force, then the revolutionary democracy should enter the battle to seize the power, and it will be sustained by the most profound strata of the people....

Gorky pointed out that both reactionary and Government newspapers were inciting the Bolsheviki to violence. An insurrection, however, would prepare the way for a new Kornilov. He urged the Bolsheviki to deny the rumours. Potressov, in the Menshevik *Dien* (Day), published a sensational story, accompanied by a map, which professed to reveal the secret Bolshevik plan of campaign.

As if by magic, the walls were covered with warnings, proclamations, appeals, from the Central Committees of the "moderate" and conservative factions and the *Tsay-ee-kah*, denouncing any "demonstrations," imploring the workers and soldiers not to listen to agitators. For instance, this from the Military Section of the Socialist Revolutionary party:

Again rumours are spreading around the town of an intended *vystuplennie*. What is the source of these rumours? What organisation authorises these agitators who preach insurrection? The Bolsheviki, to a question addressed to them in the *Tsay-ee-kah*, denied that they have anything to do with it.... But these rumours themselves carry with them a great danger. It may easily happen that, not taking into consideration the state of mind of the majority of the workers, soldiers and peasants, individual hot-heads will call out part of the workers and soldiers on the streets, inciting them to an uprising.... In this fearful time through which revolutionary Russia is passing, any insurrection can easily turn into civil war, and there can result from it the destruction of all organisations of the proletariat, built up with so much labour.... The counter-revolutionary plotters are planning to take advantage of this insurrection to destroy the Revolution, open the front to Wilhelm, and wreck the Constituent Assembly.... Stick stubbornly to your posts! Do not come out!

On October 28th, in the corridors of Smolny, I spoke with Kameniev, a little man with a reddish pointed beard and Gallic gestures. He was not at all sure that enough delegates would come. "If there *is* a Congress," he said, "it will represent the overwhelming sentiment of the people. If the majority is Bolshevik, as I think it will be, we shall demand that the power be given to the Soviets, and the Provisional Government must resign...."

Volodarsky, a tall, pale youth with glasses and a bad complexion, was more definite. "The 'Lieber-Dans' and the other compromisers are sabotaging the Congress. If they succeed in preventing its meeting,-well, then we are realists enough not to depend on *that!*"

Under date of October 29th I find entered in my notebook the following items culled from the newspapers of the day:

Moghilev (General Staff Headquarters). Concentration here of loyal Guard Regiments, the Savage Division, Cossacks and Death Battalions.

The *yunkers* of the Officers' Schools of Pavlovsk, Tsarskoye Selo and Peterhof ordered by the Government to be ready to come to Petrograd. Oranienbaum *yunkers* arrive in the city.

Part of the Armoured Car Division of the Petrograd garrism stationed in the Winter Palace.

Upon orders signed by Trotzky, several thousand rifles delivered by the Government Arms Factory at Sestroretzk to delegates of the Petrograd workmen.

At a meeting of the City Militia of the Lower Liteiny Quarter, a resolution demanding that all power be given to the Soviets.

This is just a sample of the confused events of those feverish days, when everybody knew that something was going to happen, but nobody knew just what.

At a meeting of the Petrograd Soviet in Smolny, the night of October 30th, Trotzky branded the assertions of the bourgeois press that the Soviet contemplated armed insurention as "an attempt of the reactionaries to discredit and wreck the Congress of Soviets.... The Petrograd Soviet," he declared, "had not ordered any *uystuplennie.* If it is necessary we shall do so, and we will be supported by the Petrogruad garrison.... They (the Government) are preparing a counter-revolution; and we shall answer with an offensive which will be merciless and decisive."

It is true that the Petrograd Soviet had not ordered a demonstration, but the Central Committee of the Bolshevik party was considering the question of insurrection. All night long the 23d they met. There were present all the party intellectuals, the leaders-and delegates of the Petrograd workers and garrison. Alone of the intellectuals Lenin and Trotzky stood for insurrection. Even urrection. Even | | the military men opposed it. A vote was taken. Insurrection was defeated!

Then arose a rough workman, his face convulsed with rage. "I speak for the Petrograd proletariat," he said, harshly. "We are in favour of insurrection. Have it your own way, but I tell you now that if you allow the Soviets to be destroyed, *we're through with you!*" Some soldiers joined him.... And after that they voted again-insurrection won....

However, the right wing of the Bolsheviki, led by Riazanov, Kameniev and Zinoviev, continued to campaign against an armed rising. On the morning of October 31st appeared in *Rabotchi Put* the first instalment of Lenin's "Letter to the Comrades," one of the most audacious pieces of political propaganda the world has ever seen. In it Lenin seriously presented the arguments in favour of insurrection, taking as text the objections of Kameniev and Riazonov.

"Either we must abandon our slogan, 'All Power to the Soviets,' " he wrote, "or else we must make an insurrection. There is no middle course...."

That same afternoon Paul Miliukov, leader of the Cadets, made a brilliant, bitter speech in the Council of the Republic, branding the Skobeliev *nakaz* as pro-German, declaring that the "revolutionary democracy" was destroying Russia, sneering at Terestchenko, and openly declaring that he preferred German diplomacy to Russian.... The Left benches were one roaring tumult all through....

On its part the Government could not ignore the significance of the success of the Bolshevik propaganda. On the 29th joint commission of the Government and the Council of the Republic hastily drew up two laws, one for giving the land temporarily to the peasants, and the other for pushing an energetic foreign policy of peace. The next day Kerensky suspended capital punishment in the army. That same afternoon was opened with great ceremony the first session of the new "Commission for Strengthening the Republican Régime and Fighting Against Anarchy and Counter-Revolution"-of which history shows not the slightest further trace.... The following morning with two other correspondents I interviewed Kerensky the last time he received journalists.

"The Russian people," he said, bitterly, "are suffering from economic fatigue-and from disillusionment with the Allies! The world thinks that the Russian Revolution is at an end. Do not be mistaken. The Russian Revolution is just beginning...." Words more prophetic, perhaps, than he knew.

Stormy was the all-night meeting of the Petrograd Soviet the 30th of October, at which I was present. The "moderate" Socialist intellectuals, officers, members of Army Committees, the *Tsay-ee-kah,* were there in force. Against them rose up workmen, peasants and common soldiers, passionate and simple.

A peasant told of the disorders in Tver, which he said were caused by the arrest of the Land Committees. "This Kerensky is nothing but a shield to the *pomieshtchiki* (landowners)," he cried. "They know that at the Constituent Assembly we will take the land anyway, so they are trying to destroy the Constituent Assembly!"

A machinist from the Putilov works described how the superintendents were closing down the departments one by one on the pretext that there was no fuel or raw materials. The Factory-Shop Committee, he declared, had discovered huge hidden supplies.

"It is a *provocatzia,"* said he. "They want to starve us-or drive us to violence!"

Among the soldiers one began, "Comrades! I bring you greetings from the place where men are digging their graves and call them trenches!"

Then arose a tall, gaunt young soldier, with flashing eyes, met with a roar of welcome. It was Tchudnovsky, reported killed in the July fighting, and now risen from the dead.

"The soldier masses no longer trust their officers. Even the Army Committees, who refused to call a meeting of our Soviet, betrayed us.... The masses of the soldiers want the Constituent Assembly to be held exactly when it was called for, and those who dare to postpone it will be cursed-and not only platonic curses either, for the Army has guns too...."

He told of the electoral campaign for the Constituent now raging in the Fifth Army. "The officers, and especially the Mensheviki and the Socialist Revolutionaries, are trying deliberately to cripple the Bolsheviki. Our papers are not allowed to circulate in the trenches. Our speakers are arrested-"

"Why don't you speak about the lack of bread?" shouted another soldier.

"Man shall not live by bread alone," answered Tchudnovsky, sternly....

Followed him an officer, delegate from the Vitebsk Soviet, a Menshevik *oboronetz.* "It isn't the question of who has the power. The trouble is not with the Government, but with the war.... and the war must be won before any change-" At this, hoots and ironical cheers. "These Bolshevik agitators are demagogues!" The hall rocked with laughter. "Let us for a moment forget the class struggle-" But he got no farther. A voice yelled, "Don't you wish we would!"

Petrograd presented a curious spectacle in those days. In the factories the committe-rooms were filled with stacks of rifles, couriers came and went, the Red Guard [*] drilled.... In all the [* See Notes and Explanations] barracks meetings every night, and all day long interminable hot arguments. On the streets the crowds thickened toward gloomy evening, pouring in slow voluble tides up and down the Nevsky, fighting for the newspapers.... Hold-ups increased to such an extent that it was dangerous to walk down side streets.... On the Sadovaya one afternoon I saw a crowd of several hundred people beat and trample to death a soldier caught stealing.... Mysterious individuals circulated around the shivering women who waited in *queue* long cold hours for bread and milk, whispering that the Jews had cornered the food supply-and that while the people starved, the Soviet members lived luxuriously....

At Smolny there were strict guards at the door and the outer gates, demanding everybody's pass. The committee-rooms buzzed and hummed all day and all night, hundreds of soldiers and workmen slept on the floor, wherever they could find room. Upstairs in the great hall a thousand people crowded to the uproarious sessions of the Petrograd Soviet....

Gambling clubs functioned hectically from dusk to dawn, with champagne flowing and stakes of twenty thousand rubles. In the centre of the city at night prostitutes in jewels and expensive furs walked up and down, crowded the cafés....

Monarchist plots, German spies, smugglers hatching schemes....

And in the rain, the bitter chill, the great throbbing city under grey skies rushing faster and faster toward-what?

CHAPTER III

On The Eve

IN the relations of a weak Government and a rebellious people there comes a time when every act of the authorities exasperates the masses, and every refusal to act excites their contempt....

The proposal to abandon Petrograd raised a hurricane; Kerensky's public denial that the Government had any such intention was met with hoots of derision.

Pinned to the wall by the pressure of the Revolution (cried *Rabotchi Put),* the Government of "provisional" bourgeois tries to get free by giving out lying assurances that it never thought of fleeing from Petrograd, and that it didn't wish to surrender the capital....

In Kharkov thirty thousand coal miners organised, adopting the preamble of the I. W. W. constitution: "The working class and the employing class have nothing in common." Dispersed by Cossacks, some were locked out by the mine-owners, and the rest declared a general strike. Minister of Commerce and Industry Konovalov appointed his assistant, Orlov, with plenary powers, to settle the trouble. Orlov was hated by the miners. But the *Tsay-ee-kah* not only supported his appointment, but refused to demand that the Cossacks be recalled from the Don Basin....

This was followed by the dispersal of the Soviet at Kaluga. The Bolsheviki, having secured a majority in the Soviet, set free some political prisoners. With the sanction of the Government Commissar the Municipal Duma called in troops from Minsk, and bombarded the Soviet headquarters with artillery. The Bolsheviki yielded, but as they left the building Cossacks attacked them, crying, "This is what we'll do to all the other Bolshevik Soviets, including those of Moscow and Petrograd!" This incident sent a wave of panic rage throughout Russia....

In Petrograd was ending a regional Congress of Soviets of the North, presided over by the Bolshevik Krylenko. By an immense majority it resolved that all power should be assumed by the All-Russian Congress; and concluded by greeting the Bolsheviki in prison, bidding them rejoice, for the hour of their liberation was at hand. At the same time the first All-Russian Conference of Factory-Shop Committees declared emphatically for the Soviets, and continued significantly,

After liberating themselves politically from Tsardom, the working-class wants to see the democratic régime triumphant in the sphere of its productive activity. This is best expressed by Workers' Control over industrial production, which naturally arose in the atmosphere of economic decomposition created by the criminal policy of the dominating classes....

The Union of Railwaymen was demanding the resignation of Liverovsky, Minister of Ways and Communications....

In the name of the *Tsay-ee-kah,* Skobeliev insisted that the *nakaz* be presented at the Allied Conference, and formally protested against the sending of Terestchenko to Paris. Terestchenko offered to resign....

General Verkhovsky, unable to accomplish his reorganisation of the army, only came to Cabinet meetings at long intervals....

On November 3d Burtzev's *Obshtchee Dielo* came out with great headlines:

Citizens! Save the fatherland!

I have just learned that yesterday, at a meeting of the Commission for National Defence, Minister of War General Verkhovsky, one of the principal persons responsible for the fall of Kornilov, proposed to sign a separate peace, independently of the Allies.

That is treason to Russia!

Terestchenko declared that the Provisional Government had not even examined Verkhovsky's proposition.

"You might think," said Terestchenko, "that we were in a madhouse!"

The members of the Commission were astounded at the General's words.

General Alexeyev wept.

No! It is not madness! It is worse. It is direct treason to Russia!

Kerensky, Terestchenko and Nekrassov must immediately answer us concerning the words of Verkhovsky.

Citizens, arise!

Russia is being sold!

Save her!

What Verkhovsky really said was that the Allies must be pressed to offer peace, because the Russian army could fight no longer....

Both in Russia and abroad the sensation was tremendous. Verkhovsky was given "indefinite leave of absence for illhealth," and left the Government. *Obshtchee Dielo* was suppressed....

Sunday, November 4th, was designated as the Day of the Petrograd Soviet, with immense meetings planned all over the city, ostensibly to raise money for the organisation and the press; really, to make a demonstration of strength. Suddenly it was announced that on the same day the Cossacks would hold a *Krestny Khod*-Procession of the Cross-in honour of the Ikon of 1612, through whose miraculous intervention Napoleon had been driven from Moscow. The atmosphere was electric; a spark might kindle civil war. The Petrograd Soviet issued a manifesto, headed "Brothers-Cossacks!"

You, Cossacks, are being incited against us, workers and soldiers. This plan of Cain is being put into operation by our common enemies, the oppressors, the privileged classes-generals, bankers, landlords, former officials, former servants of the Tsar.... We are hated by all grafters, rich men, princes, nobles, generals, including your Cossack generals. They are ready at any moment to destroy the Petrograd Soviet and crush the Revolution....

On the 4th of November somebody is organising a Cossack religious procession. It is a question of the free consciousness of every individual whether he will or will not take part in this procession. We do not interfere in this matter, nor do we obstruct anybody.... However, we warn you, Cossacks! Look out and see to it that under the pretext of a *Krestni Khod,* your Kaledins do not instigate you against workmen, against soldiers....

The procession was hastily called off....

In the barracks and the working-class quarters of the town the Bolsheviki were preaching, "All Power to the Soviets!" and agents of the Dark Forces were urging the people to rise and slaughter the Jews, shop-keepers, Socialist leaders....

On one side the Monarchist press, inciting to bloody repression-on the other Lenin's great voice roaring, "Insurrection!.... We cannot wait any longer!"

Even the bourgeois press was uneasy. *Birjevya Viedomosti* (Exchange Gazette) called the Bolshevik propaganda an attack on "the most elementary principles of society-personal security and the respect for private property."

[Graphic page-46 Appeal of the Petrograd Soviet]

Appeal of the Petrograd Soviet to the Cosacks to call off their *Krestny Khod*-the religious procession planned for November 4th (our calendar). "Brothers-Cossacks!" it begins. "The Petrograd Soviet of Workers' and Soldiers' Deputies addresses you."

But it was the "moderate" Socialist journals which were the most hostile. "The Bolsheviki are the most dangerous enemies of the Revolution," declared *Dielo Naroda*. Said the Menshevik *Dien*, "The Government ought to defend itself and defend us." Plekhanov's paper, *Yedinstvo* (Unity) called the attention of the Government to the fact that the Petrograd workers were being armed, and demanded stern measures against the Bolsheviki.

Daily the Government seemed to become more helpless. Even the Municipal administration broke down. The columns of the morning papers were filled with accounts of the most audacious robberies and murders, and the criminals were unmolested.

On the other hand armed workers patrolled the streets at night, doing battle with marauders and requisitioning arms wherever they found them.

On the first of November Colonel Polkovnikov, Military Commander of Petrograd, issued a proclamation:

Despite the difficult days through which the country is passing, irresponsible appeals to armed demonstrations and massacres are still being spread around Petrograd, and from day to day robbery and disorder increase.

This state of things is disorganising the life of the citizens, and hinders the systematic work of the Government and the Municipal Institutions.

In full consciousness of my responsibility and my duty before my country, I command:

1. Every military unit, in accordance with special instructions and within the territory of its garrison, to afford every assistance to the Municipality, to the Commissars, and to the militia, in the guarding of Government institutions.

2. The organisation of patrols, in co-operation with the District Commander and the representatives of the city militia, and the taking of measures for the arrest of criminals and deserters.

3. The arrest of all persons entering barracks and inciting to armed demonstrations and massacres, and their delivery to the headquarters of the Second Commander of the city.

4. To suppress any armed demonstration or riot at its start, with all armed forces at hand.

5. To afford assistance to the Commissars in preventing unwarranted searches in houses and unwarranted arrests.

6. To report immediately all that happens in the district under charge to the Staff of the Petrograd Military District.

I call upon all Army Committees and organisations to afford their help to the commanders in fulfilment of the duties with which they are charged.

In the Council of the Republic Kerensky declared that the Government was fully aware of the Bolshevik preparations, and had sufficient force to cope with any demonstration. He accused *Novaya Rus* and *Robotchi Put* of both doing the same kind of subversive work. "But owing to the absolute freedom of the press," he added, "the Government is not in a position to combat printed lies. [*]...." Declaring that these were two aspects of the same [* This was not quite candid. The Provisional Government had suppressed Bolshevik papers before, in July, and was planning to do so again.] propaganda, which had for its object the counter-revolution, so ardently desired by the Dark Forces, he went on:

"I am a doomed man, it doesn't matter what happens to me, and I have the audacity to say that the other enigmatic part is that of the unbelievable provocation created in the city by the Bolsheviki!"

On November 2d only fifteen delegates to the Congress of Soviets had arrived. Next day there were a hundred, and the morning after that a hundred and seventy-five, of whom one hundred and three were Bolsheviki.... Four hundred constituted a quorum, and the Congress was only three days off....

I spent a great deal of time at Smolny. It was no longer easy to get in. Double rows of sentries guarded the outer gates, and once inside the front door there was a long line of people waiting to be let in, four at a time, to be questioned as to their identity and their business. Passes were given out, and the pass system was changed every few hours; for spies continually sneaked through....

[Graphic page-49 Russian Pass to Reed, translation follows]

Pass to Smolny Institute, issued by the Military Revolutionary Committee, giving me the right of entry at any time. (Translation)

Military Revolutionary Committee
attached to the
Petrograd Soviet of W. & S. D.
Commandant's office

PASS

Is given by the present to John Reed, correspondent of the American Socialist press, until December 1, the right of free entry into Smolny Institute. Commandant Adjutant

One day as I came up to the outer gate I saw Trotzky and his wife just ahead of me. They were halted by a soldier. Trotzky searched through his pockets, but could find no pass.

"Never mind," he said finally. "You know me. My name is Trotzky."

"You haven't got a pass," answered the soldier stubbornly.

"You cannot go in. Names don't mean anything to me."

"But I am the president of the Petrograd Soviet."

"Well," replied the soldier, "if you're as important a fellow as that you must at least have one little paper."

Trotzky was very patient. "Let me see the Commandant," he said. The soldier hesitated, grumbling something about not wanting to disturb the Commandant for every devil that came along. He beckoned finally to the soldier in command of the guard. Trotzky explained matters to him. "My name is Trotzky," he repeated.

"Trotzky?" The other soldier scratched his head. "I've heard the name somewhere," he said at length. "I guess it's all right. You can go on in, comrade...."

In the corridor I met Karakhan, member of the Bolshevik Central Committee, who explained to me what the new Government would be like.

"A loose organisation, sensitive to the popular will as expressed through the Soviets, allowing local forces full play. At present the Provisional Government obstructs the action of the local democratic will, just as the Tsar's Government did. The initiative of the new society shall come from below.... The form of the Government will be modelled on the Constitution of the Russian Social Democratic Labour Party. The new *Tsay-ee-kah,* responsible to frequent meetings of the All-Russian Congress of Soviets, will be the parliament; the various Ministries will be headed by *collegia*-committees-instead of by Ministers, and will be directly responsible to the Soviets....

On October 30th, by appointment, I went up to a small, bare room in the attic of Smolny, to talk with Trotzky. In the middle of the room he sat on a rough chair at a bare table. Few questions from me were necessary; he talked rapidly and steadily, for more than an hour. The substance of his talk, in his own words, I give here:

"The Provisional Government is absolutely powerless. The bourgeoisie is in control, but this control is masked by a fictitious coalition with the *oborontsi* parties. Now, during the Revolution, one sees revolts of peasants who are tired of waiting for their promised land; and all over the country, in all the toiling classes, the same disgust is evident. This domination by the bourgeoisie is only possible by means of civil war. The Kornilov method is the only way by which the bourgeoisie can control. But it is force which the bourgeoisie lacks.... The Army is with us. The conciliators and pacifists, Socialist Revolutionaries and Mensheviki, have lost all authority-because the struggle between the peasants and the landlords, between the workers and the employers, between the soldiers and the officers, has become more bitter, more irreconcilable than ever. Only by the concerted action of the popular mass, only by the victory of proletarian dictatorship, can the Revolution be achieved and the people saved....

"The Soviets are the most perfect representatives of the people-perfect in their revolutionary experience, in their ideas and objects. Based directly upon the army in the trenches, the workers in the factories, and the peasants in the fields, they are the backbone of the Revolution.

"There has been an attempt to create a power without the Soviets-and only powerlessness has been created. Counter-revolutionary schemes of all sorts are now being hatched in the corridors of the Council of the Russian Republic. The Cadet party represents the counter-revolution militant. On the other side, the Soviets represent the cause of the people. Between the two camps there are no groups of serious importance.... It is the *lutte finale.* The bourgeois counter-revolution organises all its forces and waits for the moment to attack us. Our answer will be decisive. We will complete the work scarcely begun in March, and advanced during the Kornilov affair...."

He went on to speak of the new Government's foreign policy:

"Our first act will be to call for an immediate armistice on all fronts, and a conference of peoples to discuss democratic peace terms. The quantity of democracy we get in the peace settlement depends on the quantity of revolutionary response there is in Europe. If we create here a Government of the Soviets, that will be a powerful factor for immediate peace in Europe; for this Government will address itself directly and immediately to all peoples, over the heads of their Governments, proposing an armistice. At the moment of the conclusion of peace the pressure of the Russian Revolution will be in the direction of 'no annexations,# no indemnities, the right of self-determination of peoples,' and a *Federated Republic of Europe....*

34

"At the end of this war I see Europe recreated, not by the diplomats, but by the proletariat. The Federated Republic of Europe-the United States of Europe-that is what must be. National autonomy no longer suffices. Economic evolution demands the abolition of national frontiers. If Europe is to remain split into national groups, then Imperialism will recommence its work. Only a Federated Republic of Europe can give peace to the world." He smiled-that fine, faintly ironical smile of his. "But without the action of the European masses, these ends cannot be realised-now...."

Now while everybody was waiting for the Bolsheviki to appear suddenly on the streets one morning and begin to shoot down people with white collars on, the real insurrection took its way quite naturally and openly.

The Provisional Government planned to send the Petrograd garrison to the front.

The Petrograd garrison numbered about sixty thousand men, who had taken a prominent part in the Revolution. It was they who had turned the tide in the great days of March, created the Soviets of Soldiers' Deputies, and hurled back Kornilov from the gates of Petrograd.

Now a large part of them were Bolsheviki. When the Provisional Government talked of evacuating the city, it was the Petrograd garrison which answered, "If you are not capable of defending the capital, conclude peace; if you cannot conclude peace, go away and make room for a People's Government which can do both...."

It was evident that any attempt at insurrection depended upon the attitude of the Petrograd garrison. The Government's plan was to replace the garrison regiments with "dependable" troops-Cossacks, Death Battalions. The Army Committees, the "moderate" Socialists and the *Tsay-ee-kah* supported the Government. A wide-spread agitation was carried on at the Front and in Petrograd, emphasizing the fact that for eight months the Petrograd garrison had been leading an easy life in the barracks of the capital, while their exhausted comrades in the trenches starved and died.

Naturally there was some truth in the accusation that the garrison regiments were reluctant to exchange their comparative comfort for the hardships of a winter campaign. But there were other reasons why they refused to go. The Petrograd Soviet feared the Government's intentions, and from the Front came hundreds of delegates, chosen by the common soldiers, crying, "It is true we need reinforcements, but more important, we must know that Petrograd and the Revolution are well-guarded.... Do you hold the rear, comrades, and we will hold the front!"

On October 25th, behind closed doors, the Central Committee of the Petrograd Soviet discussed the formation of a special Military Committee to decide the whole question. The next day a meeting of the Soldiers' Section of the Petrograd Soviet elected a Committee, which immediately proclaimed a boycott of the bourgeois newspapers, and condemned the *Tsay-ee-kah* for opposing the Congress of Soviets. On the 29th, in open session of the Petrograd Soviet, Trotzky proposed that the Soviet formally sanction the Military Revolutionary Committee. "We ought," he said, "to create our special organisation to march to battle, and if necessary to die...." It was decided to send to the front two delegations, one from the Soviet and one from the garrison, to confer with the Soldiers' Committees and the General Staff.

At Pskov, the Soviet delegates were met by General Tcheremissov, commander of the Northern Front, with the curt declaration that he had ordered the Petrograd garrison to the trenches, and that was all. The garrison committee was not allowed to leave Petrograd....

A delegation of the Soldiers' Section of the Petrograd Soviet asked that a representative be admitted to the Staff of the Petrograd District. Refused. The Petrograd Soviet demanded that no orders be issued without the approval of the Soldiers' Section. Refused. The delegates were roughly told, "We only recognise the *Tsay-ee-kah*. We do not recognise you; if you break any laws, we shall arrest you."

On the 30th a meeting of representatives of all the Petrograd regiments passed a resolution: *"The Petrograd garrison no longer recognises the Provisional Government. The Petrograd Soviet is our Government. We will obey only the orders of the Petrograd Soviet, through the Military Revolutionary Committee."* The local military units were ordered to wait for instructions from the Soldiers' Section of the Petrograd Soviet.

Next day the *Tsay-ee-kah* summoned its own meeting, composed largely of officers, formed a Committee to cooperate with the Staff, and detailed Commissars in all quarters of the city.

A great soldier meeting at Smolny on the 3d resolved:

Saluting the creation of the Military Revolutionary Committee, the
Petrograd garrison promises it complete support in all its actions,
to unite more closely the front and the rear in the interests of the
Revolution.

The garrison moreover declares that with the revolutionary
proletariat it assures the maintenance of revolutionary order in
Petrograd. Every attempt at provocation on the part of the
Kornilovtsi or the bourgeoisie will be met with merciless resistance.

Now conscious of its power, the Military Revolutionary Committee peremptorily summoned the Petrograd Staff to submit to its control. To all printing plants it gave orders not to publish any appeals or proclamations without the Committee's authorisation. Armed

Commissars visited the Kronversk arsenal and seized great quantities of arms and ammunition, halting a shipment of ten thousand bayonets which was being sent to Novotcherkask, headquarters of Kaledin....

Suddenly awake to the danger, the Government offered immunity if the Committee would disband. Too late. At midnight November 5th Kerensky himself sent Malevsky to offer the Petrograd Soviet representation on the Staff. The Military Revolutionary Committee accepted. An hour later General Manikovsky, acting Minister of war, countermanded the offer....

Tuesday morning, November 6th, the city was thrown into excitement by the appearance of a placard signed, "Military Revolutionary Committee attached to the Petrograd Soviet of Workers' and Soldiers' Deputies."

To the Population of Petrograd. Citizens!

Counter-revolution has raised its criminal head. The Kornilovtsi are mobilising their forces in order to crush the All-Russian Congress of Soviets and break the Constituent Assembly. At the same time the *pogromists* may attempt to call upon the people of Petrograd for trouble and bloodshed. The Petrograd Soviet of Workers' and Soldiers' Deputies takes upon itself the guarding of revolutionary order in the city against counter-revolutionary and *pogrom* attempts.

The Petrograd garrison will not allow any violence or disorders. The population is invited to arrest hooligans and Black Hundred agitators and take them to the Soviet Commissars at the nearest barracks. At the first attempt of the Dark Forces to make trouble on the streets of Petrograd, whether robbery or fighting, the criminals will be wiped off the face of the earth!

Citizens! We call upon you to maintain complete quiet and self-possession. The cause of order and Revolution is in strong hands.

List of regiments where there are Commissars of the Military
Revolutionary Committee....

On the 3rd the leaders of the Bolsheviki had another historic meeting behind closed doors. Notified by Zalkind, I waited in the corridor outside the door; and Volodarsky as he came out told me what was going on.

Lenin spoke: "November 6th will be too early. We must have an all-Russian basis for the rising; and on the 6th all the delegates to the Congress will not have arrived.... On the other hand, November 8th will be too late. By that time the Congress will be organised, and it is difficult for a large organised body of people to take swift, decisive action. We must act on the 7th, the day the Congress meets, so that we may say to it, 'Here is the power! What are you going to do with it?'"

In a certain upstairs room sat a thin-faced, long-haired individual, once an officer in the armies of the Tsar, then revolutionist and exile, a certain Avseenko, called Antonov, mathematician and chess-player; he was drawing careful plans for the seizure of the capital.

On its side the Government was preparing. Inconspicuously certain of the most loyal regiments, from widely-separated divisions, were ordered to Petrograd. The *yunker* artillery was drawn into the Winter Palace. Patrols of Cossacks made their appearance in the streets, for the first time since the July days. Polkovnikov issued order after order, threatening to repress all insubordination with the "utmost energy." Kishkin, Minister of Public Instruction, the worsthated member of the Cabinet, was appointed Special Commissar to keep order in Petrograd; he named as assistants two men no less unpopular, Rutenburg and Paltchinsky. Petrograd, Cronstadt and Finland were declared in a state of siege-upon which the bourgeois *Novoye Vremya* (New Times) remarked ironically:

Why the state of siege? The Government is no longer a power. It has no moral authority and it does not possess the necessary apparatus to use force.... In the most favourable circumstances it can only negotiate with any one who consents to parley. Its authority goes no farther....

Monday morning, the 5th, I dropped in at the Marinsky Palace, to see what was happening in the Council of the Russian Republic. Bitter debate on Terestchenko's foreign policy. Echoes of the Burtzev-Verkhovski affair. All the diplomats present except the Italian ambassador, who everybody said was prostrated by the Carso disaster....

As I came in, the Left Socialist Revolutionary Karelin was reading aloud an editorial from the London *Times* which said, "The remedy for Bolshevism is bullets!" Turning to the Cadets he cried, "That's what *you* think, too!"

Voices from the Right, "Yes! Yes!"

"Yes, I know you think so," answered Karelin, hotly. "But you haven't the courage to try it!"

Then Skobeliev, looking like a matinée idol with his soft blond beard and wavy yellow hair, rather apologetically defending the Soviet *nakaz*. Terestchenko followed, assailed from the Left by cries of "Resignation! Resignation!" He insisted that the delegates of the Government and of the *Tsay-ee-kah* to Paris should have a common point of view-his own. A few words about the restoration of discipline in the army, about war to victory.... Tumult, and over the stubborn opposition of the truculent Left, the Council of the Republic passed to the simple order of the day.

There stretched the rows of Bolshevik seats-empty since that first day when they left the Council, carrying with them so much life. As I went down the stairs it seemed to me that in spite of the bitter wrangling, no real voice from the rough world outside could penetrate this high, cold hall, and that the Provisional Government was wrecked-on the same rock of War and Peace that had wrecked the Miliukov Ministry.... The doorman grumbled as he put on my coat, "I don't know what is becoming of poor Russia. All these Mensheviki and Bolsheviki and Trudoviki.... This Ukraine and this Finland and the German imperialists and the English imperialists. I am forty-five years old, and in all my life I never heard so many words as in this place...."

In the corridor I met Professor Shatsky, a rat-faced individual in a dapper frock-coat, very influential in the councils of the Cadet party. I asked him what he thought of the much-talked-of Bolshevik *vystuplennie.* He shrugged, sneering.

"They are cattle-*canaille,"* he answered. "They will not dare, or if they dare they will soon be sent flying. From our point of view it will not be bad, for then they will ruin themselves and have no power in the Constituent Assembly....

"But, my dear sir, allow me to outline to you my plan for a form of Government to be submitted to the Constituent Assembly. You see, I am chairman of a commission appointed from this body, in conjunction with the Provisional Government, to work out a constitutional project.... We will have a legislative assembly of two chambers, such as you have in the United States. In the lower chamber will be territorial representatives; in the upper, representatives of the liberal professions, zemstvos, Cooperatives-and Trade Unions...."

Outside a chill, damp wind came from the west, and the cold mud underfoot soaked through my shoes. Two companies of *yunkers* passed swinging up the Morskaya, tramping stiffly in their long coats and singing an oldtime crashing chorus, such as the soldiers used to sing under the Tsar.... At the first cross-street I noticed that the City Militiamen were mounted, and armed with revolvers in bright new holsters; a little group of people stood silently staring at them. At the corner of the Nevsky I bought a pamphlet by Lenin, "Will the Bolsheviki be Able to Hold the Power?" paying for it with one of the stamps which did duty for small change. The usual street-cars crawled past, citizens and soldiers clinging to the outside in a way to make Theodore P. Shonts green with envy.... Along the sidewalk a row of deserters in uniform sold cigarettes and sunflower seeds....

Up the Nevsky in the sour twilight crowds were battling for the latest papers, and knots of people were trying to make out the multitudes of appeals and proclamations pasted in every flat place; from the *Tsay-ee-kah,* the Peasants' Soviets, the "moderate" Socialist parties, the Army Committees-threatening, cursing, beseeching the workers and soldiers to stay home, to support the Government....

An armoured automobile went slowly up and down, siren screaming. On every corner, in every open space, thick groups were clustered; arguing soldiers and students. Night came swiftly down, the wide-spaced street-lights flickered on, the tides of people flowed endlessly.... It is always like that in Petrograd just before trouble....

The city was nervous, starting at every sharp sound. But still no sign from the Bolsheviki; the soldiers stayed in the barracks, the workmen in the factories.... We went to a moving picture show near the Kazan Cathedral-a bloody Italian film of passion and intrigue. Down front were some soldiers and sailors, staring at the screen in childlike wonder, totally unable to comprehend why there should be so much violent running about, and so much homicide....

From there I hurried to Smolny. In room 10 on the top floor, the Military Revolutionary Committee sat in continuous session, under the chairmanship of a tow-headed, eighteen-year-old boy named Lazimir. He stopped, as he passed, to shake hands rather bashfully.

"Peter-Paul Fortress has just come over to us," said he, with a pleased grin. "A minute ago we got word from a regiment that was ordered by the Government to come to Petrograd. The men were suspicious, so they stopped the train at Gatchina and sent a delegation to us. 'What's the matter?' they asked. 'What have you got to say? We have just passed a resolution, "All Power to the Soviets."'... The Military Revolutionary Committee sent back word, 'Brothers! We greet you in the name of the Revolution. Stay where you are until further instructions!'"

All telephones, he said, were cut off: but communication with the factories and barracks was established by means of military telephonograph apparatus....

A steady stream of couriers and Commissars came and went. Outside the door waited a dozen volunteers, ready to carry word to the farthest quarters of the city. One of them, a gypsy-faced man in the uniform of a lieutenant, said in French, "Everything is ready to move at the push of a button...."

There passed Podvoisky, the thin, bearded civillian whose brain conceived the strategy of insurrection; Antonov, unshaven, his collar filthy, drunk with loss of sleep; Krylenko, the squat, wide-faced soldier, always smiling, with his violent gestures and tumbling speech; and Dybenko, the giant bearded sailor with the placid face. These were the men of the hour-and of other hours to come.

Downstairs in the office of the Factory-Shop Committees sat Seratov, signing orders on the Government Arsenal for arms-one hundred and fifty rifles for each factory.... Delegates waited in line, forty of them....

In the hall I ran into some of the minor Bolshevik leaders. One showed me a revolver. "The game is on," he said, and his face was pale. "Whether we move or not the other side knows it must finish us or be finished...."

The Petrograd Soviet was meeting day and night. As I came into the great hall Trotzky was just finishing.

"We are asked," he said, "if we intend to have a *vystuplennie.* I can give a clear answer to that question. The Petrograd Soviet feels that at last the moment has arrived when the power must fall into the hands of the Soviets. This transfer of government will be accomplished by the All-Russian Congress. Whether an armed demonstration is necessary will depend on... those who wish to interfere with the All-Russian Congress....

"We feel that our Government, entrusted to the personnel of the Provisional Cabinet, is a pitiful and helpless Government, which only awaits the sweep of the broom of History to give way to a really popular Government. But we are trying to avoid a conflict, even now, to-day. We hope that the All-Russian Congress will take... into its hands that power and authority which rests upon the organised freedom of the people. If, however, the Government wants to utilise the short period it is expected to live-twenty-four, forty eight, or seventy-two hours-to attack us, then we shall answer with counter-attacks, blow for blow, steel for iron!"

Amid cheers he announced that the Left Socialist Revolutionaries had agreed to send representatives into the Military Revolutionary Committee....

As I left Smolny, at three o'clock in the morning, I noticed that two rapid-firing guns had been mounted, one on each side of the door, and that strong patrols of soldiers guarded the gates and the near-by street-corners. Bill Shatov [*] came bounding up the steps. "Well," he [* Well known in the American labor movement.] cried, "We're off! Kerensky sent the *yunkers* to close down our papers, *Soldat* and *Rabotchi Put.* But our troops went down and smashed the Government seals, and now we're sending detachments to seize the bourgeois newspaper offices!" Exultantly he slapped me on the shoulder, and ran in....

On the morning of the 6th I had business with the censor, whose office was in the Ministry of Foreign Affairs. Everywhere, on all the walls, hysterical appeals to the people to remain "calm." Polkovnikov emitted *prikaz* after *prikaz:*

I order all military units and detachments to remain in their barracks until further orders from the Staff of the Military District.... All officers who act without orders from their superiors will be court-martialled for mutiny. I forbid absolutely any execution by soldiers of instructions from other organisations....

The morning papers announced that the Government had suppressed the papers *Novaya Rus, Zhivoye Slovo, Rabotchi Put* and *Soldat,* and decreed the arrest of the leaders of the Petrograd Soviet and the members of the Military Revolutionary Committee....

As I crossed the Palace Square several batteries of *yunker* artillery came through the Red Arch at a jingling trot, and drew up before the Palace. The great red building of the General Staff was unusually animated, several armoured automobiles ranked before the door, and motors full of officers were coming and going.... The censor was very much excited, like a small boy at a circus. Kerensky, he said, had just gone to the Council of the Republic to offer his resignation. I hurried down to the Marinsky Palace, arriving at the end of that passionate and almost incoherent speech of Kerensky's, full of self-justification and bitter denunciation of his enemies.

"I will cite here the most characteristic passage from a whole series of articles published in *Rabotchi Put* by Ulianov-Lenin, a state criminal who is in hiding and whom we are trying to find.... This state criminal has invited the proletariat and the Petrograd garrison to repeat the experience of the 16th-18th of July, and insists upon the immediate necessity for an armed rising.... Moreover, other Bolshevik leaders have taken the floor in a series of meetings, and also made an appeal to immediate insurrection. Particularly should be noticed the activity of the present president of the Petrograd Soviet, Bronstein-Trotzky....

"I ought to bring to your notice... that the expressions and the style of a whole series of articles in *Rabotchi Put* and *Soldat* resemble absolutely those of *Novaya Rus....* We have to do not so much with the movement of such and such political party, as with the exploitation of the political ignorance and criminal instincts of a part of the population, a sort of organisation whose object it is to provoke in Russia, cost what it may, an inconscient movement of destruction and pillage; for given the state of mind of the masses, any movement at Petrograd will be followed by the most terrible massacres, which will cover with eternal shame the name of free Russia....

"... By the admission of Ulianov-Lenin himself, the situation of the extreme left wing of the Social Democrats in Russia is very favourable." (Here Kerensky read the following quotation from Lenin's article.):

Think of it!... The German comrades have only one Liebknecht, without newspapers, without freedom of meeting, without a Soviet.... They are opposed by the incredible hostility of all classes of society-and yet the German comrades try to act; while we, having dozens of newspapers, freedom of meeting, the majority of the Soviets, we, the best-placed international proletarians of the entire world, can we refuse to support the German revolutionists and insurrectionary organisations?...

Kerensky then continued:

"The organisers of rebellion recognise thus implicitly that the most perfect conditions for the free action of a political party obtain now in Russia, administered by a Provisional Government at the head of which is, in the eyes of this party, 'a usurper and a man who has sold himself to the bourgeoisie, the Minister-President Kerensky....'

"... The organisers of the insurrection do not come to the aid of the German proletariat, but of the German governing classes, and they open the Russian front to the iron fists of Wilhelm and his friends.... Little matter to the Provisional Government the motives of these people, little matter if they act consciously or unconsciously; but in any case, from this tribune, in full consciousness of my responsibility, I quality such acts of a Russian political party as acts of treason to Russia!

"... I place myself at the point of view of the Right, and I propose immediately to proceed to an investigation and make the necessary arrests." (Uproar from the Left.) "Listen to me!" he cried in a powerful voice. "At the moment when the state is in danger, because of conscious or unconscious treason, the Provisional Government, and myself among others, prefer to be killed rather than betray the life, the honour and the independence of Russia...."

At this moment a paper was handed to Kerensky.

"I have just received the proclamation which they are distributing to the regiments. Here is the contents." Reading: "'The Petrograd Soviet of Workers' and Soldiers' Deputies is menaced. We order immediately the regiments to mobilise on a war footing and to await new orders. All delay or non-execution of this order will be considered as an act of treason to the Revolution. The Military Revolutionary Committee. For the President, Podvoisky. The Secretary, Antonov.'

"In reality, this is an attempt to raise the populace against the existing order of things, to break the Constituent and to open the front to the regiments of the iron fist of Wilhelm....

"I say 'populace' intentionally, because the conscious democracy and its *Tsay-ee-kah,* all the Army organisations, all that free Russia glorifies, the good sense, the honour and the conscience of the great Russian democracy, protests against these things....

"I have not come here with a prayer, but to state my firm conviction that the Provisional Government, which defends at this moment our new liberty-that the new Russian state, destined to a brilliant future, will find unanimous support except among those who have never dared to face the truth....

"... The Provisional Government has never violated the liberty of all citizens of the State to use their political rights.... But now the Provisional Government.... declares: in this moment those elements of the Russian nation, those groups and parties who have dared to lift their hands against the free will of the Russian people, at the same time threatening to open the front to Germany, must be liquidated with decision!...

"Let the population of Petrograd understand that it will encounter a firm power, and perhaps at the last moment good sense, conscience and honour will triumph in the hearts of those who still possess them...."

All through this speech, the hall rang with deafening clamour. When the Minister-President had stepped down, pale-faced and wet with perspiration, and strode out with his suite of officers, speaker after speaker from the Left and Centre attacked the Right, all one angry roaring. Even the Socialist Revolutionaries, through Gotz:

"The policy of the Bolsheviki is demagogic and criminal, in their exploitation of the popular discontent. But there is a whole series of popular demands which have received no satisfaction up to now.... The questions of peace, land and the democratization of the army ought to be stated in such a fashion that no soldier, peasant or worker would have the least doubt that our Government is attempting, firmly and infallibly, to solve them....

"We Mensheviki do not wish to provoke a Cabinet crisis, and we are ready to defend the Provisional Government with all our energy, to the last drop of our blood-if only the Provisional Government, on all these burning questions, will speak the clear and precise words awaited by the people with such impatience...."

Then Martov, furious:

"The words of the Minister-President, who allowed himself to speak of 'populace' when it is question of the movement of important sections of the proletariat and the army-although led in the wrong direction-are nothing but an incitement to civil war."

The order of the day proposed by the Left was voted. It amounted practically to a vote of lack of confidence.

1. The armed demonstration which has been preparing for some days past has for its object a *coup d'etat,* threatens to provoke civil war, creates conditions favourable to *pogroms* and counterrevolution, the mobilization of counter-revolutionary forces, such as the Black Hundreds, which will inevitably bring about the impossibility of convoking the Constituent, will cause a military catastrophe, the death of the Revolution, paralyse the economic life of the country and destroy Russia;

2. The conditions favourable to this agitation have been created by delay in passing urgent measures, as well as objective conditions caused by the war and the general disorder. It is necessary before everything to promulgate at once a decree transmitting the land to the peasants' Land Committees, and to adopt an energetic course of action abroad in proposing to the Allies to proclaim their peace terms and to begin peace-parleys;

3. To cope with Monarchist manifestations and *pogromist* movements, it is indispensable to take immediate measures to suppress these movements, and for this purpose to create at Petrograd a Committee of Public Safety, composed of representatives of the Municipality and the organs of the revolutionary democracy, acting in contact with the Provisional Government....

It is interesting to note that the Mensheviki and Socialist Revolutionaries all rallied to this resolution.... When Kerensky saw it, however, he summoned Avksentiev to the Winter Palace to explain. If it expressed a lack of confidence in the Provisional Government, he begged Avksentiev to form a new Cabinet. Dan, Gotz and Avksentiev, the leaders of the "compromisers," performed their last compromise.... They explained to Kerensky that it was not meant as a criticism of the Government!

At the corner of the Morskaya and the Nevsky, squads of soldiers with fixed bayonets were stopping all private automobiles, turning out the occupants, and ordering them toward the Winter Palace. A large crowd had gathered to watch them. Nobody knew whether the soldiers belonged to the Government or the Military Revolutionary Committee. Up in front of the Kazan Cathedral the same thing was happening, machines being directed back up the Nevsky. Five or six sailors with rifles came along, laughing excitedly, and fell into conversation with two of the soldiers. On the sailors' hat bands were *Avrora* and *Zaria Svobody,*-the names of the leading Bolshevik cruisers of the Baltic Fleet. One of them said, "Cronstadt is coming!"... It was as if, in 1792, on the streets of Paris, some one had said: "The Marseillais are coming!" For at Cronstadt were twenty-five thousand sailors, convinced Bolsheviki and not afraid to die....

Rabotchi i Soldat was just out, all its front page one huge proclamation: SOLDIERS! WORKERS! CITIZENS!

The enemies of the people passed last night to the offensive. The Kornilovists of the Staff are trying to draw in from the suburbs *yunkers* and volunteer battalions. The Oranienbaum *yunkers* and the Tsarskoye Selo volunteers refused to come out. A stroke of high treason is being contemplated against the Petrograd Soviet.... The campaign of the counter-revolutionists is being directed against the All-Russian Congress of Soviets on the eve of its opening, against the Constituent Assembly, against the people. The Petrograd Soviet is guarding the Revolution. The Military Revolutionary Committee is directing the repulse of the conspirators' attack. The entire garrison and proletariat of Petrograd are ready to deal the enemy of the people a crushing blow.

The Military Revolutionary Committee decrees:

1. All regimental, division and battle-ship Committees, together with the Soviet Commissars, and all revolutionary organisations, shall meet in continuous session, concentrating in their hands all information about the plans of the conspirators.

2. Not one soldier shall leave his division without permission of the Committee.

3. To send to Smolny at once two delegates from each military unit and five from each Ward Soviet.

4. All members of the Petrograd Soviet and all delegates to the All-Russian Congress are invited immediately to Smolny for an extraordinary meeting.

Counter-revolution has raised its criminal head.

A great danger threatens all the conquests and hopes of the soldiers and workers.

But the forces of the Revolution by far exceed those of its enemies.

The cause of the People is in strong hands. The conspirators will be crushed.

No hesitation or doubts! Firmness, steadfastness, discipline, determination!

Long live the Revolution!

The Military Revolutionary Committee.

The Petrograd Soviet was meeting continuously at Smolny, a centre of storm, delegates falling down asleep on the floor and rising again to take part in the debate, Trotzky, Kameniev, Volodarsky speaking six, eight, twelve hours a day....

I went down to room 18 on the first floor where the Bolshevik delegates were holding caucus, a harsh voice steadily booming, the speaker hidden by the crowd: "The compromisers say that we are isolated. Pay no attention to them. Once it begins they must be dragged along with us, or else lose their following...."

Here he held up a piece of paper. "We are dragging them! A message has just come from the Mensheviki and Socialist Revolutionaries! They say that they condemn our action, but that if the Government attacks us they will not oppose the cause of the proletariat!" Exultant shouting....

As night fell the great hall filled with soldiers and workmen, a monstrous dun mass, deep-humming in a blue haze of smoke. The old *Tsay-ee-kah* had finally decided to welcome the delegates to that new Congress which would mean its own ruin-and perhaps the ruin of the revolutionary order it had built. At this meeting, however, only members of the *Tsay-ee-kah* could vote....

It was after midnight when Gotz took the chair and Dan rose to speak, in a tense silence, which seemed to me almost menacing.

"The hours in which we live appear in the most tragic colours," he said. "The enemy is at the gates of Petrograd, the forces of the democracy are trying to organise to resist him, and yet we await bloodshed in the streets of the capital, and famine threatens to destroy, not only our homogeneous Government, but the Revolution itself...."

"The masses are sick and exhausted. They have no interest in the Revolution. If the Bolsheviki start anything, that will be the end of the Revolution..." (Cries, "That's a lie!)" "The counter-revolutionists are waiting with the Bolsheviki to begin riots and massacres.... If there is any *vystuplennie,* there will be no Constituent Assembly...." (Cries, "Lie! Shame!")

"It is inadmissible that in the zone of military operations the Petrograd garrison shall not submit to the orders of the Staff.... You must obey the orders of the Staff and of the *Tsay-ee-kah* elected by you. All Power to the Soviets-that means death! Robbers and thieves are waiting for the moment to loot and burn.... When you have such slogans put before you, 'Enter the houses, take away the shoes and clothes from the bourgeoisie-'" (Tumult. Cries, "No such slogan! A lie! A lie!") "Well, it may start differently, but it will end that way!

"The *Tsay-ee-kah* has full power to act, and must be obeyed.... We are not afraid of bayonets.... The *Tsay-ee-kah* will defend the Revolution with its body...." (Cries, "It was a dead body long ago!")

Immense continued uproar, in which his voice could be heard screaming, as he pounded the desk, "Those who are urging this are committing a crime!"

Voice: "You committed a crime long ago, when you captured the power and turned it over to the bourgeoisie!"

Gotz, ringing the chairman's bell: "Silence, or I'll have you put out!"

Voice: "Try it!" (Cheers and whistling.)

"Now concerning our policy about peace." (Laughter.) "Unfortunately Russia can no longer support the continuation of the war. There is going to be peace, but not permanent peace-

47

not a democratic peace.... To-day, at the Council of the Republic, in order to avoid bloodshed, we passed an order of the day demanding the surrender of the land to the Land Committees and immediate peace negotiations...." (Laughter, and cries, "Too late!")

Then for the Bolsheviki, Trotzky mounted the tribune, borne on a wave of roaring applause that burst into cheers and a rising house, thunderous. His thin, pointed face was positively Mephistophelian in its expression of malicious irony.

"Dan's tactics prove that the masses-the great, dull, indifferent masses-are absolutely with him!" (Titantic mirth.) He turned toward the chairman, dramatically. "When we spoke of giving the land to the peasants, you were against it. We told the peasants, 'If they don't give it to you, take it yourselves!' and the peasants followed our advice. And now you advocate what we did six months ago....

"I don't think Kerensky's order to suspend the death penalty in the army was dictated by his ideals. I think Kerensky was persuaded by the Petrograd garrison, which refused to obey him....

"To-day Dan is accused of having made a speech in the Council of the Republic which proves him to be a secret Bolshevik.... The time may come when Dan will say that the flower of the Revolution participated in the rising of July 16th and 18th.... In Dan's resolution to-day at the Council of the Republic there was no mention of enforcing discipline in the army, although that is urged in the propaganda of his party....

"No. The history of the last seven months shows that the masses have left the Mensheviki. The Mensheviki and the Socialist Revolutionaries conquered the Cadets, and then when they got the power, they gave it to the Cadets....

"Dan tells you that you have no right to make an insurrection. Insurrection is the right of all revolutionists! When the down-trodden masses revolt, it is their right...."

Then the long-faced, cruel-tongued Lieber, greeted with groans and laughter.

"Engels and Marx said that the proletariat had no right to take power until it was ready for it. In a bourgeois revolution like this.... the seizure of power by the masses means the tragic end of the Revolution.... Trotzky, as a Social Democratic theorist, is himself opposed to what he is now advocating...." (Cries, "Enough! Down with him!")

Martov, constantly interrupted: "The Internationalists are not opposed to the transmission of power to the democracy, but they disapprove of the methods of the Bolsheviki. This is not the moment to seize the power...."

Again Dan took the floor, violently protesting against the action of the Military Revolutionary Committee, which had sent a Commissar to seize the office of *Izviestia* and censor the paper. The wildest uproar followed. Martov tried to speak, but could not be heard. Delegates of the Army and the Baltic Fleet stood up all over the hall, shouting that the Soviet was *their* Government....

Amid the wildest confusion Ehrlich offered a resolution, appealing to the workers and soldiers to remain calm and not to respond to provocations to demonstrate, recognising the necessity of immediately creating a Committee of Public Safety, and asking the Provisional Government at once to pass decrees transferring the land to the peasants and beginning peace negotiations....

Then up leaped Volodarsky, shouting harshly that the *Tsay-ee-kah,* on the eve of the Congress, had no right to assume the functions of the Congress. The *Tsay-ee-kah* was practically dead, he said, and the resolution was simply a trick to bolster up its waning power....

"As for us, Bolsheviki, we will not vote on this resolution!" Whereupon all the Bolsheviki left the hall and the resolution was passed....

Toward four in the morning I met Zorin in the outer hall, a rifle slung from his shoulder.

"We're moving!" said he, calmly but with satisfaction. "We pinched the Assistant Minister of Justice and the Minister of Religions. They're down cellar now. One regiment is on the march to capture the Telephone Exchange, another the Telegraph Agency, another the State Bank. The Red Guard is out...."

On the steps of Smolny, in the chill dark, we first saw the Red Guard-a huddled group of boys in workmen's clothes, carrying guns with bayonets, talking nervously together.

Far over the still roofs westward came the sound of scattered rifle fire, where the *yunkers* were trying to open the bridges over the Neva, to prevent the factory workers and soldiers of the Viborg quarter from joining the Soviet forces in the centre of the city; and the Cronstadt sailors were closing them again....

Behind us great Smolny, bright with lights, hummed like a gigantic hive....

CHAPTER IV

The Fall of the Provisional Government

WEDNESDAY, November 7th, I rose very late. The noon cannon boomed from Peter-Paul as I went down the Nevsky. It was a raw, chill day. In front of the State Bank some soldiers with fixed bayonets were standing at the closed gates.

"What side do you belong to?" I asked. "The Government?"

"No more Government," one answered with a grin, "*Slava Bogu!* Glory to God!" That was all I could get out of him....

The street-cars were running on the Nevsky, men, women and small boys hanging on every projection. Shops were open, and there seemed even less uneasiness among the street crowds than there had been the day before. A whole crop of new appeals against insurrection had blossomed out on the walls during the night-to the peasants, to the soldiers at the front, to the workmen of Petrograd. One read:

FROM THE PETROGRAD MUNICIPAL DUMA:

The Municipal Duma informs the citizens that in the extraordinary meeting of November 6th the Duma formed a Committee of Public Safety, composed of members of the Central and Ward Dumas, and representatives of the following revolutionary democratic organizations: The *Tsay-ee-kah,* the All-Russian Executive Committee of Peasant Deputies, the Army organisations, the *Tsentroflot,* the Petrograd Soviet of Workers' and Soldiers' Deputies (!), the Council of Trade Unions, and others.

Members of the Committee of Public Safety will be on duty in the building of the Municipal Duma. Telephones No. 15-40, 223-77, 138-36.

November 7th, 1917.

Though I didn't realize it then, this was the Duma's declaration of war against the Bolsheviki.

I bought a copy of *Rabotchi Put,* the only newspaper which seemed on sale, and a little later paid a soldier fifty kopeks for a second-hand copy of *Dien.* The Bolshevik paper, printed on large-sized sheets in the conquered office of the *Russkaya Volia,* had huge headlines: "ALL POWER-TO THE SOVIETS OF WORKERS, SOLDIERS AND PEASANTS! PEACE! BREAD! LAND!" The leading article was signed "Zinoviev,"-Lenin's companion in hiding. It began:

Every soldier, every worker, every real Socialist, every honest democrat realises that there are only two alternatives to the present situation.

Either-the power will remain in the hands of the bourgeois-landlord crew, and this will mean every kind of repression for the workers, soldiers and peasants, continuation of the war, inevitable hunger and death....

Or-the power will be transferred to the hands of the revolutionary workers, soldiers and peasants; and in that case it will mean a complete abolition of landlord tyranny, immediate check of the capitalists, immediate proposal of a just peace. Then the land is assured to the peasants, then control of industry is assured to the workers, then bread is assured to the hungry, then the end of this nonsensical war!...

Dien contained fragmentary news of the agitated night. Bolsheviki capture of the Telephone Exchange, the Baltic station, the Telegraph Agency; the Peterhof *yunkers* unable to reach Petrograd; the Cossacks undecided; arrest of some of the Ministers; shooting of Chief of the City Militia Meyer; arrests, counter-arrests, skirmishes between clashing patrols of soldiers, *yunkers* and Red Guards.

On the corner of the Morskaya I ran into Captain Gomberg, Menshevik *oboronetz,* secretary of the Military Section of his party. When I asked him if the insurrection had really happened he shrugged his shoulders in a tired manner and replied, *"Tchort znayet!* The devil knows! Well, perhaps the Bolsheviki can seize the power, but they won't be able to hold it more than three days. They haven't the men to run a government. Perhaps it's a good thing to let them try-that will furnish them...."

The Military Hotel at the corner of St. Isaac's Square was picketed by armed sailors. In the lobby were many of the smart young officers, walking up and down or muttering together; the sailors wouldn't let them leave....

Suddenly came the sharp crack of a rifle outside, followed by a scattered burst of firing. I ran out. Something unusual was going on around the Marinsky Palace, where the Council of the Russian Republic met. Diagonally across the wide square was drawn a line of soldiers, rifles ready, staring at the hotel roof.

"Provacatzia! Shot at us!" snapped one, while another went running toward the door.

At the western corner of the Palace lay a big armoured car with a red flag flying from it, newly lettered in red paint: "S.R.S.D." (*Soviet Rabotchikh Soldatskikh Deputatov*); all the guns trained toward St. Isaac's. A barricade had been heaped up across the mouth of Novaya Ulitza-boxes, barrels, an old bed-spring, a wagon. A pile of lumber barred the end of the

Moika quay. Short logs from a neighbouring wood-pile were being built up along the front of the building to form breastworks....

"Is there going to be any fighting?" I asked.

"Soon, soon," answered a soldier, nervously. "Go away, comrade, you'll get hurt. They will come from that direction," pointing toward the Admiralty.

"Who will?"

"That I couldn't tell you, brother," he answered, and spat.

Before the door of the Palace was a crowd of soldiers and sailors. A sailor was telling of the end of the Council of the Russian Republic. "We walked in there," he said, "and filled all the doors with comrades. I went up to the counter-revolutionist Kornilovitz who sat in the president's chair. 'No more Council,' I says. 'Run along home now!'" |

There was laughter. By waving assorted papers I managed to get around to the door of the press gallery. There an enormous smiling sailor stopped me, and when I showed my pass, just said, "If you were Saint Michael himself, comrade, you couldn't pass here!" Through the glass of the door I made out the distorted face and gesticulating arms of a French correspondent, locked in....

Around in front stood a little, grey-moustached man in the uniform of a general, the centre of a knot of soldiers. He was very red in the face.

"I am General Alexeyev," he cried. "As your superior officer and as a member of the Council of the Republic I demand to be allowed to pass!" The guard scratched his head, looking uneasily out of the corner of his eye; he beckoned to an approaching officer, who grew very agitated when he saw who it was and saluted before he realised what he was doing.

"*Vashe Vuisokoprevoskhoditelstvo*-your High Excellency-" he stammered, in the manner of the old régime, "Access to the Palace is strictly forbidden—I have no right-"

An automobile came by, and I saw Gotz sitting inside, laughing apparently with great amusement. A few minutes later another, with armed soldiers on the front seat, full of arrested members of the Provisional Government. Peters, Lettish member of the Military Revolutionary Committee, came hurrying across the Square.

"I thought you bagged all those gentlemen last night," said I, pointing to them.

"Oh," he answered, with the expression of a disappointed small boy. "The damn fools let most of them go again before we made up our minds...."

Down the Voskressensky Prospect a great mass of sailors were drawn up, and behind them came marching soldiers, as far as the eye could reach.

We went toward the Winter Palace by way of the Admiralteisky. All the entrances to the Palace Square were closed by sentries, and a cordon of troops stretched clear across the western end, besieged by an uneasy throng of citizens. Except for far-away soldiers who seemed to be carrying wood out of the Palace courtyard and piling it in front of the main gateway, everything was quiet.

We couldn't make out whether the sentries were pro-Government or pro-Soviet. Our papers from Smolny had no effect, however, so we approached another part of the line with an important air and showed our American passports, saying "Official business!" and shouldered through. At the door of the Palace the same old *shveitzari,* in their brass-buttoned blue uniforms with the red-and-gold collars, politely took our coats and hats, and we went up-stairs. In the dark, gloomy corridor, stripped of its tapestries, a few old attendants were lounging about, and in front of Kerensky's door a young officer paced up and down, gnawing his moustache. We asked if we could interview the Minister-president. He bowed and clicked his heels.

"No, I am sorry," he replied in French. "Alexander Feodorvitch is extremely occupied just now...." He looked at us for a moment. "In fact, he is not here...."

"Where is he?"

"He has gone to the Front. And do you know, there wasn't enough gasoline for his automobile. We had to send to the English Hospital and borrow some."

"Are the Ministers here?"

"They are meeting in some room-I don't know where.'

"Are the Bolsheviki coming?"

"Of course. Certainly, they are coming. I expect a telephone call every minute to say that they are coming. But we are ready. We have *yunkers* in the front of the Palace. Through that door there."

"Can we go in there?"

"No. Certainly not. It is not permitted." Abruptly he shook hands all around and walked away. We turned to the forbidden door, set in a temporary partition dividing the hall and locked on the outside. On the other side were voices, and somebody laughing. Except for that the vast spaces of the old Palace were silent as the grave. An old *shveitzar* ran up. "No, *barin,* you must not go in there."

"Why is the door locked?"

"To keep the soldiers in," he answered. After a few minutes he said something about having a glass of tea and went back up the hall. We unlocked the door.

Just inside a couple of soldiers stood on guard, but they said nothing. At the end of the corridor was a large, ornate room with gilded cornices and enormous crystal lustres, and beyond it several smaller ones, wainscoted with dark wood. On both sides of the parquetted floor lay rows of dirty mattresses and blankets, upon which occasional soldiers were stretched out; everywhere was a litter of cigarette-butts, bits of bread, cloth, and empty bottles with expensive French labels. More and more soldiers, with the red shoulder-straps of the *yunker*-schools, moved about in a stale atmosphere of tobacco-smoke and unwashed humanity. One had a bottle of white Burgundy, evidently filched from the cellars of the Palace. They looked at us with astonishment as we marched past, through room after room, until at last we came out into a series of great state-salons, fronting their long and dirty windows on the Square. The walls were covered with huge canvases in massive gilt frames-historical battle-scenes.... "12 October 1812" and "6 November 1812" and "16/28 August 1813." ... One had a gash across the upper right hand corner.

The place was all a huge barrack, and evidently had been for weeks, from the look of the floor and walls. Machine guns were mounted on window-sills, rifles stacked between the mattresses.

As we were looking at the pictures an alcoholic breath assailed me from the region of my left ear, and a voice said in thick but fluent French, "I see, by the way you admire the paintings, that you are foreigners." He was a short, puffy man with a baldish head as he removed his cap.

"Americans? Enchanted. I am Stabs-Capitan Vladimir Artzibashev, absolutely at your service." It did not seem to occur to him that there was anything unusual in four strangers, one a woman, wandering through the defences of an army awaiting attack. He began to complain of the state of Russia.

"Not only these Bolsheviki," he said, "but the fine traditions of the Russian army are broken down. Look around you. These are all students in the officers' training schools. But are they gentlemen? Kerensky opened the officers' schools to the ranks, to any soldier who could pass an examination. Naturally there are many, many who are contaminated by the Revolution...."

Without consequence he changed the subject. "I am very anxious to go away from Russia. I have made up my mind to join the American army. Will you please go to your Consul and make arrangements? I will give you my address." In spite of our protestations he wrote it on a piece of paper, and seemed to feel better at once. I have it still-"*Oranien-baumskaya Shkola Praporshtchikov 2nd, Staraya Peterhof.*"

"We had a review this morning early," he went on, as he guided us through the rooms and explained everything. "The Women's Battalion decided to remain loyal to the Government."

"Are the women soldiers in the Palace?"

"Yes, they are in the back rooms, where they won't be hurt if any trouble comes." He sighed. "It is a great responsibility," said he.

For a while we stood at the window, looking down on the Square before the Palace, where three companies of long-coated *yunkers* were drawn up under arms, being harangued by a tall, energetic-looking officer I recognised as Stankievitch, chief Military Commissar of the Provisional Government. After a few minutes two of the companies shouldered arms with a clash, barked three sharp shouts, and went swinging off across the Square, disappearing through the Red Arch into the quiet city.

"They are going to capture the Telephone Exchange," said some one. Three cadets stood by us, and we fell into conversation. They said they had entered the schools from the ranks, and gave their names-Robert Olev, Alexei Vasilienko and Erni Sachs, an Esthonian. But now they didn't want to be officers any more, because officers were very unpopular. They didn't seem to know what to do, as a matter of fact, and it was plain that they were not happy.

But soon they began to boast. "If the Bolsheviki come we shall show them how to fight. They do not dare to fight, they are cowards. But if we should be overpowered, well, every man keeps one bullet for himself...."

At this point there was a burst of rifle-fire not far off. Out on the Square all the people began to run, falling flat on their faces, and the *izvoshtchiki,* standing on the corners, galloped in every direction. Inside all was uproar, soldiers running here and there, grabbing up guns, rifle-belts and shouting, "Here they come! Here they come!" ... But in a few minutes it quieted down again. The *izvoshtchiki* came back, the people lying down stood up. Through the Red Arch appeared the *yunkers,* marching a little out of step, one of them supported by two comrades.

It was getting late when we left the Palace. The sentries in the Square had all disappeared. The great semi-circle of Government buildings seemed deserted. We went into the Hotel France for dinner, and right in the middle of soup the waiter, very pale in the face, came up and insisted that we move to the main dining-room at the back of the house, because they were going to put out the lights in the café. "There will be much shooting," he said.

When we came out on the Morskaya again it was quite dark, except for one flickering street-light on the corner of the Nevsky. Under this stood a big armored automobile, with racing engine and oil-smoke pouring out of it. A small boy had climbed up the side of the thing and was looking down the barrel of a machine gun. Soldiers and sailors stood around, evidently waiting for something. We walked back up to the Red Arch, where a knot of soldiers was gathered staring at the brightly-lighted Winter Palace and talking in loud tones.

"No, comrades," one was saying. "How can we shoot at them? The Women's Battalion is in there-they will say we have fired on Russian women."

As we reached the Nevsky again another armoured car came around the corner, and a man poked his head out of the turret-top.

"Come on!" he yelled. "Let's go on through and attack!"

The driver of the other car came over, and shouted so as to be heard above the roaring engine. "The Committee says to wait. They have got artillery behind the wood-piles in there...."

Here the street-cars had stopped running, few people passed, and there were no lights; but a few blocks away we could see the trams, the crowds, the lighted shop-windows and the electric signs of the moving-picture shows-life going on as usual. We had tickets to the Ballet at the Marinsky Theatre-all theatres were open-but it was too exciting out of doors....

In the darkness we stumbled over lumber-piles barricading the Police Bridge, and before the Stroganov Palace made out some soldiers wheeling into position a three-inch field-gun. Men in various uniforms were coming and going in an aimless way, and doing a great deal of talking....

Up the Nevsky the whole city seemed to be out promenading. On every corner immense crowds were massed around a core of hot discussion. Pickets of a dozen soldiers with fixed bayonets lounged at the street-crossings, red-faced old men in rich fur coats shook their fists at them, smartly-dressed women screamed epithets; the soldiers argued feebly, with embarrassed grins.... Armoured cars went up and down the street, named after the first Tsars-Oleg, Rurik, Svietoslav-and daubed with huge red letters, "R. S. D. R. P." *(Rossiskaya Partia)* [*]. At the Mikhailovsky a man appeared with an [* (Russian Social Democratic

Labor Party).] armful of newspapers, and was immediately stormed by frantic people, offering a rouble, five roubles, ten roubles, tearing at each other like animals. It was *Rabotchi i Soldat,* announcing the victory of the Proletarian Revolution, the liberation of the Bolsheviki still in prison, calling upon the Army front and rear for support... a feverish little sheet of four pages, running to enormous type, containing no news....

On the corner of the Sadovaya about two thousand citizens had gathered, staring up at the roof of a tall building, where a tiny red spark glowed and waned.

"See!" said a tall peasant, pointing to it. "It is a provocator. Presently he will fire on the people...." Apparently no one thought of going to investigate.

The massive facade of Smolny blazed with lights as we drove up, and from every street converged upon it streams of hurrying shapes dim in the gloom. Automobiles and motorcycles came and went; an enormous elephant-coloured armoured automobile, with two red flags flying from the turret, lumbered out with screaming siren. It was cold, and at the outer gate the Red Guards had built themselves a bon-fire. At the inner gate, too, there was a blaze, by the light of which the sentries slowly spelled out our passes and looked us up and down. The canvas covers had been taken off the four rapid-fire guns on each side of the doorway, and the ammunition-belts hung snakelike from their breeches. A dun herd of armoured cars stood under the trees in the court-yard, engines going. The long, bare, dimly-illuminated halls roared with the thunder of feet, calling, shouting.... There was an atmosphere of recklessness. A crowd came pouring down the staircase, workers in black blouses and round black fur hats, many of them with guns slung over their shoulders, soldiers in rough dirt-coloured coats and grey fur *shapki* pinched flat, a leader or so-Lunatcharsky, Kameniev-hurrying along in the centre of a group all talking at once, with harassed anxious faces, and bulging portfolios under their arms. The extraordinary meeting of the Petrograd Soviet was over. I stopped Kameniev-a quick moving little man, with a wide, vivacious face set close to his shoulders. Without preface he read in rapid French a copy of the resolution just passed:

The Petrograd Soviet of Workers' and Soldiers' Deputies, saluting the victorious Revolution of the Petrograd proletariat and garrison, particularly emphasises the unity, organisation, discipline, and complete cooperation shown by the masses in this rising; rarely has less blood been spilled, and rarely has an insurrection succeeded so well.

The Soviet expresses its firm conviction that the Workers' and Peasants' Government which, as the government of the Soviets, will be created by the Revolution, and which will assure the industrial proletariat of the support of the entire mass of poor peasants, will march firmly toward Socialism, the only means by which the country can be spared the miseries and unheard-of horrors of war.

The new Workers' and Peasants' Government will propose immediately a just and democratic peace to all the belligerent countries.

It will suppress immediately the great landed property, and transfer the land to the peasants. It will establish workmen's control over production and distribution of manufactured products, and will set up a general control over the banks, which it will transform into a state monopoly.

The Petrograd Soviet of Workers' and Soldiers' Deputies calls upon the workers and the peasants of Russia to support with all their energy and all their devotion the Proletarian Revolution. The Soviet expresses its conviction that the city workers, allies of the poor peasants, will assure complete revolutionary order, indispensable to the victory of Socialism. The Soviet is convinced that the proletariat of the countries of Western Europe will aid us in conducting the cause of Socialism to a real and lasting victory.

"You consider it won then?"

He lifted his shoulders. "There is much to do. Horribly much. It is just beginning....

On the landing I met Riazanov, vice-president of the Trade Unions, looking black and biting his grey beard. "It's insane! Insane!" he shouted. "The European working-class won't move! All Russia-" He waved his hand distractedly and ran off. Riazanov and Kameniev had both opposed the insurrection, and felt the lash of Lenin's terrible tongue....

It had been a momentous session. In the name of the Military Revolutionary Committee Trotzky had declared that the Provisional Government no longer existed.

"The characteristic of bourgeois governments," he said, "is to deceive the people. We, the Soviets of Workers', Soldiers' and Peasants' Deputies, are going to try an experiment unique in history; we are going to found a power which will have no other aim but to satisfy the needs of the soldiers, workers, and peasants."

Lenin had appeared, welcomed with a mighty ovation, prophesying world-wide Social Revolution.... And Zinoviev, crying, "This day we have paid our debt to the international proletariat, and struck a terrible blow at the war, a terrible body-blow at all the imperialists and particularly at Wilhelm the Executioner....

Then Trotzky, that telegrams had been sent to the front announcing the victorious insurrection, but no reply had come. Troops were said to be marching against Petrograd-a delegation must be sent to tell them the truth.

Cries, "You are anticipating the will of the All-Russian Congress of Soviets!"

Trotzky, coldly, "The will of the All-Russian Congress of Soviets has been anticipated by the rising of the Petrograd workers and soldiers!"

So we came into the great meeting-hall, pushing through the clamorous mob at the door. In the rows of seats, under the white chandeliers, packed immovably in the aisles and on the sides, perched on every window-sill, and even the edge of the platform, the representatives of the workers and soldiers of all Russia waited in anxious silence or wild exultation the ringing of the chairman's bell. There was no heat in the hall but the stifling heat of unwashed human bodies. A foul blue cloud of cigarette smoke rose from the mass and hung in the thick air. Occasionally some one in authority mounted the tribune and asked the comrades not to smoke; then everybody, smokers and all, took up the cry "Don't smoke, comrades!" and went on smoking. Petrovsky, Anarchist delegate from the Obukhov factory, made a seat for me beside him. Unshaven and filthy, he was reeling from three nights' sleepless work on the Military Revolutionary Committee.

On the platform sat the leaders of the old *Tsay-ee-kah*-for the last time dominating the turbulent Soviets, which they had ruled from the first days, and which were now risen against them. It was the end of the first period of the Russian revolution, which these men had attempted to guide in careful ways.... The three greatest of them were not there: Kerensky, flying to the front through country towns all doubtfully heaving up; Tcheidze, the old eagle, who had contemptuously retired to his own Georgian mountains, there to sicken with consumption; and the high-souled Tseretelli, also mortally stricken, who, nevertheless, would return and pour out his beautiful eloquence for a lost cause. Gotz sat there, Dan, Lieber, Bogdanov, Broido, Fillipovsky,-white-faced, hollow-eyed and indignant. Below them the second *siezd* of the All-Russian Soviets boiled and swirled, and over their heads the Military Revolutionary Committee functioned white-hot, holding in its hands the threads of insurrection and striking with a long arm.... It was 10.40 P. M.

Dan, a mild-faced, baldish figure in a shapeless military surgeon's uniform, was ringing the bell. Silence fell sharply, intense, broken by the scuffling and disputing of the people at the door....

"We have the power in our hands," he began sadly, stopped for a moment, and then went on in a low voice. "Comrades! The Congress of Soviets in meeting in such unusual circumstances and in such an extraordinary moment that you will understand why the *Tsay-ee-kah* considers it unnecessary to address you with a political speech. This will become much clearer to you if you will recollect that I am a member of the *Tsay-ee-kah,* and that at this very moment our party comrades are in the Winter Palace under bombardment, sacrificing themselves to execute the duty put on them by the *Tsay-ee-kah.*" (Confused uproar.)

"I declare the first session of the Second Congress of Soviets of Workers' and Soldiers' Deputies open!"

The election of the presidium took place amid stir and moving about. Avanessov announced that by agreement of the Bolsheviki, Left Socialist Revolutionaries and Mensheviki Internationalists, it was decided to base the presidium upon proportionality. Several Mensheviki leaped to their feet protesting. A bearded soldier shouted at them, "Remember what you did to us Bolsheviki when *we* were the minority!" Result-14 Bolsheviki, 7 Socialist Revolutionaries, 3 Mensheviki and 1 Internationalist (Gorky's group). Hendelmann, for the right and centre Socialist Revolutionaries, said that they refused to take part in the presidium; the same from Kintchuk, for the Mensheviki; and from the Mensheviki Internationalists, that until the verification of certain circumstances, they too could not enter the presidium. Scattering applause and hoots. One voice, "Renegades, you call yourselves Socialists!" A representative of the Ukrainean delegates demanded, and received, a place. Then the old *Tsay-ee-kah* stepped down, and in their places appeared Trotzky, Kameniev, Lunatcharsky, Madame Kollentai, Nogin.... The hall rose, thundering. How far they had soared, these Bolsheviki, from a despised and hunted sect less than four months ago, to this supreme place, the helm of great Russia in full tide of insurrection!

The order of the day, said Kameniev, was first, Organisation of Power; second, War and Peace; and third, the Constituent Assembly. Lozovsky, rising, announced that upon agreement of the bureau of all factions, it was proposed to hear and discuss the report of the Petrograd Soviet, then to give the floor to members of the *Tsay-ee-kah* and the different parties, and finally to pass to the order of the day.

But suddenly a new sound made itself heard, deeper than the tumult of the crowd, persistent, disquieting,-the dull shock of guns. People looked anxiously toward the clouded windows, and a sort of fever came over them. Martov, demanding the floor, croaked hoarsely, "The civil war is beginning, comrades! The first question must be a peaceful settlement of the crisis. On principle and from a political standpoint we must urgently discuss a means of averting civil war. Our brothers are being shot down in the streets! At this moment, when before the opening of the Congress of Soviets the question of Power is being settled by means of a military plot organised by one of the revolutionary parties-" for a moment he could not make himself heard above the noise, "All of the revolutionary parties must face the fact! The first *vopros* (question) before the Congress is the question of Power, and this question is already being settled by force of arms in the streets!... We must create a power which will be recognised by the whole democracy. If the Congress wishes to be the voice of the revolutionary democracy it must not sit with folded hands before the developing civil war, the result of which may be a dangerous outburst of counter-revolution.... The possibility of a peaceful outcome lies in the formation of a united democratic authority.... We must elect a delegation to negotiate with the other Socialist parties and organisation....

Always the methodical muffled boom of cannon through the windows, and the delegates, screaming at each other.... So, with the crash of artillery, in the dark, with hatred, and fear, and reckless daring, new Russia was being born.

The Left Socialist Revolutionaries and the United Social Democrats supported Martov's proposition. It was accepted. A soldier announced that the All-Russian Peasants' Soviets had refused to send delegates to the Congress; he proposed that a committee be sent with a formal invitation. "Some delegates are present," he said. "I move that they be given votes." Accepted.

Kharash, wearing the epaulets of a captain, passionately demanded the floor. "The political hypocrites who control this Congress," he shouted, "told us we were to settle the question of Power-and it is being settled behind our backs, before the Congress opens! Blows are being struck against the Winter Palace, and it is by such blows that the nails are being driven into the coffin of the political party which has risked such an adventure!" Uproar. Followed him Gharra: "While we are here discussing propositions of peace, there is a battle on in the streets.... The Socialist Revolutionaries and the Mensheviki refuse to be involved in what is happening, and call upon all public forces to resist the attempt to capture the power...." Kutchin, delegate of the 12th Army and representative of the Troudoviki: "I was sent here only for information, and I am returning at once to the Front, where all the Army Committees consider that the taking of power by the Soviets, only three weeks before the Constituent Assembly, is a stab in the back of the Army and a crime against the people-!" Shouts of "Lie! You lie!"... When he could be heard again, "Let's make an end of this adventure in Petrograd! I call upon all delegates to leave this hall in order to save the country and the Revolution!" As he went down the aisle in the midst of a deafening noise, people surged in upon him, threatening.... Then Khintchuk, an officer with a long brown goatee, speaking suavely and persuasively: "I speak for the delegates from the Front. The Army is imperfectly represented in this Congress, and furthermore, the Army does not consider the Congress of Soviets necessary at this time, only three weeks before the opening of the Constituent-" shouts and stamping, always growing more violent. "The Army does not consider that the Congress of Soviets has the necessary authority-" Soldiers began to stand up all over the hall.

"Who are you speaking for? What do you represent?" they cried.

"The Central Executive Committee of the Soviet of the Fifth Army, the Second F- regiment, the First N- Regiment, the Third S- Rifles...."

"When were you elected? You represent the officers, not the soldiers! What do the soldiers say about it?" Jeers and hoots.

"We, the Front group, disclaim all responsibility for what has happened and is happening, and we consider it necessary to mobilise all self-conscious revolutionary forces for the salvation of the Revolution! The Front group will leave the Congress.... The place to fight is out on the streets!"

Immense bawling outcry. "You speak for the Staff-not for the Army!"

"I appeal to all reasonable soldiers to leave this Congress!"

"Kornilovitz! Counter-revolutionist! Provocator!" were hurled at him.

On behalf of the Mensheviki, Khintchuk then announced that the only possibility of a peaceful solution was to begin negotiations with the Provisional Government for the formation of a new Cabinet, which would find support in all strata of society. He could not proceed for several minutes. Raising his voice to a shout he read the Menshevik declaration:

"Because the Bolsheviki have made a military conspiracy with the aid of the Petrograd Soviet, without consulting the other factions and parties, we find it impossible to remain in the Congress, and therefore withdraw, inviting the other groups to follow us and to meet for discussion of the situation!"

"Deserter!" At intervals in the almost continuous disturbance Hendelman, for the Socialist Revolutionaries, could be heard protesting against the bombardment of the Winter Palace.... "We are opposed to this kind of anarchy...."

Scarcely had he stepped down than a young, lean-faced soldier, with flashing eyes, leaped to the platform, and dramatically lifted his hand:

"Comrades!" he cried and there was a hush. "My *familia* (name) is Peterson-I speak for the Second Lettish Rifles. You have heard the statements of two representatives of the Army committees; these statements would have some value *if their authors had been representatives of the Army-*" Wild applause. *"But they do not represent the soldiers!"* Shaking his fist. "The Twelfth Army has been insisting for a long time upon the re-election of the Great Soviet and the Army Committee, but just as your own *Tsay-ee-kah,* our Committee refused to call a meeting of the representatives of the masses until the end of September, so that the reactionaries could elect their own false delegates to this Congress. I tell you now, the Lettish soldiers have many times said, 'No more resolutions! No more talk! We want deeds-the Power must be in our hands!' Let these impostor delegates leave the Congress! The Army is not with them!"

The hall rocked with cheering. In the first moments of the session, stunned by the rapidity of events, startled by the sound of cannon, the delegates had hesitated. For an hour hammer-blow after hammer-blow had fallen from that tribune, welding them together but beating them down. Did they stand then alone? Was Russia rising against them? Was it true that the Army was marching on Petrograd? Then this clear-eyed young soldier had spoken, and in a flash they knew it for the truth.... *This* was the voice of the soldiers-the stirring millions of uniformed workers and peasants were men like them, and their thoughts and feelings were the same...

More soldiers ... Gzhelshakh; for the Front delegates, announcing that they had only decided to leave the Congress by a small majority, and that *the Bolshevik members had not even taken part in the vote,* as they stood for division according to political parties, and not groups. "Hundreds of delegates from the Front," he said, "are being elected without the participation of the soldiers because the Army Committees are no longer the real representatives of the rank and file...." Lukianov, crying that officers like Kharash and Khintchuk could not represent the Army in this congress,-but only the high command. "The real inhabitants of the trenches want with all their hearts the transfer of Power into the hands of the Soviets, and they expect very much from it!"... The tide was turning.

Then came Abramovitch, for the *Bund,* the organ of the Jewish Social Democrats-his eyes snapping behind thick glasses, trembling with rage.

"What is taking place now in Petrograd is a monstrous calamity! The *Bund* group joins with the declaration of the Mensheviki and Socialist Revolutionaries and will leave the Congress!" He raised his voice and hand. "Our duty to the Russian proletariat doesn't permit us to remain here and be responsible for these crimes. Because the firing on the Winter Palace doesn't cease, the Municipal Duma together with the Mensheviki and Socialist Revolutionaries, and the Executive Committee of the Peasants' Soviet, has decided to perish with the Provisional Government, and we are going with them! Unarmed we will expose our breasts to the machine guns of the Terrorists.... We invite all delegates to this Congress-" The rest was lost in a storm of hoots, menaces and curses which rose to a hellish pitch as fifty delegates got up and pushed their way out....

Kameniev jangled the bell, shouting, "Keep your seats and we'll go on with our business!" And Trotzky, standing up with a pale, cruel face, letting out his rich voice in cool contempt, "All these so-called Socialist compromisers, these frightened Mensheviki, Socialist Revolutionaries, *Bund*-let them go! They are just so much refuse which will be swept into the garbage-heap of history!"

Riazanov, for the Bolsheviki, stated that at the request of the City Duma the Military Revolutionary Committee had sent a delegation to offer negotiations to the Winter Palace. "In this way we have done everything possible to avoid blood-shed...."

We hurried from the place, stopping for a moment at the room where the Military Revolutionary Committee worked at furious speed, engulfing and spitting out panting couriers, despatching Commissars armed with power of life and death to all the corners of the city, amid the buzz of the telephonographs. The door opened, a blast of stale air and cigarette smoke rushed out, we caught a glimpse of dishevelled men bending over a map under the glare of a shaded electric-light.... Comrade Josephov-Dukhvinski, a smiling youth with a mop of pale yellow hair, made out passes for us.

When we came into the chill night, all the front of Smolny was one huge park of arriving and departing automobiles, above the sound of which could be heard the far-off slow beat of the cannon. A great motor-truck stood there, shaking to the roar of its engine. Men were tossing bundles into it, and others receiving them, with guns beside them.

"Where are you going?" I shouted.

"Down-town-all over-everywhere!" answered a little workman, grinning, with a large exultant gesture.

We showed our passes. "Come along!" they invited. "But there'll probably be shooting-" We climbed in; the clutch slid home with a raking jar, the great car jerked forward, we all toppled backward on top of those who were climbing in; past the huge fire by the gate, and then the fire by the outer gate, glowing red on the faces of the workmen with rifles who squatted around it, and went bumping at top speed down the Suvorovsky Prospect, swaying from side to side.... One man tore the wrapping from a bundle and began to hurl handfuls of l handfuls of | | papers into the air. We imitated him, plunging down through the dark street with a tail of white papers floating and eddying out behind. The late passerby stooped to pick them up; the patrols around bonfires on the corners ran out with uplifted arms to catch them. Sometimes armed men loomed up ahead, crying "*Shtoi!*" and raising their guns, but our chauffeur only yelled something unintelligible and we hurtled on....

I picked up a copy of the paper, and under a fleeting street-light read:

TO THE CITIZENS OF RUSSIA!

The Provisional Government is deposed. The State Power has passed into the hands of the organ of the Petrograd Soviet of Workers' and Soldiers' Deputies, the Military Revolutionary Committee, which stands at the head of the Petrograd proletariat and garrison.

The cause for which the people were fighting: immediate proposal of a democratic peace, abolition of landlord property-rights over the land, labor control over production, creation of a Soviet Government-that cause is securely achieved.

LONG LIVE THE REVOLUTION OF WORKMEN, SOLDIERS AND PEASANTS!

Military Revolutionary Committee

Petrograd Soviet of Workers' and Soldiers' Deputies.

[Graphic page-96 Proclamation in Russian, title follows] | *111* |

Proclamation of the Fall of the Provisional Government issued by the Military Revolutionary Committee on the night of November 7th (our calendar), which we helped to distribute from a motor-truck just after the surrender of the Winter Palace.

A slant-eyed, Mongolian-faced man who sat beside me, dressed in a goat-skin Caucasian cape, snapped, "Look out! Here the provocators always shoot from the windows!" We turned into Znamensky Square, dark and almost deserted, careened around Trubetskoy's brutal statue and swung down the wide Nevsky, three men standing up with rifles ready, peering at the windows. Behind us the street was alive with people running and stooping. We could no longer hear the cannon, and the nearer we drew to the Winter Palace end of the city the quieter and more deserted were the streets. The City Duma was all brightly lighted. Beyond that we made out a dark mass of people, and a line of sailors, who yelled furiously at us to stop. The machine slowed down, and we climbed out.

It was an astonishing scene. Just at the corner of the Ekaterina Canal, under an arc-light, a cordon of armed sailors was drawn across the Nevsky, blocking the way to a crowd of people in column of fours. There were about three or four hundred of them, men in frock coats, well-dressed women, officers-all sorts and conditions of people. Among them we recognised many of the delegates from the Congress, leaders of the Mensheviki and Socialist Revolutionaries; Avksentiev, the lean, red-bearded president of the Peasants' Soviets, Sarokin, Kerensky's spokesman, Khintchuk, Abramovitch; and at the head white-bearded old Schreider, Mayor of Petrograd, and Prokopovitch, Minister of Supplies in the Provisional Government, arrested that morning and released. I caught sight of Malkin, reporter for the *Russian Daily News.* "Going to die in the Winter Palace," he shouted cheerfully. The procession stood still, but from the front of it came loud argument. Schreider and Prokopovitch were bellowing at the big sailor who seemed in command.

"We demand to pass!" they cried. "See, these comrades come from the Congress of Soviets! Look at their tickets! We are going to the Winter Palace!"

The sailor was plainly puzzled. He scratched his head with an enormous hand, frowning. "I have orders from the Committee not to let anybody go to the Winter Palace," he grumbled. "But I will send a comrade to telephone to Smolny...."

"We Insist upon passing! We are unarmed! We will march on whether you permit us or not!" cried old Schreider, very much excited.

65

"I have orders-" repeated the sailor sullenly.

"Shoot us if you want to! We will pass! Forward!" came from all sides. "We are ready to die, if you have the heart to fire on Russians and comrades! We bare our breasts to your guns!"

"No," said the sailor, looking stubborn, "I can't allow you to pass."

"What will you do if we go forward? Will you shoot?"

"No, I'm not going to shoot people who haven't any guns. We won't shoot unarmed Russian people...."

"We will go forward! What can you do?"

"We will do something,"replied the sailor, evidently at a loss. "We can't let you pass. We will do something."

"What will you do? What will you do?"

Another sailor came up, very much irritated. "We will spank you!" he cried, energetically. "And if necessary we will shoot you too. Go home now, and leave us in peace!"

At this there was a great clamour of anger and resentment, Prokopovitch had mounted some sort of box, and, waving his umbrella, he made a speech:

"Comrades and citizens!" he said. "Force is being used against us! We cannot have our innocent blood upon the hands of these ignorant men! It is beneath our dignity to be shot down here in the street by switchmen-" (What he meant by "switchmen" I never discovered.) "Let us return to the Duma and discuss the best means of saving the country and the Revolution!"

Whereupon, in dignified silence, the procession marched around and back up the Nevsky, always in column of fours. And taking advantage of the diversion we slipped past the guards and set off in the direction of the Winter Palace.

Here it was absolutely dark, and nothing moved but pickets of soldiers and Red Guards grimly intent. In front of the Kazan Cathedral a three-inch field-gun lay in the middle of the street, slewed sideways from the recoil of its last shot over the roofs. Soldiers were standing in every doorway talking in low tones and peering down toward the Police Bridge. I heard one voice saying: "It is possible that we have done wrong...." At the corners patrols stopped all passersby-and the composition of these patrols was interesting, for in command of the regular troops was invariably a Red Guard.... The shooting had ceased.

Just as we came to the Morskaya somebody was shouting: "The *yunkers* have sent word they want us to go and get them out!" Voices began to give commands, and in the thick gloom we made out a dark mass moving forward, silent but for the shuffle of feet and the clinking of arms. We fell in with the first ranks.

Like a black river, filling all the street, without song or cheer we poured through the Red Arch, where the man just ahead of me said in a low voice: "Look out, comrades! Don't trust them. They will fire, surely!" In the open we began to run, stooping low and bunching together, and jammed up suddenly behind the pedestal of the Alexander Column.

"How many of you did they kill?" I asked.

"I don't know. About ten...."

After a few minutes huddling there, some hundreds of men, the army seemed reassured and without any orders suddenly began again to flow forward. By this time, in the light that streamed out of all the Winter Palace windows, I could see that the first two or three hundred men were Red Guards, with only a few scattered soldiers. Over the barricade of firewood we clambered, and leaping down inside gave a triumphant shout as we stumbled on a heap of rifles thrown down by the *yunkers* who had stood there. On both sides of the main gateway the doors stood wide open, light streamed out, and from the huge pile came not the slightest sound.

Carried along by the eager wave of men we were swept into the right hand entrance, opening into a great bare vaulted room, the cellar of the East wing, from which issued a maze of corridors and stair-cases. A number of huge packing cases stood about, and upon these the Red Guards and soldiers fell furiously, battering them open with the butts of their rifles, and pulling out carpets, curtains, linen, porcelain plates, glassware.... One man went strutting around with a bronze clock perched on his shoulder; another found a plume of ostrich feathers, which he stuck in his hat. The looting was just beginning when somebody cried, "Comrades! Don't touch anything! Don't take anything! This is the property of the People!" Immediately twenty voices were crying, "Stop! Put everything back! Don't take anything! Property of the People!" Many hands dragged the spoilers down. Damask and tapestry were snatched from the arms of those who had them; two men took away the bronze clock. Roughly and hastily the things were crammed back in their cases, and self-appointed sentinels stood guard. It was all utterly spontaneous. Through corridors and up stair-cases the cry could be heard growing fainter and fainter in the distance, "Revolutionary discipline! Property of the People...."

We crossed back over to the left entrance, in the West wing. There order was also being established. "Clear the Palace!" bawled a Red Guard, sticking his head through an inner door. "Come, comrades, let's show that we're not thieves and bandits. Everybody out of the Palace except the Commissars, until we get sentries posted."

Two Red Guards, a soldier and an officer, stood with revolvers in their hands. Another soldier sat at a table behind them, with pen and paper. Shouts of "All out! All out!" were heard far and near within, and the Army began to pour through the door, jostling, expostulating, arguing. As each man appeared he was seized by the self-appointed committee, who went through his pockets and looked under his coat. Everything that was plainly not his property was taken away, the man at the table noted it on his paper, and it was carried into a little room. The most amazing assortment of objects were thus confiscated; statuettes, bottles of ink, bed-spreads worked with the Imperial monogram, candles, a small oil-painting, desk blotters, gold-handled swords, cakes of soap, clothes of every description, blankets. One Red Guard carried three rifles, two of which he had taken away from *yunkers;* another had four portfolios bulging with written documents. The culprits either sullenly surrendered or pleaded like children. All talking at once the committee explained that stealing was not worthy of the people's champions; often those who had been caught turned around and began to help go through the rest of the comrades.

Yunkers came out, in bunches of three or four. The committee seized upon them with an excess of zeal, accompanying the search with remarks like, "Ah, Provocators! Kornilovists! Counter-revolutionists! Murderers of the People!" But there was no violence done, although the *yunkers* were terrified. They too had their pockets full of small plunder. It was carefully noted down by the scribe, and piled in the little room.... The *yunkers* were disarmed. "Now, will you take up arms against the People any more?" demanded clamouring voices.

"No," answered the *yunkers,* one by one. Whereupon they were allowed to go free.

We asked if we might go inside. The committee was doubtful, but the big Red Guard answered firmly that it was forbidden. "Who are you anyway?" he asked. "How do I know that you are not all Kerenskys? (There were five of us, two women.)

"*Pazhal'st', touarishtchi!* Way, Comrades!" A soldier and a Red Guard appeared in the door, waving the crowd aside, and other guards with fixed bayonets. After them followed single file half a dozen men in civilian dress-the members of the Provisional Government. First came Kishkin, his face drawn and pale, then Rutenberg, looking sullenly at the floor; Terestchenko was next, glancing sharply around; he stared at us with cold fixity.... They passed in silence; the victorious insurrectionists crowded to see, but there were only a few angry mutterings. It was only later that we learned how the people in the street wanted to lynch them, and shots were fired-but the sailors brought them safely to Peter-Paul....

In the meanwhile unrebuked we walked into the Palace. There was still a great deal of coming and going, of exploring new-found apartments in the vast edifice, of searching for hidden garrisons of *yunkers* which did not exist. We went upstairs and wandered through room after room. This part of the Palace had been entered also by other detachments from the side of the Neva. The paintings, statues, tapestries and rugs of the great state apartments were unharmed; in the offices, however, every desk and cabinet had been ransacked, the papers scattered over the floor, and in the living rooms beds had been stripped of their coverings and ward-robes wrenched open. The most highly prized loot was clothing, which the working people needed. In a room where furniture was stored we came upon two soldiers ripping the elaborate Spanish leather upholstery from chairs. They explained it was to make boots with....

The old Palace servants in their blue and red and gold uniforms stood nervously about, from force of habit repeating, "You can't go in there, *barin!* It is forbidden-" We penetrated at length to the gold and malachite chamber with crimson brocade hangings where the Ministers had been in session all that day and night, and where the *shveitzari* had betrayed them to the Red Guards. The long table covered with green baize was just as they had left it, under arrest. Before each empty seat was pen and ink and paper; the papers were scribbled over with beginnings of plans of action, rough drafts of proclamations and manifestos. Most of these were scratched out, as their futility became evident, and the rest of the sheet covered with absent-minded geometrical designs, as the writers sat despondently listening while Minister after Minister proposed chimerical schemes. I took one of these scribbled pages, in the hand writing of Konovalov, which read, "The Provisional Government appeals to all classes to support the Provisional Government-"

All this time, it must be remembered, although the Winter Palace was surrounded, the Government was in constant communication with the Front and with provincial Russia. The Bolsheviki had captured the Ministry of War early in the morning, but they did not know of the military telegraph office in the attic, nor of the private telephone line connecting it with the Winter Palace. In that attic a young officer sat all day, pouring out over the country a flood of appeals and proclamations; and when he heard that the Palace had fallen, put on his hat and walked calmly out of the building....

Interested as we were, for a considerable time we didn't notice a change in the attitude of the soldiers and Red Guards around us. As we strolled from room to room a small group followed us, until by the time we reached the great picture-gallery where we had spent the afternoon with the *yunkers,* about a hundred men surged in after us. One giant of a soldier stood in our path, his face dark with sullen suspicion.

[Graphic page-104 Doodling by Konavalov, title follows]

Facsimile of the beginning of a proclamation, written in pencil by A.I. Konovalov, Minister of Commerce and Industry in he Provisional Government, and then scratched out as the hopelessness of the situation became more and more evident. The geometrical figure beneath was probably idly drawn while the Ministers were waiting for the end.

"Who are you?" he growled. "What are you doing here?" The others massed slowly around, staring and beginning to mutter. *"Provocatori!"* I heard somebody say. "Looters!" I produced our passes from the Military Revolutionary Committee. The soldier took them gingerly, turned them upside down and looked at them without comprehension. Evidently he could not read. He handed them back and spat on the floor. *"Bumagi!* Papers!" said he with contempt. The mass slowly began to close in, like wild cattle around a cowpuncher on foot. Over their heads I caught sight of an officer, looking helpless, and shouted to him. He made for us, shouldering his way through.

"I'm the Commissar," he said to me. "Who are you? What is it?" The others held back, waiting. I produced the papers.

"You are foreigners?" he rapidly asked in Franch. "It is very dangerous...." Then he turned to the mob, holding up our documents. "Comrades!" he cried. "These people are foreign comrades-from America. They have come here to be able to tell their countrymen about the bravery and the revolutionary discipline of the proletarian army!"

"How do you know that?" replied the big soldier. "I tell you they are provocators! They say they came here to observe the revolutionary discipline of the proletarian army, but they have been wandering freely through the Palace, and how do we know they haven't got their pockets full of loot?"

"Pravilno!" snarled the others, pressing forward.

"Comrades! Comrades!" appealed the officer, sweat standing out on his forehead. "I am Commissar of the Military Revolutionary Committee. Do you trust me? Well, I tell you that these passes are signed with the same names that are signed to my pass!"

He led us down through the Palace and out through a door opening onto the Neva quay, before which stood the usual committee going through pockets... "You have narrowly escaped," he kept muttering, wiping his face.

"What happened to the Women's Battalion?" we asked.

"Oh-the women!" He laughed. "They were all huddled up in a back room. We had a terrible time deciding what to do with them-many were in hysterics, and so on. So finally we marched them up to the Finland Station and put them on a train for Levashovo, where they have a camp.....

We came out into the cold, nervous night, murmurous with obscure armies on the move, electric with patrols. From across the river, where loomed the darker mass of Peter-Paul, came a hoarse shout.... Underfoot the sidewalk was littered with broken stucco, from the cornice of the Palace where two shells from the battleship *Avrora* had struck; that was the only damage done by the bombardment....

It was now after three in the morning. On the Nevsky all the street-lights were again shining, the cannon gone, and the only signs of war were Red Guards and soldiers squatting around fires. The city was quiet-probably never so quiet in its history; on that night not a single hold-up occurred, not a single robbery.

But the City Duma Building was all illuminated. We mounted to the galleried Alexander Hall, hung with its great, gold-framed, red-shrouded Imperial portraits. About a hundred people were grouped around the platform, where Skobeliev was speaking. He urged that the Committee of Public Safety be expanded, so as to unite all the anti-Bolshevik elements in one huge organisation, to be called the Committee for Salvation of Country and Revolution. And as we looked on, the Committee for Salvation was formed-that Committee which was to develop into the most powerful enemy of the Bolsheviki, appearing, in the next week, sometimes under its own partisan name, and sometimes as the strictly non-partisan Committee of Public Safety....

Dan, Gotz, Avkesntiev were there, some of the insurgent Soviet delegates, members of the Executive Committee of the Peasants' Soviets, old Prokopovitch, and even members of the Council of the Republic-among whom Vinaver and other Cadets. Lieber cried that the convention of Soviets was not a legal convention, that the old *Tsay-ee-kah* was still in office.... An appeal to the country was drafted.

We hailed a cab. "Where to?" But when we said "Smolny," the *izvoshtchik* shook his head. *"Niet!"* said he, "there are devils...." It was only after weary wandering that we found a driver willing to take us-and he wanted thirty rubles, and stopped two blocks away.

The windows of Smolny were still ablaze, motors came and went, and around the still-leaping fires the sentries huddled close, eagerly asking everybody the latest news. The corridors were full of hurrying men, hollow-eyed and dirty. In some of the committee-rooms people lay sleeping on the floor, their guns beside them. In spite of the seceding delegates, the hall of meetings was crowded with people, roaring like the sea. As we came in, Kameniev was reading the list of arrested Ministers. The name of Terestchenko was greeted with thunderous applause, shouts of satisfaction, laughter; Rutenburg came in for less; and at the mention of Paltchinsky, a storm of hoots, angry cries, cheers burst forth.... It was announced that Tchudnovsky had been appointed Commissar of the Winter Palace.

Now occurred a dramatic interruption. A big peasant, his bearded face convulsed with rage, mounted the platform and pounded with his fist on the presidium table.

"We, Socialist Revolutionaries, insist upon the immediate release of the Socialist Ministers arrested in the Winter Palace! Comrades! Do you know that four comrades who risked their lives and their freedom fighting against tyranny of the Tsar, have been flung into Peter-Paul prison-the historical tomb of Liberty?" In the uproar he pounded and yelled. Another delegate climbed up beside him, and pointed at the presidium.

71

"Are the representatives of the revolutionary masses going to sit quietly here while the *Okhrana* of the Bolsheviki tortures their leaders?"

Trotzky was gesturing for silence. "These 'comrades' who are now caught plotting the crushing of the Soviets with the adventurer Kerensky-is there any reason to handle them with gloves? After July 16th and 18th they didn't use much ceremony with us!" With a triumphant ring in his voice he cried, "Now that the *oborontsi* and the faint-hearted have gone, and the whole task of defending and saving the Revolution rests on our shoulders, it is particularly necessary to work-work-work! We have decided to die rather than give up!"

Followed him a Commissar from Tsarskoye Selo, panting and covered with the mud of his ride. "The garrison of Tsarskoye Selo is on guard at the gates of Petrograd, ready to defend the Soviets and the Military Revolutionary Committee!" Wild cheers. "The Cycle Corps sent from the front has arrived at Tsarskoye, and the soldiers are now with us; they recognise the power of the Soviets, the necessity of immediate transfer of land to the peasants and industrial control to the workers. The Fifth Battalion of Cyclists, stationed at Tsarskoye, is ours...."

Then the delegate of the Third Cycle Battalion. In the midst of delirious enthusiasm he told how the cycle corps had been ordered *three days before* from the South-west front to the "defence of Petrograd." They suspected, however, the meaning of the order; and at the station of Peredolsk were met by representatives of the Fifth Battalion from Tsarskoye. A joint meeting was held, and it was discovered that "among the cyclists not a single man was found willing to shed the blood of his brothers, or to support a Government of bourgeois and land-owners!"

Kapelinski, for the Mensheviki Internationalists, proposed to elect a special committee to find a peaceful solution to the civil war. "There isn't any peaceful solution!" bellowed the crowed. "Victory is the only solution!" The vote was overwhelmingly against, and the Mensheviki Internationalists left the Congress in a Whirlwind of Jocular insults. There was no longer any panic fear.... Kameniev from the platform shouted after them, "The Mensheviki Internationalists claimed 'emergency' for the question of a 'peaceful solution,' but they always voted for suspension of the order of the day in favour of declarations of factions which wanted to leave the Congress. It is evident," finished Kameniev, "that the withdrawal of all these renegades was decided upon beforehand!"

The assembly decided to ignore the withdrawal of the factions, and proceed to the appeal to the workers, soldiers and peasants of all Russia:

TO WORKERS, SOLDIERS AND PEASANTS

The Second All-Russian Congress of Soviets of Workers' and Soldiers' Deputies has opened. It represents the great majority of the Soviets. There are also a number of Peasant deputies. Based upon the will of the great majority of the workers', soldiers and peasants, based upon the triumphant uprising of the Petrograd workmen and soldiers, the Congress assumes the Power.

The Provisional Government is deposed. Most of the members of the Provisional Government are already arrested.

The Soviet authority will at once propose an immediate democratic peace to all nations, and an immediate truce on all fronts. It will assure the free transfer of landlord, crown and monastery lands to the Land Committees, defend the soldiers rights, enforcing a complete democratisation of the Army, establish workers' control over production, ensure the convocation of the Constituent Assembly at the proper date, take means to supply bread to the cities and articles of first necessity to the villages, and secure to all nationalities living in Russia a real right to independent existence.

The Congress resolves: that all local power shall be transferred to the Soviets of Workers', Soldiers' and Peasants' Deputies, which must enforce revolutionary order.

The Congress calls upon the soldiers in the trenches to be watchful and steadfast. The Congress of Soviets is sure that the revolutionary Army will know how to defend the Revolution against all attacks of Imperialism, until the new Government shall have brought about the conclusion of the democratic peace which it will directly propose to all nations. The new Government will take all necessary steps to secure everything needful to the revolutionary Army, by means of a determined policy of requisition and taxation of the propertied classes, and also to improve the situation of soldiers' families.

The Kornilovitz-Kerensky, Kaledin and others, are endeavouring to lead troops against Petrograd. Several regiments, deceived by Kerensky, have sided with the insurgent People.

Soldiers! Make active resistance to the Kornilovitz-Kerensky! Be on guard!

Railway men! Stop all troop-trains being sent by Kerensky against Petrograd!

Soldiers, Workers, Clerical employees! The destiny of the Revolution and democratic peace is in your hands!

Long live the Revolution!

The All-Russian Congress of Soviets of Workers' and Soldiers' Deputies. Delegates from the Peasants' Soviets.

It was exactly 5:17 A.M. when Krylenko, staggering with fatigue, climbed to the tribune with a telegram in his hand.

"Comrades! From the Northern Front. The Twelfth Army sends greetings
to the Congress of Soviets, announcing the formation of a Military
Revolutionary Committee which has taken over the command of the
Northern Front!" Pandemonium, men weeping, embracing each other.
"General Tchermissov has recognised the Committee-Commissar of the
Provisional Government Voitinsky has resigned!"

So. Lenin and the Petrograd workers had decided on insurrection, the Petrograd Soviet had overthrown the Provisional Government, and thrust the *coup d'etat* upon the Congress of Soviets. Now there was all great Russia to win-and then the world! Would Russia follow and rise? And the world-what of it? Would the peoples answer and rise, a red world-tide?

Although it was six in the morning, night was yet heavy and chill. There was only a faint unearthly pallor stealing over the silent streets, dimming the watch-fires, the shadow of a terrible dawn grey-rising over Russia....

CHAPTER V

Plunging Ahead

THURSDAY, November 8th. Day broke on a city in the wildest excitement and confusion, a whole nation having up in long hissing swells of storm. Superficially all was quiet; hundreds of thousands of people retired at a prudent hour, got up early, and went to work. In Petrograd the street-cars were running, the stores and restaurants open, theatres going, an exhibition of paintings advertised.... All the complex routine of common life-humdrum even in war-time-proceeded as usual. Nothing is so astounding as the vitality of the social organism-how it persists, feeding itself, clothing itself, amusing itself, in the face of the worst calamities....

The air was full of rumours about Kerensky, who was said to have raised the Front, and to be leading a great army against the capital. *Volia Naroda* published a *prikaz* launched by him at Pskov:

The disorders caused by the insane attempt of the Bolsheviki place the country on the verge of a precipice, and demand the effort of our entire will, our courage and the devotion of every one of us, to win through the terrible trial which the fatherland is undergoing....

Until the declaration of the composition of the new Government-if one is formed-every one ought to remain at his post and fulfil his duty toward bleeding Russia. It must be remembered that the least interference with existing Army organisations can bring on irreparable misfortunes, by opening the Front to the enemy. Therefore it is indispensable to preserve at any price the morale of the troops, by assuring complete order and the preservation of the Army from new shocks, and by maintaining absolute confidence between officers and their subordinates. I order all the chiefs and Commissars, in the name of the safety of the country, to stay at their posts, as I myself retain the post of Supreme Commander, until the Provisional Government of the Republic shall declare its will....

In answer, this placard on all the walls:

FROM THE ALL-RUSSIAN CONGRESS OF SOVIETS

"The ex-Ministers Konovalov, Kishkin, Terestchenko, Maliantovitch, Nikitin and others have been arrested by the Military Revolutionary Committee. Kerensky has fled. All Army organisations are ordered to take every measure for the immediate arrest of Kerensky and his conveyance to Petrograd.

"All assistance given to Kerensky will be punished as a serious crime against the state."

With brakes released the Military Revolutionary Committee whirled, throwing off orders, appeals, decrees, like sparks. ... Kornilov was ordered brought to Petrograd. Members of the Peasant Land Committees imprisoned by the Provisional Government were declared free. Capital punishment in the army was abolished. Government employees were ordered to continue their work, and threatened with severe penalties if they refused. All pillage, disorder and speculation were forbidden under pain of death. Temporary Commissars were appointed to the various Ministries: Foreign Affairs, Vuritsky and Trotzky; Interior and Justice, Rykov; Labor, Shliapnikov; Finance, Menzhinsky; Public Welfare, Madame Kollontai; Commerce, Ways and Communications, Riazanov; Navy, the sailor Korbir; Posts and Telegraphs, Spiro; Theatres, Muraviov; State Printing Office, Gherbychev; for the City of Petrograd, Lieutenant Nesterov; for the Northern Front, Pozern....

To the Army, appeal to set up Military Revolutionary Committees. To the railway workers, to maintain order, especially not to delay the transport of food to the cities and the front.... In return, they were promised representation in the Ministry of Ways and Communications.

Cossack brothers! (said one proclamation). You are being led against Petrograd. They want to force you into battle with the revolutionary workers and soldiers of the capital. Do not believe a word that is said by our common enemies, the land-owners and the capitalists.

At our Congress are represented all the conscious organisations of workers, soldiers and peasants of Russia. The Congress wishes also to welcome into its midst the worker-Cossacks. The Generals of the Black Band, henchmen of the land-owners, of Nicolai the Cruel, are our enemies.

They tell you that the Soviets wish to confiscate the lands of the Cossacks. This is a lie. It is only from the great Cossack landlords that the Revolution will confiscate the land to give it to the people.

Organise Soviets of Cossacks' Deputies! Join with the Soviets of
Workers' and Soldiers' Deputies!

Show the Black Band that you are not traitors to the People, and that you do not wish to be cursed by the whole of revolutionary Russia!...

Cossack brothers, execute no orders of the enemies of the people.
Send your delegates to Petrograd to talk it over with us.... The
Cossacks of the Petrograd garrison, to their honour, have not
justified the hope of the People's enemies....

Cossack brothers! The All-Russian Congress of Soviets extends to you a fraternal hand. Long live the brotherhood of the Cossacks with the soldiers, workers and peasants of all Russia!

On the other side, what a storm of proclamations posted up, hand-bills scattered everywhere, newspapers-screaming and cursing and prophesying evil. Now raged the battle of the printing press-all other weapons being in the hands of the Soviets.

First, the appeal of the Committee for Salvation of Country and Revolution, flung broadcast over Russia and Europe:

TO THE CITIZENS OF THE RUSSIAN REPUBLIC!

Contrary to the will of the revolutionary masses, on November 7th the Bolsheviki of Petrograd criminally arrested part of the Provisional Government, dispersed the Council of the Republic, and proclaimed an illegal power. Such violence committed against the Government of revolutionary Russia at the moment of its greatest external danger, is an indescribable crime against the fatherland.

The insurrection of the Bolsheviki deals a mortal blow to the cause of national defence, and postpones immeasurably the moment of peace so greatly desired.

Civil war, begun by the Bolsheviki, threatens to deliver the country to the horrors of anarchy and counter-revolution, and cause the failure of the Constituent Assembly, which must affirm the republican régime and transmit to the People forever their right to the land.

Preserving the continuity of the only legal Governmental power, the Committee for Salvation of Country and Revolution, established on the night of November 7th, takes the initiative in forming a new Provisional Government; which, basing itself on the forces of democracy, will conduct the country to the Constituent Assembly and save it from anarchy and counter-revolution. The Committee for Salvation summons you, citizens, to refuse to recognise the power of violence. Do not obey its orders!

Rise for the defence of the country and Revolution!

Support the Committee for Salvation!

Signed by the Council of the Russian Republic, the Municipal Duma of Petrograd, the *Tsay-ee-kah (First Congress),* the Executive Committee of the Peasants' Soviets, and from the Congress itself the Front group, the factions of Socialist Revolutionaries, Mensheviki, Populist Socialists, Unified Social Democrats, and the group "Yedinstvo."

Then posters from the Socialist Revolutionary party, the Mensheviki *oborontsi,* Peasants' Soviets again; from the Central Army Committee, the *Tsentroflot....*

... Famine will crush Petrograd! (they cried). The German armies will trample on our liberty. Black Hundred *pogroms* will spread over Russia, if we all-conscious workers, soldiers, citizens-do not unite....

Do not trust the promises of the Bolsheviki! The promise of immediate peace-is a lie! The promise of bread-a hoax! The promise of land-a fairy tale!...

They were all in this manner.

Comrades! You have been basely and cruelly deceived! The seizure of power has been accomplished by the Bolsheviki alone.... They concealed their plot from the other Socialist parties composing the Soviet....

You have been promised land and freedom, but the counter-revolution will profit by the anarchy called forth by the Bolsheviki, and will deprive you of land and freedom....

The newspapers were as violent.

Our duty (said the *Dielo Naroda*) is to unmask these traitors to the working-class. Our duty is to mobilise all our forces and mount guard over the cause of the Revolution!...

Izviestia, for the last time speaking in the name of the old *Tsay-ee-kah,* threatened awful retribution.

As for the Congress of Soviets, we affirm that there has been no Congress of Soviets! We affirm that it was merely a private conference of the Bolshevik faction! And in that case, they have no right to cancel the powers of the *Tsay-ee-kah....*

Novaya Zhizn, while pleading for a new Government that should unite all the Socialist parties, criticised severely the action of the Socialist Revolutionaries and the Mensheviki in quitting the Congress, and pointed out that the Bolshevik insurrection meant one thing very clearly: that all illusions about coalition with the bourgeoisie were henceforth demonstrated vain...

Rabotchi Put blossomed out as *Pravda,* Lenin's newspaper which had been suppressed in July. It crowed, bristling:

Workers, soldiers, peasants! In March you struck down the tyranny of the clique of nobles. Yesterday you struck down the tyranny of the bourgeois gang....

The first task now is to guard the approaches to Petrograd.

The second is definitely to disarm the counter-revolutionary elements of Petrograd.

The third is definitely to organise the revolutionary power and assure the realisation of the popular programme...

What few Cadet organs appeared, and the bourgeoisie generally, adopted a detached, ironical attitude toward the whole business, a sort of contemptuous "I-told-you-so" to the other parties. Influential Cadets were to be seen hovering around the Municipal Duma, and on the outskirts of the Committee for Salvation. Other than that, the bourgeoisie lay low, biding its hour-which could not far off. That the Bolsheviki would remain in power longer than three days never occurred to anybody-except perhaps to Lenin, Trotzky, the Petrograd workers and the simpler soldiers....

In the high, amphitheatrical Nicolai Hall that afternoon I saw the Duma sitting in *permanence,* tempestuous, grouping around it all the forces of opposition. The old Mayer, Schreider, majestic with his white hair and beard, was describing his visit to Smolny the night before, to protest in the name of the Municipal Self-Government. "The Duma, being the only existing legal Government in the city, elected by equal, direct and secret suffrage, would not recognise the new power," he had told Trotzky. And Trotzky had answered, "There is a constitutional remedy for that. The Duma can be dissolved and re-elected...." At this report there was a furious outcry.

"If one recognises a Government by bayonet," continued the old man, addressing the Duma, "well, we have one; but I consider legitimate only a Government recognised by the majority, and not one created by the usurpation of a minority!" Wild applause on all benches except those of the Bolsheviki. Amid renewed tumult the Mayor announced that the Bolsheviki already were violating Municipal autonomy by appointing Commissars in many departments.

The Bolshevik speaker shouted, trying to make himself heard, that the decision of the Congress of Soviets meant that all Russia backed up the action of the Bolsheviki.

"You!" he cried. "You are not the real representative of the people of Petrograd!" Shrieks of "Insult! Insult!" The old Mayor, with dignity, reminded him that the Duma was elected by the freest possible popular vote. "Yes," he answered, "but that was a long time ago-like the *Tsay-ee-kah*-like the Army Committee."

"There has been no new Congress of Soviets!" they yelled at him.

"The Bolshevik faction refuses to remain any longer in this nest of counter-revolution-" Uproar. "-and we demand a re-election of the Duma...." Whereupon the Bolsheviki left the chamber, followed by cries of "German agents! Down with the traitors!"

Shingariov, Cadet, then demanded that all Municipal functionaries who had consented to be Commissars of the Military Revolutionary Committee be discharged from their position and indicted. Schreider was on his feet, putting a motion to the effect that the Duma protested against the menace of the Bolsheviki to dissolve it, and as the legal representative of the population, it would refuse to leave its post.

Outside, the Alexander Hall was crowded for the meeting of the Committee for Salvation, and Skobeliev was again speaking. "Never yet," he said, "was the fate of the Revolution so acute, never yet did the question of the existence of the Russian state excite so much anxiety, never yet did history put so harshly and categorically the question-is Russia to be or not to be! The great hour for the salvation of the Revolution has arrived, and in consciousness thereof we observe the close union of the live forces of the revolutionary democracy, by whose organised will a centre for the salvation of the country and the Revolution has already been created...." And much of the same sort. "We shall die sooner than surrender our post!"

Amid violent applause it was announced that the Union of Railway Workers had joined the Committee for Salvation. A few moments later the Post and Telegraph Employees came in; then some Mensheviki Internationalists entered the hall, to cheers. The Railway men said they did not recognise the Bolsheviki and had taken the entire railroad apparatus into their own hands, refusing to entrust it to any usurpatory power. The Telegraphers' delegate declared that the operators had flatly refused to work their instruments as long as the Bolshevik Commissar was in the office. The Postmen would not deliver or accept mail at Smolny.... All the Smolny telephones were cut off. With great glee it was reported how Uritzky had gone to the Ministry of Foreign Affairs to demand the secret treaties, and how Neratov had put him out. The Government employees were all stopping work....

It was war-war deliberately planned, Russian fashion; war by strike and sabotage. As we sat there the chairman read a list of names and assignments; so-and-so was to make the round of the Ministries; another was to visit the banks; some ten or twelve were to work the barracks and persuade the soldiers to remain neutral-"Russian soldiers, do not shed the blood of your brothers!"; a committee was to go and confer with Kerensky; still others were despatched to provincial cities, to form branches of the Committee for Salvation, and link together the anti-Bolshevik elements.

The crowd was in high spirits. "These Bolsheviki *will* try to dictate to the *intelligentzia?* We'll show them!"... Nothing could be more striking than the contrast between this assemblage and the Congress of Soviets. There, great masses of shabby soldiers, grimy workmen, peasants-poor men, bent and scarred in the brute struggle for existence; here the Menshevik and Social Revolutionary leaders-Avksentievs, Dans, Liebers,-the former Socialist Ministers-Skobelievs, Tchernovs,-rubbed shoulders with Cadets like oily Shatsky, sleek Vinaver; with journalists, students, intellectuals of almost all camps. This Duma crowd was well-fed, well-dressed; I did not see more than three proletarians among them all....

News came. Kornilov's faithful *Tekhintsi* [*] had slaughtered his [* See Notes and Explanations] guards at Bykhov, and he had escaped. Kaledin was marching north.... The Soviet of Moscow had set up a Military Revolutionary Committee, and was negotiating with the commandant of the city for possession of the arsenal, so that the workers might be armed.

With these facts was mixed an astounding jumble of rumours,
distortions, and plain lies. For instance, an intelligent young
Cadet, formerly private secretary to Miliukov and then to
Terestchenko, drew us aside and told us all about the taking of the
Winter Palace.

"The Bolsheviki were led by German and Austrian officers," he affirmed.

"Is that so?" we replied, politely. "How do you know?"

"A friend of mine was there and saw them."

"How could he tell they were German officers?"

"Oh, because they wore German uniforms!"

There were hundreds of such absurd tales, and they were not only solemnly published by the anti-Bolshevik press, but believed by the most unlikely persons-Socialist Revolutionaries and Mensheviki who had always been distinguished by their sober devotion to facts....

But more serious were the stories of Bolshevik violence and terrorism. For example, it was said printed that the Red Guards had not only thoroughly looted the Winter Palace, but that they had massacred the *yunkers* after disarming them, had killed some of the Ministers in cold blood; and as for the woman soldiers, most of them had been violated, and many had committed suicide because of the tortures they had gone through.... All these stories were swallowed whole by the crowd in the Duma. And worse still, the mothers and fathers of the students and of the women read these frightful details, *often accompanied by lists of names,* and toward nightfall the Duma began to be besieged by frantic citizens....

A typical case is that of Prince Tumanov, whose body, it was announced in many newspapers, had been found floating in the Moika Canal. A few hours later this was denied by the Prince's family, who added that the Prince was under arrest so the press identified the dead man as General Demissov. The General having also come to life, we investigated, and could find no trace of any body found whatever....

As we left the Duma building two boy scouts were distributing hand-bills to the enormous crowd which blocked the Nevsky in front of the door-a crowd composed almost entirely of business men, shop-keepers, *tchinouniki,* clerks. One read!

FROM THE MUNICIPAL DUMA

The Municipal Duma in its meeting of October 26th, in view of the events of the day decrees: To announce the inviolability of private dwellings. Through the House Committees it calls upon the population of the town of Petrograd to meet with decisive repulse all attempts to enter by force private apartments, not stopping at the use of arms, in the interests of the self-defence of citizens.

Up on the corner of the Liteiny, five or six Red Guards and a couple of sailors had surrounded a news-dealer and were demanding that he hand over his copies of the Menshevik *Rabot-chaya Gazeta* (Workers' Gazette). Angrily he shouted at them, shaking his fist, as one of the sailors tore the papers from his stand. An ugly crowd had gathered around, abusing the patrol. One little workman kept explaining doggedly to the people and the news-dealer, over and over again, "It has Kerensky's proclamation in it. It says we killed Russian people. It will make bloodshed...."

Smolny was tenser than ever, if that were possible. The same running men in the dark corridors, squads of workers with rifles, leaders with bulging portfolios arguing, explaining, giving orders as they hurried anxiously along, surrounded by friends and lieutenants. Men literally out of themselves, living prodigies of sleeplessness and work-men unshaven, filthy, with burning eyes, who drove upon their fixed purpose full speed on engines of exaltation. So much they had to do, so much! Take over the Government, organise the City, keep the garrison loyal, fight the Duma and the Committee for Salvation, keep out the Germans, prepare to do battle with Kerensky, inform the provinces what had happened, Propagandise from Archangel to Vladivostok.... Government and Municipal employees refusing to obey their Commissars, post and telegraph refusing them communication, railroads roads stonily ignoring their appeals for trains, Kerensky coming, the garrison not altogether to be trusted, the Cossacks waiting to come out.... Against them not only the organised bourgeoisie, but all the other Socialist parties except the Left Socialist Revolutionaries, a few Mensheviki Internationalists and the Social Democrat Internationalists, and even they undecided whether to stand by or not. With them, it is true, the workers and the soldier-masses-the peasants an unknown quantity-but after all the Bolsheviki were a political faction not rich in trained and educated men....

Riazanov was coming up the front steps, explaining in a sort of humorous panic that he, Commissar of Commerce, knew nothing whatever of business. In the upstairs cafe sat a man all by himself in the corner, in a goat-skin cape and clothes which had been-I was going to say "slept in," but of course he hadn't slept-and a three days' growth of beard. He was anxiously figuring on a dirty envelope, and biting his pencil meanwhile. This was

Menzhinsky, Commissar of Finance, whose qualifications were that he had once been clerk in a French bank.... And these four half-running down the hall from the office of the Military Revolutionary Committee, and scribbling on bits of paper as they run-these were Commissars despatched to the four corners of Russia to carry the news, argue, or fight-with whatever arguments or weapons came to hand....

The Congress was to meet at one o'clock, and long since the great meeting-hall had filled, but by seven there was yet no sign of the presidium.... The Bolshevik and Left Social Revolutionary factions were in session in their own rooms. All the livelong afternoon Lenin and Trotzky had fought against compromise. A considerable part of the Bolsheviki were in favour of giving way so far as to create a joint all-Socialist government. "We can't hold on!" they cried.

"Too much is against us. We haven't got the men. We will be isolated, and the whole thing will fall." So Kameniev, Riazanov and others.

But Lenin, with Trotzky beside him, stood firm as a rock. "Let the compromisers accept our programme and they can come in! We won't give way an inch. If there are comrades here who haven't the courage and the will to dare what we dare, let them leave with the rest of the cowards and conciliators! Backed by the workers and soldiers we shall go on."

At five minutes past seven came word from the left Socialist Revolutionaries to say that they would remain in the Military Revolutionary Committee.

"See!" said Lenin. "They are following!"

A little later, as we sat at the press table in the big hall, an Anarchist who was writing for the bourgeois papers proposed to me that we go and find out what had become of the presidium. There was nobody in the *Tsay-ee-kah* office, nor in the bureau of the Petrograd Soviet. From room to room we wandered, through vast Smolny. Nobody seemed to have the slightest idea where to find the governing body of the Congress. As we went my companion described his ancient revolutionary activities, his long and pleasant exile in France.... As for the Bolsheviki, he confided to me that they were common, rude, ignorant persons, without aesthetic sensibilities. He was a real specimen of the Russian *intelligentzia*.... So he came at last to Room 17, office of the Military Revolutionary Committee, and stood there in the midst of all the furious coming and going. The door opened, and out shot a squat, flat-faced man in a uniform without insignia, who seemed to be smiling-which smile, after a minute, one saw to be the fixed grin of extreme fatigue. It was Krylenko.

My friend, who was a dapper, civilized-looking young man, gave a cry of pleasure and stepped forward.

"Nicolai Vasilievitch!" he said, holding out his hand. "Don't you remember me, comrade? We were in prison together."

Krylenko made an effort and concentrated his mind and sight. "Why yes," he answered finally, looking the other up and down with an expression of great friendliness. "You are S-. *Zdra'stvuitye!*" They kissed. "What are you doing in all this?" He waved his arm around.

"Oh, I'am just looking on.... You seem very successful."

"Yes," replied Krylenko, with a sort of doggedness, "The proletarian Revolution is a great success." He laughed. "Perhaps-perhaps, however, we'll meet in prison again!"

When we got out into the corridor again my friend went on with his explanations. "You see, I'am a follower of Kropotkin. To us the Revolution is a great failure; it has not aroused the patriotism of the masses. Of course that only proves that the people are not ready for Revolution...."

It was just 8.40 when a thundering wave of cheers announced the entrance of the presidium, with Lenin-great Lenin-among them. A short, stocky figure, with a big head set down in his shoulders, bald and bulging. Little eyes, a snubbish nose, wide, generous mouth, and heavy chin; clean-shaven now, but already beginning to bristle with the well-known beard of his past and future. Dressed in shabby clothes, his trousers much too long for him. Unimpressive, to be the idol of a mob, loved and revered as perhaps few leaders in history have been. A strange popular leader-a leader purely by virtue of intellect; colourless, humourless, uncompromising and detached, without picturesque idiosyncrasies-but with the power of explaining profound ideas in simple terms, of analysing a concrete situation. And combined with shrewdness, the greatest intellectual audacity.

Kameniev was reading the report of the actions of the Military Revolutionary Committee; abolition of capital punishment in the Army, restoration of the free right of propaganda, release of officers and soldiers arrested for political crimes, orders to arrest Kerensky and confiscation of food supplies in private store-houses.... Tremendous applause.

Again the representative of the *Bund.* The uncompromising attitude of the Bolsheviki would mean the crushing of the Revolution; therefore, the *Bund* delegates must refuse any longer to sit in the Congress. Cries from the audience, "We thought you walked out last night! How many times are you going to walk out?"

Then the representative of the Mensheviki Internationalists. Shouts, "What! You here still?" The speaker explained that only part of the Mensheviki Internationalists left the Congress; the rest were going to stay-

"We consider it dangerous and perhaps even mortal for the Revolution to transfer the power to the Soviets"-Interruptions-"but we feel it our duty to remain in the Congress and vote against the transfer here!"

Other speakers followed, apparently without any order. A delegate of the coal-miners of the Don Basin called upon the Congress to take measures against Kaledin, who might cut off coal and food from the capital. Several soldiers just arrived from the Front brought the enthusiastic greetings of their regiments.... Now Lenin, gripping the edge of the reading stand, letting his little winking eyes travel over the crowd as he stood there waiting, apparently oblivious to the long-rolling ovation, which lasted several minutes. When it finished, he said simply, "We shall now proceed to construct the Socialist order!" Again that overwhelming human roar.

"The first thing is the adoption of practical measures to realise peace.... We shall offer peace to the peoples of all the belligerent countries upon the basis of the Soviet terms-no annexations, no indemnities, and the right of self-determination of peoples. At the same time, according to our promise, we shall publish and repudiate the secret treaties.... The question of War and Peace is so clear that I think that I may, without preamble, read the project of a Proclamation to the Peoples of All the Belligerent Countries...."

His great mouth, seeming to smile, opened wide as he spoke; his voice was hoarse-not unpleasantly so, but as if it had hardened that way after years and years of speaking-and went on monotonously, with the effect of being able to go on forever.... For emphasis he bent forward slightly. No gestures. And before him, a thousand simple faces looking up in intent adoration.

PROCLAMATION TO THE PEOPLES AND GOVERNMENTS OF ALL THE BELLIGERENT NATIONS.

The Workers' and Peasants' Government, created by the revolution of November 6th and 7th and based on the Soviets of Workers', Soldiers' and Peasants' Deputies, proposes to all the belligerent peoples and to their Governments to begin immediately negotiations for a just and democratic peace.

The Government means by a just and democratic peace, which is desired by the immense majority of the workers and the labouring classes, exhausted and depleted by the war-that peace which the Russian workers and peasants, after having struck down the Tsarist monarchy, have not ceased to demand categorically-immediate peace without annexations (that is to say, without conquest of foreign territory, without forcible annexation of other nationalities), and without indemnities.

The Government of Russia Proposes to all the belligerent peoples immediately to conclude such a peace, by showing themselves willing to enter upon the decisive steps of negotiations aiming at such a peace, at once, without the slightest delay, before the definitive ratification of all the conditions of such a peace by the authorised assemblies of the people of all countries and of all nationalities.

By annexation or conquest of foreign territory, the Government means-conformably to the conception of democratic rights in general, and the rights of the working-class in particular-all union to a great and strong State of a small or weak nationality, without the voluntary, clear and precise expression of its consent and desire; whatever be the moment when such an annexation by force was accomplished, whatever be the degree civilisation of the nation annexed by force or maintained outside the frontiers of another State, no matter if that nation be in Europe or in the far countries across the sea.

If any nation is retained by force within the limits of another State; if, in spite of the desire expressed by it, (it matters little if that desire be expressed by the press, by popular meetings, decisions of political parties, or by disorders and riots against national oppression), that nation is not given the right of deciding by free vote-without the slightest constraint, after the complete departure of the armed forces of the nation which has annexed it or wishes to annex it or is stronger in general-the form of its national and political organisation, such a union constitutes an annexation-that is to say, conquest and an act of violence.

To continue this war in order to permit the strong and rich nations to divide among themselves the weak and conquered nationalities is considered by the Government the greatest possible crime against humanity; and the Government solemnly proclaims its decision to sign a treaty of peace which will put an end to this war upon the above conditions, equally fair for all nationalities without exception.

The Government abolishes secret diplomacy, expressing before the whole country its firm decision to conduct all the negotiations in the light of day before the people, and will proceed immediately to the full publication of all secret treaties confirmed or concluded by the Government of land-owners and capitalists, from March until November 7th, 1917. All the clauses of the secret treaties which, as occur in a majority of cases, have for their object to procure advantages and privileges for Russian capitalists, to maintain or augment the annexations of the Russian imperialists, are denounced by the Government immediately and without discussion.

In proposing to all Governments and all peoples to engage in public negotiations for peace, the Government declares itself ready to carry on these negotiations by telegraph, by post, or by pourparlers between the representatives of the different countries, or at a conference of these representatives. To facilitate these pourparlers, the Government appoints its authorised representatives in the neutral countries.

The Government proposes to all the governments and to the peoples of all the belligerent countries to conclude an immediate armistice, at the same time suggesting that the armistice ought to last three months, during which time it is perfectly possible, not only to hold the necessary pourparlers between the representatives of all the nations and nationalities without exception drawn into the war or forced to take part in it, but also to convoke authorised assemblies of representatives of the people of all countries, for the purpose of the definite acceptance of the conditions of peace.

In addressing this offer of peace to the Governments and to the peoples of all the belligerent countries, the Provisional Workers' and Peasants' Government of Russia addresses equally and in particular the conscious workers of the three nations most devoted to humanity and the three most important nations among those taking part in the present war-England, France, and Germany. The workers of these countries have rendered the greatest services to the cause of progress and of Socialism. The splendid examples of the Chartist movement in England, the series of revolutions, of world-wide historical significance, accomplished by the French proletariat-and finally, in Germany, the historic struggle against the Laws of Exception, an example for the workers of the whole world of prolonged and stubborn action, and the creation of the formidable organisations of German proletarians-all these models of proletarian heroism, these monuments of history, are for us a sure guarantee that the workers of these countries will understand the duty imposed upon them to liberate humanity from the horrors and consequences of war; and that these workers, by decisive, energetic and continued action, will help us to bring to a successful conclusion the cause of peace-and at the same time, the cause of the liberation of the exploited working masses from all slavery and all exploitation.

When the grave thunder of applause had died away, Lenin spoke again:

"We propose to the Congress to ratify this declaration. We address ourselves to the Governments as well as to the peoples, for a declaration which would be addressed only to the peoples of the belligerent countries might delay the conclusion of peace. The conditions of peace, drawn up during the armistice, will be ratified by the Constituent Assembly. In fixing the duration of the armistice at three months, we desire to give to the peoples as long a rest as possible after this bloody extermination, and ample time for them to elect their representatives. This proposal of peace will meet with resistance on the part of the imperialist governments-we don't fool ourselves on that score. But we hope that revolution will soon break out in all the belligerent countries; that is why we address ourselves especially to the workers of France, England and Germany....

"The revolution of November 6th and 7th," he ended, "has opened the era of the Social Revolution.... The labour movement, in the name of peace and Socialism, shall win, and fulfil its destiny....

There was something quiet and powerful in all this, which stirred the souls of men. It was understandable why people believed when Lenin spoke...."

By crowd vote it was quickly decided that only representatives of political factions should be allowed to speak on the motion and that speakers should be limited to fifteen minutes.

First Karelin for the Left Socialist Revolutionaries. "Our faction had no opportunity to propose amendments to the text of the proclamation; it is a private document of the Bolsheviki. But we will vote for it because we agree with its spirit...."

For the Social Democrats Internationalists Kramarov, long, stoop-shouldered and near-sighted-destined to achieve some notoriety as the Clown of the Opposition. Only a Government composed of all the Socialist parties, he said, could possess the authority to take such important action. If a Socialist coalition were formed, his faction would support the entire programme; if not, only part of it. As for the proclamation, the Internationalists were in thorough accord with its main points....

Then one after another, amid rising enthusiasm; Ukrainean Social Democracy, support; Lithuanian Social Democracy, support; Populist Socialists, support; Polish Social Democracy, support; Polish Socialists support-but would prefer a Socialist coalition; Lettish Social Democracy, support.... Something was kindled in these men. One spoke of the "coming World-Revolution, of which we are the advance-guard"; another of "the new age of brotherhood, when all the peoples will become one great family...." An individual member claimed the floor. "There is contradiction here," he said. "First you offer peace without annexations and indemnities, and then you say you will consider all peace offers. To consider means to accept...."

Lenin was on his feet. "We want a just peace, but we are not afraid of a revolutionary war.... Probably the imperialist Governments will not answer our appeal-but we shall not issue an ultimatum to which it will be easy to say no.... If the German proletariat realises that we are ready to consider all offers of peace, that will perhaps be the last drop which overflows the bowl-revolution will break out in Germany....

"We consent to examine all conditions of peace, but that doesn't mean that we shall accept them.... For some of our terms we shall fight to the end-but possibly for others will find it impossible to continue the war.... Above all, we want to finish the war...."

It was exactly 10:35 when Kameniev asked all in favour of the proclamation to hold up their cards. One delegate dared to raise his hand against, but the sudden sharp outburst around him brought it swiftly down.... Unanimous.

Suddenly, by common impulse, we found ourselves on our feet, mumbling together into the smooth lifting unison of the *Internationale.* A grizzled old soldier was sobbing like a child. Alexandra Kollontai rapidly winked the tears back. The immense sound rolled through the hall, burst windows and doors and seared into the quiet sky. "The war is ended! The war is ended!" said a young workman near me, his face shining. And when it was over, as we stood there in a kind of awkward hush, some one in the back of the room ck of the room | | shouted, "Comrades! Let us remember those who have died for liberty!" So we began to sing the Funeral March, that slow, melancholy and yet triumphant chant, so Russian and so moving. The *Internationale* is an alien air, after all. The Funeral March seemed the very soul of those dark masses whose delegates sat in this hall, building from their obscure visions a new Russia-and perhaps more.

You fell in the fatal fight

For the liberty of the people, for the honour of the people....

You gave up your lives and everything dear to you,

You suffered in horrible prisons,

You went to exile in chains....

Without a word you carried your chains because you could not ignore your suffering brothers,

Because you believed that justice is stronger than the sword....

The time will come when your surrendered life will count

That time is near; when tyranny falls the people will rise, great and free!

Farewell, brothers, you chose a noble path,

You are followed by the new and fresh army ready to die and to suffer....

Farewell, brothers, you chose a noble path,

At your grave we swear to fight, to work for freedom and the people's happiness....

For this did they lie there, the martyrs of March, in their cold Brotherhood Grave on Mars Field; for this thousands and tens of thousands had died in the prisons, in exile, in Siberian mines. It had not come as they expected it would come, nor as the *intelligentzia* desired it;

89

but it had come-rough, strong, impatient of formulas, contemptuous of sentimentalism; real....

Lenin was reading the Decree on Land:

(1.) All private ownership of land is abolished immediately without compensation.

(2.) All land_owners' estates, and all lands belonging to the Crown, to monasteries, church lands with all their live stock and inventoried property, buildings and all appurtenances, are transferred to the disposition of the township Land Committees and the district Soviets of Peasants' Deputies until the Constituent Assembly meets.

(3.) Any damage whatever done to the confiscated property which from now on belongs to the whole People, is regarded as a serious crime, punishable by the revolutionary tribunals. The district Soviets of Peasants' Deputies shall take all necessary measures for the observance of the strictest order during the taking over of the land-owners' estates, for the determination of the dimensions of the plots of land and which of them are subject to confiscation, for the drawing up of an inventory of the entire confiscated property, and for the strictest revolutionary protection of all the farming property on the land, with all buildings, implements, cattle, supplies of products, etc., passing into the hands of the People.

(4.) For guidance during the realisation of the great land reforms until their final resolution by the Constituent Assembly, shall serve the following peasant *nakaz* (instructions), drawn up on the basis of 242 local peasant *nakazi* by the editorial board of the "*Izviestia* of the All-Russian Soviet of Peasants' Deputies," and published in No.88 of said "*Izviestia*" (Petrograd, No.88, August 19th, 1917).

The lands of peasants and of Cossacks serving in the Army shall not be confiscated.

"This is not," explained Lenin, "the project of former Minister Tchernov, who spoke of 'erecting a frame-work' and tried to realise reforms from above. From below, on the spot, will be decided the questions of division of the land. The amount of land received by each peasant will vary according to the locality...."

"Under the Provisional Government, the *pomieshtchiki* flatly refused to obey the orders of the Land Committees-those Land Committees projected by Lvov, brought into existence by Shingariov, and administered by Kerensky!"

Before the debates could begin a man forced his way violently through the crowd in the aisle and climbed upon the platform. It was Pianikh, member of the Executive Committee of the Peasants' Soviets, and he was mad clean through.

"The Executive Committee of the All-Russian Soviets of Peasants' Deputies protests against the arrest of our comrades, the Ministers Salazkin and Mazlov!" he flung harshly in the faces of the crowd, "We demand their instant release! They are now in Peter-Paul fortress. We must have immediate action! There is not a moment to lose!"

Another followed him, a soldier with disordered beard and flaming eyes. "You sit here and talk about giving the land to the peasants, and you commit an act of tyrants and usurpers against the peasants' chosen representatives! I tell you-" he raised his fist, "If one hair of their heads is harmed, you'll have a revolt on your hands!" The crowd stirred confusedly.

Then up rose Trotzky, calm and venomous, conscious of power, greeted with a roar. "Yesterday the Military Revolutionary Committee decided to release the Socialist Revolutionary and Menshevik Ministers, Mazlov, Salazkin, Gvozdov and Maliantovitch-on principle. That they are still in Peter-Paul is only because we have had so much to do.... They will, however, be detained at their homes under arrest until we have investigated their complicity in the treacherous acts of Kerensky during the Kornilov affair!"

"Never," shouted Pianikh, "in any revolution have such things been seen as go on here!"

"You are mistaken," responded Trotzky. "Such things have been seen even in this revolution. Hundreds of our comrades were arrested in the July days.... When Comrade Kollontai was released from prison by the doctor's orders, Avksentiev placed at her door two former agents of the Tsar's secret police!" The peasants withdrew, muttering, followed by ironical hoots.

The representative of the Left Socialist Revolutionaries spoke on the Land Decree. While agreeing in principle, his faction could not vote on the question until after discussion. The Peasants' Soviets should be consulted....

The Mensheviki Internationalists, too, insisted on a party caucus.

Then the leader of the Maximalists, the Anarchist wing of the peasants: "We must do honour to a political party which puts such an act into effect the first day, without jawing about it!"

A typical peasant was in the tribune, long hair, boots and sheep-skin coat, bowing to all corners of the hall. "I wish you well, comrades and citizens," he said. "There are some Cadets walking around outside. You arrested our Socialist peasants-why not arrest them?"

This was the signal for a debate of excited peasants. It was precisely like the debate of soldiers of the night before. Here were the real proletarians of the land....

"Those members of our Executive Committee, Avksentiev and the rest, whom we thought were the peasants' protectors-they are only Cadets too! Arrest them! Arrest them!"

Another, "Who are these Pianikhs, these Avksentievs? They are not peasants at all! They only wag their tails!"

How the crowd rose to them, recognising brothers!

The Left Socialist Revolutionaries proposed a half-hour intermission. As the delegates streamed out, Lenin stood up in his place.

"We must not lose time, comrades! News all-important to Russia must be on the press to-morrow morning. No delay!"

And above the hot discussion, argument, shuffling of feet could be heard the voice of an emissary of the Military Revolutionary Committee, crying, "Fifteen agitators wanted in room 17 at once! To go to the Front!"hellip;

It was almost two hours and a half later that the delegates came straggling back, the presidium mounted the platform, and the session recommenced by the reading of telegrams from regiment after regiment, announcing their adhesion to the Military Revolutionary Committee.

In leisurely manner the meeting gathered momentum. A delegate from the Russian troops on the Macedonian front spoke bitterly of their situation. "We suffer there more from the friendship of our 'Allies' than from the enemy," he said. Representatives of the Tenth and Twelfth Armies, just arrived in hot haste, reported, "We support you with all our strength!" A peasant-soldier protested against the release of "the traitor Socialists, Mazlov and Salazkin"; as for the Executive Committee of the Peasants' Soviets, it should be arrested _en masse!_Here was real revolutionary talk.... A deputy from the Russian Army in Persia declared he was instructed to demand all power to the Soviets.... A Ukrainean officer, speaking in his native tongue: "There is no nationalism in this crisis.... *Da zdravstvuyet* the proletarian dictatorship of all lands!" Such a deluge of high and hot thoughts that surely Russia would never again be dumb!

Kameniev remarked that the anti-Bolshevik forces were trying to stir up disorders everywhere, and read an appeal of the Congress to all the Soviets of Russia:

The All-Russian Congress of Soviets of Workers' and Soldiers' Deputies, including some Peasants' Deputies, calls upon the local Soviets to take immediate energetic measures to oppose all counter-revolutionary anti-Jewish action and all *pogroms,* whatever they may be.

The honour of the Workers', Peasants' and Soldiers' Revolution demands that no *pogrom* be tolerated.

The Red Guard of Petrograd, the revolutionary garrison and the sailors have maintained complete order in the capital.

Workers, soldiers and peasants, you should follow everywhere the example of the workers and soldiers of Petrograd.

Comrade soldiers and Cossacks, on us falls the duty of assuring real revolutionary order.

All revolutionary Russia and the entire world have their eyes on us....

At two o'clock the Land Decree was put to vote, with only one against and the peasant delegates wild with joy.... So plunged the Bolsheviki ahead, irresistible, over-riding hesitation and opposition-the only people in Russia who had a definite programme of action while the others talked for eight long months.

Now arose a soldier, gaunt, ragged and eloquent, to protest against the clause of the *nakaz* tending to deprive military deserters from a share in village land allotments. Bawled at and hissed at first, his simple, moving speech finally made silence. "Forced against his will into the butchery of the trenches," he cried, "which you yourselves, in the Peace decree, have voted senseless as well as horrible, he greeted the Revolution with hope of peace and freedom. Peace? The Government of Kerensky forced him again to go forward into Galicia to slaughter and be slaughtered; to his pleas for peace, Terestchenko simply laughed.... Freedom? Under Kerensky he found his Committees suppressed, his newspapers cut off, his party speakers put in prison.... At home in his village, the landlords were defying his Land Committees, jailing his comrades.... In Petrograd the bourgeoisie, in alliance with the Germans, were sabotaging the food and ammunition for the Army.... He was without boots, or clothes.... Who forced him to desert? The Government of Kerensky, which you have overthrown!" At the end there was applause.

But another soldier hotly denounced it: "The Government of Kerensky is not a screen behind which can be hidden dirty work like desertion! Deserters are scoundrels, who run away home and leave their comrades to die in the trenches alone! Every deserter is a traitor, and should be punished...." Uproar, shouts of *"Do volno! Teesche!"* Kameniev hastily proposed to leave the matter to the Government for decision.

At 2.30 A. M. fell a tense hush. Kameniev was reading the decree of the Constitution of Power:

93

Until the meeting of the Constituent Assembly, a provisional Workers' and Peasants' Government is formed, which shall be named the Council of People's Commissars.

The administration of the different branches of state activity shall be intrusted to commissions, whose composition shall be regulated to ensure the carrying out of the programme of the Congress, in close union with the mass-organisations of working-men, working-women, sailors, soldiers, peasants and clerical employees. The governmental power is vested in a *collegium* made up of the chairmen of these commissions, that is to say, the Council of People's Commissars.

Control over the activities of the People's Commissars, and the right to replace them, shall belong to the All-Russian Congress of Soviets of Workers', Peasants' and Soldiers' Deputies, and its Central Executive Committee.

Still silence; as he read the list of Commissars, bursts of applause after each name, Lenin's and Trotzky's especially.

President of the Council: Vladimir Ulianov *(Lenin)*

Interior: A. E. Rykov

Agriculture: V. P. Miliutin

Labour: A. G. Shliapnikov

Military and Naval Affairs-a committee composed of V. A.

Avseenko (Antonov), N. V. Krylenko, and F. M. Dybenko.

Commerce and Industry: V. P. Nogin

Popular Education: A. V. Lunatcharsky

Finance: E. E. Skvortsov *(Stepanov)*

Foreign Affairs: L. D. Bronstein *(Trotzky)*

Justice: G. E. Oppokov *(Lomov)*

Supplies: E. A. Teodorovitch

Post and Telegraph: N. P. Avilov *(Gliebov)*

Chairman for Nationalities: I. V. Djougashvili *(Stalin)*

Railroads: To be filled later.

There were bayonets at the edges of the room, bayonets pricking up among the delegates; the Military Revolutionary Committee was arming everybody, Bolshevism was arming for the decisive battle with Kerensky, the sound of whose trumpets came up the south-west wind.... In the meanwhile nobody went home; on the contrary hundreds of newcomers filtered in, filling the great room solid with stern-faced soldiers and workmen who stood for hours and hours, indefatigably intent. The air was thick with cigarette smoke, and human breathing, and the smell of coarse clothes and sweat.

Avilov of the staff of *Novaya Zhizn* was speaking in the name of the Social Democrat Internationalists and the remnant of the Mensheviki Internationalists; Avilov, with his young, intelligent face, looking out of place in his smart frock-coat.

"We must ask ourselves where we are going.... The ease with which the Coalition Government was upset cannot be explained by the strength of the left wing of the democracy, but only by the incapacity of the Government to give the people peace and bread. And the left wing cannot maintain itself in power unless it can solve these questions....

"Can it give bread to the people? Grain is scarce. The majority of the peasants will not be with you, for you cannot give them the machinery they need. Fuel and other primary necessities are almost impossible to procure....

"As for peace, that will be even more difficult. The allies refused to talk with Skobeliev. They will never accept the proposition of a peace conference from *you.* You will not be recognised either in London and Paris, or in Berlin....

"You cannot count on the effective help of the proletariat of the Allied countries, because in most countries it is very far from the revolutionary struggle; remember, the Allied democracy was unable even to convoke the Stockholm Conference. Concerning the German Social Democrats, I have just talked with Comrade Goldenberg, one of our delegates to Stockholm; he was told by the representatives of the Extreme Left that revolution in Germany was impossible during the war...." Here interruptions began to come thick and fast, but Avilov kept on.

"The isolation of Russia will fatally result either in the defeat of the Russian Army by the Germans, and the patching up of a peace between the Austro-German coalition and the Franco-British coalition *at the expense of Russia*-or in a separate peace with Germany.

"I have just learned that the Allied ambassadors are preparing to leave, and that Committees for Salvation of Country and Revolution are forming in all the cities of Russia....

"No one party can conquer these enormous difficulties. The majority of the people, supporting a government of Socialist coalition, can alone accomplish the Revolution....

"He then read the resolution of the two factions:

Recognising that for the salvation of the conquests of the Revolution it is indispensable immediately to constitute a government based on the revolutionary democracy organised in the Soviets of Workers,' Soldiers' and Peasants' Deputies, recognising moreover that the task of this government is the quickest possible attainment of peace, the transfer of the land into the hands of the agrarian committees, the organisation of control over industrial production, and the convocation of the Constituent Assembly on the date decided, the Congress appoints an executive committee to constitute such a government after an agreement with the groups of the democracy which are taking part in the Congress.

In spite of the revolutionary exaltation of the triumphant crowd, Avilov's cool tolerant reasoning had shaken them. Toward the end, the cries and hisses died away, and when he finished there was even some clapping.

Karelin followed him-also young, fearless, whose sincerity no one doubted-for the Left Socialist Revolutionaries, the party of Maria Spiridonova, the party which almost alone followed the Bolsheviki, and which represented the revolutionary peasants.

"Our party has refused to enter the Council of People's Commissars because we do not wish forever to separate ourselves from the part of the revolutionary army which left the Congress, a separation which would make it impossible for us to serve as intermediaries between the Bolsheviki and the other groups of the democracy.... And that is our principal duty at this moment. We cannot sustain any government except a government of Socialist coalition....

"We protest, moreover, against the tyrannical conduct of the Bolsheviki. Our Commissars have been driven from their posts. Our only organ, *Znamia Truda* (Banner of Labour), was forbidden to appear yesterday....

"The Central Duma is forming a powerful Committee for Salvation of Country and Revolution, to fight you. Already you are isolated, and your Government is without the support of a single other democratic group....

And now Trotzky stood upon the raised tribune, confident and dominating, with that sarcastic expression about his mouth which was almost a sneer. He spoke, in a ringing voice, and the great crowd rose to him.

"These considerations on the dangers of isolation of our party are not new. On the eve of insurrection our fatal defeat was also predicted. Everybody was against us; only a faction of the Socialist Revolutionaries of the left was with us in the Military Revolutionary Committee. How is it that we were able to overturn the Government almost without bloodshed?.... That fact is the most striking proof that we *were not isolated.* In reality the Provisional Government was isolated; the democratic parties which march against us were isolated, are isolated, and forever cut off from the proletariat!

"They speak of the necessity for a coalition. There is only one coalition possible-the coalition of the workers, soldiers and poorest peasants; and it is our party's honour to have realised that coalition.... What sort of coalition did Avilov mean? A coalition with those who supported the Government of Treason to the People? Coalition doesn't always add to strength. For example, could we have organised the insurrection with Dan and Avksentiev in our ranks?" Roars of laughter.

"Avksentiev gave little bread. Will a coalition with the *oborontsi* furnish more? Between the peasants and Avksentiev, who ordered the arrest of the Land Committees, we choose the peasants! Our Revolution will remain the classic revolution of history....

"They accuse us of repelling an agreement with the other democratic parties. But is it we who are to blame? Or must we, as Karelin put it, blame it on a 'misunderstanding'? No, comrades. When a party in full tide of revolution, still wreathed in powder-smoke, comes to say, 'Here is the Power-take it!'-and when those to whom it is offered go over to the enemy, that is not a misunderstanding.... that is a declaration of pitiless war. And it isn't we who have declared war....

"Avilov menaces us with failure of our peace efforts-if we remain 'isolated.' I repeat, I don't see how a coalition with Skobeliev, or even Terestchenko, can help us to get peace! Avilov tries to frighten us by the threat of a peace at our expense. And I answer that in any case, if Europe continues to be ruled by the imperialist bourgeoisie, revolutionary Russia will inevitably be lost....

"There are only two alternatives; either the Russian Revolution will create a revolutionary movement in Europe, or the European powers will destroy the Russian Revolution!"

They greeted him with an immense crusading acclaim, kindling to the daring of it, with the thought of championing mankind. And from that moment there was something conscious and decided about the insurrectionary masses, in all their actions, which never left them.

But on the other side, too, battle was taking form. Kameniev recognised a delegate from the Union of Railway Workers, a hardfaced, stocky man with an attitude of implacable hostility. He threw a bombshell.

"In the name of the strongest organisation in Russia I demand the right to speak, and I say to you: the _Vikzhel_charges me to make known the decision of the Union concerning the constitution of Power. The Central Committee refuses absolutely to support the Bolsheviki if they persist in isolating themselves from the whole democracy of Russia!" Immense tumult all over the hall.

"In 1905, and in the Kornilov days, the Railway Workers were the best defenders of the Revolution. But you did not invite us to your Congress-" Cries, "It was the old *Tsay-ee-kah* which did not invite you!" The orator paid no attention. "We do not recognise the legality of this Congress; since the departure of the Mensheviki and Socialist Revolutionaries there is not a legal quorum.... The Union supports the old *Tsay-ee-Kah,* and declares that the Congress has no right to elect a new Committee....

"The Power should be a Socialist and revolutionary Power, responsible before the authorised organs of the entire revolutionary democracy. Until the constitution of such a power, the Union of Railway Workers, which refuses to transport counter-revolutionary troops to Petrograd, at the same time forbids the execution of any order whatever without the consent of the *Vikzhel.* The *Vikzhel* also takes into its hands the entire administration of the railroads of Russia."

At the end he could hardly be heard for the furious storm of abuse which beat upon him. But it was a heavy blow-that could be seen in the concern on the faces of the presidium. Kameniev, however, merely answered that there could be no doubt of the legality of the Congress, as even the quorum established by the old *Tsay-ee-Kah* was exceeded-in spite of the secession of the Mensheviki and Socialist Revolution arises....

Then came the vote on the Constitution of Power, which carried the Council of People's Commissars into office by an enormous majority....

The election of the new *Tsay-ee-kah,* the new parliament of the Russian Republic, took barely fifteen minutes. Trotzky announced its composition: 100 members, of which 70 Bolsheviki.... As for the peasants, and the seceding factions, places were to be reserved for them. "We welcome into the Government all parties and groups which will adopt our programme," ended Trotzky.

And thereupon the Second All-Russian Congress of Soviets was dissolved, so that the members might hurry to their homes in the four corners of Russia and tell of the great happenings....

It was almost seven when we woke the sleeping conductors and motor-men of the street-cars which the Street-Railway Workers' Union always kept waiting at Smolny to take the Soviet delegates to their homes. In the crowded car there was less happy hilarity than the night before, I thought. Many looked anxious; perhaps they were saying to themselves, "Now we are masters, how can we do our will?"

At our apartment-house we were held up in the dark by an armed patrol of citizens and carefully examined. The Duma's proclamation was doing its work....

The landlady heard us come in, and stumbled out in a pink silk wrapper.

The House Committee has again asked that you take your turn on guard-duty with the rest of the men," she said.

"What's the reason for this guard-duty?"

"To protect the house and the women and children."

"Who from?"

"Robbers and murderers."

"But suppose there came a Commissar from the Military Revolutionary Committee to search for arms?"

"Oh, that's what they'll *say* they are.... And besides, what's the difference?"

I solemnly affirmed that the Consul had forbidden all American citizens to carry arms-especially in the neighbourhood of the Russian *intelligentzia*....

CHAPTER VI

The Committee for Salvation

FRIDAY, November 9th....

Novotcherkask, November 8th.

In view of the revolt of the Bolsheviki, and their attempt to depose the Provisional Government and to seize the power in Petrograd... the Cossack Government declares that it considers these acts criminal and absolutely inadmissible. In consequence, the Cossacks will lend all their support to the Provisional Government, which is a government of coalition. Because of these circumstances, and until the return of the Provisional Government to power, and the restoration of order in Russia, I take upon myself, beginning November 7th, all the power in that which concerns the region of the Don.

Signed: ATAMAN KALEDIN

President of the Government of the Cossack Troops.

Prikaz of the Minister-President Kerensky, dated at Gatchina:

I, Minister-President of the Provisional Government, and Supreme Commander of all the armed forces of the Russian Republic, declare that I am at the head of regiments from the Front who have remained faithful to the fatherland.

I order all the troops of the Military District of Petrograd, who through mistake or folly have answered the appeal of the traitors to the country and the Revolution, to return to their duty without delay.

This order shall be read in all regiments, battalions and squadrons.

Signed: *Minister-President of the Provisional*

Government and Supreme Commander

A. F. KERENSKY.

Telegram from Kerensky to the General in Command of the Northern Front:

The town of Gatchina has been taken by the loyal regiments without bloodshed. Detachments of Cronstadt sailors, and of the Semionovsky and Ismailovsky regiments, gave up their arms without resistance and joined the Government troops.

I order all the designated units to advance as quickly as possible. The Military Revolutionary Committee has ordered its troops to retreat....

Gatchina, about thirty kilometers south-west, had fallen during the night. Detachments of the two regiments mentioned-not the sailors-while wandering captainless in the neighbourhood, had indeed been surrounded by Cossacks and given up their arms; but it was not true that they had joined the Government troops. At this very moment crowds of them, bewildered and ashamed, were up at Smolny trying to explain. They did not think the Cossacks were so near.... They had tried to argue with the Cossacks....

Apparently the greatest confusion prevailed along the revolutionary front. The garrisons of all the little towns southward had split hopelessly, bitterly into two factions-or three: the high command being on the side of Kerensky, in default of anything stronger, the majority of the rank and file with the Soviets, and the rest unhappily wavering.

Hastily the Military Revolutionary Committee appointed to command the defence of Petrograd an ambitious regular Army Captain, Muraviov, the same Muraviov who had organised the Death Battalions during the summer, and had once been heard to advise the Government that "it was too lenient with the Bolsheviki; they must be wiped out." A man of military mind, who admired power and audacity, perhaps sincerely....

Beside my door when I came down in the morning were posted two new orders of the Military Revolutionary Committee, directing that all shops and stores should open as usual, and that all empty rooms and apartments should be put at the disposal of the Committee....

For thirty-six hours now the Bolsheviki had been cut off from provincial Russia and the outside world. The railway men and telegraphers refused to transmit their despatches, the postmen would not handle their mail. Only the Government wireless at Tsarskoye Selo launched half-hourly bulletins and manifestoes to the four corners of heaven; the Commissars of Smolny raced the Commissars of the City Duma on speeding trains half across the earth; and two aeroplanes, laden with propaganda, fled high up toward the Front....

But the eddies of insurrection were spreading through Russia with a swiftness surpassing any human agency. Helsingfors Soviet passed resolutions of support; Kiev Bolsheviki captured the arsenal and the telegraph station, only to be driven out by delegates to the Congress of Cossacks, which happened to be meeting there; in Kazan, a Military Revolutionary Committee arrested the local garrison staff and the Commissar of the Provisional Government; from far Krasnoyarsk, in Siberia, came news that the Soviets were in control of the Municipal institutions; at Moscow, where the situation was aggravated by a great strike of leather-workers on one side, and a threat of general lock-out on the other, the Soviets had voted overwhelmingly to support the action of the Bolsheviki in Petrograd.... Already a Military Revolutionary Committee was functioning.

Everywhere the same thing happened. The common soldiers and the industrial workers supported the Soviets by a vast majority; the officers, *yunkers* and middle class generally were on the side of the Government-as were the bourgeois Cadets and the "moderate" Socialist parties. In all these towns sprang up Committees for Salvation of Country and Revolution, arming for civil war....

Vast Russia was in a state of solution. As long ago as 1905 the process had begun; the March Revolution had merely hastened it, and giving birth to a sort of forecast of the new order, had ended by merely perpetuating the hollow structure of the old regime. Now, however, the Bolsheviki, in one night, had dissipated it, as one blows away smoke. Old Russia was no more; human society flowed molten in primal heat, and from the tossing sea of flame was emerging the class struggle, stark and pitiless-and the fragile, slowly-cooling crust of new planets....

In Petrograd sixteen Ministries were on strike, led by the Ministries of Labour and of Supplies-the only two created by the all-Socialist Government of August.

If ever men stood alone the "handful of Bolsheviki" apparently stood alone that grey chill morning, with all storms towering over them. Back against the wall, the Military Revolutionary Committee struck-for its life. *"De l'audace, encore de l'audace, et toujours de l'audace....* At five in the morning the Red Guards entered the printing office of the City Government, confiscated thousands of copies of the Appeal-Protest of the Duma, and suppressed the official Municipal organ-the *Viestnik Gorodskovo Samoupravleniya* (Bulletin of the Municipal Self-Government). All the bourgeois newspapers were torn from the presses, even the *Golos Soldata,* journal of the old *Tsay-ee-kah*-which, however, changing its name to *Soldatski Golos,* appeared in an edition of a hundred thousand copies, bellowing rage and defiance:

The men who began their stroke of treachery in the night, who have suppressed the newspapers, will not keep the country in ignorance long. The country will know the truth! It will appreciate you, Messrs. the Bolsheviki! We shall see!...

As we came down the Nevsky a little after midday the whole street before the Duma building was crowded with people. Here and there stood Red Guards and sailors, with bayonetted rifles, each one surrounded by about a hundred men and women-clerks, students, shopkeepers, *tchinovniki*-shaking their fists and bawling insults and menaces. On the steps stood boy-scouts and officers, distributing copies of the *Soldatski Golos.* A workman with a red band around his arm and a revolver in his hand stood trembling with rage and nervousness in the middle of a hostile throng at the foot of the stairs, demanding the surrender of the papers.... Nothing like this, I imagine, ever occurred in history. On one side a handful of workmen and common soldiers, with arms in their hands, representing a victorious insurrection-and perfectly miserable; on the other a frantic mob made up of the kind of people that crowd the sidewalks of Fifth Avenue at noon-time, sneering, abusing, shouting, "Traitors! Provocators! *Opritchniki!* [*]" [* Savage body-guards if Ian the Terrible, 17th century]

The doors were guarded by students and officers with white arm-bands lettered in red, "Militia of the Committee of Public Safety," and half a dozen boy-scouts came and went. Upstairs the place was all commotion. Captain Gomberg was coming down the stairs. "They're going to dissolve the Duma," he said. "The Bolshevik Commissar is with the Mayor now." As we reached the top Riazanov came hurrying out. He had been to demand that the Duma recognise the Council of peoples' Commissars, and the Mayor had given him a flat refusal.

In the offices a great babbling crowd, hurrying, shouting, gesticulating-Government officials, intellectuals, journalists, foreign correspondents, French and British officers.... "The City Engineer pointed to them triumphantly. "The Embassies recognise the Duma as the only power now," he explained. "For these Bolshevik murderers and robbers it is only a question of hours. All Russia is rallying to us....

In the Alexander Hall a monster meeting of the Committee for Salvation. Fillipovsky in the chair and Skobeliev again in the tribune, reporting, to immense applause, new adhesions to the Committee; Executive Committee of Peasants' Soviets, old *Tsay-ee-kah*, Central Army Committee, *Tsentroflot*, Menshevik, Socialist Revolutionary and Front group delegates from the Congress of Soviets, Central Committees of the Menshevik, Socialist Revolutionary, Populist Socialist parties. "Yedinstvo" group, Peasants' Union, Cooperatives, Zemstvos, Municipalities, Post and Telegraph Unions, *Vikzhel*, Council of the Russian Republic, Union of Unions, [*] Merchants' and Manufacturers' Association.... [* See Notes and Explanations.]

".... The power of the Soviets is not democratic power, but a dictatorship-and not the dictatorship of the proletariat, but *against* the proletariat. All those who have felt or know how to feel revolutionary enthusiasm must join now for the defence of the Revolution....

"The problem of the day is not only to render harmless irresponsible demagogues, but to fight against the counter-revolution.... If rumours are true that certain generals in the provinces are attempting to profit by events in order to march on Petrograd with other designs, it is only one more proof that we must establish a solid base of democratic government. Otherwise, troubles with the Right will follow troubles from the Left....

"The garrison of Petrograd cannot remain indifferent when citizens buying the *Golos Soldata* and newsboys selling the *Rabotchaya Gazeta* are arrested in the streets....

"The hour of resolutions has passed.... Let those who have no longer faith in the Revolution retire.... To establish a united power, we must again restore the prestige of the Revolution....

"Let us swear that either the Revolution shall be saved-or we shall perish!"

The hall rose, cheering, with kindling eyes. There was not a single proletarian anywhere in sight....

Then Weinstein:

"We must remain calm, and not act until public opinion is firmly grouped in support of the Committee for Salvation-then we can pass from the defensive to action!"

The *Vikzhel* representative announced that his organisation was taking the initiative in forming the new Government, and its delegates were now discussing the matter with Smolny.... Followed a hot discussion: were the Bolsheviki to be admitted to the new Government? Martov pleaded for their admission; after all, he said, they represented an important political party. Opinions were very much divided upon this, the right wing Mensheviki and Socialist Revolutionaries, as well as the Populist Socialists, the Cooperatives and the bourgeois elements being bitterly against....

"They have betrayed Russia," one speaker said. "They have started civil war and opened the front to the Germans. The Bolsheviki must be mercilessly crushed...."

Skobeliev was in favor of excluding both the Bolsheviki and the
Cadets.

We got into conversation with a young Socialist Revolutionary, who
had walked out of the Democratic Conference to gether with the
Bolsheviki, that night when Tseretelli and the "compromisers" forced
Coalition upon the democracy of Russia.

"You here?" I asked him.

His eyes flashed fire. "Yes!" he cried. "I left the Congress with my party Wednesday night. I have not risked my life for twenty years and more to submit now to the tyranny of the Dark People. Their methods are intolerable. But they have not counted on the peasants.... When the peasants begin to act, then it is a question of minutes before they are done for."

"But the peasants-will they act? Doesn't the Land decree settle the peasants? What more do they want?"

"Ah, the Land decree!" he said furiously. "Yes, do you know what that Land decree is? It is *our* decree-it is the Socialist Revolutionary programme, intact! My party framed that policy, after the most careful compilation of the wishes of the peasants themselves. It is an outrage...."

"But if it is your own policy, why do you object? If it is the peasants' wishes, why will they oppose it?"

"You don't understand! Don't you see that the peasants will immediately realise that it is all a trick-that these usurpers have stolen the Socialist Revolutionary programme?"

I asked if it were true that Kaledin was marching north.

He nodded, and rubbed his hands with a sort of bitter satisfaction.
"Yes. Now you see what these Bolsheviki have done. They have raised
the counter-revolution against us. The Revolution is lost. The
Revolution is lost."

"But won't you defend the Revolution?"

"Of course we will defend it-to the last drop of our blood. But we won't cooperate with the Bolsheviki in any way...."

"But if Kaledin comes to Petrograd, and the Bolsheviki defend the city. Won't you join with them?"

"Of course not. We will defend the city also, but we won't support the Bolsheviki. Kaledin is the enemy of the Revolution, but the Bolsheviki are equally enemies of the Revolution."

"Which do you prefer-Kaledin or the Bolsheviki?"

"It is not a question to be discussed!" he burst out impatiently. "I tell you, the Revolution is lost. And it is the Bolsheviki who are to blame. But listen-why should we talk of such things? Kerensky is comming.... Day after tomorrow we shall pass to the offensive.... Already Smolny has sent delegates inviting us to form a new Government. But we have them now-they are absolutely impotent.... We shall not cooperate...."

Outside there was a shot. We ran to the windows. A Red Guard, finally exasperated by the taunts of the crowd, had shot into it, wounding a young girl in the arm. We could see her being lifted into a cab, surrounded by an excited throng, the clamour of whose voices floated up to us. As we looked, suddenly an armoured automobile appeared around the corner of the Mikhailovsky, its guns sluing this way and that. Immediately the crowd began to run, as

Petrograd crowds do, falling down and lying still in the street, piled in the gutters, heaped up behind telephone-poles. The car lumbered up to the steps of the Duma and a man stuck his head out of the turret, demanding the surrender of the *Soldatski Golos.* The boy-scouts jeered and scuttled into the building. After a moment the automobile wheeled undecidedly around and went off up the Nevsky, while some hundreds of men and women picked themselves up and began to dust their clothes....

Inside was a prodigious running-about of people with armfuls of *Soldatski Golos,* looking for places to hide them....

A journalist came running into the room, waving a paper.

"Here's a proclamation from Krasnov!" he cried. Everybody crowded around. "Get it printed-get it printed quick, and around to the barracks!"

By the order of the Supreme Commander I am appointed commandant of the troops concentrated under Petrograd.

Citizens, soldiers, valorous Cossacks of the Don, of the Kuban, of the Transbaikal, of the Amur, of the Yenissei, to all you who have remained faithful to your oath I appeal; to you who have sworn to guard inviolable your oath of Cossack-I call upon you to save Petrograd from anarchy, from famine, from tyranny, and to save Russia from the indelible shame to which a handful of ignorant men, bought by the gold of Wilhelm, are trying to submit her.

The Provisional Government, to which you swore fidelity in the great days of March, is not overthrown, but by violence expelled from the edifice in which it held its meetings. However the Government, with the help of the Front armies, faithful to their duty, with the help of the Council of Cossacks, which has united under its command all the Cossacks and which, strong with the morale which reigns in its ranks, and acting in accordance with the will of the Russian people, has sworn to serve the country as its ancestors served it in the Troublous Times of 1612, when the Cossacks of the Don delivered Moscow, menaced by the Swedes, the Poles, and the Lithuanians. Your Government still exists....

The active army considers these criminals with horror and contempt. Their acts of vandalism and pillage, their crimes, the German mentality with which they regard Russia-stricken down but not yet surrendered-have alienated from them the entire people.

Citizens, soldiers, valorous Cossacks of the garrison of Petrograd; send me your delegates so that I may know who are traitors to their country and who are not, that there may be avoided an effusion of innocent blood.

Almost the same moment word ran from group to group that the building was surrounded by Red Guards. An officer strode in, a red band around his arm, demanding the Mayor. A few minutes later he left and old Schreider came out of his office, red and pale by turns.

"A special meeting of the Duma!" he cried. "Immediately!"

In the big hall proceedings were halted. "All members of the Duma for a special meeting!"

"What's the matter?"

"I don't know-going to arrest us-going to dissolve the Duma-arresting members at the door-" so ran the excited comments.

In the Nicolai Hall there was barely room to stand. The Mayor announced that troops were stationed at all the doors, prohibiting all exit and entrance, and that a Commissar had threatened arrest and the dispersal of the Municipal Duma. A flood of impassioned speeches from members, and even from the galleries, responded. The freely-elected City Government could not be dissolved by *any* power; the Mayor's person and that of all the members were inviolable; the tyrants, the provocators, the German agents should never be recognised; as for these threats to dissolve us, let them try-only over our dead bodies shall they seize this chamber, where like the Roman senators of old we await with dignity the coming of the Goths....

Resolution, to inform the Dumas and Zemstvos of all Russia by telegraph. Resolution, that it was impossible for the Mayor or the Chairman of the Duma to enter into any relations whatever with representatives of the Military Revolutionary Committee or with the so-called Council of People's Commissars. Resolution, to address another appeal to the population of Petrograd to stand up for the defence of their elected town government. Resolution, to remain in permanent session....

In the meanwhile one member arrived with the information that he had telephoned to Smolny, and that the Military Revolutionary Committee said that no orders had been given to surround the Duma, that the troops would be withdrawn....

As we went downstairs Riazanov burst in through the front door, very agitated.

"Are you going to dissolve the Duma?" I asked.

"My God, no!" he answered. "It is all a mistake. I told the Mayor this morning that the Duma would be left alone....

Out on the Nevsky, in the deepening dusk, a long double file of cyclists came riding, guns slung on their shoulders. They halted, and the crowd pressed in and deluged them with questions.

"Who are you? Where do you come from?" asked a fat old man with a cigar in his mouth.

"Twelfth Army. From the front. We came to support the Soviets against the damn' bourgeoisie!"

"Ah!" were furious cries. "Bolshevik gendarmes! Bolshevik Cossacks!"

A little officer in a leather coat came running down the steps. "The garrison is turning!" he muttered in my ear. "It's the beginning of the end of the Bolsheviki. Do you want to see the turn of the tide? Come on!" He started at a half-trot up the Mikhailovsky, and we followed.

"What regiment is it?"

"The *brunnoviki*...." Here was indeed serious trouble. The *brunnoviki* were the Armoured Car troops, the key to the situation; whoever controlled the *brunnoviki* controlled the city. "The Commissars of the Committee for Salvation and the Duma have been talking to them. There's a meeting on to decide....

"Decide what? Which side they'll fight on?"

"Oh, no. That's not the way to do it. They'll never fight against the Bolsheviki. They will vote to remain neutral-and then the *yunkers* and Cossacks-"

The door of the great Mikhailovsky Riding-School yawned blackly. Two sentinels tried to stop us, but we brushed by hurriedly, deaf to their indignant expostulations. Inside only a single arc-light burned dimly, high up near the roof of the enormous hall, whose lofty pilasters and rows of windows vanished in the gloom. Around dimly squatted the monstrous shapes of the armoured cars. One stood alone in the centre of the place, under the light, and round it were gathered some two thousand dun-colored soldiers, almost lost in the immensity of that imperial building. A dozen men, officers, chairmen of the Soldiers' Committees and speakers, were perched on top of the car, and from the central turret a soldier was speaking. This was Khanjunov, who had been president of last summer's all-Russian Congress of *Brunnoviki*. A lithe, handsome figure in his leather coat with lieutenant's shoulder-straps, he stood pleading eloquently for neutrality.

"It is an awful thing," he said, "for Russians to kill their Russian brothers. There must not be civil war between soldiers who stood shoulder to shoulder against the Tsar, and conquered the foreign enemy in battles which will go down in history! What have we, soldiers, got to do with these squabbles of political parties? I will not say to you that the Provisional Government was a democratic Government; we want no coalition with the bourgeoisie-no. But we must have a Government of the united democracy, or Russia is lost! With such a Government there will be no need for civil war, and the killing of brother by brother!"

This sounded reasonable-the great hall echoed to the crash of hands and voices.

A soldier climbed up, his face white and strained, "Comrades!" he cried, "I came from the Rumanian front, to urgently tell you all: there must be peace! Peace at once! Whoever can give us peace, whether it be the Bolsheviki or this new Government, we will follow. Peace! We at the front cannot fight any longer. We cannot fight either Germans or Russians-" With that he leaped down, and a sort of confused agonised sound rose up from all that surging mass, which burst into something like anger when the next speaker, a Menshevik *oboronetz,* tried to say that the war must go on until the Allies were victorious.

"You talk like Kerensky!" shouted a rough voice.

A Duma delegate, pleading for neutrality. Him they listened to, muttering uneasily, feeling him not one of them. Never have I seen men trying so hard to understand, to decide. They never moved, stood staring with a sort of terrible intentness at the speaker, their brows wrinkled with the effort of thought, sweat standing out on their foreheads; great giants of men with the innocent clear eyes of children and the faces of epic warriors....

Now a Bolshevik was speaking, one of their own men, violently, full of hate. They liked him no more than the other. It was not their mood. For the moment they were lifted out of the ordinary run of common thoughts, thinking in terms of Russia, of Socialism, the world, as if it depended on them whether the Revolution were to live or die....

Speaker succeeded speaker, debating amid tense silence, roars of approval, or anger: should we come out or not? Khanjunov returned, persuasive and sympathetic. But wasn't he an officer, and an *oboronotz,* however much he talked of peace? Then a workman from Vasili Ostrov, but him they greeted with, "And are *you* going to give us peace, working-man?" Near us some men, many of them officers, formed a sort of *claque* to cheer the advocates of Neutrality. They kept shouting, "Khanjunov! Khanjunov!" and whistled insultingly when the Bolsheviki tried to speak.

Suddenly the committeemen and officers on top of the automobile began to discuss something with great heat and much gesticulation. The audience shouted to know what was the matter, and all the great mass tossed and stirred. A soldier, held back by one of the officers, wrenched himself loose and held up his hand.

109

"Comrades!" he cried, "Comrade Krylenko is here and wants to speak to us." An outburst of cheers, whistlings, yells of *"Prosim! Prosim! Dolby!* Go ahead! Go ahead! Down with him!" in the midst of which the People's Commissar for Military Affairs clambered up the side of the car, helped by hands before and behind, pushed and pulled from below and above. Rising he stood for a moment, and then walked out on the radiator, put his hands on his hips and looked around smiling, a squat, short-legged figure, bare-headed, with-out insignia on his uniform.

The *claque* near me kept up a fearful shouting, "Khanjunov! We want Khanjunov! Down with him! Shut up! Down with the traitor!" The whole place seethed and roared. Then it began to move, like an avalanche bearing down upon us, great black-browed men forcing their way through.

"Who is breaking up our meeting?" they shouted. "Who is whistling here?" The *claque,* rudely burst asunder, went flying-nor did it gather again....

"Comrade soliders!" began Krylenko, in a voice husky with fatigue. "I cannot speak well to you; I am sorry; but I have not had any sleep for four nights....

"I don't need to tell you that I am a soldier. I don't need to tell you that I want peace. What I must say is that the Bolshevik party, successful in the Workers' and Soldiers' Revolution, by the help of you and of all the rest of the brave comrades who have of you and of all the rest of the brave comrades who have hurled down forever the power of the blood-thirsty bourgeoisie, promised to offer peace to all the peoples, and that has already been done-to-day!" Tumultuous applause.

"You are asked to remain neutral—to remain neutral while the *yunkers* and the Death Battalions, who are *never* neutral, shoot us down in the streets and bring back to Petrograd Kerensky-or perhaps some other of the gang. Kaledin is marching from the Don. Kerensky is coming from the front. Kornilov is raising the *Tekhintsi* to repeat his attempt of August. All these Mensheviki and Socialist Revolutionaries who call upon you now to prevent civil war-how have they retained the power except by civil war, that civil war which has endured ever since last July, and in which they constantly stood on the side of the bourgeoisie, as they do now?

"How can I persuade you, if you have made up your minds? The question is very plain. On one side are Kerensky, Kaledin, Kornilov, the Mensheviki, Socialist Revolutionaries, Cadets, Dumas, officers.... They tell us that their objects are good. On the other side are the workers, the soldiers and sailors, the poorest peasants. The Government is in your hands. You are the masters. Great Russia belongs to you. Will you give it back?"

While he spoke, he kept himself up by sheer evident effort of will, and as he went on the deep sincere feeling back of his words broke through the tired voice. At the end he totered,

110

almost falling; a hundred hands reached up to help him down, and the great dim spaces of the hall gave back the surf of sound that beat upon him.

Khanjunov tried to speak again, but "Vote! Vote! Vote!" they cried. At length, giving in, he read the resolution: that the *brunnoviki* withdraw their representative from the Military Revolutionary Committee, and declare their neutrality in the present civil war. All those in favour should go to the right; those opposed, to the left. There was a moment of hesitation, a still expectancy, and then the crowd began to surge faster and faster, stumbling over one another, to the left, hundreds of big soldiers in a solid mass rushing across the dirt floor in the faint light…. Near us about fifty men were left stranded, stubbornly in favour, and even as the high roof shook under the shock of victorious roaring, they turned and rapidly walked out of the building-and, some of them, out of the Revolution….

Imagine this struggle being repeated in every barracks of the city, the district, the whole front, all Russia. Imagine the sleepless Krylenkos, watching the regiments, hurrying from place to place, arguing, threatening, entreating. And then imaging the same in all the locals of every labour union, in the factories, the villages, on the battle-ships of the far-flung Russian fleets; think of the hundreds of thousands of Russian men staring up at speakers all over the vast country, workmen, peasants, soldiers, sailors, trying so hard to understand and to choose, thinking so intensely-and deciding so unanimously at the end. So was the Russian Revolution….

Up at Smolny the new Council of People's Commissars was not idle. Already the first decree was on the presses, to be circulated in thousands through the city streets that night, and shipped in bales by every train southward and east:

In the name of the Government of the Russian Republic, chosen by the All-Russian Congress of Soviets of Workers' and Soldiers' Deputies with participation of peasant deputies, the Council of People's Commissars decrees:

1. The elections for the Constituent Assembly shall take place at the date determined upon-November 12.

2. All electoral commissions, organs of local self-government, Soviets of Workers', Soldiers' and Peasants' Deputies, and soldiers' organisations on the front should make every effort to assure free and regular elections at the date determined upon.

In the name of the Government of the Russian Republic, *The President of the Council of People's Commissars,*

VLADIMIR ULIANOV-LENIN.

In the Municipal building the Duma was in full blast. A member of the Council of the Republic was talking as we came in. The Council, he said, did not consider itself dissolved at all, but merely unable to continue its labours until it secured a new meeting-place. In the meanwhile, its Committee of Elders had determined to enter *en masse* the Committee for Salvation.... This, I may remark parenthetically, is the last time history mentions the Council of the Russian Republic....

Then followed the customary string of delegates from the Ministries, the *Vikzhel,* the Union of Posts and Telegraphs, for the hundredth time reiterating their determination not to work for the Bolshevik usurpers. A *yunker* who had been in the Winter Palace told a highly-coloured tale of the heroism of himself and his comrades, and disgraceful conduct of the Red Guards-all of which was devoutly believed. Somebody read aloud an account in the Socialist Revolutionary paper *Narod,* which stated that five hundred million rubles' worth of damage had been done in the Winter Palace, and describing in great detail the loot and breakage.

From time to time couriers came from the telephone with news. The four Socialist Ministers had been released from prison. Krylenko had gone to Peter-Paul to tell Admiral Verderevsky that the Ministry of Marine was deserted, and to beg him, for the sake of Russia, to take charge under the authority of the Council of People's Commissars; and the old seaman had consented.... Kerensky was advancing north from Gatchina, the Bolshevik garrisons falling back before him. Smolny had issued another decree, enlarging the powers of the City Dumas to deal with food supplies.

This last piece of insolence caused an outburst of fury. He, Lenin, the usurper, the tyrant, whose Commissars had seized the Municipal garage, entered the Municipal ware houses, were interfering with the Supply Committees and the distribution of food-he presumed to define the limits of power of the free, independent, autonomous City Government! One member, shaking his fist, moved to cut off the food of the city if the Bolsheviki dared to interfere with the Supply Committees.... Another, representative of the Special Supply Committee, reported that the food situation was very grave, and asked that emissaries be sent out to hasten food trains.

Diedonenko announced dramatically that the garrison was wavering. The Semionovsky regiment had already decided to submit to the orders of the Socialist Revolutionary party; the crews of the torpedo-boats on the Neva were shaky. Seven members were at once appointed to continue the propaganda....

Then the old Mayor stepped into the tribune: "Comrades and citizens! I have just learned that the prisoners in Peter Paul are in danger. Fourteen *yunkers* of the Pavlovsk school have been stripped and tortured by the Bolshevik guards. One has gone mad. They are threatening to lynch the Ministers!" There was a whirlwind of indignation and horror, which only grew more violent when a stocky little woman dressed in grey demanded the

112

floor, and lifted up her hard, metallic voice. This was Vera Slutskaya, veteran revolutionist and Bolshevik member of the Duma.

"That is a lie and a provocation!" she said, unmoved at the torrent of abuse. "The Workers' and Peasants' Government, which has abolished the death penalty, cannot permit such deeds. We demand that this story be investigated, at once; if there is any truth in it, the Government will take energetic measures!"

A commission composed of members of all parties was immediately appointed, and with the Mayor, sent to Peter Paul to investigate. As we followed them out, the Duma was appointing another commission to meet Kerensky—to try and avoid bloodshed when he entered the capital....

It was midnight when we bluffed our past the guards at the gate of the fortress, and went forward under the faint glimmer of rare electric lights along the side of the church where lie the tombs of the Tsars, beneath the slender golden spire and the chimes, which, for months, continued to play *Bozhe Tsaria Khrani [*]* every day at [* "God Save the Tsar." noon.... The place was deserted; in most of the windows there were not even lights. Occasionally we bumped into a burly figure stumbling along in the dark, who answered questions with the usual, *"Ya nieznayu."*

[Graphic page-166 Pass to Reed fromDepartment of Prisons
   translation follows]

Pass from the Department of Prisons of the Soviet Government to visit freely all prisons of Petrograd and Cronstadt. (Translation)

Commissar
Chief Bureau of Prisons
6th of November, 1917.
        No. 213
Petrograd, Smolny
Institute, room No. 56-

PASS To the representative of the American Socialist press, JOHN REED, to visit all places of confinement in the cities of Petrograd and Cronstadt, for the purpose of generally investigating the condition of the prisoners, and for thorough social information for the purpose of stopping the flood of newspaper lies against demorcracy. Chief Commissar Secretary

On the left loomed the low dark outline of Trubetskoi Bastion, that living grave in which so many martyrs of liberty had lost their lives or their reason in the days of the Tsar, where the

Provisional Government had in turn shut up the Ministers of the Tsar, and now the Bolsheviki had shut up the Ministers of the Provisional Government.

A friendly sailor led us to the office of the commandant, in a little house near the Mint. Half a dozen Red Guards, sailors and soldiers were sitting around a hot room full of smoke, in which a samovar steamed cheerfully. They welcomed us with great cordiality, offering tea. The commandant was not in; he was escorting a commission of *"sabotazhniki"* (sabotageurs) from the City Duma, who insisted that the *yunkers* were all being murdered. This seemed to amuse them very much. At one side of the room sat a bald-headed, dissipated-looking little man in a frock-coat and a rich fur coat, biting his moustache and staring around him like a cornered rat. He had just been arrested. Somebody said, glancing carelessly at him, that he was a Minister or something.... The little man didn't seem to hear it; he was evidently terrified, although the occupants of the room showed no animosity whatever toward him.

I went across and spoke to him in French. "Count Tolstoy," he answered, bowing stiffly. "I do not understand why I was arrested. I was crossing the Troitsky Bridge on my way home when two of these-of these-persons held me up. I was a Commissar of the Provisional Government attached to the General Staff, but in no sense a member of the Government..."

"Let him go,"said a sailor. "He's harmless...."

"No," responded the soldier who had brought the prisoner. "We must ask the commandant."

"Oh, the commandant!" sneered the sailor. "What did you make a revolution for? To go on obeying officers?"

A *praporshtchik* of the Pavlovsky regiment was telling us how the insurrection started. "The *polk* (regiment) was on duty at the General Staff the night of the 6th. Some of my comrades and I were standing guard; Ivan Pavlovitch and another man-I don't remember his name-well, they hid behind the window-curtains in the room where the Staff was having a meeting, and they heard a great many things. For any things. For | | example, they heard orders to bring the Gatchina *yunkers* to Petrograd by night, and an order for the Cossacks to be ready to march in the morning.... The principal points in the city were to be occupied before dawn. Then there was the business of opening the bridges. But when they began to talk about surrounding Smolny, then Ivan Pavlovitch couldn't stand it any longer. That minute there was a good deal of coming and going, so he slipped out and came down to the guard-room,leaving the other comrade to pick up what he could.

"I was already suspicious that something was going on. Automobiles full of officers kept coming, and all the Ministers were there. Ivan Pavlovitch told me what he had heard. It was half-past two in the morning. The secretary of the regimental Committee was there, so we told him and asked what to do.

114

"'Arrest everybody coming and going!#' he says. So we began to do it. In an hour we had some officers and a couple of Ministers, whom we sent up to Smolny right away. But the Military Revolutionary Committee wasn't ready; they didn't know what to do; and pretty soon back came the order to let everybody go and not arrest anybody else. Well, we ran all the way to Smolny, and I guess we talked for an hour before they finally saw that it was war. It was five o'clock when we got back to the Staff, and by that time most of them were gone. But we got a few, and the garrison was all on the march...."

A Red Guard from Vasili Ostrov described in great detail what had happened in his district on the great day of the rising. "We didn't have any machine-guns over there," he said, laughing, "and we couldn't get any from Smolny. Comrade Zalking, who was a member of the *Uprava* (Central Bureau) of the Ward Duma, remembered all at once that there was lying in the meeting-room of the *Uprava* a machinegun which had been captured from the Germans. So he and I and another comrade went there. The Mensheviki and Socialist Revolutionaries were having a meeting. Well, we opened the door and walked right in on them, as they sat around the table-twelve or fifteen of them, three of us. When they saw us they stopped talking and just stared. We walked right across the room, uncoupled the machine-gun; Comrade Zalkind picked up one part, I the other, we put them on our shoulders and walked out-and not a single man said a word!"

"Do you know how the Winter Palace was captured?" asked a third man, a sailor. "Along about eleven o'clock we found out there weren't any more *yunkers* on the Neva side. So we broke in the doors and filtered up the different stairways one by one, or in little bunches. When we got to the top of the stairs the *yunkers* held us up and took away our guns. Still our fellows kept coming up, little by little, until we had a majority. Then we turned around and took away the *yunkers'* guns...."

Just then the commandant entered-a merry-looking young non-commissioned officer with his arm in a sling, and deep circles of sleeplessness under his eyes. His eye fell first on the prisoner, who at once began to explain.

"Oh, yes," interrupted the other. "You were one of the committee who refused to surrender the Staff Wednesday afternoon. However, we don't want you, citizen. Apologies-" He opened the door and waved his arm for Count Tolstoy to leave. Several of the others, especially the Red Guards, grumbled protests, and the sailor remarked triumphantly, *"Vot!* There! Didn't I say so?"

Two soldiers now engaged his attention. They had been elected a committee of the fortress garrison to protest. The prisoners, they said, were getting the same food as the guards, when there wasn't even enough to keep a man from being hungry. "Why should the counter-revolutionists be treated so well?"

"We are revolutionists, comrades, not bandits," answered the commandant. He turned to us. We explained that rumours were going about that the *yunkers* were being tortured, and the lives of the Ministers threatened. Could we perhaps see the prisoners, so as to be able to prove to the world-?"

"No," said the young soldier, irritably. "I am not going to disturb the prisoners again. I have just been compelled to wake them up-they were sure we were going to massacre them.... Most of the *yunkers* have been released anyway, and the rest will go out to-morrow." He turned abruptly away.

"Could we talk to the Duma commission, then?"

The Commandant, who was pouring himself a glass of tea, nodded. "They are still out in the hall," he said carelessly.

Indeed they stood there just outside the door, in the feeble light of an oil lamp, grouped around the Mayor and talking excitedly.

"Mr. Mayor," I said, "we are American correspondents. Will you please tell us officially the result of your investigations?"

He turned to us his face of venerable dignity.

"There is no truth in the reports," he said slowly. "Except for the incidents which occurred as the Ministers were being brought here, they have been treated with every consideration. As for the *yunkers,* not one has received the slightest injury...."

Up the Nevsky, in the empty after-midnight gloom, an interminable column of soldiers shuffled in silence-to battle with Kerensky. In dim back streets automobiles without lights flitted to and fro, and there was furtive activity in Fontanka 6, headquarters of the Peasants' Soviet, in a certain apartment of a huge building on the Nevsky, and in the *Injinierny Zamok* (School of Engineers); the Duma was illuminated....

In Smolny Institute the Military Revolutionary Committee flashed baleful fire, pounding like an over-loaded dynamo....

CHAPTER VII

The Revolutionary Front

SATURDAY, November 10th....

Citizens!

The Military Revolutionary Committee declares that it will not tolerate any violation of revolutionary order....

Theft, brigandage, assaults and attempts at massacre will be severely punished....

Following the example of the Paris Commune, the Committee will destroy without mercy any looter or instigator of disorder....

Quiet lay the city. Not a hold-up, not a robbery, not even a drunken fight. By night armed patrols went through the silent streets, and on the corners soldiers and Red Guards squatted around little fires, laughing and singing. In the daytime great crowds gathered on the sidewalks listening to interminable hot debates between students and soldiers, business men and workmen.

Citizens stopped each other on the street.

"The Cossacks are coming?"

"No...."

"What's the latest?"

"I don't know anything. Where's Kerensky?"

"They say only eight versts from Petrograd.... Is it true that the Bolsheviki have fled to the battleship *Avrora?*"

"They say so...."

Only the walls screamed, and the few newspapers; denunciation, appeal, decree....

An enormous poster carried the hysterical manifesto of the Executive Committee of the Peasant' Soviets:

....They (the Bolsheviki) dare to say that they are supported by the Soviets of Peasants' Deputies, and that they are speaking on behalf of the Soviets of Peasants' Deputies....

Let all working-class Russia know that this is a LIE, AND THAT ALL THE WORKING PEASANTS-in the person of-the EXECUTIVE COMMITTEE OF THE ALL-RUSSIAN SOVIETS OF PEASANTS' DEPUTIES-refutes with indignation all participation of the organised peasantry in this criminal violation of the will of the working-classes....

From the Soldier Section of the Socialist Revolutionary party:

The insane attempt of the Bolsheviki is on the eve of collapse. The garrison is divided.... The Ministries are on strike and bread is getting scarcer. All factions except the few Bolsheviki have left the Congress. The Bolsheviki are alone....

We call upon all sane elements to group themselves around the
Committee for Salvation of Country and Revolution, and to prepare
themselves seriously to be ready at the first call of the Central
Committee....

In a hand-bill the Council of the Republic recited its wrongs:

Ceding to the force of bayonets, the Council of the Republic has been obliged to separate, and temporarily to interrupt its meetings.

The usurpers, with the words "Liberty and Socialism" on their lips, have set up a rule of arbitrary violence. They have arrested the members of the Provisional Government, closed the newspapers, seized the printing-shops....This power must be considered the enemy of the people and the Revolution; it is necessary to do battle with it, and to pull it down....

The Council of the Republic, until the resumption of its labours, invites the citizens of the Russian Republic to group themselves around the....local Committees for Salvation of Country and Revolution, which are organising the overthrow of the Bolsheviki and the creation of a Government capable of leading the country to the Constituent Assembly.

_Dielo Naroda_said:

A revolution is a rising of all the people.... But here what have we?
Nothing but a handful of poor fools deceived by Lenin and Trotzky....
Their decrees and their appeals will simply add to the museum of
historical curiosities....

And *Narodnoye Slovo*(People'sWord-PopulistSocialist):

"Workers' and Peasants' Government?" That is only a pipedream; nobody, either in Russia or in the countries of our Allies, will recognise this "Government"-or even in the enemy countries....

The bourgeois press had temporarily disappeared....*Pravada* had an account of the first meeting of the new *Tsay-ee-kah,* now the parliament of the Russian Soviet Republic. Miliutin, Commissar of Agriculture, remarked that the Peasants' Executive Committee had called an All-Russian Peasant Congress for December 13th.

"But we cannot wait," he said. "We must have the backing of the peasants. I propose that *we* call the Congress of Peasants, and do it immediately...." The Left Socialist Revolutionaries agreed. An Appeal to the Peasants of Russia was hastily drafted, and a committee of five elected to carry out the project.

The question of detailed plans for distributing the land, and the question of Workers' Control of Industry, were postponed until the experts working on them should submit a report.

Three decrees were read and approved: first, Lenin's "General Rules For the Press," ordering the suppression of all newspapers inciting to resistance and disobedience to the new Government, inciting to criminal acts, or deliberately perverting the news; the Decree of Moratorium for House-rents; and the Decree Establishing a Workers' Militia. Also orders, one giving the Municipal Duma power to requisition empty apartments and houses, the other directing the unloading of freight cars in the railroad terminals, to hasten the distribution of necessities and to free the badly-needed rolling-stock....

Two hours later the Executive Committee of the Peasants' Soviets was sending broadcast over Russia the following telegram:

The arbitrary organisation of the Bolsheviki, which is called "Bureau of Organisation for the National Congress of Peasants,"is inviting all the Peasants' Soviets to send delegates to the Congress at Petrograd....

The Executive Committee of the Soviets of Peasants' Deputies declares that it considers, now as well as before, that it would be dangerous to take away from the provinces at this moment the forces necessary to prepare for elections to the Constituent Assembly, which is the only salvation of the working-class and the country. We confirm the date of the Congress of Peasants, *December 13th.*

At the Duma all was excitement, officers coming and going, the Mayor in conference with the leaders of the Committee for Salvation. A Councillor ran in with a copy of Kerensky's proclamation, dropped by hundreds from an aeroplane low flying down the Nevsky, which threatened terrible vengeance on all who did not submit, and ordered soldiers to lay down their arms and assemble immediately in Mars Field.

The Minister-President had taken Tsarskoye Selo, we were told, and was already in the Petrograd campagna, five miles away. He would enter the city to-morrow-in a few hours. The Soviet troops in contact with his Cossacks were said to be going over to the Provisional Government. Tchernov was somewhere in between, trying to organise the "neutral" troops into a force to halt the civil war.

In the city the garrison regiments were leaving the Bolsheviki, they said. Smolny was already abandoned…. All the Governmental machinery had stopped functioning. The employees of the State Bank had refused to work under Commissars from Smolny, refused to pay out money to them. All the private banks were closed. The Ministries were on strike. Even now a committee from the Duma was making the rounds of business houses, collecting a fund to pay the salaries of the strikers….

Trotzky had gone to the Ministry of Foreign Affairs and ordered the clerks to translate the Decree on Peace into foreign languages; six hundred functionaries had hurled their resignations in his face…. Shliapnikov, Commissar of Labour, had commanded all the employees of his Ministry to return to their places within twenty-four hours, or lose their places and their pension-rights; only the door-servants had responded…. Some of the branches of the Special Food Supply Committee had suspended work rather than submit to the Bolsheviki…. In spite of lavish promises of high wages and better conditions, the operators at the Telephone Exchange would not connect Soviet headquarters….

The Socialist Revolutionary Party had voted to expel all members who had remained in the Congress of Soviets, and all who were taking part in the insurrection….

News from the provinces. Moghilev had declared against the Bolsheviki. At Kiev the Cossacks had overthrown the Soviets and arrested all the insurrectionary leaders. The Soviet and garrison of Luga, thirty thousand strong, affirmed its loyalty to the Provisional Government, and appealed to all Russia to rally around it. Kaledin had dispersed all Soviets and Unions in the Don Basin, and his forces were moving north….

Said a representative of the Railway Workers: "Yesterday we sent a telegram all over Russia demanding that war between the political parties cease at once, and insisting on the formation of a coalition Socialist Government. Otherwise we shall call a strike to-morrow night…. In the morning there will be a meeting of all factions to consider the question. The Bolsheviki seem anxious for an agreement…."

"If they last that long!" laughed the City Engineer, a stout, ruddy man….

As we came up to Smolny-not abandoned, but busier than ever, throngs of workers and soldiers running in and out, and doubled guards everywhere-we met the reporters for the bourgeois and "moderate" Socialist papers.

"Threw us out!" cried one, from *Volia Naroda.* "Bonch-Bruevitch came down to the Press Bureau and told us to leave! Said we were spies!" They all began to talk at once: "Insult! Outrage! Freedom of the press!"

In the lobby were great tables heaped with stacks of appeals, proclamations and orders of the Military Revolutionary Committee. Workmen and soldiers staggered past, carrying them to waiting automobiles.

One began:

TO THE PILLORY!

In this tragic moment through which the Russian masses are living, the Mensheviki and their followers and the Right Socialist Revolutionaries have betrayed the working-class. They have enlisted on the side of Kornilov, Kerensky and Savinkov....

They are printing orders of the traitor Kerensky and creating a panic in the city, spreading the most ridiculous rumours of mythical victories by that renegade....

Citizens! Don't believe these false rumours. No power can defeat the People's Revolution.... Premier Kerensky and his followers await speedy and well-deserved punishment....

We are putting them in the Pillory. We are abandoning them to the enmity of all workers, soldiers, sailors and peasants, on whom they are trying to rivet the ancient chains. They will never be able to wash from their bodies the stain of the people's hatred and contempt.

Shame and curses to the traitors of the People!...

The Military Revolutionary Committee had moved into larger quarters, room 17 on the top floor. Red Guards were at the door. Inside, the narrow space in front of the railing was crowded with well-dressed persons, outwardly respectful but inwardly full of murder-bourgeois who wanted permits for their automobiles, or passports to leave the city, among them many foreigners.... Bill Shatov and Peters were on duty. They suspended all other business to read us the latest bulletins.

The One Hundred Seventy-ninth Reserve Regiment offers its unanimous support. Five thousand stevedores at the Putilov wharves greet the new Government. Central Committee of the Trade Unions-enthusiastic support. The garrison and squadron at Reval elect Military

Revolutionary Committees to cooperate, and despatch troops. Military Revolutionary Committees control in Pskov and Minsk. Greetings from the Soviets of Tsaritzin, Rovensky-on-Don, Tchernogorsk, Sevastopol.... The Finland Division, the new Committees of the Fifth and Twelfth Armies, offer allegiance....

From Moscow the news is uncertain. Troops of the Military Revolutionary Committee occupy the strategic points of the city; two companies on duty in the Kremlin have gone over to the Soviets, but the Arsenal is in the hands of Colonel Diabtsev and his *yunkers.* The Revolutionary Committee demanded arms for the workers, and Riabtsev parleyed with them until this morning, when suddenly he sent an ultimatum to the Committee, ordering Soviet troops to surrender and the Committee to disband. Fighting has begun....

In Petrograd the Staff submitted to Smolny's Commissars at once. The *Tsentroflot,* refusing, was stormed by Dybenko and a company of Cronstadt sailors, and a new *Tsentroflot* set up, supported by the Baltic and the Black Sea battleships....

But beneath all the breezy assurance there was a chill premonition, a feeling of uneasiness in the air. Kerensky's Cossacks were coming fast; they had artillery. Skripnik, Secretary of the Factory-Shop Committees, his face drawn and yellow, assured me that there was a whole army corps of them, but he added, fiercely, "They'll never take us alive!" Petrovsky laughed weariedly, "To-morrow maybe we'll get a sleep-a long one...." Lozovsky, with his emaciated, red-bearded face, said, "What chance have we? All alone.... A mob against trained soldiers!"

South and south-west the Soviets had fled before Kerensky, and the garrisons of Gatchina, Pavlovsk, Tsarskoye Selo were divided-half voting to remain neutral, the rest, without officers, falling back on the capital in the wildest disorder.

In the halls they were pasting up bulletins:

FROM KRASNOYE SELO, NOVEMBER 10TH, 8 A.M.

To be communicated to all Commanders of Staffs, Commanders in Chief, Commanders, everywhere and to all, all, all.

The ex-Minister Kerensky has sent a deliberately false telegram to every one everywhere to the effect that the troops of revolutionary Petrograd have voluntarily surrendered their arms and joined the armies of the former Government, the Government of Treason, and that the soldiers have been ordered by the Military Revolutionary Committee to retreat. The troops of a free people do not retreat nor do they surrender.

Our troops have left Gatchina in order to avoid bloodshed between themselves and their mistaken brother-Cossacks, and in order to take a more convenient position, which is at present so strong that if Kerensky and his companions in arms should even increase their forces ten times, still there would be no cause for anxiety. The spirit of our troops is excellent.

In Petrograd all is quiet.

Chief of the Defence of Petrograd and the Petrograd District,

Lieutenant-Colonel Muraviov.

As we left the Military Revolutionary Committee Antonov entered, a paper in his hand, looking like a corpse.

"Send this," said he.

TO ALL DISTRICT SOVIETS OF WORKERS' DEPUTIES AND FACTORYSHOP COMMITTEES

The Kornilovist bands of Kerensky are threatening the approaches to the capital. All the necessary orders have been given to crush mercilessly the counter-revolutionary attempt against the people and its conquests.

The Army and the Red Guard of the Revolution are in need of the immediate support of the workers.

WE ORDER THE WARD SOVIETS AND FACTORY-SHOP COMMITTEES:

1. To move out the greatest possible number of workers for the digging of trenches, the erection of barricades and reinforcing of wire entanglements.

2. Wherever it shall be necessary for this purpose to stop work at the factories this shall be done immediately.

3. All common and barbed wire available must be assembled, and also all implements for the digging of trenches and the erection of barricades.

4. All available arms must be taken.

5. THE STRICTEST DISCIPLINE IS TO BE OBSERVED, AND EVERY ONE MUST BE READY TO SUPPORT THE ARMY OF THE REVOLUTION BY ALL MEANS.

Chairman of the Petrograd Soviet of Worker's and Soldiers' Deputies,

People's Commissar LEON TROTZKY.

Chairman of the Military Revolutionary Committee,

Commander in Chief PODVOISKY.

As we came out into the dark and gloomy day all around the grey horizon factory whistles were blowing, a hoarse and nervous sound, full of foreboding. By tens of thousands the working-people poured out, men and women; by tens of thousands the humming slums belched out their dun and miserable hordes. Red Petrograd was in danger! Cossacks! South and southwest they poured through the shabby streets toward the Moskovsky Gate, men, women and children, with rifles, picks, spades, rolls of wire, cartridge-belts over their working clothes.... Such an immense, spontaneous outpouring of a city never was seen! They rolled along torrent-like, companies of soldiers borne with them, guns, motor-trucks, wagons-the revolutionary proletariat defending with its breast the capital of the Workers' and Peasants' Republic!

Before the door of Smolny was an automobile. A slight man with thick glasses magnifying his red-rimmed eyes, his speech a painful effort, stood leaning against a mud-guard with his hands in the pockets of a shabby raglan. A great bearded sailor, with the clear eyes of youth, prowled restlessly about, absently toying with an enormous blue-steel revolver, which never left his hand. These were Antonov and Dybenko.

Some soldiers were trying to fasten two military bicycles on the running-board. The chauffeur violently protested; the enamel would get scratched, he said. True, he was a Bolshevik, and the automobile was commandeered from a bourgeois; true, the bicycles were for the use of orderlies. But the chauffeur's professional pride was revolted.... So the bicycles were abandoned....

The People's Commissars for War and Marine were going to inspect the revolutionary front-wherever that was. Could we go with them? Certainly not. The automobile only held five-the two Commissars, two orderlies and the chauffeur. However, a Russian acquaintance of mine, whom I will call Trusishka, calmly got in and sat down, nor could any argument dislodge him....

I see no reason to doubt Trusishka's story of the journey. As they went down the Suvorovsky Prospect some one mentioned food. They might be out three or four days, in a country indifferently well provisioned. They stopped the car. Money? The Commissar of War looked through his pockets-he hadn't a kopek. The Commissar of Marine was broke. So was the chauffeur. Trusishka bought the provisions....

Just as they turned into the Nevsky a tire blew out.

"What shall we do?" asked Antonov.

"Commandeer another machine!" suggested Dybenko, waving his revolver. Antonov stood in the middle of the street and signalled a passing machine, driven by a soldier.

"I want that machine," said Antonov.

"You won't get it," responded the soldier.

"Do you know who I am?" Antonov produced a paper upon which was written that he had been appointed Commander-in-Chief of all the armies of the Russian Republic, and that every one should obey him without question.

"I don't care if you're the devil himself," said the soldier, hotly. "This machine belongs to the First Machine-Gun Regiment, and we're carrying ammunition in it, and you can't have it...."

The difficulty, however, was solved by the appearance of an old battered taxi-cab, flying the Italian flag. (In time of trouble private cars were registered in the name of foreign consulates, so as to be safe from requisition.) From the interior of this was dislodged a fat citizen in an expensive fur coat, and the party continued on its way.

Arrived at Narvskaya Zastava, about ten miles out, Antonov called for the commandant of the Red Guard. He was led to the edge of the town, where some few hundred workmen had dug trenches and were waiting for the Cossacks.

"Everything all right here, comrade?" asked Antonov.

"Everything perfect, comrade," answered the commandant.

"The troops are in excellent spirits.... Only one thing-we have no ammunition...."

"In Smolny there are two billion rounds," Antonov told him. "I will give you an order." He felt in his pockets. "Has any one a piece of paper?"

Dybenko had none-nor the couriers. Trusishka had to offer his note-book....

"Devil! I have no pencil!" cried Antonov. "Who's got a pencil?"
Needless to say, Trusishka had the only pencil in the crowd....

We who were left behind made for the Tsarskoye Selo station. Up the Nevsky, as we passed, Red Guards were marching, all armed, some with bayonets and some without. The early twilight of winter was falling. Heads up they tramped in the chill mud, irregular lines of four, without music, without drums. A red flag crudely lettered in gold, "Peace! Land!" floated over them. They were very young. The expression on their faces was that of who know they are going to die.... Half-fearful, half-contemptuous, the crowds on the sidewalk watched them pass, in hateful silence....

[Graphic page-184 Pass to the Northern Front]

This pass was issued upon the recommendation of Trotzky three days after the Bolshevik Revolution. It gives me the right of free travel to the Northern front-and an added note on the back extends the permission to all fronts. It will be noticed that the speaks of the *Petersburg*, instead of the *Petrograd* Soviet; it was the fashion among thorough-going internationalists to abolish all names which smacked of "patriotism"; but at the same time, it would not do to restore the "Saint."... (Translation) Executive Committee Petrograd Soviet of Workers' and Soldiers' Deputies Military Section 28th October, 1917 No. 1435 CERTIFICATE The present certificate is given to the representative of the American Social Democracy, the internationalist comrade JOHN REED. The Military Revolutionary Committee of the Petersburg Soviet of Workers' and Soldiers' Deputies gives him the right of free travel through the entire Northern front, for the purpose of reporting to our American comrades-internationalists concerning events in Russia. For the President For the Secretary

At the railroad station nobody knew just where Kerensky was, or where the front lay. Trains went no further, however, than Tsarskoye....

Our car was full of commuters and country people going home, laden with bundles and evening papers. The talk was all of the Bolshevik rising. Outside of that, however, one would never have realised that civil war was rending mighty Russia in two, and that the train was headed into the zone of battle. Through the window we could see, in the swiftly-deepening darkness, masses of soldiers going along the muddy road toward the city, flinging out their arms in argument. A freight-train, swarming with troops and lit up by huge bonfires, was halted on a siding. That was all. Back along the flat horizon the glow of the city's lights faded down the night. A street-car crawled distantly along a far-flung suburb....

Tsarskoye Selo-station was quiet, but knots of soldiers stood here and there talking in low tones and looking uneasily down the empty track in the direction of Gatchina. I asked some of them which side they were on. "Well," said one, "we don't exactly know the rights of the matter…. There is no doubt that Kerensky is a provocator, but we do not consider it right for Russian men to be shooting Russian men."

In the station commandant's office was a big, jovial, bearded common soldier, wearing the red arm-band of a regimental committee. Our credentials from Smolny commanded immediate respect. He was plainly for the Soviets, but bewildered.

"The Red Guards were here two hours ago, but they went away again. A Commissar came this morning, but he returned to Petrograd when the Cossacks arrived."

"The Cossacks are here then?"

He nodded, gloomily. "There has been a battle. The Cossacks came early in the morning. They captured two or three hundred of our men, and killed about twenty-five."

"Where are the Cossacks?"

"Well, they didn't get this far. I don't know just where they are. Off that way…." He waved his arm vaguely westward.

We had dinner-an excellent dinner, better and cheaper than could be got in Petrograd-in the station restaurant. Nearby sat a French officer who had just come on foot from Gatchina. All was quiet there, he said. Kerensky held the town. "Ah, these Russians," he went on, "they are original! What a civil war! Everything except the fighting!"

We sallied out into the town. Just at the door of the station stood two soldiers with rifles and bayonets fixed. They were surrounded by about a hundred business men, Government officials and students, who attacked them with passionate argument and epithet. The soldiers were uncomfortable and hurt, like children unjustly scolded.

A tall young man with a supercilious expression, dressed in the uniform of a student, was leading the attack.

"You realise, I presume," he said insolently, "that by taking up arms against your brothers you are making your-selves the tools of murderers and traitors?"

"Now brother,"answered the soldier earnestly, "you don't understand. There are two classes, don't you see, the proletariat and the bourgeoisie. We—"

"Oh, I know that silly talk!" broke in the student rudely. "A bunch of ignorant peasants like you hear somebody bawling a few catch-words. You don't understand what they mean. You just echo them like a lot of parrots." The crowd laughed. "I'm a Marxian student. And I tell you that this isn't Socialism you are fighting for. It's just plain pro-German anarchy!"

"Oh, yes, I know," answered the soldier, with sweat dripping from his brow. "You are an educated man, that is easy to see, and I am only a simple man. But it seems to me—"

"I suppose," interrupted the other contemptuously, "that you believe Lenin is a real friend of the proletariat?"

"Yes, I do," answered the soldier, suffering.

"Well, my friend, do you know that Lenin was sent through Germany in a closed car? Do you know that Lenin took money from the Germans?"

"Well, I don't know much about that," answered the soldier stubbornly, "but it seems to me that what he says is what I want to hear, and all the simple men like me. Now there are two classes, the bourgeoisie and the proletariat—"

"You are a fool! Why, my friend, I spent two years in Schlüsselburg for revolutionary activity, when you were still shooting down revolutionists and singing 'God Save the Tsar!' My name is Vasili Georgevitch Panyin. Didn't you ever hear of me?"

"I'm sorry to say I never did," answered the soldier with humility.
"But then, I am not an educated man. You are probably a great hero."

"I am," said the student with conviction. "And I am opposed to the Bolsheviki, who are destroying our Russia, our free Revolution. Now how do you account for that?"

The soldier scratched his head. "I can't account for it at all," he said, grimacing with the pain of his intellectual processes. "To me it seems perfectly simple-but then, I'm not well educated. It seems like there are only two classes, the proletariat and the bourgeoisie—"

"There you go again with your silly formula!" cried the student.

"—only two classes," went on the soldier, doggedly.

ldquo;And whoever isn't on one side is on the other..."

We wandered on up the street, where the lights were few and far between, and where people rarely passed. A threatening silence hung over the place-as of a sort of purgatory between heaven and hell, a political No Man's Land. Only the barber shops were all brilliantly lighted and crowded, and a line formed at the doors of the public bath; for it was

Saturday night, when all Russia bathes and perfumes itself. I haven't the slightest doubt that Soviet troops and Cossacks mingled in the places where these ceremonies were performed.

The nearer we came to the Imperial Park, the more deserted were the streets. A frightened priest pointed out the headquarters of the Soviet, and hurried on. It was in the wing of one of the Grand Ducal palaces, fronting the Park. The windows were dark, the door locked. A soldier, lounging about with his hands in the top of his trousers, looked us up and down with gloomy suspicion. "The Soviet went away two days ago," said he. "Where?" A shrug. *"Nie znayu.* I don't know."

A little further along was a large building, brightly illuminated. From within came a sound of hammering. While we were hesitating, a soldier and a sailor came down the street, hand in hand. I showed them my pass from Smolny. "Are you for the Soviets?" I asked. They did not answer, but looked at each other in a frightened way.

"What is going on in there?" asked the sailor, pointing to the building.

"I don't know."

Timidly the soldier put out his hand and opened the door a crack. Inside a great hall hung with bunting and evergreens, rows of chairs, a stage being built.

A stout woman with a hammer in her hand and her mouth full of tacks came out. "What do you want?" she asked.

"Is there a performance to-night?" said the sailor, nervously.

"There will be private theatricals Sunday night," she answered severely. "Go away."

We tried to engage the soldier and sailor in conversation, but they seemed frightened and unhappy, and drew off into the darkness.

We strolled toward the Imperial Palaces, along the edge of the vast, dark gardens, their fantastic pavilions and ornamental bridges looming uncertainly in the night, and soft water splashing from the fountains. At one place, where a ridiculous iron swan spat unceasingly from an artificial grotto, we were suddenly aware of observation, and looked up to encounter the sullen, suspicious gaze of half a dozen gigantic armed soldiers, who stared moodily down from a grassy terrace. I climbed up to them. "Who are you?" I asked.

"We are the guard," answered one. They all looked very depressed, as undoubtedly they were, from weeks and weeks of all-day all-night argument and debate.

"Are you Kerensky's troops, or the Soviets'?"

There was silence for a moment, as they looked uneasily at each other. Then, "We are neutral," said he.

We went on through the arch of the huge Ekaterina Palace, into the Palace enclosure itself, asking for headquarters. A sentry outside a door in a curving white wing of the Palace said that the commandant was inside.

In a graceful, white, Georgian room, divided into unequal parts by a two-sided fire-place, a group of officers stood anxiously talking. They were pale and distracted, and evidently hadn't slept. To one, an oldish man with a white beard, his uniform studded with decorations, who was pointed out as the Colonel, we showed our Bolshevik papers.

He seemed surprised. "How did you get here without being killed?" he asked politely. "It is very dangerous in the streets just now. Political passion is running very high in Tsarskoye Selo. There was a battle this morning, and there will be another to-morrow morning. Kerensky is to enter the town at eight o'clock."

"Where are the Cossacks?"

"About a mile over that way." He waved his arm.

"And you will defend the city against them?"

"Oh dear no." He smiled. "We are holding the city for Kerensky." Our hearts sank, for our passes stated that we were revolutionary to the core. The Colonel cleared his throat. "About those passes of yours," he went on. "Your lives will be in danger if you are captured. Therefore, if you want to see the battle, I will give you an order for rooms in the officers' hotel, and if you will come back here at seven o'clock in the morning, I will give you new passes."

"So you are for Kerensky?" we said.

"Well, not exactly *for* Kerensky." The Colonel hesitated. "You see, most of the soldiers in the garrison are Bolsheviki, and to-day, after the battle, they all went away in the direction of Petrograd, taking the artillery with them. You might say that none of the *soldiers* are for Kerensky; but some of them just don't want to fight at all. The *officers* have almost all gone over to Kerensky's forces, or simply gone away. We are-ahem-in a most difficult position, as you see...."

We did not believe that there would be any battle.... The Colonel courteously sent his orderly to escort us to the railroad station. He was from the South, born of French immigrant parents in Bessarabia. "Ah," he kept saying, "it is not the danger or the hardships I mind, but being so long, three years, away from my mother...."

Looking out of the window of the train as we sped through the cold dark toward Petrograd, I caught glimpses of clumps of soldiers gesticulating in the light of fires, and of clusters of armoured cars halted together at cross-roads, the chauffeurs hanging out of the turrets and shouting to each other....

All the troubled night over the bleakflats leaderless bands of soldiers and Red Guards wandered, clashing and confused, and the Commissars of the Military Revolutionary Committee hurried from one group to another, trying to organise a defence....

Back in town excited throngs were moving in tides up and down the Nevsky. Something was in the air. From the Warsaw Railway station could be heard far-off cannonade. In the *yunker* schools there was feverish activity. Duma members went from barracks to barracks, arguing and pleading, narrating fearful stories of Bolshevik violence-massacre of the *yunkers* in the Winter Palace, rape of the women soldiers, the shooting of the girl before the Duma, the murder of Prince Tumanov.... In the Alexander Hall of the Duma building the Committee for Salvation was in special session; Commissars came and went, running.... All the journalists expelled from Smolny were there, in high spirits. They did not believe our report of conditions in Tsarskoye. Why, everybody knew that Tsarskoye was in Kerensky's hands, and that the Cossacks were now at Pulkovo. A committee was being elected to meet Kerensky at the railway station in the morning....

One confided to me, in strictest secrecy, that the counter-revolution would begin at midnight. He showed me two proclamations, one signed by Gotz and Polkovnikov, ordering the *yunker* schools, soldier convalescents in the hospitals, and the Knights of St. George to mobilise on a war footing and wait for orders from the Committee for Salvation; the other from the Committee for Salvation itself, which read as follows:

To the Population of Petrograd!

Comrades, workers, soldiers and citizens of revolutionary Petrograd! nary Petrograd! | |

The Bolsheviki, while appealing for peace at the front, are inciting to civil war in the rear.

Do not dig their provocatory appeals!

Do not dig trenches!

Down with the traitorous barricades!

Lay down your arms!

Soldiers, return to your barracks!

The war begun in Petrograd-is the death of the Revolution!

In the name of liberty, land, and peace, unite around the Committee for Salvation of Country and Revolution!

As we left the Duma a company of Red Guards, stern-faced and desperate, came marching down the dark, deserted street with a dozen prisoners-members of the local branch of the Council of Cossacks, caught red-handed plotting counter-revolution in their headquarters....

A soldier, accompanied by a small boy with a pail of paste, was sticking up great flaring notices:

By virtue of the present, the city of Petrograd and its suburbs are declared in a state of siege. All assemblies or meetings in the streets, and generally in the open air, are forbidden until further orders.

N. PODVOISKY, President of the Military

Revolutionary Committee.

As we went home the air was full of confused sound-automobile horns, shouts, distant shots. The city stirred uneasily, wakeful.

In the small hours of the morning a company of *yunkers,* disguised as soldiers of the Semionovsky Regiment, presented themselves at the Telephone Exchange just before the hour of changing guard. They had the Bolshevik password, and took charge without arousing suspicion. A few minutes later Antonov appeared, making a round of inspection. Him they captured and locked in a small room. When the relief came it was met by a blast of rifle-fire, several being killed.

Counter-revolution had begun...

CHAPTER VIII

Counter-Revolution

NEXT morning, Sunday the 11th, the Cossacks entered Tsarskoye Selo, Kerensky himself riding a white horse and all the church-bells clamouring. From the top of a little hill outside the town could be seen the golden spires and many-coloured cupolas, the sprawling grey immensity of the capital spread along the dreary plain, and beyond, the steely Gulf of Finland.

There was no battle. But Kerensky made a fatal blunder. At seven in the morning he sent word to the Second Tsarskoye Selo Rifles to lay down their arms. The soldiers replied that they would remain neutral, but would not disarm. Kerensky gave them ten minutes in which to obey. This angered the soldiers; for eight months they had been governing themselves by committee, and this smacked of the old régime.... A few minutes later Cossack artillery opened fire on the barracks, killing eight men. From that moment there were no more "neutral" soldiers in Tsarskoye....

Petrograd woke to bursts of rifle-fire, and the tramping thunder of men marching. Under the high dark sky a cold wind smelt of snow. At dawn the Military Hotel and the Telegraph Agency had been taken by large forces of *yunkers,* and bloodily recaptured. The Telephone Station was besieged by sailors, who lay behind barricades of barrels, boxes and tin sheets in the middle of the Morskaya, or sheltered themselves at the corner of the Gorokhovaya and of St. Isaac's Square, shooting at anything that moved. Occasionally an automobile passed in and out, flying the Red Cross flag. The sailors let it pass....

Albert Rhys Williams was in the Telephone Exchange. He went out with the Red Cross automobile, which was ostensibly full of wounded. After circulating about the city, the car went by devious ways to the Mikhailovsky *yunker* school, headquarters of the counter-revolution. A French officer, in the court-yard, seemed to be in command.... By this means ammunition and supplies were conveyed to the Telephone Exchange. Scores of these pretended ambulances acted as couriers and ammunition trains for the *yunkers.*

Five or six armoured cars, belonging to the disbanded British Armoured Car Division, were in their hands. As Louise Bryant was going along St. Isaac's Square one came rolling up from the Admiralty, on its way to the Telephone Exchange. At the corner of the Gogolia, right in front of her, the engine stalled. Some sailors ambushed behind wood-piles began shooting. The machine-gun in the turret of the thing slewed around and spat a hail of bullets indiscriminately into the wood-piles and the crowd. In the archway where Miss Bryant stood seven people were shot dead, among them two little boys. Suddenly, with a shout, the sailors leaped up and rushed into the flaming open; closing around the monster, they thrust their bayonets into the loop-holes, again and again, yelling... The chauffeur pretended to be wounded, and they let him go free-to run to the Duma and swell the tale of Bolshevik atrocities....Among the dead was a British Officer....

Later the newspapers told of another French officer, captured in a *yunker* armoured car and sent to Peter-Paul. The French Embassy promptly denied this, but one of the City Councillors told me that he himself had procured the officer's release from prison....

Whatever the official attitude of the Allied Embassies, individual French and British officers were active these days, even to the extent of giving advice at executive sessions of the Committee for Salvation.

All day long in every quarter of the city there were skirmishes between *yunkers* and Red Guards, battles between armoured cars.... Volleys, single shots and the shrill chatter of machine-guns could be heard, far and near. The iron shutters of the shops were drawn, but business still went on. Even the moving-picture shows, all outside lights dark, played to crowded houses. The street-cars ran. The telephones were all working; when you called Central, shooting could be plainly heard over the wire.... Smolny was cut off, but the Duma and the Committee for Salvation were in constant communication with all the *yunker* schools and with Kerensky at Tsarskoye.

At seven in the morning the Vladimir *yunker* school was visited by a patrol of soldiers, sailors and Red Guards, who gave the *yunkers* twenty minutes to lay down their arms. The ultimatum was rejected. An hour later the *yunkers* got ready to march, but were driven back by a violent fusillade from the corner of the Grebetskaya and the Bolshoy Prospekt. Soviet troops surrounded the building and opened fire, two armoured cars cruising back and forth with machine guns raking it. The *yunkers* telephoned for help. The Cossacks replied that they dare not come, because a large body of sailors with two cannon commanded their barracks. The Pavlovsk school was surrounded. Most of the Mikhailov *yunkers* were fighting in the streets....

At half-past eleven three field-pieces arrived. Another demand to surrender was met by the *yunkers* shooting down two of the Soviet delegates under the white flag. Now began a real bombardment. Great holes were torn in the walls of the school. The *yunkers* defended themselves desperately; shouting waves of Red Guards, assaulting, crumpled under the withering blast.... Kerensky telephoned from Tsarskoye to refuse all parley with the Military Revolutionary Committee.

Frenzied by defeat and their heaps of dead, the Soviet troops opened a tornado of steel and flame against the battered building. Their own officers could not stop the terrible bombardment. A Commissar from Smolny named Kirilov tried to halt it; he was threatened with lynching. The Red Guards' blood was up.

At half-past two the *yunkers* hoisted a white flag; they would surrender if they were guaranteed protection. This was promised. With a rush and a shout thousands of soldiers and Red Guards poured through windows, doors and holes in the wall. Before it could be stopped five *yunkers* were beaten and stabbed to death. The rest, about two hundred, were taken to Peter-Paul under escort, in small groups so as to avoid notice. On the way a mob set upon one party, killing eight more *yunkers*.... More than a hundred Red Guards and soldiers had fallen....

Two hours later the Duma got a telephone message that the victors were marching toward the *Injinierny Zamok*-the Engineers' school. A dozen members immediately set out to distribute among them armfuls of the latest proclamation of the Committee for Salvation. Several did not come back.... All the other schools surrendered without resistance, and the *yunkers* were sent unharmed to Peter-Paul and Cronstadt....

The Telephone Exchange held out until afternoon, when a Bolshevik armoured car appeared, and the sailors stormed the place. Shrieking, the frightened telephone girls ran to and fro; the *yunkers* tore from their uniforms all distinguishing marks, and one offered Williams *anything* for the loan of his overcoat, as a disguise.... "They will massacre us! They will massacre us!" they cried, for many of them had given their word at the Winter Palace not to take up arms against the People. Williams offered to mediate if Antonov were released. This was immediately done; Antonov and Williams made speeches to the victorious sailors, inflamed by their many dead-and once more the *yunkers* went free.... All but a few, who in their panic tried to flee over the roofs, or to hide in the attic, and were found and hurled into the street.

Tired, bloody, triumphant, the sailors and workers swarmed into the switchboard room, and finding so many pretty girls, fell back in an embarrassed way and fumbled with awkward feet. Not a girl was injured, not one insulted. Frightened, they huddled in the corners, and then, finding themselves safe, gave vent to their spite. "Ugh! The dirty, ignorant people! The fools!"... The sailors and Red Guards were embarrassed. "Brutes! Pigs!" shrilled the girls, indignantly putting on their coats and hats. Romantic had been their experience passing up cartridges and dressing the wounds of their dashing young defenders, the *yunkers,* many of them members of noble families, fighting to restore their beloved Tsar! These were just common workmen, peasants, "Dark People."...

The Commissar of the Military Revolutionary Committee, little Vishniak, tried to persuade the girls to remain. He was effusively polite. "You have been badly treated," he said. "The telephone system is controlled by the Municipal Duma. You are paid sixty rubles a month, and have to work ten hours and more.... From now on all that will be changed. The Government intends to put the telephones under control of the Ministry of Posts and Telegraphs. Your wages will be immediately raised to one hundred and fifty rubles, and your working-hours reduced. As members of the working-class you should be happy—"

Members of the *working-class* indeed! Did he mean to infer that there was anything in common between these-these animals-and *us?* Remain? Not if they offered a thousand rubles!... Haughty and spiteful the girls left the place....

The employees of the building, the line-men and labourers-they stayed. But the switch-boards must be operated-the telephone was vital.... Only half a dozen trained operators were available. Volunteers were called for; a hundred responded, sailors, soldiers, workers. The six girls scurried backward and forward, instructing, helping, scolding.... So, crippled, halting, but *going,* the wires slowly began to hum. The first thing was to connect Smolny with the barracks and the factories; the second, to cut off the Duma and the *yunker* schools.... Late in the afternoon word of it spread through the city, and hundreds of bourgeois called up to scream, "Fools! Devils! How long do you think you will last? Wait till the Cossacks come!"

Dusk was already falling. On the almost deserted Nevsky, swept by a bitter wind, a crowd had gathered before the Kazan Cathedral, continuing the endless debate; a few workmen, some soldiers and the rest shop-keepers, clerks and the like.

"But Lenin won't get Germany to make peace!" cried one.

A violent young soldier replied. "And whose fault is it? Your damn
Kerensky, dirty bourgeois! To hell with Kerensky! We don't want him!
We want Lenin...."

Outside the Duma an officer with a white arm-band was tearing down posters from the wall, swearing loudly. One read:

To the Population of Petrograd!

At this dangerous hour, when the Municipal Duma ought to use every means to calm the population, to assure it bread and other necessities, the Right Socialist Revolutionaries and the Cadets, forgetting their duty, have turned the Duma into a counter-revolutionary meeting, trying to raise part of the population against the rest, so as to facilitate the victory of Kornilov-Kerensky. Instead of doing their duty, the Right Socialist Revolutionaries and the Cadets have transformed the Duma into an arena of political attack upon the Soviets of Workers', Soldiers' and Peasants' Deputies, against the revolutionary Government of peace, bread and liberty.

Citizens of Petrograd, we, the Bolshevik Municipal Councillors elected by you-we want you to know that the Right Socialist Revolutionaries and the Cadets are engaged in counter-revolutionary action, have forgotten their duty, and are leading the population to famine, to civil war. We, elected by 183,000 votes, consider it our duty to bring to the attention of our constituents what is going on in the Duma, and declare that we disclaim all responsibility for the terrible but inevitable consequences....

Far away still sounded occasional shots, but the city lay quiet, cold, as if exhausted by the violent spasms which had torn it.

In the Nicolai Hall the Duma session was coming to an end. Even the truculent Duma seemed a little stunned. One after another the Commissars reported-capture of the Telephone Exchange, street-fighting, the taking of the Vladimir school.... "The Duma," said Trupp, "is on the side of the democracy in its struggle against arbitrary violence; but in any case, whichever side wins, the Duma will always be against lynchings and torture...."

Konovski, Cadet, a tall old man with a cruel face: "When the troops of the legal Government arrive in Petrograd, they will shoot down these insurgents, and that will not be lynching!" Protests all over the hall, even from his own party.

Here there was doubt and depression. The counter-revolution was being put down. The Central Committee of the Socialist Revolutionary party had voted lack of confidence in its officers; the left wing was in control; Avksentiev had resigned. signed. A courier reported that the Committee of Welcome sent to meet Kerensky at the railway station had been arrested. In the streets could be heard the dull rumble of distant cannonading, south and southwest. Still Kerensky did not come...

Only three newspapers were out-*Pravda, Dielo Naroda* and *Novaya Zhizn.* All of them devoted much space to the new "coalition" Government. The Socialist Revolutionary paper demanded a Cabinet without either Cadets or Bolsheviki. Gorky was hopeful; Smolny had made concessions. A purely Socialist Government was taking shape-all elements except the bourgeoisie. As for *Pravda,* it sneered:

We ridicule these coalitions with political parties whose most prominent members are petty journalists of doubtful reputation; our "coalition" is that of the proletariat and the revolutionary Army with the poor peasants...

On the walls a vainglorious announcement of the *Vikzhel,* threatening to strike if both sides did not compromise:

The conquerors of these riots, the saviours of the wreck of our
country, these will be neither the Bolsheviki, nor the Committee for
Salvation, nor the troops of Kerensky-but we, the Union of
Railwaymen...

Red Guards are incapable of handling a complicated business like the railways; as for the Provisional Government, it has shown itself incapable of holding the power...

We refuse to lend our services to any party which does not act by authority of ... a Government based on the confidence of all the democracy....

Smolny thrilled with the boundless vitality of inexhaustible humanity in action.

In Trade Union headquarters Lozovsky introduced me to a delegate of the Railway Workers of the Nicolai line, who said that the men were holding huge mass-meetings, condemning the action of their leaders.

"All power to the Soviets!" he cried, pounding on the table.
"The_oborontsi_ in the Central Committee are playing
Ko&rgrave;nilov's game. They tried to send a mission to the Stavka,
but we arrested them at Minsk.... Our branch has demanded an
All-Russian Convention, and they refuse to call it...."

The same situation as in the Soviets, the Army Committees. One after another the various democratic organisations, all over Russia, were cracking and changing. The Cooperatives were torn by internal struggles; the meetings of the Peasants' Executive broke up in stormy wrangling; even among the Cossacks there was trouble....

On the top floor the Military Revolutionary Committee was in full blast, striking and slacking not. Men went in, fresh and vigorous; night and day and night and day they threw themselves into the terrible machine; and came out limp, blind with fatigue, hoarse and filthy, to fall on the floor and sleep.... The Committee for Salvation had been outlawed. Great piles of new proclamations littered the floor:

... The conspirators, who have no support among the garrison or the working-class, above all counted on the suddenness of their attack. Their plan was discovered in time by Sub-Lieutenant Blagonravov, thanks to the revolutionary vigilance of a soldier of the Red Guard, whose name shall be made public. At the centre of the plot was the Committee for Salvation. Colonel Polkovnikov was in command of their forces, and the orders were signed by Gotz, former member of the Provisional Government, allowed at liberty on his word of honour....

Bringing these facts to the attention of the Petrograd population, the Military Revolutionary Committee orders the arrest of all concerned in the conspiracy, who shall be tried before the Revolutionary Tribunal....

From Moscow, word that the *yunkers* and Cossacks had surrounded the Kremlin and ordered the Soviet troops to lay down their arms. The Soviet forces complied, and as they were leaving the Kremlin, were set upon and shot down. Small forces of Bolsheviki had been driven from the Telephone and Telegraph offices; the *yunkers* now held the centre of the city. ... But all around them the Soviet troops were mustering. Street-fighting was slowly gathering way; all attempts at compromise had failed.... On the side of the Soviet, ten thousand garrison soldiers and a few Red Guards; on the side of the Government, six thousand *yunkers,* twenty-five hundred Cossacks and two thousand White Guards.

The Petrograd Soviet was meeting, and next door the new *Tsay-ee-kah,* acting on the decrees and orders which came down in a steady stream from the Council of People's Commissars in session upstairs; on the Order in Which Laws Are to be Ratified and Published, Establishing an Eight hour Days for Workers, and Lunatcharsky's "Basis for a System of Popular Education." Only a few hundred people were present at the two meetings, most of them armed. Smolny was almost deserted, except for the guards, who were busy at the hall windows, setting up machine-guns to command the flanks of the building.

In the *Tsay-ee-kah* a delegate of the *Vikzhel* was speaking: "We refuse to transport the troops of either party.... We have sent a committee to Kerensky to say that if he continues to march on Petrograd we will break his lines of communication...."

He made the usual plea for a conference of all the Socialist parties to form a new Government....

Kameniev answered discreetly. The Bolsheviki would be very glad to attend the conference. The centre of gravity, however, lay not in composition of such a Government, but in its acceptance of the programme of the Congress of Soviets.

... The *Tsay-ee-kah* had deliberated on the declaration made by the Left Socialist Revolutionaries and the Social Democrats Internationalists, and had accepted the proposition of proportional representation at the conference, even including delegates from the Army Committees and the Peasants' Soviets....

In the great hall, Trotzky recounted the events of the day.

"We offered the Vladimir *yunkers* a chance to surrender," he said. "We wanted to settle matters without bloodshed. But now that blood has been spilled there is only one way-pitiless struggle. It would be childish to think we can win by any other means.... The moment is decisive. Everybody must cooperate with the Military Revolutionary Committee, report where there are stores of barbed wire, benzine, guns.

... We've won the power; now we must keep it!"

The Menshevik Yoffe tried to read his party's declaration, but Trotzky refused to allow "a debate about principle."

"Our debates are now in the streets," he cried. "The decisive step has been taken. We all, and I in particular, take the responsibility for what is happening...."

Soldiers from the front, from Gatchina, told their stories. One from the Death Battalion, Four Hundred Eighty-first Artillery: "When the trenches hear of this, they will cry, 'This is *our* Government!'" A *yunker* from Peterhof said that he and two others had refused to march against the Soviets; and when his comrades had returned from the defence of the Winter Palace they appointed him their Commissar, to go to Smolny and offer their services to the *real* Revolution....

Then Trotzky again, fiery, indefatigable, giving orders, answering questions.

"The petty bourgeoisie, in order to defeat the workers, soldiers and peasants, would combine with the devil himself!" he said once. Many cases of drunkenness had been remarked the last two days. "No drinking, comrades! No one must be on the streets after eight in the evening, except the regular guards. All places suspected of having stores of liquor should be searched, and the liquor destroyed. No mercy to the sellers of liquor...."

The Military Revolutionary Committee sent for the delegation from the Viborg section; then for the members from Putilov. They clumped out hurriedly.

"For each revolutionist killed," said Trotzky, "we shall kill five counter-revolutionists!"

Down-town again. The Duma brilliantly illuminated and great crowds pouring in. In the lower hall wailing and cries of grief; the throng surged back and forth before the bulletin board, where was posted a list of *yunkers* killed in the day's fighting-or supposed to be killed, for most of the dead afterward turned up safe and sound.... Up in the Alexander Hall the Committee for Salvation held forth. The gold and red epaulettes of officers were conspicuous, the familiar faces of the Menshevik and Socialist Revolutionary intellectuals, the hard eyes and bulky magnificence of bankers and diplomats, officials of the old régime, and well-dressed women....

The telephone girls were testifying. Girl after girl came to the tribune-over-dressed, fashion-aping little girls, with pinched faces and leaky shoes. Girl after girl, flushing with pleasure at the applause of the "nice" people of Petrograd, of the officers, the rich, the great names of politics-girl after girl, to narrate her sufferings at the hands of the proletariat, and proclaim her loyalty to all that was old, established and powerful....

The Duma was again in session in the Nicolai Hall. The Mayor said hopefully that the Petrograd regiments were ashamed of their actions; propaganda was making headway.

[Graphic page-205 Proclamation for "wine pogroms"]

Revolutionary law and order. A proclamation of the Finland Regiment, in December, 1917, announcing desperate remedies for "wine pogroms." For translation see Appendix 5.

... Emissaries came and went, reporting horrible deeds by the Bolsheviki, interceding to save the *yunkers,* busily investigating....

"The Bolsheviki," said Trupp, "will be conquered by moral force, and not by bayonets....."

Meanwhile all was not well on the revolutionary front. The enemy had brought up armoured trains, mounted with cannon. The Soviet forces, mostly raw Red Guards, were without officers and without a definite plan. Only five thousand regular soldiers had joined them; the rest of the garrison was either busy suppressing the *yunker* revolt, guarding the city, or undecided what to do. At ten in the evening Lenin addressed a meeting of delegates from the city regiments, who voted overwhelmingly to fight. A Committee of five soldiers was elected to serve as General Staff, and in the small hours of the morning the regiments left their barracks in full battle array.... Going home I saw them pass, swinging along with the regular tread of veterans, bayonets in perfect alignment, through the deserted streets of the conquered city....

At the same time, in the headquarters of the *Vikzhel* down on the Sadovaya, the conference of all the Socialist parties to form a new Government was under way. Abramovitch, for the centre Mensheviki, said that there should be neither conquerors nor conquered-that bygones should be bygones. ...In this were agreed all the left wing parties. Dan, speaking in the name of the right Mensheviki, proposed to the Bolsheviki the following conditions for a truce: The Red Guard to be disarmed, and the Petrograd garrison to be placed at the orders of the Duma; the troops of Kerensky not to fire a single shot or arrest a single man; a Ministry of all the Socialist parties *except the Bolsheviki.* For Smolny Riazanov and Kameniev declared that a coalition ministry of all parties was acceptable, but protested at Dan's proposals. The Socialist Revolutionaries were divided; but the Executive Committee of the Peasants's Soviets and the Populist Socialists flatly refused to admit the Bolsheviki.... After bitter quarrelling a commission was elected to draw up a workable plan....

All that night the commission wrangled, and all the next day, and the next night. Once before, on the 9th of November, there had been a similar effort at conciliation, led by Martov and Gorky; but at the approach of Kerensky and the activity of the Committee for Salvation, the right wing of the Mensheviki, Socialist Revolutionaries and Populist Socialists suddenly withdrew. Now they were awed by the crushing of the *yunker* rebellion...

Monday the 12th was a day of suspense. The eyes of all Russia were fixed on the grey plain beyond the gates of Petrograd, where all the available strength of the old order faced the unorganised power of the new, the unknown. In Moscow a truce had been declared; both sides parleyed, awaiting the result in the capital. Now the delegates to the Congress of Soviets, hurrying on speeding trains to the farthest reaches of Asia, were coming to their homes, carrying the fiery cross. In wide-spreading ripples news of the miracle spread over the face of the land, and in its wake towns, cities and far villages stirred and broke, Soviets and Military Revolutionary Committees against Dumas, Zemstvos and Government Commissars-Red Guards against White-street fighting and passionate speech.... The result waited on the word from Petrograd....

Smolny was almost empty, but the Duma was thronged and noisy. The old Mayor, in his dignified way, was protesting against the Appeal of the Bolshevik Councillors.

"The Duma is not a centre of counter-revolution," he said, warmly. "The Duma takes no part in the present struggle between the parties. But at a time when there is no legal power in the land, the only centre of order is the Municipal Self-Government. The peaceful population recognises this fact; the foreign Embassies recognise only such documents as are signed by the Mayor of the town. The mind of a European does not admit of any other situation, as the Municipal self-government is the only organ which is capable of protecting the interests of the citizens. The City is bound to show hospitality, to all organisations which desire to profit by such hospitality, and therefore the Duma cannot prevent the distribution of any newspapers whatever within the Duma building. The sphere of our work is increasing, and we must be given full liberty of action, and our rights must be respected by both parties....

"We are perfectly neutral. When the Telephone Exchange was occupied by the *yunkers* Colonel Polkovnikov ordered the telephones to Smolny disconnected, but I protested, and the telephones were kept going...."

At this there was ironic laughter from the Bolshevik benches, and imprecations from the right.

"And yet," went on Schreider, "they look upon us as counter-revolutionaries and report us to the population. They deprive us of our means of transport by taking away our last motor-cars. It will not be our fault if there is famine in the town. Protests are of no use...."

Kobozev, Bolshevik member of the Town Board, was doubtful whether the Military Revolutionary Committee had requisitioned the Municipal automobiles. Even granting the fact, it was probably done by some unauthorised individual, in the emergency.

"The Mayor," he continued, "tells us that we must not make political meetings out of the Duma. But every Menshevik and Socialist Revolutionary here talks nothing but party propaganda, and at the door they distribute their illegal newspapers, *Iskri* (Sparks),

Soldatski Golos and *Rabotchaya Gazeta,* inciting to insurrection. What if we Bolsheviki should also begin to distribute our papers here? But this shall not be, for we respect the Duma. We have not attacked the Municipal Self-Government, and we shall not do so. But you have addressed an Appeal to the population, and we are entitled also to do so....

Followed him Shingariov, Cadet, who said that there could be no common language with those who were liable to be brought before the Attorney General for indictment, and who must be tried on the charge of treason.... He proposed again that all Bolshevik members should be expelled from the Duma. This was tabled, however, for there were no personal charges against the members, and they were active in the Municipal administration.

Then two Mensheviki Internationalists, declaring that the Appeal of the Bolshevik Councillors was a direct incitement to massacre. "If everything that is against the Bolsheviki is counter-revolutionary," said Pinkevitch, "then I do not know the difference between revolution and anarchy.... The Bolsheviki are depending upon the passions of the unbridled masses; we have nothing but moral force. We will protest against massacres and violence from both sides, as our task is to find a peaceful issue."

"The notice posted in the streets under the heading 'To the Pillory,' which calls upon the people to destroy the Mensheviki and Socialist Revolutionaries," said Nazariev, "is a crime which you, Bolsheviki, will not be able to wash away. Yesterday's horrors are but a preface to what you are preparing by such a proclamation.... I have always tried to reconcile you with the other parties, but at present I feel for you nothing but contempt!"

The Bolshevik Councillors were on their feet, shouting angrily, assailed by hoarse, hateful voices and waving arms....

Outside the hall I ran into the City Engineer, the Menshevik Gomberg and three or four reporters. They were all in high spirits.

"See!" they said. "The cowards are afraid of us. They don't dare arrest the Duma! Their Military Revolutionary Committee doesn't dare to send a Commissar into this building. Why, on the corner of the Sadovaya to-day, I saw a Red Guard try to stop a boy selling *Soldatski Golos*.... The boy just laughed at him, and a crowd of people wanted to lynch the bandit. It's only a few hours more, now. Even if Kerensky wouldn't come they haven't the men to run a Government. Absurd! I understand they're even fighting among themselves at Smolny!"

A Socialist Revolutionary friend of mine drew me aside. "I know where the Committee for Salvation is hiding," he said. "Do you want to go and talk with them?"

By this time it was dusk. The city had again settled down to normal-shop-shutters up, lights shining, and on the streets great crowds of people slowly moving up and down and arguing....

At Number 86 Nevsky we went through a passage into a courtyard, surrounded by tall apartment buildings. At the door of apartment 229 my friend knocked in a peculiar way. There was a sound of scuffling; an inside door slammed; then the front door opened a crack and a woman's face appeared. After a minute's observation she led us in-a placid-looking, middle-aged lady who at once cried, "Kyril, it's all right!" In the dining-room, where a samovar steamed on the table and there were plates full of bread and raw fish, a man in uniform emerged from behind the window-curtains, and another, dressed like a workman, from a closet. They were delighted to meet an American reporter. With a certain amount of gusto both said that they would certainly be shot if the Bolsheviki caught them. They would not give me their names, but both were Socialist Revolutionaries....

"Why," I asked, "do you publish such lies in your newspapers?"

Without taking offence the officer replied, "Yes, I know; but what can we do?" He shrugged. "You must admit that it is necessary for us to create a certain frame of mind in the people...."

The other man interrupted. "This is merely an adventure on the part of the Bolsheviki. They have no intellectuals. ... The Ministries won't work.... Russia is not a city, but a whole country.... Realising that they can only last a few days, we have decided to come to the aid of the strongest force opposed to them-Kerensky-and help to restore order."

"That is all very well," I said. "But why do you combine with the Cadets?"

The pseudo-workman smiled frankly. "To tell you the truth, at this moment the masses of the people are following the Bolsheviki. We have no following-now. We can't mobilise a handful of soldiers. There are no arms available.... The Bolsheviki are right to a certain extent; there are at this moment in Russia only two parties with any force-the Bolsheviki and the reactionaries, who are all hiding under the coat-tails of the Cadets. The Cadets think they are using us; but it is really we who are using the Cadets. When we smash the Bolsheviki we shall turn against the Cadets...."

"Will the Bolsheviki be admitted into the new Government?"

He scratched his head. "That's a problem," he admitted. "Of course if they are not admitted, they'sll probably do this all over again. At any rate, they will have a chance to hold the balance of power in the Constituent-that is, if there *is* a Constituent."

"And then, too," said the officer, "that brings up the question of admitting the Cadets into the new Government-and for the same reasons. You know the Cadets do not really want the Constituent Assembly-not if the Bolsheviki can be destroyed now." He shook his head. "It is not easy for us Russians, politics. You Americans are born politicians; you have had politics all your lives. But for us-well, it has only been a year, you know!"

"What do you think of Kerensky?" I asked.

"Oh, Kerensky is guilty of the sins of the Provisional Government," answered the other man. "Kerensky himself forced us to accept coalition with the bourgeoisie. If he had resigned, as he threatened, it would have meant a new Cabinet crisis only sixteen weeks before the Constituent Assembly, and that we wanted to avoid."

"But didn't it amount to that anyway?"

"Yes, but how were we to know? They tricked us-the Kerenskys and Avksentievs. Gotz is a little more radical. I stand with Tchernov, who is a real revolutionist.... Why, only to-day Lenin sent word that he would not object to Tchernov entering the Government.

"We wanted to get rid of the Kerensky Government too, but we thought it better to wait for the Constituent.... At the beginning of this affair I was with the Bolsheviki, but the Central Committee of my party voted unanimously against it-and what could I do? It was a matter of party discipline....

"In a week the Bolshevik Government will go to pieces; if the Socialist Revolutionaries could only stand aside and wait, the Government would fall into their hands. But if we wait a week the country will be so disorganised that the German imperialists will be victorious. That is why we began our revolt with only two regiments of soldiers promising to support us-and they turned against us.... That left only the *yunkers*...."

"How about the Cossacks?"

The officer sighed. "They did not move. At first they said they would come out if they had infantry support. They said moreover that they had their men with Kerensky, and that they were doing their part.... Then, too, they said that the Cossacks were always accused of being the hereditary enemies of democracy.... And finally, 'The Bolsheviki promise that they will not take away our land. There is no danger to us. We remain neutral.'"

During this talk people were constantly entering and leaving-most of them officers, their shoulder-straps torn off. We could see them in the hall, and hear their low, vehement voices. Occasionally, through the half-drawn portières, we caught a glimpse of a door opening into a bath-room, where a heavily-built officer in a colonel's uniform sat on the toilet, writing something on a pad held in his lap. I recognised Colonel Polkovnikov, former commandant of Petrograd, for whose arrest the Military Revolutionary Committee would have paid a fortune.

"Our programme?" said the officer. "This is it. Land to be turned over to the Land Committees. Workmen to have full representation in the control of industry. An energetic peace programme, but not an ultimatum to the world such as the Bolsheviki issued. The Bolsheviki cannot keep their promises to the masses, even in the country itself. We won't let them.... They stole our land programme in order to get the support of the peasants. That is dishonest. If they had waited for the Constituent Assembly-"

"It doesn't matter about the Constituent Assembly!" broke in the officer. "If the Bolsheviki want to establish a Socialist state here, we cannot work with them in any event! Kerensky made the great mistake. He let the Bolsheviki know what he was going to do by announcing in the Council of the Republic that he had ordered their arrest...."

"But what," I said, "do you intend to do now?"

The two men looked at one another. "You will see in a few days. If there are enough troops from the front on our side, we shall not compromise with the Bolsheviki. If not, perhaps we shall be forced to...."

Out again on the Nevsky we swung on the step of a streetcar bulging with people, its platforms bent down from the weight and scraping along the ground, which crawled with agonising slowness the long miles to Smolny.

Meshkovsky, a neat, frail little man, was coming down the hall, looking worried. The strikes in the Ministries, he told us, were having their effect. For instance, the Council of People's Commissars had promised to publish the Secret Treaties; but Neratov, the functionary in charge, had disappeared, taking the documents with him. They were supposed to be hidden in the British Embassy....

Worst of all, however, was the strike in the banks. "Without money," said Menzhinsky, "we are helpless. The wages of the railroad men, of the postal and telegraph employees, must be paid.... The banks are closed; and the key to the situation, the State Bank, is also shut. All the bank-clerks in Russia have been bribed to stop work...."

"But Lenin has issued an order to dynamite the State Bank vaults, and there is a Decree just out, ordering the private banks to open to-morrow, or we will open them ourselves!"

The Petrograd Soviet was in full swing, thronged with armed men, Trotzky reporting:

"The Cossacks are falling back from Krasnoye Selo." (Sharp, exultant cheering.) "But the battle is only beginning. At Pulkovo heavy fighting is going on. All available forces must be hurried there....

"From Moscow, bad news. The Kremlin is in the hands of the *yunkers,* and the workers have only a few arms. The result depends upon Petrograd.

"At the front, the decrees on Peace and Land are provoking great enthusiasm. Kerensky is flooding the trenches with tales of Petrograd burning and bloody, of women and children massacred by the Bolsheviki. But no one believes him....

"The cruisers *Oleg, Avrora* and *Respublica* are anchored in the Neva, their guns trained on the approaches to the city...."

"Why aren't you out there with the Red Guards?" shouted a rough voice.

"I'm going now!" answered Trotzky, and left the platform. His face a little paler than usual, he passed down the side of the room, e room, | | surrounded by eager friends, and hurried out to the waiting automobile.

Kameniev now spoke, describing the proceedings of the reconciliation conference. The armistice conditions proposed by the Mensheviki, he said, had been contemptuously rejected. Even the branches of the Railwaymen's Union had voted against such a proposition....

"Now that we've won the power and are sweeping all Russia," he declared, "all they ask of us are three little things: 1. To surrender the power. 2. To make the soldiers continue the war. 3. To make the peasants forget about the land...."

Lenin appeared for a moment, to answer the accusations of the Socialist Revolutionaries:

"They charge us with stealing their land programme.... If that is so, we bow to them. It is good enough for us...."

So the meeting roared on, leader after leader explaining, exhorting, arguing, soldier after soldier, workman after workman, standing up to speak his mind and his heart.... The audience flowed, changing and renewed continually. From time to time men came in, yelling for the members of such and such a detachment, to go to the front; others, relieved, wounded, or coming to Smolny for arms and equipment, poured in....

It was almost three o'clock in the morning when, as we left the hall, Holtzman, of the Military Revolutionary Committee, came running down the hall with a transfigured face.

"It's all right!" he shouted, grabbing my hands. "Telegram from the front. Kerensky is smashed! Look at this!"

He held out a sheet of paper, scribbled hurriedly in pencil, and then, seeing we couldn't read it, he declaimed aloud:

Pulkovo. Staff. 2.10 A.M.

The night of October 30th to 31st will go down in history. The attempt of Kerensky to move counter-revolutionary troops against the capital of the Revolution has been decisively repulsed. Kerensky is retreating, we are advancing. The soldiers, sailors and workers of Petrograd have shown that they can and will with arms in their hands enforce the will and authority of the democracy. The bourgeoisie tried to isolate the revolutionary army. Kerensky attempted to break it by the force of the Cossacks. Both plans met a pitiful defeat.

The grand idea of the domination of the worker and peasant democracy closed the ranks of the army and hardened its will. All the country from now on will be convinced that the Power of the Soviets is no ephemeral thing, but an invincible fact.... The repulse of Kerensky is the repulse of the land-owners, the bourgeoisie and the Kornilovists in general. The repulse of Kerensky is the confirmation of the right of the people to a peaceful free life, to land, bread and power. The Pulkovo detachment by its valorous blow has strengthened the cause of the Workers' and Peasants's Revolution. There is no return to the past. Before us are struggles, obstacles and sacrifices. But the road is clear and victory is certain.

Revolutionary Russia and the Soviet Power can be proud of their
Pulkovo detachment, acting under the command of Colonel Walden.
Eternal memory to those who fell! Glory to the warriors of the
Revolution, the soldiers and the officers who were faithful to the
People!

Long live revolutionary, popular, Socialist Russia!

In the name of the Council,

L. TROTZKY, People's Commissar....

Driving home across Znamensky Square, we made out an unusual crowd in front of the Nicolai Railway Station. Several thousand sailors were massed there, bristling with rifles.

Standing on the steps, a member of the *Vikzhel* was pleading with them.

"Comrades, we cannot carry you to Moscow. We are neutral. We do not carry troops for either side. We cannot take you to Moscow, where already there is terrible civil war...."

All the seething Square roared at him; the sailors began to surge forward. Suddenly another door was flung wide; in it stood two or three brakeman, a fireman or so.

"This way, comrades!" cried one. "We will take you to Moscow-or Vladivostok, if you like! Long live the Revolution!"

CHAPTER IX

Victory

Order Number I

To the Troops of the Pulkovo Detachment.

November 13, 1917. 38 minutes past 9 a. m.

After a cruel fight the troops of the Pulkovo detachment completely routed the counter-revolutionary forces, who retreated from their positions in disorder, and under cover of Tsarskoye Selo fell back toward Pavlovsk II and Gatchina.

Our advanced units occupied the northeastern extremity of Tsarskoye Selo and the station Alexandrovskaya. The Colpinno detachment was on our left, the Krasnoye Selo detachment to our right.

I ordered the Pulkovo forces to occupy Tsarskoye Selo, to fortify its approaches, especially on the side of Gatchina.

Also to pass and occupy Pavlovskoye, fortifying its southern side, and to take up the railroad as far as Dno.

The troops must take all measures to strengthen the positions occupied by them, arranging trenches and other defensive works.

They must enter into close liaison with the detachments of Colpinno and Krasnoye Selo, and also with the Staff of the Commander in Chief for the Defence of Petrograd.

Signed,

Commander in Chief aver all Forces acting against the Counter-revolutionary Troops of Kerensky,

Lieutenant-Colonel MURAVIOV.

Tuesday morning. But how is this? Only two days ago the Petrograd campagna was full of leaderless bands, wandering aimlessly; without food, without artillery, without a plan. What had fused that disorganised mass of undisciplined Red Guards, and soldiers without officers, into an army obedient to its own elected high command, tempered to meet and break the assault of cannon and Cossack cavalry?

People in revolt have a way of defying military precedent. The ragged armies of the French Revolution are not forgotten-Valmy and the Lines of Weissembourg. Massed against the Soviet forces were *yunkers,* Cossacks, land-owners, nobility, Black Hundreds-the Tsar come again, *Okhrana* and Siberian chains; and the vast and terrible menace of the Germans.... Victory, in the words of Carlyle, meant "Apotheosis and Millennium without end!"

Sunday night, the Commissars of the Military Revolutionary Committee returning desperately from the field, the garrison of Petrograd elected its Committee of Five, its Battle Staff, three soldiers and two officers, all certified free from counter-revolutionary taint. Colonel Muraviov, ex-patriot, was in command-an efficient man, but to be carefully watched. At Colpinno, at Obukhovo, at Pulkovo and Krasnoye Selo were formed provisional detachments, increased in size as the stragglers came in from the surrounding country-mixed soldiers, sailors and Red Guards, parts of regiments, infantry, cavalry and artillery all together, and a few armoured cars.

Day broke, and the pickets of Kerensky's Cossacks came in touch. Scattered rifle-fire, summons to surrender. Over the bleak plain on the cold quiet air spread the sound of battle, falling upon the ears of roving bands as they gathered about their little fires, waiting.... So it was beginning! They made toward the battle; and the worker hordes pouring out along the straight roads quickened their pace.... Thus upon all the points of attack automatically converged angry human swarms, to be met by Commissars and assigned positions, or work to do. This was *their* battle, for *their* world; the officers in command were elected by *them*. For the moment that incoherent multiple will was one will....

Those who participated in the fighting described to me how the sailors fought until they ran out of cartridges, and then stormed; how the untrained workmen rushed the charging Cossacks and tore them from their horses; how the anonymous hordes of the people, gathering in the darkness around the battle, rose like a tide and poured over the enemy.... Before midnight of Monday the Cossacks broke and were fleeing, leaving their artillery behind them, and the army of the proletariat, on a long ragged front, moved forward and rolled into Tsarskoye, before the enemy had a chance to destroy the great Government wireless station, from which now the Commissars of Smolny were hurling out to the world paeans of triumph....

TO ALL SOVIETS OF WORKERS' AND SOLDIERS' DEPUTIES

The 12th of November, in a bloody combat near Tsarskoye Selo, the revolutionary army defeated the counter-revolutionary troops of Kerensky and Kornilov. In the name of the Revolutionary Government I order all regiments to take the offensive against the enemies of the revolutionary democracy, and to take all measures to arrest Kerensky, and also to oppose any adventure which might menace the conquests of the Revolution and the victory of the proletariat.

151

Long live the Revolutionary Army!
MURAVIOV.

News from the provinces....

At Sevastopol the local Soviet had assumed the power; a huge meeting of the sailors on the battleships in the harbour had forced their officers to line up and swear allegiance to the new Government. At Nizhni Novgorod the Soviet was in control. From Kazan came reports of a battle in the streets, *yunkers* and a brigade of artillery against the Bolshevik garrison....

Desperate fighting had broken out again in Moscow. The *yunkers* and White Guards held the Kremlin and the centre of the town, beaten upon from all sides by the troops of the Military Revolutionary Committee. The Soviet artillery was stationed in Skobeliev Square, bombarding the City Duma building, the Prefecture and the Hotel Metropole. The cobblestones of the Tverskaya and Nikitskaya had been torn up for trenches and barricades. A hail of machine-gun fire swept the quarters of the great banks and commercial houses. There were no lights, no telephones; the bourgeois population lived in the cellars.... The last bulletin said that the Military Revolutionary Committee had delivered an ultimatum to the Committee of Public Safety, demanding the immediate surrender of the Kremlin, or bombardment would follow.

"Bombard the Kremlin?" cried the ordinary citizen. "They dare not!"

From Vologda to Chita in far Siberia, from Pskov to Sevastopol on the Black Sea, in great cities and little villages, civil war burst into flame. From thousands of factories, peasant communes, regiments and armies, ships on the wide sea, greetings poured into Petrograd-greetings to the Government of the People.

The Cossack Government at Novotcherkask telegraphed to Kerensky, *"The Government of the Cossack troops invites the Provisional Government and the members of the Council of the Republic to come, if possible, to Novotcherkask, where we can organise in common the struggle against the Bolsheviki."*

In Finland, also, things were stirring. The Soviet of Helsingfors and the *Tsentrobalt* (Central Committee of the Baltic Fleet), jointly proclaimed a state of siege, and declared that all attempts to interfere with the Bolshevik forces, and all armed resistance to its orders, would be severely repressed. At the same time the Finnish Railway Union called a countrywide general strike, to put into operation the laws passed by the Socialist Diet of June, 1917, dissolved by Kerensky....

Early in the morning I went out to Smolny. Going up the long wooden sidewalk from the outer gate I saw the first thin, hesitating snow-flakes fluttering down from the grey, windless sky. "Snow!" cried the soldier at the door, grinning with delight. "Good for the health!" Inside, the long, gloomy halls and bleak rooms seemed deserted. No one moved in all the enormous pile. A deep, uneasy sound came to my ears, and looking around, I noticed that everywhere on the floor, along the walls, men were sleeping. Rough, dirty men, workers and soldiers, spattered and caked with mud, sprawled alone or in heaps, in the careless attitudes of death. Some wore ragged bandages marked with blood. Guns and cartridge-belts were scattered about.... The victorious proletarian army!

In the upstairs buffet so thick they lay that one could hardly walk. The air was foul. Through the clouded windows a pale light streamed. A battered samovar, cold, stood on the counter, and many glasses holding dregs of tea. Beside them lay a copy of the Military Revolutionary Committee's last bulletin, upside down, scrawled with painful hand-writing. It was a memorial written by some soldier to his comrades fallen in the fight against Kerensky, just as he had set it down before falling on the floor to sleep. The writing was blurred with what looked like tears....

Alexei Vinogradov

D. Maskvin

S. Stolbikov

A. Voskressensky

D. Leonsky

D. Preobrazhensky

V. Laidansky

M. Berchikov

These men were drafted into the Army on November 15th, 1916. Only three are left of the above.

Mikhail Berchikov

Alexei Voskressensky

Dmitri Leonsky

Sleep, Warrior eagles, sleep with peaceful soul.

You have deserved, our own ones, happiness and

Eternal peace. Under the earth of the grave

You have straitly closed your ranks. Sleep, Citizens!

Only the Military Revolutionary Committee still functioned, unsleeping. Skripnik, emerging from the inner room, said that Gotz had been arrested, but had flatly denied signing the proclamation of the Committee for Salvation, as had Avksentiev; and the Committee for Salvation itself had repudiated the Appeal to the garrison. There was still disafiection among the city regiments, Skripnik reported; the Volhynsky Regiment had refused to fight against Kerensky.

Several detachments of "neutral" troops, with Tchernov at their head, were at Gatchina, trying to persuade Kerensky to halt his attack on Petrograd.

Skripnik laughed. "There can be no 'neutrals' now," he said. "We've won!" His sharp, bearded face glowed with an almost religious exaltation. "More than sixty delegates have arrived from the Front, with assurances of support by all the armies except the troops on the Rumanian front, who have not been heard from. The Army Committees have suppressed all news from Petrograd, but we now have a regular system of couriers...."

[Graphic page-224 Certificate approving telegram transmission]
Order given me at Staff headquarters by command of the Council of
People's Commissars, to transmit the first despatch out of Perograd
after the November Revolution, over the Government wires to America.
                    (Translation)
          STAFF
Military Revolutionary
          Commitee
Sov. W. & S. D.
2 November, 1917
          No. 1860
                    CERTIFICATE
Is given by the present to the journalist of
the New York Socialist press JOHN REED, that the text of the
telegram (herewith) has been examined by the Government of People's
Commissars, and there is no objection to its transmission, and also
it is recommended that all cooperate in every way to transmit same
to its destination.
                    For the Commander in Chief, ANTONOV
                    Chief of Staff, VLAD. BONCH-BRUEVITCH

Down in the front hall Kameniev was just entering, worn out by the all-night session of the Conference to Form a New Government, but happy. "Already the Socialist Revolutionaries are inclined to admit us into the new Government," he told me. "The right wing groups are frightened by the Revolutionary Tribunals; they demand, in a sort of panic, that we dissolve them before going any further. ... We have accepted the proposition of the *Vikzhel* to form a homogeneous Socialist Ministry, and they're working on that now. You see, it all springs from our victory. When we were down, they would't have us at any price; not everybody's in favour of some agreement with the Soivets.... What we need is a really decisive victory. Kerensky wants an armistice, but he'll have to surrender ...."

That was the temper of the Bolshevik leaders. To a foreign journalist who asked Trotzky what statement he had to make to the world, Trotzky replied: "At this moment the only statement possible is the one we are making through the mouths of our cannon!"

But there was an undercurrent of real anxiety in the tide of victory; the question of finances. Instead of opening the banks, as had been ordered by the Military Revolutionary Committee, the Union of Bank Employees had held a meeting and declared a formal strike. Smolny had demanded some thirty-five millions of rubles from the State Bank, and the cashier had locked the vaults, only paying out money to the representatives of the Provisional Government. The reactionaries were using the State Bank as a political weapon; for instance, when the *Vikzhel* demanded money to pay the salaries of the employees of the Government railroads, it was told to apply to Smolny....

I went to the State Bank to see the new Commissar, a redhaired Ukrainean Bolshevik named Petrovitch. He was trying to bring order out of the chaos in which affairs had been left by the striking clerks. In all the offices of the huge place perspiring volunteer workers, soldiers and sailors, their tongues sticking out of their mouths in the intensity of their effort, were poring over the great ledgers with a bewildered air....

The Duma building was crowded. There were still isolated cases of defiance toward the new Government, but they were rare. The Central Land Committee had appealed to the Peasants, ordering them not to recognise the Land Decree passed by the Congress of the Soviets, because it would cause confusion and civil war. Mayor Schreider announced that because of the Bolshevik insurrection, the elections to the Constituent Assembly would have to be indefinitely postponed.

Two questions seemed to be uppermost in all minds, shocked by the ferocity of the civil war; first, a truce to the bloodshed -second, the creation of a new Government. There was no longer any talk of "destroying the Bolsheviki"-and very little about excluding them from the Government, except from the Populist Socialists and the Peasants' Soviets. Even the Central Army Committee at the *Stavka,* the most determined enemy of Smolny, telephoned from Moghilev: "If, to constitute the new Ministry, it is necessary to come to an understanding with the Bolsheviki, we agree to admit them *in a minority* to the Cabinet."

155

Pravda, ironically calling attention to Kerensky's "humanitarian sentiments," published his despatch to the Committee for Salvation:

In accord with the proposals of the Committee for Salvation and all the democratic organisations united around it, I have halted all military action against the rebels. A delegate of the Committee has been sent to enter into negotiations. Take all measures to stop the useless shedding of blood.

The *Vikzhel* sent a telegram to all Russia:

The Conference of the Union of Railway Workers with the representatives of both the belligerent parties, who admit the necessity of an agreement, protest energetically against the use of political terrorism in the civil war, especially when it is carried on between different factions of the revolutionary democracy, and declare that political terrorism, in whatever form, is in contradiction to the very idea of the negotiations for a new Government....

[Graphic page-227 Leaflet]

Popular leaflet sold in the streets just after the Bolshevik insurrection, containing rhymes and jokes about the defeated bourgeoisie and the "moderate" Socialist leaders, Called, "How THE BOORZHUI (BOURGEOISIE) LOST THE POWER."

Delegations from the Conference were sent to the Front, to Gatchina. In the Conference itself everything seemed on the point of final settlement. It had even been decided to elect a Provisional People's Council, composed of about four hundred members-seventy-five representing Smolny, seventy-five the old *Tsay-ee-kah,* and the rest split up among the Town Dumas, the Trade Unions, Land Committees and political parties. Tchernov was mentioned as the new Premier. Lenin and Trotzky, rumour said, were to be excluded....

About noon I was again in front of Smolny, talking with the driver of an ambulance bound for the revolutionary front. Could I go with him? Certainly! He was a volunteer, a University student, and as we rolled down the street shouted over his shoulder to me phrases of execrable German: *"Also, gut! Wir nach die Kasernen zu essen gehen!"* I made out that there would be lunch at some barracks.

On the Kirotchnaya we turned into an immense courtyard surrounded by military buildings, and mounted a dark stairway to a low room lit by one window. At a long wooden table were seated some twenty soldiers, eating *shtchi* (cabbage soup) from a great tin wash-tub with wooden spoons, and talking loudly with much laughter.

"Welcome to the Battalion Committee of the Sixth Reserve Engineers' Battalion!" cried my friend, and introduced me as an American Socialist. Whereat every one rose to shake my hand, and one old soldier put his arms around me and gave me a hearty kiss. A wooden spoon was produced and I took my place at the table. Another tub, full of *kasha,* was brought in, a huge loaf of black bread, and of course the inevitable tea-pots. At once every one began asking me questions about America: Was it true that people in a free country sold their votes for *money?* If so, how did they get what they wanted? How about this "Tammany"? Was it true that in a free country a little group of people could control a whole city, and exploited it for their personal benefit? Why did the people stand it? Even under the Tsar such things could not happen in Russia; true, here there was always graft, but to buy and sell a whole city full of people! And in a free country! Had the people no revolutionary feeling? I tried to explain that in my country people tried to change things by law.

"Of course," nodded a young sergeant, named Baklanov, who spoke French. "But you have a highly developed capitalist class? Then the capitalist class must control the legislatures and the courts. How then can the people change things? I am open to conviction, for I do not know your country; but to me it is incredible...."

I said that I was going to Tsarskoye Selo. "I, too," said Baklanov, suddenly. "And I-and I-" The whole roomful decided on the spot to go to Tsarskoye Selo.

Just then came a knock on the door. It opened, and in it stood the figure of the Colonel. No one rose, but all shouted a greeting. "May I come in?" asked the Colonel. "*Prosim! Prosim!*" they answered heartily. He entered, smiling, a tall, distinguished figure in a goat-skin cape embroidered with gold. "I think I heard you say that you were going to Tsarskoye Selo, comrades," he said. "Could I go with you?"

Baklanov considered. "I do not think there is anything to be done here to-day," he answered. "Yes, comrade, we shall be very glad to have you." The Colonel thanked him and sat down, filling a glass of tea.

In a low voice, for fear of wounding the Colonel's pride, Baklanov explained to me. "You see, I am the chairman of the Committee. We control the Battalion absolutely, except in action, when the Colonel is delegated by us to command. In action his orders must be obeyed, but he is strictly responsible to us. In barracks he must ask our permission before taking any action.... You might call him our Executive Officer...."

Arms were distributed to us, revolvers and rifles-"we might meet some Cossacks, you know"-and we all piled into the ambulance, together with three great bundles of newspapers for the front. Straight down the Liteiny we rattled, and along the Zagorodny Prospekt. Next to me sat a youth with the shoulder-straps of a Lieutenant, who seemed to speak all European languages with equal fluency. He was a member of the Battalion Committee.

"I am not a Bolshevik," he assured me, emphatically. "My family is a very ancient and noble one. I, myself, am, you might say, a Cadet...."

"But how—?" I began, bewildered.

"Oh, yes, I am a member of the Committee. I make no secret of my political opinions, but the others do not mind, because they know I do not believe in opposing the will of the majority.... I have refused to take any action in the present civil war, however, for I do not believe in taking up arms against my brother Russians...."

"Provocator! Kornilovitz!" the others cried at him gaily, slapping him on the shoulder....

Passing under the huge grey stone archway of the Moskovsky Gate, covered with golden hieroglyphics, ponderous Imperial eagles and the names of Tsars, we sped out on the wide straight highway, grey with the first light fall of snow. It was thronged with Red Guards, stumbling along on foot toward the revolutionary front, shouting and singing; and others, greyfaced and muddy, coming back. Most of them seemed to be mere boys. Women with spades, some with rifles and bandoleers, others wearing the Red Cross on their arm-bands-the bowed, toil-worm women of the slums. Squads of soldiers marching out of step, with an affectionate jeer for the Red Guards; sailors, grim-looking; children with bundles of food for their fathers and mothers; all these, coming and going, trudged through the whitened mud that covered the cobbles of the highway inches deep. We passed cannon, jingling southward with their caissons; trucks bound both ways, bristling with armed men; ambulances full of wounded from the direction of the battle, and once a peasant cart, creaking slowly along, in which sat a white-faced boy bent over his shattered stomach and screaming monotonously. In the fields on either side women and old men were digging trenches and stringing barbed wire entanglements.

Back northward the clouds rolled away dramatically, and the pale sun came out. Across the flat, marshy plain Petrograd glittered. To the right, white and gilded and coloured bulbs and pinnacles; to the left, tall chimneys, some pouring out black smoke; and beyond, a lowering sky over Finland. On each side of us were churches, monasteries.... Occasionally a monk was visible, silently watching the pulse of the proletarian army throbbing on the road.

At Pulkovo the road divided, and there we halted in the midst of a great crowd, where the human streams poured from three directions, friends meeting, excited and congratulatory, describing the battle to one another. A row of houses facing the cross-roads was marked with bullets, and the earth was trampled into mud half a mile around. The fighting had been furious here.... In the near distance riderless Cossack horses circled hungrily, for the grass of the plain had died long ago. Right in front of us an awkward Red Guard was trying to ride one, falling off again and again, to the childlike delight of a thousand rough men.

The left road, along which the remnants of the Cossacks had retreated, led up a little hill to a hamlet, where there was a glorious view of the immense plain, grey as a windless sea, tumultuous clouds towering over, and the imperial city disgorging its thousands along all the roads. Far over to the left lay the little hill of Kranoye Selo, the parade-ground of the Imperial Guards' summer camp, and the Imperial Dairy. In the middle distance nothing broke the flat monotony but a few walled monasteries and convents, some isolated factories, and several large buildings with unkempt grounds that were asylums and orphanages....

"Here," said the driver, as we went on over a barren hill, "here was where Vera Slutskaya died. Yes, the Bolshevik member of the Duma. It happened early this morning. She was in an automobile, with Zalkind and another man. There was a truce, and they started for the front trenches. They were talking and laughing, when all of a sudden, from the armoured train in which Kerensky himself was riding, somebody saw the automobile and fired a cannon. The shell struck Vera Slutskaya and killed her...."

And so we came into Tsarskoye, all bustling with the swaggering heroes of the proletarian horde. Now the palace where the Soviet had met was a busy place. Red Guards and sailors filled the court-yard, sentries stood at the doors, and a stream of couriers and Commissars pushed in and out. In the Soviet room a samovar had been set up, and fifty or more workers, soldiers, sailors and officers stood around, drinking tea and talking at the top of their voices. In one corner two clumsy-handed workingmen were trying to make a multigraphing machine go. At the centre table, the huge Dybenko bent over a map, marking out positions for the troops with red and blue pencils. In his free hand he carried, as always, the enormous bluesteel revolver. Anon he sat himself down at a typewriter and pounded away with one finger; every little while he would pause, pick up the revolver, and lovingly spin the chamber.

A couch lay along the wall, and on this was stretched a young workman. Two Red Guards were bending over him, but the rest of the company did not pay any attention. In his breast was a hole; through his clothes fresh blood came welling up with every heart-beat. His eyes were closed and his young, bearded face was greenish-white. Faintly and slowly he still breathed, with every breath sighing, *Mir boudit! Mir boudit!* (Peace is coming! Peace is coming!)"

Dybenko looked up as we came in. "Ah," he said to Baklanov. "Comrade, will you go up to the Commandant's headquarters and take charge? Wait; I will write you credentials." He went to the typewriter and slowly picked out the letters.

The new Commandant of Tsarskoye Selo and I went toward the Ekaterina Palace, Baklanov very excited and important. In the same ornate, white room some Red Guards were rummaging curiously around, while my old friend, the Colonel, stood by the window biting his moustache. He greeted me like a long-lost brother. At a table near the door sat the French Bessarabian. The Bolsheviki had ordered him to remain, and continue his work.

"What could I do?" he muttered. "People like myself cannot fight on either side in such a war as this, no matter how much we may instinctively dislike the dictatorship of the mob.... I only regret that I am so far from my mother in Bessarabia!"

Baklanov was formally taking over the office from the Commandant. "Here," said the Colonel nervously, "are the keys to the desk."

A Red Guard interrupted. "Where's the money?" he asked rudely. The Colonel seemed surprised. "Money? Money? Ah, you mean the chest. There it is," said the Colonel, "just as I found it when I took possession three days ago. Keys?" The Colonel shrugged. "I have no keys."

The Red Guard sneered knowingly. "Very convenient," he said.

"Let us open the chest," said Baklanov. "Bring an axe. Here is an American comrade. Let him smash the chest open, and write down what he finds there."

I swung the axe. The wooden chest was empty.

"Let's arrest him," said the Red Guard, venomously. "He is
Kerensky's man. He has stolen the money and given it to Kerensky."

Baklanov did not want to. "Oh, no," he said. "It was the Kornilovitz before him. He is not to blame.

"The devil!" cried the Red Guard. "He is Kerensky's man, I tell you.
If *you* won't arrest him, then *we* will, and we'll take him to
Petrograd and put him in Peter-Paul, where he belongs!" At this the
other Red Guards growled assent. With a piteous glance at us the
Colonel was led away....

Down in front of the Soviet palace an auto-truck was going to the front. Half a dozen Red Guards, some sailors, and a soldier or two, under command of a huge workman, clambered in, and shouted to me to come along. Red Guards issued from headquarters, each of them staggering under an arm-load of small, corrugated-iron bombs, filled with *grubit*-which, they say, is ten times as strong, and five times as sensitive as dynamite; these they threw into the truck. A three-inch cannon was loaded and then tied onto the tail of the truck with bits of rope and wire.

We started with a shout, at top speed of course; the heavy truck swaying from side to side. The cannon leaped from one wheel to the other, and the *grubit* bombs went rolling back and forth over our feet, fetching up against the sides of the car with a crash.

The big Red Guard, whose name was Vladimir Nicolaievitch, plied me with questions about America. "Why did America come into the war? Are the American workers ready to throw over the capitalists? What is the situation in the Mooney case now? Will they extradite Berkman to San Francisco?" and other, very difficult to answer, all delivered in a shout above the roaring of the truck, while we held on to each other and danced amid the caroming bombs.

Occasionally a patrol tried to stop us. Soldiers ran out into the road before us, shouted *"Shtoi!"* and threw up their guns.

We paid no attention. "The devil take you!" cried the Red Guards. "We don't stop for anybody! We're Red Guards!" And we thundered imperiously on, while Vladimir Nicolaievitch bellowed to me about the internationalisation of the Panama Canal, and such matters....

About five miles out we saw a squad of sailors marching back, and slowed down.

"Where's the front, brothers?"

The foremost sailor halted and scratched his head. "This morning," he said, "it was about half a kilometer down the road. But the damn thing isn't anywhere now. We walked and walked and walked, but we couldn't find it."

They climbed into the truck, and we proceeded. It must have been about a mile further that Vladimir Nicolaievitch cocked his ear and shouted to the chauffeur to stop.

"Firing!" he said. "Do you hear it?" For a moment dead silence, and then, a little ahead and to the left, three shots in rapid succession. Along here the side of the road was heavily wooded. Very much excited now, we crept along, speaking in whispers, until the truck was nearly opposite the place where the firing had come from. Descending, we spread out, and every man carrying his rifle, went stealthily into the forest.

Two comrades, meanwhile, detached the cannon and slewed it around until it aimed as nearly as possible at our backs.

It was silent in the woods. The leaves were gone, and the tree-trunks were a pale wan colour in the low, sickly autumn sun. Not a thing moved, except the ice of little woodland pools shivering under our feet. Was it an ambush?

161

We went uneventfully forward until the trees began to thin, and paused. Beyond, in a little clearing, three soldiers sat around a small fire, perfectly oblivious.

Vladimir Nicolaievitch stepped forward. *"Zra'zvuitye,* comrades!" he greeted, while behind him one cannon, twenty rifles and a truck-load of *grubit* bombs hung by a hair. The soldiers scrambled to their feet.

"What was the shooting going on around here?"

One of the soldiers answered, looking relieved, "Why we were just shooting a rabbit or two, comrade...."

The truck hurtled on toward Romanov, through the bright, empty day. At the first cross-roads two soldiers ran out in front of us, waving their rifles. We slowed down, and stopped.

"Passes, comrades!"

The Red Guards raised a great clamour. "We are Red Guards. We don't need any passes.... Go on, never mind them!"

But a sailor objected. "This is wrong, comrades. We must have revolutionary discipline. Suppose some counterrevolutionaries came along in a truck and said: 'We don't need any passes?' The comrades don't know you."

At this there was a debate. One by one, however, the sailors and soldiers joined with the first. Grumbling, each Red Guard produced his dirty *bumaga* (paper). All were alike except mine, which had been issued by the Revolutionary Staff at Smolny. The sentries declared that I must go with them. The Red Guards objected strenuously, but the sailor who had spoken first insisted. "This comrade we know to be a true comrade," he said. "But there are orders of the Committee, and these orders must be obeyed. That is revolutionary discipline...."

In order not to make any trouble, I got down from the truck, and watched it disappear careening down the road, all the company waving farewell. The soldiers consulted in low tones for a moment, and then led me to a wall, against which they placed me. It flashed upon me suddenly; they were going to shoot me!

In all three directions not a human being was in sight. The only sign of life was smoke from the chimney of a *datchya,* a rambling wooden house a quarter of a mile up the side road. The two soldiers were walking out into the road. Desperately I ran after them.

"But comrades! See! Here is the seal of the Military Revolutionary Committee!"

They stared stupidly at my pass, then at each other.

"It is different from the others," said one, sullenly. "We cannot read, brother."

I took him by the arm. "Come!" I said. "Let's go to that house. Some one there can surely read." They hesitated. "No," said one. The other looked me over. "Why not?" he muttered. "After all, it is a serious crime to kill an innocent man."

We walked up to the front door of the house and knocked. A short, stout woman opened it, and shrank back in alarm, babbling, "I don't know anything about them! I don't know anything about them!" One of my guards held out the pass. She screamed. "Just to read it, comrade." Hesitatingly she took the paper and read aloud, swiftly:

The bearer of this pass, John Reed, is a representative of the American Social-Democracy, an internationalist....

Out on the road again the two soldiers held another consultation. "We must take you to the Regimental Committee," they said. In the fast-deepening twilight we trudged along the muddy road. Occasionally we met squads of soldiers, who stopped and surrounded me with looks of menace, handling my pass around and arguing violently as to whether or not I should be killed....

It was dark when we came to the barracks of the Second Tsarskoye Selo Rifles, low sprawling buildings huddled along the post-road. A number of soldiers slouching at the entrance asked eager questions. A spy? A provocator? We mounted a winding stair and emerged into a great, bare room with a huge stove in the centre, and rows of cots on the floor, where about a thousand soldiers were playing cards, talking, singing, and asleep. In the roof was a jagged hole made by Kerensky's cannon....

I stood in the doorway, and a sudden silence ran among the groups, who turned and stared at me. Of a sudden they began to move, slowly and then with a rush, thundering, with faces full of hate. "Comrades! Comrades!" yelled one of my guards. "Committee! Committee!" The throng halted, banked around me, muttering. Out of them shouldered a lean youth, wearing a red arm-band.

"Who is this?" he asked roughly. The guards explained. "Give me the paper!" He read it carefully, glancing at me with keen eyes. Then he smiled and handed me the pass. "Comrades, this is an American comrade. I am Chairman of the Committee, and I welcome you to the Regiment...." A sudden general buzz grew into a roar of greeting, and they pressed forward to shake my hand.

"You have not dined? Here we have had our dinner. You shall go to the Officers' Club, where there are some who speak your language...."

He led me across the court-yard to the door of another building. An aristocratic-looking youth, with the shoulder straps of a Lieutenant, was entering. The Chairman presented me, and shaking hands, went back.

"I am Stepan Georgevitch Morovsky, at your service," said the Lieutenant, in perfect French. From the ornate entrance hall a ceremonial staircase led upward, lighted by glittering lustres. On the second floor billiard-rooms, card-rooms, a library opened from the hall. We entered the dining-room, at a long table in the centre of which sat about twenty officers in full uniform, wearing their gold- and silver-handled swords, the ribbons and crosses of Imperial decorations. All rose politely as I entered, and made a place for me beside the Colonel, a large, impressive man with a grizzled beard. Orderlies were deftly serving dinner. The atmosphere was that of any officers' mess in Europe. Where was the Revolution?

"You are not Bolsheviki?" I asked Morovsky.

A smile went around the table, but I caught one or two glancing furtively at the orderly.

"No," answered my friend. "There is only one Bolshevik officer in this regiment. He is in Petrograd to-night. The Colonel is a Menshevik. Captain Kherlov there is a Cadet. I myself am a Socialist Revolutionary of the right wing.... I should say that most of the officers in the Army are not Bolsheviki, but like me they believe in democracy; they believe that they must follow the soldier-masses...."

Dinner over, maps were brought, and the Colonel spread them out on the table. The rest crowded around to see.

"Here," said the Colonel, pointing to pencil marks, "were our positions this morning. Vladimir Kyrilovitch, where is your company?"

Captain Kherlov pointed. "According to orders, we occupied the position along this road. Karsavin relieved me at five o'clock."

Just then the door of the room opened, and there entered the Chairman of the Regimental Committee, with another soldier. They joined the group behind the Colonel, peering at the map. map. | |

"Good," said the Colonel. "Now the Cossacks have fallen back ten kilometres in our sector. I do not think it is necessary to take up advanced positions. Gentlemen, for to-night you will hold the present line, strengthening the positions by—"

"If you please," interrupted the Chairman of the Regimental Committee. "The orders are to advance with all speed, and prepare to engage the Cossacks north of Gatchina in the morning. A crushing defeat is necessary. Kindly make the proper dispositions."

There was a short silence. The Colonel again turned to the map. "Very well," he said, in a different voice. "Stepan Georgevitch, you will please—" Rapidly tracing lines with a blue pencil, he gave his orders, while a sergeant made shorthand notes. The sergeant then withdrew, and ten minutes later returned with the orders typewritten, and one carbon copy. The Chairman of the Committee studied the map with a copy of the orders before him.

"All right," he said, rising. Folding the carbon copy, he put it in his pocket. Then he signed the other, stamped it with a round seal taken from his pocket, and presented it to the Colonel....

Here was the Revolution!

I returned to the Soviet palace in Tsarskoye in the Regimental Staff automobile. Still the crowds of workers, soldiers and sailors pouring in and out, still the choking press of trucks, armoured cars, cannon before the door, and the shouting, the laughter of unwonted victory. Half a dozen Red Guards forced their way through, a priest in the middle. This was Father Ivan, they said, who had blessed the Cossacks when they entered the town. I heard afterward that he was shot....

Dybenko was just coming out, giving rapid orders right and left. In his hand he carried the big revolver. An automobile stood with racing engine at the kerb. Alone, he climbed in the rear seat, and was off-off to Gatchina, to conquer Kerensky.

Toward nightfall he arrived at the outskirts of the town, and went on afoot. What Dybenko told the Cossacks nobody knows, but the fact is that General Krasnov and his staff and several thousand Cossacks surrendered, and advised Kerensky to do the same.

As for Kerensky-I reprint here the deposition made by General Krasnov on the morning of November 14th:

"Gatchina, November 14, 1917. To-day, about three o'clock (A. M.), I was summoned by the Supreme Commander (Kerensky). He was very agitated, and very nervous.

"'General,' he said to me, 'you have betrayed me. Your Cossacks declare categorically that they will arrest me and deliver me to the sailors.'

"'Yes,' I answered, 'there is talk of it, and I know that you have no sympathy anywhere.'

"'But the officers say the same thing.'

"'Yes, most of all it is the officers who are discontented with you.'

"'What shall I do? I ought to commit suicide!'

"'If you are an honorable man, you will go immediately to Petrograd with a white flag, you will present yourself to the Military Revolutionary Committee, and enter into negotiations as Chief of the Provisional Government.'

"'All right. I will do that, General.'

"'I will give you a guard and ask that a sailor go with you.'

"'No, no, not a sailor. Do you know whether it is true that Dybenko is here?'

"'I don't know who Dybenko is.'

"'He is my enemy.

"'There is nothing to do. If you play for high stakes you must know how to take a chance.'

"'Yes. I'll leave to-night!'

"'Why? That would be a flight. Leave calmly and openly, so that every one can see that you are not running away.'

"'Very well. But you must give me a guard on which I can count.'

"'Good.'

"I went out and called the Cossack Russkov, of the Tenth Regiment of the Don, and ordered him to pick out ten Cossacks to accompany the Supreme Commander. Half an hour later the Cossacks came to tell me that Kerensky was not in his quarters, that he had run away.

"I gave the alarm and ordered that he be searched for, supposing that he could not have left Gatchina, but he could not be found...."

And so Kerensky fled, alone, "disguised in the uniform of a sailor," and by that act lost whatever popularity he had retained among the Russian masses....

I went back to Petrograd riding on the front seat of an auto truck, driven by a workman and filled with Red Guards. We had no kerosene, so our lights were not burning. The road was crowded with the proletarian army going home, and new reserves pouring out to take their places. Immense trucks like ours, columns of artillery, wagons, loomed up in the night, without lights, as we were. We hurtled furiously on, wrenched right and left to avoid collisions that seemed inevitable, scraping wheels, followed by the epithets of pedestrians.

Across the horizon spread the glittering lights of the capital, immeasurably more splendid by night than by day, like a dike of jewels heaped on the barren plain.

The old workman who drove held the wheel in one hand, while with the other he swept the far-gleaming capital in an exultant gesture.

"Mine!" he cried, his face all alight. "All mine now! My Petrograd!"

CHAPTER X

Moscow

The Military Revolutionary Committee, with a fierce intensity, followed up its victory:

November 14th.

To all Army, corps, divisional and regimental Committees, to all Soviets of Workers', Soldiers' and Peasants' Deputies, to all, all, all.

Conforming to the agreement between the Cossacks, *yunkers,* soldiers, sailors and workers, it has been decided to arraign Alexander Feodorvitch Kerensky before a tribunal of the people. We demand that Kerensky be arrested, and that he be ordered, in the name of the organisations hereinafter mentioned, to come immediately to Petrograd and present himself to the tribunal.

Signed,

The Cossacks of the First Division of Ussuri Cavalry; the Committee of Yunkers of the Petrograd detachment of Franc-Tireurs; the delegate of the Fifth Army.

People's Commissar DYBENKO.

The Committee for Salvation, the Duma, the Central Committee of the Socialist Revolutionary party-proudly claiming Kerensky as a member-all passionately protested that he could only be held responsible to the Constituent Assembly.

On the evening of November 16th I watched two thousand Red Guards swing down the Zagorodny Prospekt behind a military band playing the *Marseillaise*-and how appropriate it sounded-with blood-red flags over the dark ranks of workmen, to welcome home again their brothers who had defended "Red Petrograd." In the bitter dusk they tramped, men and women, their tall bayonets swaying; through streets faintly lighted and slippery with mud, between silent crowds of bourgeois, contemptuous but fearful....

All were against them-business men, speculators, investors, land-owners, army officers, politicians, teachers, students, professional men, shop-keepers, clerks, agents. The other Socialist parties hated the Bolsheviki with an implacable hatred. On the side of the Soviets were the rank and file of the workers, the sailors, all the undemoralised soldiers, the landless peasants, and a few-a very few-intellectuals....

From the farthest corners of great Russia, whereupon desperate street-fighting burst like a wave, news of Kerensky's defeat came echoing back the immense roar of proletarian victory. Kazan, Saratov, Novgorod, Vinnitza-where the streets had run with blood; Moscow, where the Bolsheviki had turned their artillery against the last strong-hold of the bourgeoisie-the Kremlin.

"They are bombarding the Kremlin!" The news passed from mouth to mouth in the streets of Petrograd, almost with a sense of terror. Travellers from "white and shining little mother Moscow" told fearful tales. Thousands killed; the Tverskaya and the Kuznetsky Most in flames; the church of Vasili Blazheiny a smoking ruin; Usspensky Cathedral crumbling down; the Spasskaya Gate of the Kremlin tottering; the Duma burned to the ground.

Nothing that the Bolsheviki had done could compare with this fearful blasphemy in the heart of Holy Russia. To the ears of the devout sounded the shock of guns crashing in the face of the Holy Orthodox Church, and pounding to dust the sanctuary of the Russian nation....

On November 15th, Lunatcharsky, Commissar of Education, broke into tears at the session of the Council of People's Commissars, and rushed from the room, crying, "I cannot stand it! I cannot bear the monstrous destruction of beauty and tradition...."

That afternoon his letter of resignation was published in the newspapers:

I have just been informed, by people arriving from Moscow, what has happened there.

The Cathedral of St. Basil the Blessed, the Cathedral of the Assumption, are being bombarded. The Kremlin, where are now gathered the most important art treasures of Petrograd and of Moscow, is under artillery fire. There are thousands of victims.

The fearful struggle there has reached a pitch of bestial ferocity.

What is left? What more can happen?

I cannot bear this. My cup is full. I am unable to endure these horrors. It is impossible to work under the pressure of thoughts which drive me mad!

That is why I am leaving the Council of People's Commissars.

I fully realise the gravity of this decision. But I can bear no more....

That same day the White Guards and *yunkers* in the Kremlin surrendered, and were allowed to march out unharmed. The treaty of peace follows:

1. The Committee of Public Safety ceases to exist.

2. The White Guard gives up its arms and dissolves. The officers retain their swords and regulations side-arms. In the Military Schools are retained only the arms necessary for instruction; all others are surrendered by the *yunkers*. The Military Revolutionary Committee guarantees the liberty and inviolability of the person.

3. To settle the question of disarmament, as set forth in section 2, a special commission is appointed, consisting of representatives from all organisations which took part in the peace negotiations.

4. From the moment of the signature of this peace treaty, both parties shall immediately give order to cease firing and halt all military operations, taking measures to ensure punctual obedience to this order.

5. At the signature of the treaty, all prisoners made by the two parties shall be released....

For two days now the Bolsheviki had been in control of the city. The frightened citizens were creeping out of their cellars to seek their dead; the barricades in the streets were being removed. Instead of diminishing, however, the stories of destruction in Moscow continued to grow.... And it was under the influence of these fearful reports that we decided to go there.

Petrograd, after all, in spite of being for a century the seat of Government, is still an artificial city. Moscow is real Russia, Russia as it was and will be; in Moscow we would get the true feeling of the Russian people about the Revolution. Life was more intense there.

For the past week the Petrograd Military Revolutionary Committee, aided by the rank and file of the Railway Workers, had seized control of the Nicolai Railroad, and hurled trainload after trainload of sailors and Red Guards southwest.... We were provided with passes from Smolny, without which no one could leave the capital.... When the train backed into the station, a mob of shabby soldiers, all carrying huge sacks of eatables, stormed the doors, smashed the windows, and poured into all the compartments, filling up the aisles and even climbing onto the roof. Three of us managed to wedge our way into a compartment, but almost immediately about twenty soldiers entered.... There was room for only four people; we argued, expostulated, and the conductor joined us-but the soldiers merely laughed. Were they to bother about the comfort of a lot of *boorzhui* (bourgeois)? We produced the passes from Smolny; instantly the soldiers changed their attitude.

"Come, comrades," cried one, "these are American *tovarishtchi*. They have come thirty thousand versts to see our Revolution, and they are naturally tired...."

With polite and friendly apologies the soldiers began to leave. Shortly afterward we heard them breaking into a compartment occupied by two stout, well-dressed Russians, who had bribed the conductor and locked their door....

About seven o'clock in the evening we drew out of the station, an immense long train drawn by a weak little locomotive burning wood, and stumbled along slowly, with many stops. The soldiers on the roof kicked with their heels and sang whining peasant songs; and in the corridor, so jammed that it was impossible to pass, violent political debates raged all night long. Occasionally the conductor came through, as a matter of habit, looking for tickets. He found very few except ours, and after a half-hour of futile wrangling, lifted his arms despairingly and withdrew. The atmosphere was stifling, full of smoke and foul odours; if it hadn't been for the broken windows we would doubtless have smothered during the night.

In the morning, hours late, we looked out upon a snowy world. It was bitter cold. About noon a peasant woman got on with a basket-full of bread-chunks and a great can of luke warm coffee-substitute. From then on until dark there was nothing but the packed train, jolting and stopping, and occasional stations where a ravenous mob swooped down on the scantily-furnished buffet and swept it clean.... At one of these halts I ran into Nogin and Rykov, the seceding Commissars, who were returning to Moscow to put their grievances before their own Soviet, 1and further along was Bukharin, a short, red-bearded man with the eyes of a fanatic-"more Left than Lenin," they said of him....

Then the three strokes of the bell and we made a rush for the train, worming our way through the packed and noisy aisle.... A good-natured crowd, bearing the discomfort with humorous patience, interminably arguing about everything from the situation in Petrograd to the British Trade-Union system, and disputing loudly with the few *boorzhui* who were on board. Before we reached Moscow almost every car had organised a Committee to secure and distribute food, and these Committees became divided into political factions, who wrangled over fundamental principles....

The station at Moscow was deserted. We went to the office of the Commissar, in order to arrange for our return tickets. He was a sullen youth with the shoulder-straps of a Lieutenant; when we showed him our papers from Smolny, he lost his temper and declared that he was no Bolshevik, that he represented the Committee of Public Safety.... It was characteristic-in the general turmoil attending the conquest of the city, the chief railway station had been forgotten by the victors....

Not a cab in sight. A few blocks down the street, however, we woke up a grotesquely-padded *izvostchik* asleep upright on the box of his little sleigh. "How much to the centre of the town?"

He scratched his head. "The *barini* won't be able to find a room in any hotel," he said. "But I'll take you around for a hundred rubles...." Before the Revolution it cost *two!* We objected,

171

but he simply shrugged his shoulders. "It takes a good deal of courage to drive a sleigh nowadays," he went on. We could not beat him down below fifty.... As we sped along the silent, snowy half-lighted streets, he recounted his adventures during the six days' fighting. "Driving along, or waiting for a fare on the corner," he said, "all of a sudden *pooff!* a cannon ball exploding here, *pooff!* a cannon ball there, *ratt-ratt!* a machine-gun.... I gallop, the devils shooting all around. I get to a nice quiet street and stop, doze a little, *pooff!* another cannon ball, *ratt-ratt*.... Devils! Devils! Devils! Brrr!"

In the centre of the town the snow-piled streets were quiet with the stillness of convalescence. Only a few arc-lights were burning, only a few pedestrians hurried along the side-walks. An icy wind blew from the great plain, cutting to the bone. At the first hotel we entered an office illuminated by two candles.

"Yes, we have some very comfortable rooms, but all the windows are shot out. If the *gospodin* does not mind a little fresh air...."

Down the Tverskaya the shop-windows were broken, and there were shell-holes and torn-up paving stones in the street. Hotel after hotel, all full, or the proprietors still so frightened that all they could say was, "No, no, there is no room! There is no room!" On the main streets, where the great banking-houses and mercantile houses lay, the Bolshevik artillery had been indiscriminately effective. As one Soviet official told me, "Whenever we didn't know just where the *yunkers* and White Guards were, we bombarded their pocketbooks...."

At the big Hotel National they finally took us in; for we were foreigners, and the Military Revolutionary Committee had promised to protect the dwellings of foreigners.... On the top floor the manager showed us where shrapnel had shattered several windows. "The animals!" said he, shaking his first at imaginary Bolsheviki. "But wait! Their time will come; in just a few days now their ridiculous Government will fall, and then we shall make them suffer!"

We dined at a vegetarian restaurant with the enticing name, "I Eat Nobody," and Tolstoy's picture prominent on the walls, and then sallied out into the streets.

The headquarters of the Moscow Soviet was in the palace of the former Governor-General, an imposing white building fronting Skobeliev Square. Red Guards stood sentry at the door. At the head of the wide, formal stairway, whose walls were plastered with announcements of committee-meetings and addresses of political parties, we passed through a series of lofty ante-rooms, hung with red-shrouded pictures in gold frames, to the splendid state salon, with its magnificent crystal lustres and gilded cornices. A low-voiced hum of talk, underlaid with the whirring bass of a score of sewing machines, filled the place. Huge bolts of red and black cotton cloth were unrolled, serpentining across the parqueted floor and over tables, at which sat half a hundred women, cutting and sewing streamers and banners for the Funeral of the Revolutionary Dead. The faces of these women were roughened and scarred with life at its most difficult; they worked now sternly, many of them with eyes red from weeping.... The losses of the Red Army had been heavy.

At a desk in one corner was Rogov, an intelligent, bearded man with glasses, wearing the black blouse of a worker. He invited us to march with the Central Executive Committee in the funeral procession next morning....

"It is impossible to teach the Socialist Revolutionaries and the Mensheviki anything!" he exclaimed. "They compromise from sheer habit. Imagine! They proposed that we hold a joint funeral with the *yunkers!*"

[Graphic page-251 Questionairre for the Bourgeoioisie]

Distributed to all bourgeois households in Moscow by the Moscow Military Revolutionary Commitee, so as to provide a basis for the requisition of clothing for the Army and the poor workers.

Across the hall came a man in a ragged soldier-coat and *shapka,* whose face was familiar; I recognised Melnichansky, whom I had known as the watch-maker George Melcher in Bayonne, New Jersey, during the great Standard Oil strike. Now, he told me, he was secretary of the Moscow Metal-Workers' Union, and a Commissar of the Military Revolutionary Committee during the fighting....

"You see me!" he cried, showing his decrepit clothing. "I was with the boys in the Kremlin when the *yunkers* came the first time. They shut me up in the cellar and swiped my overcoat, my money, watch and even the ring on my finger. This is all I've got to wear!"

From him I learned many details of the bloody six-day battle which had rent Moscow in two. Unlike in Petrograd, in Moscow the City Duma had taken command of the *yunkers* and White Guards. Rudnev, the Mayor, and Minor, president of the Duma, had directed the activities of the Committee of Public Safety and the troops. Riabtsev, Commandant of the city, a man of democratic instincts, had hesitated about opposing the Military Revolutionary Committee; but the Duma had forced him.... It was the Mayor who had urged the occupation of the Kremlin; "They will never dare fire on you there," he said....

One garrison regiment, badly demoralised by long inactivity, had been approached by both sides. The regiment held a meeting to decide what action to take. Resolved, that the regiment remain neutral, and continue its present activities-which consisted in peddling rubbers and sunflower seeds!

"But worst of all," said Melnichansky, "we had to organise while we were fighting. The other side knew just what it wanted; but here the soldiers had their Soviet and the workers theirs.... There was a fearful wrangle over who should be Commander-in-chief; some regiments talked for days before they decided what to do; and when the officers suddenly deserted us, we had no battle-staff to give orders...."

Vivid little pictures he gave me. On a cold grey day he had stood at a corner of the Nikitskaya, which was swept by blasts of machine-gun fire. A throng of little boys were gathered there-street waifs who used to be newsboys. Shrill, excited as if with a new game, they waited until the firing slackened, and then tried to run across the street.... Many were killed, but the rest dashed backward and forward, laughing, daring each other....

Late in the evening I went to the *Dvorianskoye Sobranie*-the Nobles'
Club-where the Moscow Bolsheviki were to meet and consider the report
of Nogin, Rykov and the others who had left the Council of People's
Commissars.

The meeting-place was a theatre, in which, under the old régime, to audiences of officers and glittering ladies, amateur presentations of the latest French comedy had once taken place.

At first the place filled with the intellectuals-those who lived near the centre of the town. Nogin spoke, and most of his listeners were plainly with him. It was very late before the workers arrived; the working-class quarters were on the outskirts of the town, and no street-cars were running. But about midnight they began to clump up the stairs, in groups of ten or twenty-big, rough men, in coarse clothes, fresh from the battle-line, where they had fought like devils for a week, seeing their comrades fall all about them.

Scarcely had the meeting formally opened before Nogin was assailed with a tempest of jeers and angry shouts. In vain he tried to argue, to explain; they would not listen. He had left the Council of People's Commissars; he had deserted his post while the battle was raging. As for the bourgeois press, here in Moscow there was no more bourgeois press; even the City Duma had been dissolved. Bukharin stood up, savage, logical, with a voice which plunged and struck, plunged and struck.... Him they listened to with shining eyes. Resolution, to support the action of the Council of People's Commissars, passed by overwhelming majority. So spoke Moscow....

[Graphic page-254 Pass to the Kremlin] By this the Military Revolutionary Commitee requests to give a pass for the purpose of investigating the Kremlin, the representatives of the American Socialist party attached to the Socialist press, comrades Reed and Bryant. Chief of the Military Revolutionary Committee For the Secretary

Late in the night we went through the empty streets and under the Iberian Gate to the great Red Square in front of the Kremlin. The church of Vasili Blazheiny loomed fantastic, its bright-coloured, convoluted and blazoned cupolas vague in the darkness. There was no sign of any damage.... Along one side of the square the dark towers and walls of the Kremlin stood up. On the high walls flickered redly the light of hidden flames; voices reached us across the immense place, and the sound of picks and shovels. We crossed over.

Mountains of dirt and rock were piled high near the base of the wall. Climbing these we looked down into two massive pits, ten or fifteen feet deep and fifty yards long, where hundreds of soldiers and workers were digging in the light of huge fires.

A young student spoke to us in German. "The Brotherhood Grave," he explained. "To-morrow we shall bury here five hundred proletarians who died for the Revolution."

He took us down into the pit. In frantic haste swung the picks and shovels, and the earth-mountains grew. No one spoke. Overhead the night was thick with stars, and the ancient Imperial Kremlin wall towered up immeasurably.

"Here in this holy place," said the student, "holiest of all Russia, we shall bury our most holy. Here where are the tombs of the Tsars, our Tsar-the People-shall sleep...." His arm was in a sling, from a bullet-wound gained in the fighting. He looked at it. "You foreigners look down on us Russians because so long we tolerated a mediæval monarchy," said he. "But we saw that the Tsar was not the only tyrant in the world; capitalism was worse, and in all the countries of the world capitalism was Emperor.... Russian revolutionary tactics are best...."

As we left, the workers in the pit, exhausted and running with sweat in spite of the cold, began to climb wearily out. Across the Red Square a dark knot of men came hurrying. They swarmed into the pits, picked up the tools and began digging, digging, without a word....

So, all the long night volunteers of the People relieved each other, never halting in their driving speed, and the cold light of the dawn laid bare the great Square, white with snow, and the yawning brown pits of the Brotherhood Grave, quite finished.

We rose before sunrise, and hurried through the dark streets to Skobeliev Square. In all the great city not a human being could be seen; but there was a faint sound of stirring, far and near, like a deep wind coming. In the pale half-light a little group of men and women were gathered before the Soviet headquarters, with a sheaf of gold-lettered red banners-the Central Executive Committee of the Moscow Soviets. It grew light. From afar the vague stirring sound deepened and became louder, a steady and tremendous bass. The city was rising. We set out down the Tverskaya, the banners flapping overhead. The little street chapels along our way were locked and dark, as was the Chapel of the Iberian Virgin, which each new Tsar used to visit before he went to the Kremlin to crown himself, and which, day or night, was always open and crowded, and brilliant with the candles of the devout gleaming on the gold and silver and jewels of the ikons. Now, for the first time since Napoleon was in Moscow, they say, the candles were out.

The Holy Orthodox Church had withdrawn the light of its countenance from Moscow, the nest of irreverent vipers who had bombarded the Kremlin. Dark and silent and cold were the churches; the priests had disappeared. There were no popes to officiate at the Red Burial, there had been no sacrament for the dead, nor were any prayers to be said over the grave of the blasphemers. Tikhon, Metropolitan of Moscow, was soon to excommunicate the Soviets....

Also the shops were closed, and the propertied classes stayed at home-but for other reasons. This was the Day of the People, the rumour of whose coming was thunderous as surf....

Already through the Iberian Gate a human river was flowing, and the vast Red Square was spotted with people, thousands of them. I remarked that as the throng passed the Iberian Chapel, where always before the passerby had crossed himself, they did not seem to notice it....

We forced our way through the dense mass packed near the Kremlin wall, and stood upon one of the dirt-mountains. Already several men were there, among them Muranov, the soldier who had been elected Commandant of Moscow-a tall, simple-looking, bearded man with a gentle face.

Through all the streets to the Red Square the torrents of people poured, thousands upon thousands of them, all with the look of the poor and the toiling. A military band came marching up, playing the *Internationale,* and spontaneously the song caught and spread like wind-ripples on a sea, slow and solemn. From the top of the Kremlin wall gigantic banners unrolled to the ground; red, with great letters in gold and in white, saying, "Martyrs of the Beginning of World Social Revolution," and "Long Live the Brotherhood of Workers of the World."

A bitter wind swept the Square, lifting the banners. Now from the far quarters of the city the workers of the different factories were arriving, with their dead. They could be seen coming through the Gate, the blare of their banners, and the dull red-like blood-of the coffins they carried. These were rude boxes, made of unplaned wood and daubed with crimson, borne high on the shoulders of rough men who marched with tears streaming down their faces, and followed by women who sobbed and screamed, or walked stiffly, with white, dead faces. Some of the coffins were open, the lid carried behind them; others were covered with gilded or silvered cloth, or had a soldier's hat nailed on the top. There were many wreaths of hideous artificial flowers....

Through an irregular lane that opened and closed again the procession slowly moved toward us. Now through the Gate was flowing an endless stream of banners, all shades of red, with silver and gold lettering, knots of crepe hanging from the top-and some Anarchist flags, black with white letters. The band was playing the Revolutionary Funeral March, and against the immense singing of the mass of people, standing uncovered, the paraders sang hoarsely, choked with sobs....

Between the factory-workers came companies of soldiers with their coffins, too, and squadrons of cavalry, riding at salute, and artillery batteries, the cannon wound with red and black-forever, it seemed. Their banners said, "Long live the Third International!" or "We Want an Honest, General, Democratic Peace!"

Slowly the marchers came with their coffins to the entrance of the grave, and the bearers clambered up with their burdens and went down into the pit. Many of them were women-squat, strong proletarian women. Behind the dead came other women-women young and broken, or old, wrinkled women making noises like hurt animals, who tried to follow their sons and husbands into the Brotherhood Grave, and shrieked when compassionate hands restrained them. The poor love each other so!

All the long day the funeral procession passed, coming in by the Iberian Gate and leaving the Square by way of the Nikolskaya, a river of red banners, bearing words of hope and brotherhood and stupendous prophecies, against a back-ground of fifty thousand people,-under the eyes of the world's workers and their descendants forever....

One by one the five hundred coffins were laid in the pits. Dusk fell, and still the banners came drooping and fluttering, the band played the Funeral March, and the huge assemblage chanted. In the leafless branches of the trees above the grave the wreaths were hung, like strange, multi-coloured blossoms. Two hundred men began to shovel in the dirt. It rained dully down upon the coffins with a thudding sound, audible beneath the singing....

The lights came out. The last banners passed, and the last moaning women, looking back with awful intensity as they went. Slowly from the great Square ebbed the proletarian tide....

I suddenly realised that the devout Russian people no longer needed priests to pray them into heaven. On earth they were building a kingdom more bright than any heaven had to offer, and for which it was a glory to die....

CHAPTER XI

The Conquest of Power

DECLARATION OF THE RIGHTS OF THE PEOPLES OF RUSSIA

... The first Congress of Soviets, in June of this year, proclaimed the right of the peoples of Russia to self-determination.

The second Congress of Soviets, in November last, confirmed this inalienable right of the peoples of Russia more decisively and definitely.

Executing the will of these Congresses, the Council of People's Commissars has resolved to establish as a basis for its activity in the question of Nationalities, the following principles:

(1) The equality and sovereignty of the peoples of Russia.

(2) The right of the peoples of Russia to free self-determination, even to the point of separation and the formation of an independent state.

(3) The abolition of any and all national and national religious privileges and disabilities.

(4) The free development of national minorities and ethnographic groups inhabiting the territory of Russia.

Decrees will be prepared immediately upon the formation of a Commission on Nationalities.

In the name of the Russian Republic,

People's Commissar for Nationalities

YUSSOV DJUGASHVILI-STALIN

President of the Council of People's Commissars

V. ULIANOV (LENIN)

The Central Rada at Kiev immediately declared Ukraine an independent Republic, as did the Government of Finland, through the Senate at Helsingfors. Independent "Governments" spring up in Siberia and the

Caucasus. The Polish Chief Military Committee swiftly gathered
together the Polish troops in the Russian army, abolished their
Committees and established an iron discipline....

All these "Governments" and "movements" had two characteristics in common; they were
controlled by the propertied classes, and they feared and detested Bolshevism....

Steadily, amid the chaos of shocking change, the Council of People's
Commissars hammered at the scaffolding of the Socialist order.
Decree on Social Insurance, on Workers' Control, Regulations for
Volost Land Committees, Abolition of Ranks and Titles, Abolition of
Courts and the Creation of People's Tribunals....

Army after army, fleet after fleet, sent deputations, "joyfully to greet the new Government of
the People."

In front of Smolny, one day, I saw a ragged regiment just come from the trenches. The
soldiers were drawn up before the great gates, thin and grey-faced, looking up at the
building as if God were in it. Some pointed out the Imperial eagles over the door, laughing....
Red Guards came to mount guard. All the soldiers turned to look, curiously, as if they had
heard of them but never seen them. They laughed good-naturedly and pressed out of line to
slap the Red Guards on the back, with half-joking, half-admiring remarks....

The Provisional Government was no more. On November 15th, in all the churches of the
capital, the priests stopped praying for it. But as Lenin himself told the *Tsay-ee-kah*, that was
"only the beginning of the conquest of power." Deprived of arms, the opposition, which still
controlled the economic life of the country, settled down to organise disorganisation, with
all the Russian genius for cooperative action-to obstruct, cripple and discredit the Soviets.

The strike of Government employees was well organised, financed by the banks and
commercial establishments. Every move of the Bolsheviki to take over the Government
apparatus was resisted.

Trotzky went to the Ministry of Foreign Affairs; the functionaries refused to recognise him,
locked themselves in, and when the doors were forced, resigned. He demanded the keys of
the archives; only when he brought workmen to force the locks were they given up. Then it
was discovered that Neratov, former assistant Foreign Minister, had disappeared with the
Secret Treaties....

Shliapnikov tried to take possession of the Ministry of Labour. It was bitterly cold, and there
was no one to light the fires. Of all the hundreds of employees, not one would show him
where the office of the Minister was....

Alexandra Kollontai, appointed the 13th of November Commissar of Public Welfare-the department of charities and public institutions-was welcomed with a strike of all but forty of the functionaries in the Ministry. Immediately the poor of the great cities, the inmates of institutions, were plunged in miserable want: delegations of starving cripples, of orphans with blue, pinched faces, besieged the building. With tears streaming down her face, Kollontai arrested the strikers until they should deliver the keys of the office and the safe; when she got the keys, however, it was discovered that the former Minister, Countess Panina, had gone off with all the funds, which she refused to surrender except on the order of the Constituent Assembly.

In the Ministry of Agriculture, the Ministry of Supplies, the Ministry of Finance, similar incidents occurred. And the employees, summoned to return or forfeit their positions and their pensions, either stayed away or returned to sabotage.... Almost all the *intelligentzia* being anti-Bolshevik, there was nowhere for the Soviet Government to recruit new staffs....

The private banks remained stubbornly closed, with a back door open for speculators. When Bolshevik Commissars entered, the clerks left, secreting the books and removing the funds. All the employees of the State Bank struck except the clerks in charge of the vaults and the manufacture of money, who refused all demands from Smolny and privately paid out huge sums to the Committee for Salvation and the City Duma.

Twice a Commissar, with a company of Red Guards, came formally to insist upon the delivery of large sums for Government expenses. The first time, the City Duma members and the Menshevik and Socialist Revolutionary leaders were present in imposing numbers, and spoke so gravely of the consequences that the Commissar was frightened. The second time he arrived with a warrant, which he proceeded to read aloud in due form; but some one called his attention to the fact that it had no date and no seal, and the traditional Russian respect for "documents" forced him again to withdraw....

The officials of the Credit Chancery destroyed their books, so that all record of the financial relations of Russia with foreign countries was lost.

The Supply Committees, the administrations of the Municipal-owned public utilities, either did not work at all, or sabotaged. And when the Bolsheviki, compelled by the desperate needs of the city population, attempted to help or to control the public service, all the employees went on strike immediately, and the Duma flooded Russia with telegrams about Bolshevik "violation of Municipal autonomy."

At Military headquarters, and in the offices of the Ministries of War and Marine, where the old officials had consented to work, the Army Committees and the high command blocked the Soviets in every way possible, even to the extent of neglecting the troops at the front. The *Vikzhel* was hostile, refusing to transport Soviet troops; every troop-train that left

Petrograd was taken out by force, and railway officials had to be arrested each time-whereupon the *Vikzhel* threatened an immediate general strike unless they were released....

Smolny was plainly powerless. The newspapers said that all the factories of Petrograd must shut down for lack of fuel in three weeks; the *Vikzhel* announced that trains must cease running by December first; there was food for three days only in Petrograd, and no more coming in; and the Army on the Front was starving.... The Committee for Salvation, the various Central Committees, sent word all over the country, exhorting the population to ignore the Government decrees. And the Allied Embassies were either coldly indifferent, or openly hostile....

The opposition newspapers, suppressed one day and reappearing next morning under new names, heaped bitter sarcasm on the new regime. Even *Novaya Zhizn* characterised it as "a combination of demagoguery and impotence."

From day to day (it said) the Government of the People's Commissars sinks deeper and deeper into the mire of superficial haste. Having easily conquered the power... the Bolsheviki can not make use of it.

Powerless to direct the existing mechanism of Government, they are unable at the same time to create a new one which might work easily and freely according to the theories of social experimenters.

Just a little while ago the Bolsheviki hadn't enough men to run their growing party-a work above all of speakers and writers; where then are they going to find trained men to execute the diverse and complicated functions of government?

The new Government acts and threatens, it sprays the country with decrees, each one more radical and more "socialist" than the last. But in this exhibition of Socialism on Paper-more likely designed for the stupefaction of our descendants-there appears neither the desire nor the capacity to solve the immediate problems of the day!

Meanwhile the *Vikzhel's* Conference to Form a New Government continued to meet night and day. Both sides had already agreed in principle to the basis of the Government; the composition of the People's Council was being discussed; the Cabinet was tentatively chosen, with Tchernov as Premier; the Bolsheviki were admitted in a large minority, but Lenin and Trotzky were barred. The Central Committees of the Menshevik and Socialist Revolutionary parties, the Executive Committee of the Peasant's Soviets, resolved that, although unalterably opposed to the "criminal politics" of the Bolsheviki, they would, "in order to halt the fratricidal bloodshed," not oppose their entrance into the People's Council.

The flight of Kerensky, however, and the astounding success of the Soviets everywhere, altered the situation. On the 16th, in a meeting of the *Tsay-ee-kah,* the Left Socialist Revolutionaries insisted that the Bolsheviki should form a coalition Government with the other Socialist parties; otherwise they would withdraw from the Military Revolutionary Committee and the *Tsay-ee-kah.* Malkin said, "The news from Moscow, where our comrades are dying on both sides of the barricades, determines us to bring up once more the question of organisation of power, and it is not only our right to do so, but our duty.... We have won the right to sit with the Bolsheviki here within the walls of Smolny Institute, and to speak from this tribune. After the bitter internal party struggle, we shall be obliged, if you refuse to compromise, to pass to open battle outside.... We must propose to the democracy terms of an acceptable compromise...."

After a recess to consider this ultimatum, the Bolsheviki returned with a resolution, read by Kameniev:

The *Tsay-ee-kah* considers it necessary that there enter into the Government representatives of *all the Socialist parties composing the Soviets of Workers', Soldiers' and Peasants' Deputies who recognise the conquests of the Revolution of November 7th-that is to say, the establishment of a Government of Soviets, the decrees on peace, land, workers' control over industry, and the arming of the working-class.* The *Tsay-ee-kah* therefore resolves to propose negotiations concerning the constitution of the Government to all parties *of the Soviet,* and insists upon the following conditions as a basis:

The Government is responsible to the *Tsay-ee-kah.* The *Tsay-ee-kah* shall be enlarged to 150 members. To these 150 delegates of the Soviets of Workers' and Soldiers' Deputies shall be added 75 delegates of the *Provincial* Soviets of Peasants' Deputies, 80 from the Front organisations of the Army and Navy, 40 from the Trade Unions (25 from the various All-Russian Unions, in proportion to their importance, 10 from the *Vikzhel,* and 5 from the Post and Telegraph Workers), and 50 delegates from the Socialist groups in the Petrograd City Duma. In the Ministry itself, at least one-half the portfolios must be reserved to the Bolsheviki. The Ministries of Labour, Interior and Foreign Affairs must be given to the Bolsheviki. The command of the garrisons of Petrograd and Moscow must remain in the hands of delegates of the Moscow and Petrograd Soviets.

The Government undertakes the systematic arming of the workers of all Russia.

It is resolved to insist upon the candidature of comrades Lenin and
Trotzky.

Kameniev explained. "The so-called 'People's Council,'" he said, "proposed by the Conference, would consist of about 420 members, of which about 150 would be Bolsheviki. Besides, there would be delegates from the counter-revolutionary old *Tsay-ee-kah,* 100 members chosen by the Municipal Dumas-Kornilovtsi all; 100 delegates from the Peasants'

Soviets-appointed by Avksentiev, and 80 from the old Army Committees, who no longer represent the soldier masses.

"We refuse to admit the old *Tsay-ee-kah*, and also the representatives of the Municipal Dumas. The delegates from the Peasants' Soviets shall be elected by the Congress of Peasants, which we have called, and which will at the same time elect a new Executive Committee. The proposal to exclude Lenin and Trotzky is a proposal to decapitate our party, and we do not accept it. And finally, we see no necessity for a 'People's Council' anyway; the Soviets are open to all Socialist parties, and the *Tsay-ee-kah* represents them in their real proportions among the masses...."

Karelin, for the Left Socialist Revolutionaries, declared that his party would vote for the Bolshevik resolution, reserving the right to modify certain details, such as the representation of the peasants, and demanding that the Ministry of Agriculture be reserved for the Left Socialist Revolutionaries. This was agreed to....

Later, at a meeting of the Petrograd Soviet, Trotzky answered a question about the formation of the new Government:

"I don't know anything about that. I am not taking part in the negotiations.... However, I don't think that they are of great importance...."

That night there was great uneasiness in the Conference. The delegates of the City Duma withdrew....

But at Smolny itself, in the ranks of the Bolshevik party, a formidable opposition to Lenin's policy was growing. On the night of November 17th the great hall was packed and ominous for the meeting of the *Tsay-ee-kah.*

Larin, Bolshevik, declared that the moment of elections to the Constituent Assembly approached, and it was time to do away with "political terrorism."

"The measures taken against the freedom of the press should be modified. They had their reason during the struggle, but now they have no further excuse. The press should be free, except for appeals to riot and insurrection."

In a storm of hisses and hoots from his own party, Larin offered the following resolution:

The decree of the Council of People's Commissars concerning the
Press is herewith repealed.

Measures of political repression can only be employed subject to decision of a special tribunal, elected by the *Tsay-ee-kah* proportionally to the strength of the different parties represented; and this tribunal shall have the right also to reconsider measures of repression already taken.

This was met by a thunder of applause, not only from the Left Socialist Revolutionaries, but also from a part of the Bolsheviki.

Avanessov, for the Leninites, hastily proposed that the question of the Press be postponed until after some compromise between the Socialist parties had been reached. Overwhelmingly voted down.

"The revolution which is now being accomplished," went on Avanessov, "has not hesitated to attack private property; and it is as private property that we must examine the question of the Press...."

Thereupon he read the official Bolshevik resolution:

The suppression of the bourgeois press was dictated not only by purely military needs in the course of the insurrection, and for the checking of counter-revolutionary action, but it is also necessary as a measure of transition toward the establishment of a new régime with regard to the Press-a régime under which the capitalist owners of printing-presses and of paper cannot be the all-powerful and exclusive manufacturers of public opinion.

We must further proceed to the confiscation of private printing plants and supplies of paper, which should become the property of the Soviets, both in the capital and in the provinces, so that the political parties and groups can make use of the facilities of printing in proportion to the actual strength of the ideas they represent-in other words, proportionally to the number of their constituents.

The reëstablishment of the so-called "freedom of the press," the simple return of printing presses and paper to the capitalists,-poisoners of the mind of the people-this would be an inadmissible surrender to the will of capital, a giving up of one of the most important conquests of the Revolution; in other words, it would be a measure of unquestionably counter-revolutionary character.

Proceeding from the above, the *Tsay-ee-kah* categorically rejects all propositions aiming at the reëstablishment of the old régime in the domain of the Press, and unequivocally supports the point of view of the Council of People's Commissars on this question, against pretentions and ultimatums dictated by petty bourgeois prejudices, or by evident surrender to the interests of the counter-revolutionary bourgeoisie.

The reading of this resolution was interrupted by ironical shouts from the Left Socialist Revolutionaries, and bursts of indignation from the insurgent Bolsheviki. Karelin was on his feet, protesting. "Three weeks ago the Bolsheviki were the most ardent defenders of the freedom of the Press... The arguments in this resolution suggest singularly the point of view of the old Black Hundreds and the censors of the Tsarist régime-for they also talked of 'poisoners of the mind of the people.'"

Trotzky spoke at length in favour of the resolution. He distinguished between the Press during the civil war, and the Press after the victory. "During civil war the right to use violence belongs only to the oppressed...." (Cries of "Who's the oppressed now? Cannibal!").

"The victory over our adversaries is not yet achieved, and the newspapers are arms in their hands. In these conditions, the closing of the newspapers is a legitimate measure of defence...." Then passing to the question of the Press after the victory, Trotzky continued:

"The attitude of Socialists on the question of freedom of the Press should be the same as their attitude toward the freedom of business.... The rule of the democracy which is being established in Russia demands that the domination of the Press by private property must be abolished, just as the domination of industry by private property.... The power of the Soviets should confiscate all printing-plants." (Cries, "Confiscate the printing-shop of *Pravda!*")

"The monopoly of the Press by the bourgeoisie must be abolished. Otherwise it isn't worth while for us to take the power! Each group of citizens should have access to print shops and paper.... The ownership of print-type and of paper belongs first to the workers and peasants, and only afterwards to the bourgeois parties, which are in a minority.... The passing of the power into the hands of the Soviets will bring about a radical transformation of the essential conditions of existence, and this transformation will necessarily be evident in the Press.... If we are going to nationalise the banks, can we then tolerate the financial journals? The old régime must die; that must be understood once and for all...." Applause and angry cries.

Karelin declared that the *Tsay-ee-kah* had no right to pass upon this important question, which should be left to a special committee. Again, passionately, he demanded that the Press be free.

Then Lenin, calm, unemotional, his forehead wrinkled, as he spoke slowly, choosing his words; each sentence falling like a hammer-blow. "The civil war is not yet finished; the enemy is still with us; consequently it is impossible to abolish the measures of repression against the Press.

"We Bolsheviki have always said that when we reached a position of power we would close the bourgeois press. To tolerate the bourgeois newspapers would mean to cease being a Socialist. When one makes a Revolution, one cannot mark time; one must always go forward-or go back. He who now talks about the 'freedom of the Press' goes backward, and halts our headlong course toward Socialism.

"We have thrown off the yoke of capitalism, just as the first revolution threw off the yoke of Tsarism. *If the first revolution had the right to suppress the Monarchist papers,* then we have the right to suppress the bourgeois press. It is impossible to separate the question of the freedom of the Press from the other questions of the class struggle. We have promised to close these newspapers, and we shall do it. The immense majority of the people is with us!

"Now that the insurrection is over, we have absolutely no desire to suppress the papers of the other Socialist parties, except inasmuch as they appeal to armed insurrection, or to disobedience to the Soviet Government. However, we shall not permit them, under the pretence of freedom of the Socialist press, to obtain, through the secret support of the bourgeoisie, a monopoly of printing-presses, ink and paper.... These essentials must become the property of the Soviet Government, and be apportioned, first of all, to the Socialist parties in strict proportion to their voting strength...."

Then the vote. The resolution of Larin and the Left Socialist Revolutionaries was defeated by 31 to 22; the Lenin motion was carried by 34 to 24. Among the minority were the Bolsheviki Riazanov and Lozovsky, who declared that it was impossible for them to vote against any restriction on the freedom of the Press.

Upon this the Left Socialist Revolutionaries declared they could no longer be responsible for what was being done, and withdrew from the Military Revolutionary Committee and all other positions of executive responsibility.

Five members-Nogin, Rykov, Miliutin, Teodorovitch and Shiapnikov-resigned from the Council of People's Commissars, declaring:

We are in favour of a Socialist Government composed of all the parties in the Soviets. We consider that only the creation of such a Government can possibly guarantee the results of the heroic struggle of the working-class and the revolutionary army. Outside of that, there remains only one way: the constitution of a purely Bolshevik Government by means of political terrorism. This last is the road taken by the Council of People's Commissars. We cannot and will not follow it. We see that this leads directly to the elimination from political life of many proletarian organisations, to the establishment of an irresponsible régime, and to the destruction of the Revolution and the country. We cannot take the responsibility for such a policy, and we renounce before the *Tsay-ee-kah* our function as People's Commissars.

Other Commissars, without resigning their positions, signed the declaration-Riazanov, Derbychev of the Press Department, Arbuzov, of the Government Printing-plant, Yureniev, of the Red Guard, Feodorov, of the Commissariat of Labour, and Larin, secretary of the Section of Elaboration of Decrees.

At the same time Kameniev, Rykov, Miliutin, Zinoviev and Nogin resigned from the Central Committee of the Bolshevik party, making public their reasons:

... The constitution of such a Government (composed of all the parties of the Soviet) is indispensable to prevent a new flow of blood, the coming famine, the destruction of the Revolution by the Kaledinists, to assure the convocation of the Constituent Assembly at the proper time, and to apply effectively the programme adopted by the Congress of Soviets....

We cannot accept the responsibility for the disastrous policy of the Central Committee, carried on against the will of an enormous majority of the proletariat and the soldiers, who are eager to see the rapid end of the bloodshed between the different political parties of the democracy.... We renounce our title as members of the Central Committee, in order to be able to say openly our opinion to the masses of workers and soldiers....

We leave the Central Committee at the moment of victory; we cannot calmly look on while the policy of the chiefs of the Central Committee leads toward the loss of the fruits of victory and the crushing of the proletariat....

The masses of the workers, the soldiers of the garrison, stirred restlessly, sending their delegations to Smolny, to the Conference for Formation of the New Government, where the break in the ranks of the Bolsheviki caused the liveliest joy.

But the answer of the Leninites was swift and ruthless. Shliapnikov and Teodorovitch submitted to party discipline and returned to their posts. Kameniev was stripped of his powers as president of the *Tsay-ee-kah*, and Sverdlov elected in his place. Zinoviev was deposed as president of the Petrograd Soviet. On the morning of the 5th, *Pravda* contained a ferocious proclamation to the people of Russia, written by Lenin, which was printed in hundreds of thousands of copies, posted on the walls everywhere, and distributed over the face of Russia.

The second All-Russian Congress of Soviets gave the majority to the Bolshevik party. Only a Government formed by this party can therefore be a Soviet Government. And it is known to all that the Central Committee of the Bolshevik party, a few hours before the formation of the new Government and before proposing the list of its members to the All-Russian Congress of Soviets, invited to its meeting three of the most eminent members of the Left Socialist Revolutionary group, comrades Kamkov, Spiro and Karelin, and ASKED THEM to participate in the new Government. We regret infinitely that the invited comrades refused; we consider their refusal inadmissible for revolutionists and champions of the working-class; we are willing at any time to include the Left Socialist Revolutionaries in the Government; but we declare that, as the party of the majority at the second All-Russian Congress of Soviets, we are entitled and BOUND before the people to form a Government....

... Comrades! Several members of the Central Committee of our party and the Council of People's Commissars, Kameniev, Zinoviev, Nogin, Rykov, Miliutin and a few others left yesterday, November 17th, the Central Committee of our party, and the last three, the Council of People's Commissars....

The comrades who left us acted like deserters, because they not only abandoned the posts entrusted to them, but also disobeyed the direct instructions of the Central Committee of our party, to the effect that they should await the decisions of the Petrograd and Moscow party organisations before retiring. We blame decisively such desertion. We are firmly convinced that all conscious workers, soldiers and peasants, belonging to our party or sympathising with it, will also disapprove of the behaviour of the deserters....

Remember, comrades, that two of these deserters, Kameniev and Zinoviev, even before the uprising in Petrograd, appeared as deserters and strike-breakers, by voting at the decisive meeting of the Central Committee, October 23d, 1917, against the insurrection; and even AFTER the resolution passed by the Central Committee, they continued their campaign at a meeting of the party workers.... But the great impulse of the masses, the great heroism of millions of workers, soldiers and peasants, in Moscow, Petrograd, at the front, in the trenches, in the villages, pushed aside the deserters as a railway train scatters saw-dust....

Shame upon those who are of little faith, hesitate, who doubt, who allow themselves to be frightened by the bourgeoisie, or who succumb before the cries of the latter's direct or indirect accomplices! There is NOT A SHADOW of hesitation in the MASSES of Petrograd, Moscow, and the rest of Russia....

... We shall not submit to any ultimatums from small groups of intellectuals which are not followed by the masses, which are PRACTICALLY only supported by Kornilovists, Savinkovists, *yunkers,* and so forth....

The response from the whole country was like a blast of hot storm. The insurgents never got a chance to "say openly their opinion to the masses of workers and soldiers." Upon the *Tsay-ee-kah* rolled in like breakers the fierce popular condemnation of the "deserters." For days Smolny was thronged with angry delegations and committees, from the front, from the Volga, from the Petrograd factories. "Why did they dare leave the Government? Were they paid by the bourgeoisie to destroy the Revolution? They must return and submit to the decisions of the Central Committee!"

Only in the Petrograd garrison was there still uncertainty. A great soldier meeting was held on November 24th, addressed by representatives of all the political parties. By a vast majority Lenin's policy was sustained, and the Left Socialist Revolutionaries were told that they must enter the government.....

The Mensheviki delivered a final ultimatum, demanding that all Ministers and *yunkers* be released, that all newspapers be allowed full freedom, that the Red Guard be disarmed and the garrison put under command of the Duma. To this Smolny answered that all the Socialist Ministers and also all but a very few *yunkers* had been already set free, that all newspapers were free except the bourgeois press, and that the Soviet would remain in command of the armed forces.... On the 19th the Conference to Form a New Government disbanded, and the opposition one by one slipped away to Moghilev, where, under the wing of the General Staff, they continued to form Government after Government, until the end....

[Graphic Page-276 Meeting announcement]

Announcement, posted on the walls of Petrograd, of the result of a meeting of representatives of the garrison regiments, called to consider the question of forming a new Government.

Meanwhile the Bolsheviki had been undermining the power of the *Vikzhel*. An appeal of the Petrograd Soviet to all railway workers called upon them to force the *Vikzhel* to surrender its powers. On the 15th, the *Tsay-ee-kah*, following its procedure toward the peasants, called an All-Russian Congress of Railway Workers for December 1st; the *Vikzhel* immediately called its own Congress for two weeks later. On November 16th, the *Vikzhel* members took their seats in the *Tsay-ee-kah*. On the night of December 2d, at the opening session of the All-Russian Congress of Railway Workers, the *Tsay-ee-kah* formally offered the post of Commissar of Ways and Communications to the *Vikzhel*-which accepted....

Having settled the question of power, the Bolsheviki turned their attention to problems of practical administration. First of all the city, the country, the Army must be fed. Bands of sailors and Red Guards scoured the warehouses, the railway terminals, even the barges in the canals, unearthing and confiscating thousands of *poods* 1 of food held by private speculators. Emissaries were sent to the provinces, where with the assistance of the Land Committees they seized the store-houses of the great grain-dealers. Expeditions of sailors, heavily armed, were sent out in groups of five thousand, to the South, to Siberia, with roving commissions to capture cities still held by the White Guards, establish order, and *get food*. Passenger traffic on the Trans-Siberian Railroad was suspended for two weeks, while thirteen trains, loaded with bolts of cloth and bars of iron assembled by the Factory-Shop Committees, were sent out eastward, each in charge of a Commissar, to barter with the Siberian peasants for grain and potatoes....

Kaledin being in possession of the coal-mines of the Don, the fuel question became urgent. Smolny shut off all electric lights in theatres, shops and restaurants, cut down the number of street cars, and confiscated the private stores of fire-wood held by the fuel-dealers.... And when the factories of Petrograd were about to close down for lack of coal, the sailors of the Baltic Fleet turned over to the workers two hundred thousand *poods* from the bunkers of battle-ships....

Toward the end of November occurred the "wine-pogroms" -looting of the wine-cellars- beginning with the plundering of the Winter Palace vaults. For days there were drunken soldiers on the streets.... In all this was evident the hand of the counter-revolutionists, who distributed among the regiments plans showing the location of the stores of liquor. The Commissars of Smolny began by pleading and arguing, which did not stop the growing disorder, followed by pitched battles between soldiers and Red Guards.... Finally the Military Revolutionary Committee sent out companies of sailors with machine-guns, who fired mercilessly upon the rioters, killing many; and by executive order the wine-cellars were invaded by Committees with hatchets, who smashed the bottles-or blew them up with dynamite....

Companies of Red Guards, disciplined and well-paid, were on duty at the headquarters of the Ward Soviets day and night, replacing the old Militia. In all quarters of the city small elective Revolutionary Tribunals were set up by the workers and soldiers to deal with petty crime....

The great hotels, where the speculators still did a thriving business, were surrounded by Red Guards, and the speculators thrown into jail. ...

Alert and suspicious, the working-class of the city constituted itself a vast spy system, through the servants prying into bourgeois households, and reporting all information to the Military Revolutionary Committee, which struck with an iron hand, unceasing. In this way was discovered the Monarchist plot led by former Duma-member Purishkevitch and a group of nobles and officers, who had planned an officers' uprising, and had written a letter inviting Kaledin to Petrograd.).... In this way was unearthed the conspiracy of the Petrograd Cadets, who were sending money and recruits to Kaledin....

Neratov, frightened at the outburst of popular fury provoked by his flight, returned and surrendered the Secret Treaties to Trotzky, who began their publication in *Pravda,* scandalising the world....

[Graphic Page-279 Proclamation]

Bolshevik order. A proclamation of the Committee to Fight against
Pogroms, attached to the Petrograd Soviet. For translation

The restrictions on the Press were increased by a decree
 making advertisements a monopoly of the official
Government newspaper. At this all the other papers suspended
publication as a protest, or disobeyed the law and were closed....
Only three weeks later did they finally submit.

Still the strike of the Ministries went on, still the sabotage of the old officials, the stoppage of normal economic life. Behind Smolny was only the will of the vast, unorganised popular masses; and with them the Council of People's Commissars dealt, directing revolutionary mass-action against its enemies. In eloquent proclamations, couched in simple words and spread over Russia, Lenin explained the Revolution, urged the people to take the power into their own hands, by force to break down the resistance of the propertied classes, by force to take over the institutions of Government. Revolutionary order. Revolutionary discipline! Strict accounting and control! No strikes! No loafing!

[Graphic Page-281 Appeal to work hard]

Appeal of the Petrograd Soviet, the Petrograd Council of
Professional Unions, and the Petrograd Council of Factory Shop
Committees, to the Workers of Petro. grad, urging them to work hard
and not to strike. For translation .

On the 20th of November the Military Revolutionary Committee issued a warning:

The rich classes oppose the power of the Soviets-the Government of workers, soldiers and peasants. Their sympathisers halt the work of the employees of the Government and the Duma, incite strikes in the banks, try to interrupt communication by the railways, the post and the telegraph....

We warn them that they are playing with fire. The country and the Army are threatened with famine. To fight against it, the regular functioning of all services is indispensable. The Workers' and Peasants' Government is taking every measure to assure the country and the Army all that is necessary. Opposition to these measures is a crime against the People. We warn the rich classes and their sympathisers that, if they do not cease their sabotage and their provocation in halting the transportation of food, they will be the first to suffer. They will be deprived of the right of receiving food. All the reserves which they possess will be requisitioned. The property of the principal criminals will be confiscated.

We have done our duty in warning those who play with fire.

We are convinced that in case decisive measures become necessary, we shall be solidly supported by all workers, soldiers, and peasants.

On the 22d of November the walls of the city were placarded with a sheet headed "EXTRAORDINARY COMMUNICATION":

The Council of People's Commissars has received an urgent telegram from the Staff of the Northern Front....

191

"There must be no further delay; do not let the Army die of hunger; the armies of the Northern Front have not received a crust of bread now for several days, and in two or three days they will not have any more biscuits-which are being doled out to them from reserve supplies until now never touched.... Already delegates from all parts of the Front are talking of a necessary removal of part of the Army to the rear, foreseeing that in a few days there will be headlong flight of the soldiers, dying from hunger, ravaged by the three years' war in the trenches, sick, insufficiently clothed, bare-footed, driven mad by superhuman misery."

The Military Revolutionary Committee brings this to the notice of the Petrograd garrison and the workers of Petrograd. The situation at the Front demands the most urgent and decisive measures. ... Meanwhile the higher functionaries of the Government institutions, banks, railroads, post and telegraph, are on strike and impeding the work of the Government in supplying the Front with provisions.... Each hour of delay may cost the life of thousands of soldiers. The counter-revolutionary functionaries are the most dishonest criminals toward their hungry and dying brethren on the Front....

The MILITARY REVOLUTIONARY COMMITTEE GIVES THESE CRIMINALS A LAST WARNING. In event of the least resistance or opposition on their part, the harshness of the measures which will be adopted against them will correspond to the seriousness of their crime....

——————————+—————+

The masses of workers and soldiers responded by a savage tremor of rage, which swept all Russia. In the capital the Government and bank employees got out hundreds of proclamations and appeals, protesting, defending themselves, such as this one:

TO THE ATTENTION OF ALL CITIZENS.

THE STATE BANK IS CLOSED!

WHY?

Because the violence exercised by the Bolsheviki against the State
Bank has made it impossible for us to work. The first act of the
People's Commissars was to DEMAND TEN MILLION RUBLES, and on
November 27th THEY DEMANDED TWENTY-FIVE MILLIONS, without any
indication as to where this money was to go.

... We functionaries cannot take part in plundering the people's property. We stopped work.

CITIZENS! The money in the State Bank is yours, the people's money, acquired by your labour, your sweat and blood. CITIZENS! Save the people's property from robbery, and us from violence, and we shall immediately resume work.

EMPLOYEES OF THE STATE BANK.

From the Ministry of Supplies, the Ministry of Finance, from the Special Supply Committee, declarations that the Military Revolutionary Committee made it impossible for the employees to work, appeals to the population to support them against Smolny.... But the dominant worker and soldier did not believe them; it was firmly fixed in the popular mind that the employees were sabotaging, starving the Army, starving the people.... In the long bread lines, which as formerly stood in the iron winter streets, it was not *the Government* which was blamed, as it had been under Kerensky, but the *tchinovniki*, the sabotageurs; for the Government was *their* Government, *their* Soviets-and the functionaries of the Ministries were against it....

At the centre of all this opposition was the Duma, and its militant organ, the Committee for Salvation, protesting against all the decrees of the Council of People's Commissars, voting again and again not to recognise the Soviet Government, openly cooperating with the new counter-revolutionary "Governments" set up at Moghilev.... On the 17th of November, for example, the Committee for Salvation addressed "all Municipal Governments, Zemstvos, and all democratic and revolutionary organisations of peasants, workers, soldiers and other citizens," in these words:

Do not recognise the Government of the Bolsheviki, and struggle against it.

Form local Committees for Salvation of Country and Revolution, who will unite all democratic forces, so as to aid the All-Russian Committee for Salvation in the tasks which it has set itself....

Meanwhile the elections for the Constituent Assembly in Petrograd gave an enormous plurality to the Bolsheviki; so that even the Mensheviki Internationalists pointed out that the Duma ought to be re-elected, as it no longer represented the political composition of the Petrograd population.... At the same time floods of resolutions from workers' organisations, from military units, even from the peasants in the surrounding country, poured in upon the Duma, calling it "counter-revolutionary, Kornilovitz," and demanding that it resign. The last days of the Duma were stormy with the bitter demands of the Municipal workers for decent living wages, and the threat of strikes....

On the 23d a formal decree of the Military Revolutionary Committee dissolved the Committee for Salvation. On the 29th, the Council of

People's Commissars ordered the dissolution and re-election of the Petrograd City Duma:

In view of the fact that the Central Duma of Petrograd, elected September 2d, ... has definitely lost the right to represent the population of Petrograd, being in complete disaccord with its state of mind and its aspirations ... and in view of the fact that the personnel of the Duma majority, although having lost all political following, continues to make use of its prerogatives to resist in a counter-revolutionary manner the will of the workers, soldiers and peasants, to sabotage and obstruct the normal work of the Government-the Council of People's Commissars considers it its duty to invite the population of the capital to pronounce judgment on the policy of the organ of Municipal autonomy.

To this end the Council of People's Commissars resolves:

(1) To dissolve the Municipal Duma; the dissolution to take effect November 30th, 1917.

(2) All functionaries elected or appointed by the present Duma shall remain at their posts and fulfil the duties confided to them, until their places shall be filled by representatives of the new Duma.

(3) All Municipal employees shall continue to fulfil their duties; those who leave the service of their own accord shall be considered discharged.

(4) The new elections for the Municipal Duma of Petrograd are fixed for December 9th, 1917....

(5) The Municipal Duma of Petrograd shall meet December 11th, 1917, at two o'clock.

(6) Those who disobey this decree, as well as those who intentionally harm or destroy the property of the Municipality, shall be immediately arrested and brought before the Revolutionary Tribunals....

The Duma met defiantly, passing resolutions to the effect that it would "defend its position to the last drop of its blood," and appealing desperately to the population to save their "own elected City Government." But the population remained indifferent or hostile. On the 31st Mayor Schreider and several members were arrested, interrogated, and released. That day and the next the Duma continued to meet, interrupted frequently by Red Guards and sailors, who politely requested the assembly to disperse. At the meeting of December 2d, an officer and some sailors entered the Nicolai Hall while a member was speaking, and ordered the members to leave, or force would be used. They did so, protesting to the last, but finally "ceding to violence."

The new Duma, which was elected ten days later, and for which the
"Moderate" Socialists refused to vote, was almost entirely
Bolshevik....

There remained several centres of dangerous opposition, such as the "republics" of Ukraine and Finland, which were showing definitely anti-Soviet tendencies. Both at Helsingfors and at Kiev the Governments were gathering troops which could be depended upon, and entering upon campaigns of crushing Bolshevism, and of disarming and expelling Russian troops. The Ukrainean Rada had taken command of all southern Russia, and was furnishing Kaledin reinforcements and supplies. Both Finland and Ukraine were beginning secret negotiations with the Germans, and were promptly recognised by the Allied Governments, which loaned them huge sums of money, joining with the propertied classes to create counter-revolutionary centres of attack upon Soviet Russia. In the end, when Bolshevism had conquered in both these countries, the defeated bourgeoisie called in the Germans to restore them to power....

But the most formidable menace to the Soviet Government was internal and two-headed-the Kaledin movement, and the Staff at Moghilev, where General Dukhonin had assumed command.

Graphic Page-287 Education Proclamation]

Proclamation of the Commission of Public Education attached to the
City Duma, concerning the strike of school-teachers, just before the
Christmas holidays. The Duma had been re-elected, and was composed
almost entirely of Bolsheviki. For translation .

The ubiquitous Muraviov was appointed commander of the war against the Cossacks, and a Red Army was recruited from among the factory workers. Hundreds of propagandists were sent to the Don. The Council of People's Commissars issued a proclamation to the Cossacks, explaining what the Soviet Government was, how the propertied classes, the *tchin ovniki,* landlords, bankers and their allies, the Cossack princes, land-owners and Generals, were trying to destroy the Revolution, and prevent the confiscation of their wealth by the people.

On November 27th a committee of Cossacks came to Smolny to see Trotzky and Lenin. They demanded if it were true that the Soviet Government did not intend to divide the Cossack lands among the peasants of Great Russia? "No," answered Trotzky. The Cossacks deliberated for a while. "Well," they asked, "does the Soviet Government intend to confiscate the estates of our great Cossack land-owners and divide them among the working Cossacks?" To this Lenin replied. "That," he said, "is for *you* to do. We shall support the working Cossacks in all their actions.... The best way to begin is to form Cossacks Soviets; you will be given representation in the *Tsay-ee-kah,* and then it will be *your* Government, too....

The Cossacks departed, thinking hard. Two weeks later General Kaledin received a deputation from his troops. "Will you," they asked, "promise to divide the great estates of the Cossack landlords among the working Cossacks?"

"Only over my dead body," responded Kaledin. A month later, seeing his army melt away before his eyes, Kaledin blew out his brains. And the Cossack movement was no more....

Meanwhile at Moghilev were gathered the old *Tsay-ee-kah* the "moderate" Socialist leaders-from Avksentiev to Tchernov-the active chiefs of the old Army Committees, and the reactionary officers. The Staff steadily refused to recognise the Council of People's Commissars. It had united about it the Death Battalions, the Knights of St. George, and the Cossacks of the Front, and was in close and secret touch with the Allied military attachès, and with the Kaledin movement and the Ukrainean Rada....

The Allied Governments had made no reply to the Peace decree of November 8th, in which the Congress of Soviets had asked for a general armistice.

On November 20th Trotzky addressed a note to the Allied Ambassadors:

I have the honour to inform you, Mr. Ambassador, that the
All-Russian Congress of Soviets... on November 8th constituted a new
Government of the Russian Republic, in the form of the Council of
People's Commissars. The President of this Government is Vladimir
Ilyitch Lenin. The direction of Foreign Affairs has been entrusted
to me, People's Commissar for Foreign Affairs....

In drawing your attention to the text, approved by the All-Russian Congress, of the proposition for an armistice and a democratic peace without annexations or indemnities, based on the right of self-determination of peoples, I have the honour to request you to consider that document as a formal proposal of an immediate armistice on all fronts, and the opening of immediate peace negotiations; a proposal which the authorised Government of the Russian Republic addresses at the same time to all the belligerent peoples and their Governments.

Please accept, Mr. Ambassador, the profound assurance of the esteem of the Soviet Government toward your people, who cannot but wish for peace, like all the other peoples exhausted and drained by this unexampled butchery....

The same night the Council of People's Commissars telegraphed to
General Dukhonin:

... The Council of People's Commissars considers it indispensable without delay to make a formal proposal of armistice to all the powers, both enemy and Allied. A declaration conforming to this decision has been sent by the Commissar for Foreign Affairs to the representatives of the Allied powers at Petrograd.

The Council of People's Commissars orders you, Citizen Commander,... to propose to the enemy military authorities immediately to cease hostilities, and enter into negotiations for peace.

In charging you with the conduct of these preliminary pourparlers, the Council of People's Commissars orders you:

1. To inform the Council by direct wire immediately of any and all steps in the pourparlers with the representatives of the enemy armies.

2. Not to sign the act of armistice until it has been passed upon by the Council of People's Commissars.

The Allied Ambassadors received Trotzky's note with contemptuous silence, accompanied by anonymous interviews in the newspapers, full of spite and ridicule. The order to Dukhonin was characterised openly as an act of treason....

As for Dukhonin, he gave no sign. On the night of November 22nd he was communicated with by telephone, and asked if he intended to obey the order. Dukhonin answered that he could not, unless it emanated from "a Government sustained by the Army and the country."

By telegraph he was immediately dismissed from the post of Supreme Commander, and Krylenko appointed in his place. Following his tactics of appealing to the masses, Lenin sent a radio to all regimental, divisional and corps Committees, to all soldiers and sailors of the Army and the Fleet, acquainting them with Dukhonin's refusal, and ordering that "the regiments on the front shall elect delegates to begin negotiations with the enemy detachments opposite their positions...."

On the 23d, the military attaches of the Allied nations, acting on instructions from their Governments, presented a note to Dukhonin, in which he was solemnly warned not to "violate the conditions of the treaties concluded between the Powers of the Entente." The note went on to say that if a separate armistice with Germany were concluded, that act "would result in the most serious consequences" to Russia. This communication Dukhonin at once sent out to all the soldiers' Committees....

Next morning Trotzky made another appeal to the troops, characterising the note of the Allied representatives as a flagrant interference in the internal affairs of Russia, and a bald attempt "to force by threats the Russian Army and the Russian people to continue the war in execution of the treaties concluded by the Tsar...."

From Smolny poured out proclamation after proclamation, denouncing Dukhonin and the counter-revolutionary officers about him, denouncing the reactionary politicians gathered at Moghilev, rousing, from one end of the thousand-mile Front to the other, millions of angry, suspicious soldiers. And at the same time Krylenko, accompanied by three detachments of fanatical sailors, set out for the *Stavka,* breathing threats of vengeance, and received by the soldiers everywhere with tremendous ovations-a triumphal progress. The Central Army Committee issued a declaration in favour of Dukhonin; and at once ten thousand troops moved upon Moghilev....

On December 2d the garrison of Moghilev rose and seized the city, arresting Dukhonin and the Army Committee, and going out with victorious red banners to meet the new Supreme Commander. Krylenko entered Moghilev next morning, to find a howling mob gathered about the railway-car in which Dukhonin had been imprisoned. Krylenko made a speech in which he implored the soldiers not to harm Dukhonin, as he was to be taken to Petrograd and judged by the Revolutionary Tribunal. When he had finished, suddenly Dukhonin himself appeared at the window, as if to address the throng. But with a savage roar the people rushed the car, and falling upon the old General, dragged him out and beat him to death on the platform....

So ended the revolt of the *Stavka*....

Immensely strengthened by the collapse of the last important stronghold of hostile military power in Russia, the Soviet Government began with confidence the organisation of the state. Many of the old functionaries flocked to its banner, and many members of other parties entered the Government service. The financially ambitious, however, were checked by the decree on Salaries of Government Employees, fixing the salaries of the People's Commissars-the highest-at five hundred rubles (about fifty dollars) a month.... The strike of Government Employees, led by the Union of Unions, collapsed, deserted by the financial and commercial interests which had been backing it. The bank clerks returned to their jobs....

With the decree on the Nationalisation of Banks, the formation of the Supreme Council of People's Economy, the putting into practical operation of the Land decree in the villages, the democratic reorganisation of the Army, and the sweeping changes in all branches of the Government and of life,-with all these, effective only by the will of the masses of workers, soldiers and peasants, slowly began, with many mistakes and hitches, the moulding of proletarian Russia.

Not by compromise with the propertied classes, or with the other political leaders; not by conciliating the old Government mechanism, did the Bolsheviki conquer the power. Nor by the organized violence of a small clique. If the masses all over Russia had not been ready for insurrection it must have failed. The only reason for Bolshevik success lay in their accomplishing the vast and simple desires of the most profound strata of the people, calling them to the work of tearing down and destroying the old, and afterward, in the smoke of falling ruins, cooperating with them to erect the frame-work of the new....

CHAPTER XII

The Peasants' Congress

IT was on November 18th that the snow came. In the morning we woke to window-ledges heaped white, and snowflakes falling so whirling thick that it was impossible to see ten feet ahead. The mud was gone; in a twinkling the gloomy city became white, dazzling. The *droshki* with their padded coachmen turned into sleights, bounding along the uneven street at headlong speed, their drivers' beards stiff and frozen.... In spite of Revolution, all Russia plunging dizzily into the unknown and terrible future, joy swept the city with the coming of the snow. Everybody was smiling; people ran into the streets, holding out their arms to the soft, falling flakes, laughing. Hidden was all the greyness; only the gold and coloured spires and cupolas, with heightened barbaric splendour, gleamed through the white snow.

Even the sun came out, pale and watery, at noon. The colds and rheumatism of the rainy months vanished. The life of the city grew gay, and the very Revolution ran swifter....

I sat one evening in a *traktir*-a kind of lower-class inn-across the street from the gates of Smolny; a low-ceilinged, loud place called "Uncle Tom's Cabin," much frequented by Red Guards. They crowded it now, packed close around the little tables with their dirty table-cloths and enormous china tea-pots, filling the place with foul cigarette-smoke, while the harassed waiters ran about crying *"Seichass! Seichass!* In a minute! Right away!"

In one corner sat a man in the uniform of a captain, addressing the assembly, which interrupted him at every few words.

"You are no better than murderers!" he cried. "Shooting down your Russian brothers on the streets!"

"When did we do that?" asked a worker.

"Last Sunday you did it, when the *yunkers*—"

"Well, didn't they shoot us?" One man exhibited his arm in a sling. "Haven't I got something to remember them by, the devils?"

The captain shouted at the top of his voice. "You should remain neutral! You should remain neutral! Who are you to destroy the legal Government? Who is Lenin? A German—"

"Who are you? A counter-revolutionist! A provocator!" they bellowed at him.

200

When he could make himself heard the captain stood up. "All right!" said he. "You call yourselves the people of Russia. But you're *not* the people of Russia. The *peasants* are the people of Russia. Wait until the peasants—"

"Yes," they cried, "wait until the peasants speak. We know what the peasants will say.... Aren't they workingmen like ourselves?"

In the long run, everything depended upon the peasants. While the peasants had been politically backward, still they had their own peculiar ideas, and they constituted more than eighty per cent of the people of Russia. The Bolsheviki had a comparatively small following among the peasants; and a permanent dictatorship of Russia by the industrial workers was impossible.... The traditional peasant party was the Socialist Revolutionary party; of all the parties now supporting the Soviet Government, the Left Socialist Revolutionaries were the logical inheritors of peasant leadership-and the Left Socialist Revolutionaries, who were at the mercy of the organised city proletariat, desperately needed the backing of the peasants....

Meanwhile Smolny had not neglected the peasants. After the Land decree, one of the first actions of the new *Tsay-ee-kah* had been to call a Congress of Peasants, over the head of the Executive Committee of the Peasants' Soviets. A few days later was issued detailed Regulations for the *Volost* (Township) Land Committees, followed by Lenin's "Instruction to Peasants," which explained the Bolshevik revolution and the new Government in simple terms; and on November 16th, Lenin and Miliutin published the "Instructions to Provincial Emissaries," of whom thousands were sent by the Soviet Government into the villages.

1. Upon his arrival in the province to which he is accredited, the emissary should call a joint meeting of the Central Executive Committees of the Soviets of Workers', Soldiers' and Peasants' Deputies, to whom he should make a report on the agrarian laws, and then demand that a joint plenary session of the Soviets be summoned....

2. He must study the aspects of the agrarian problem in the province.

a. Has the land-owners' property been taken over, and if so, in what districts?

b. Who administers the confiscated land-the former proprietor, or the Land Committees?

c. What has been done with the agricultural machinery and with the farm-animals?

3. Has the ground cultivated by the peasants been augmented?

4. How much and in what respect does the amount of land now under cultivation differ from the amount fixed by the Government as an average minimum?

5. The emissary must insist that, after the peasants have received the land, it is imperative that they increase the amount of cultivated land as quickly as possible, and that they hasten the sending of grain to the cities, as the only means of avoiding famine.

6. What are the measures projected or put into effect for the transfer of land from the land-owners to the Land Committees and similar bodies appointed by the Soviets?

7. It is desirable that agricultural properties well appointed and well organised should be administered by Soviets composed of the regular employees of those properties, under the direction of competent agricultural scientists.

All through the villages a ferment of change was going on, caused not only by the electrifying action of the Land decree, but also by thousands of revolutionary-minded peasant-soldiers returning from the front.... These men, especially, welcomed the call to a Congress of Peasants.

Like the old *Tsay-ee-kah* in the matter of the second Congress of Workers' and Soldiers' Soviets, the Executive Committee tried to prevent the Peasant Congress summoned by Smolny. And like the old *Tsay-ee-kah,* finding its resistance futile, the Executive Committee sent frantic telegrams ordering the election of Conservative delegates. Word was even spread among the peasants that the Congress would meet at Moghilev, and some delegates went there; but by November 23d about four hundred had gathered in Petrograd, and the party caucuses had begun....

The first session took place in the Alexander Hall of the Duma building, and the first vote showed that more than half of all the delegates were Left Socialist Revolutionaries, while the Bolsheviki controlled a bare fifth, the conservative Socialist Revolutionaries a quarter, and all the rest were united only in their opposition to the old Executive Committee, dominated by Avksentiev, Tchaikovsky and Peshekhonov....

The great hall was jammed with people and shaken with continual clamour; deep, stubborn bitterness divided the delegates into angry groups. To the right was a sprinkling of officers' epaulettes, and the patriarchal, bearded faces of the older, more substantial peasants; in the centre were a few peasants, non-commissioned officers, and some soldiers; and on the left almost all the delegates wore the uniforms of common soldiers. These last were the young generation, who had been serving in the army.... The galleries were thronged with workers-who, in Russia, still remember their peasant origin....

Unlike the old *Tsay-ee-kah,* the Executive Committee, in opening the session, did not recognise the Congress as official; the official Congress was called for December 13th; amid a hurricane of applause and angry cries, the speaker declared that this gathering was merely "Extraordinary Conference"... But the "Extraordinary Conference" soon showed its attitude toward the Executive Committee by electing as presiding officer Maria Spiridonova, leader of the Left Socialist Revolution aries.

Most of the first day was taken up by a violent debate as to whether the representatives of *Volost* Soviets should be seated, or only delegates from the Provincial bodies; and just as in the Workers' and Soldiers' Congress, an overwhelming majority declared in favour of the widest possible representation. Whereupon the old Executive Committee left the hall....

Almost immediately it was evident that most of the delegates were hostile to the Government of the People's Commissars. Zinoviev, attempting to speak for the Bolsheviki, was hooted down, and as he left the platform, amid laughter, there were cries, "There's how a People's Commissar sits in a mudpuddle!"

"We Left Socialist Revolutionaries refuse," cried Nazariev, a delegate from the Provinces, "to recognise this so-called Workers' and Peasants' Government until the peasants are represented in it. At present it is nothing but a dictatorship of the workers.... We insist upon the formation of a new Government which will represent the entire democracy!"

The reactionary delegates shrewdly fostered this feeling, declaring, in the face of protests from the Bolshevik benches, that the Council of People's Commissars intended either to control the Congress or dissolve it by force of arms-an announcement which was received by the peasants with bursts of fury....

On the third day Lenin suddenly mounted the tribune; for ten minutes the room went mad. "Down with him!" they shrieked. "We will not listen to any of your People's Commissars! We don't recognise your Government!"

Lenin stood there quite calmly, gripping the desk with both hands, his little eyes thoughtfully surveying the tumult beneath. Finally, except for the right side of the hall, the demonstration wore itself out somewhat.

"I do not come here as a member of the Council of People's
Commissars," said Lenin, and waited again for the noise to subside,
"but as a member of the Bolshevik faction, duly elected to this
Congress." And he held his credentials up to that all might see them.

"However," he went on, in an unmoved voice, "nobody will deny that the present Government of Russia has been formed by the Bolshevik party-" he had to wait a moment, "so that for all purposes it is the same thing...." Here the right benches broke into deafening clamour, but the centre and left were curious, and compelled silence.

Lenin's argument was simple. "Tell me frankly, you peasants, to whom we have given the lands of the *pomieshtchiki;* do you want now to prevent the workers from getting control of industry? This is class war. The *pomieshtchiki* of course oppose the peasants, and the manufactures oppose the workers. Are you going to allow the ranks of the proletariat to be divided? Which side will you be on?

"We, the Bolsheviki, are the party of the proletariat-of the peasant proletariat as well as the industrial proletariat. We, the Bolsheviki, are the protectors of the Soviets-of the Peasants' Soviets as well as those of the Workers and Soldiers. The present Government is a Government of Soviets; we have not only invited the Peasants' Soviets to join that Government, but we have also invited representatives of the Left Socialist Revolutionaries to enter the Council of People's Commissars....

"The Soviets are the most perfect representatives of the people-of the workers in the factories and mines, of the workers in the fields. Anybody who attempts to destroy the Soviets is guilty of an anti-democratic and counter-revolutionary act. And I serve notice here on you, comrades *Right* Socialist Revolutionaries-and on you, Messrs. Cadets-that if the Constituent Assembly attempts to destroy the Soviets, we shall not permit the Constituent Assembly to do this thing!"

On the afternoon of November 25th Tchernov arrived in hot haste from Moghilev, summoned by the Executive Committee. Only two months before considered an extreme revolutionist, and very popular with the peasants, he was now called to check the dangerous drift of the Congress toward the Left. Upon his arrival Tchernov was arrested and taken to Smolny, where, after a short conversation, he was released.

His first act was to bitterly rebuke the Executive Committee for leaving the Congress. They agreed to return, and Tchernov entered the hall, welcomed with great applause by the majority, and the hoots and jeers of the Bolsheviki.

"Comrades! I have been away. I participated in the Conference of the Twelfth Army on the question of calling a Congress of all the Peasant delegates of the armies of the Western Front, and I know very little about the insurrection which occurred here—"

Zinoviev rose in his seat, and shouted, "Yes, you were away-for a few minutes!" Fearful tumult. Cries, "Down with the Bolsheviki!"

Tchernov continued. "The accusation that I helped lead an army on Petrograd has no foundation, and is entirely false. Where does such an accusation come from? Show me the source!"

Zinoviev: "*Izviestia* and *Dielo Naroda*-your own paper -that's where it comes from!"

Tchernov's wide face, with the small eyes, waving hair and greyish beard, became red with wrath, but he controlled himself and went on. "I repeat, I know practically nothing about what has happened here, and I did not lead any army except this army, (he pointed to the peasant delegates), which I am largely responsible for bringing here!" Laughter, and shouts of "Bravo!"

"Upon my return I visited Smolny. No such accusation was made against me there.... After a brief conversation I left-and that's all! Let any one present make such an accusation!"

An uproar followed, in which the Bolsheviki and some of the Left Socialist Revolutionaries were on their feet all at once, shaking their fists and yelling, and the rest of the assembly tried to yell them down.

"This is an outrage, not a session!" cried Tchernov, and he left the hall; the meeting was adjourned because of the noise and disorder....

Meanwhile, the question of the status of the Executive Committee was agitating all minds. By declaring the assembly "Extraordinary Conference," it had been planned to block the reelection of the Executive Committee. But this worked both ways; the Left Socialist Revolutionists decided that if the Congress had no power over the Executive Committee, then the Executive Committee had no power over the Congress. On November 25th the assembly resolved that the powers of the Executive Committee be assumed by the Extraordinary Conference, in which only members of the Executive who had been elected as delegates might vote....

The next day, in spite of the bitter opposition of the Bolsheviki, the resolution was amended to give all the members of the Executive Committee, whether elected as delegates or not, voice and vote in the assembly.

On the 27th occurred the debate on the Land question, which revealed the differences between the agrarian programme of the Bolsheviki and the Left Socialist Revolutionaries.

Kolchinsky, for the Left Socialist Revolutionaries, outlined the history of the Land question during the Revolution. The first Congress of Peasants' Soviets, he said, had voted a precise and formal resolution in favour of putting the landed estates immediately into the hands of the Land Committees. But the directors of the Revolution, and the bourgeois in the Government, had insisted that the question could not be solved until the Constituent Assembly met.... The second period of the Revolution, the period of "compromise,"was signalled by the entrance of Tchernov into the Cabinet. The peasants were convinced that now the practical solution of the Land question would begin; but in spite of the imperative decision of the first Peasant Congress, the reactionaries and conciliators in the Executive Committee had prevented any action. This policy provoked a series of agrarian disorders, which appeared as the natural expression of impatience and thwarted energy on the part of the peasants. The peasants understood the exact meaning of the Revolution-they tried to turn words into action....

"The recent events," said the orator, "do not indicate a simple riot, or a 'Bolshevik adventure,' but on the contrary, a real popular rising, which has been greeted with sympathy by the whole country....

"The Bolsheviki in general took the correct attitude toward the Land question; but in recommending that the peasants seize the land by force, they committed a profound error.... From the first days, the Bolsheviki declared that the peasants should take over the land 'by revolutionary massacre.' This is nothing but anarchy; the land can be taken over in an organised manner.... For the Bolsheviki it was important that the problems of the Revolution should be solved in the quickest possible manner-but the Bolsheviki were not interested in *how* these problems were to be solved....

"The Land decree of the Congress of Soviets is identical in its fundamentals with the decisions of the first Peasants' Congress. Why then did not the new Government follow the tactics outlined by that Congress? Because the Council of People's Commissars wanted to hasten the settlement of the Land question, so that the Constituent Assembly would have nothing to do....

"But also the Government saw that it was necessary to adopt practical measures, so without further reflection, it adopted the Regulations for Land Committees, thus creating a strange situation; for the Council of People's Commissars abolished private property in land, but the Regulations drawn up by the Land Committees are based on private property.... However, no harm has been done by that; for the Land Committees are paying no attention to the Soviet decrees, but are putting into operation their own practical decisions-decisions based on the will of the vast majority of the peasants....

"These Land Committees are not attempting the legislative solution of the Land question, which belongs to the Constituent Assembly alone.... But will the Constituent Assembly desire to do the will of the Russian peasants? Of that we cannot be sure.... All we can be sure of is that the revolutionary determination of the peasants is now aroused, and that the Constituent will be *forced* to settle the Land question the way the peasants want it settled.... The Constituent Assembly will not dare to break with the will of the people...."

Followed him Lenin, listened to now with absorbing intensity. "At this moment we are not only trying to solve the Land question, but the question of Social Revolution-not only here in Russia, but all over the world. The Land question cannot be solved independently of the other problems of the Social Revolution.... For example, the confiscation of the landed estates will provoke the resistance not only of Russian land-owners, but also of foreign capital-with whom the great landed properties are connected through the intermediary of the banks....

"The ownership of the land in Russia is the basis for immense oppression, and the confiscation of the land by the peasants is the most important step of our Revolution. But it cannot be separated from the other steps, as is clearly manifested by the stages through which the Revolution has had to pass. The first stage was the crushing of autocracy and the crushing of the power of the industrial capitalists and land-owners, whose interests are closely related. The second stage was the strengthening of the Soviets and the political compromise with the bourgeoisie. The mistake of the Left Socialist Revolutionaries lies in the fact that at that time they did not oppose the policy of compromise, because they held the theory that the consciousness of the masses was not yet fully developed....

"If Socialism can only be realised when the intellectual development of all the people permits it, then we shall not see Socialism for at least five hundred years.... The Socialist political party-this is the vanguard of the working-class; it must not allow itself to be halted by the lack of education of the mass average, but it must lead the masses, using the Soviets as organs of revolutionary initiative.... But in order to lead the wavering, the comrades Left Socialist Revolutionaries themselves must stop hesitating....

"In July last a series of open breaks began between the popular masses and the 'compromisers'; but now, in November, the Left Socialist Revolutionaries are still holding out their hand to Avksentiev, who is pulling the people with his little finger.... If Compromise continues, the Revolution disappears. No compromise with the bourgeoisie is possible; its power must be absolutely crushed....

"We Bolsheviki have not changed our Land programme; we have not given up the abolition of private property in the land, and we do not intend to do so. We adopted the Regulations for Land Committees,-which are *not* based on private property at all-because we want to accomplish the popular will in the way the people have themselves decided to do it, so as to draw closer the coalition of all the elements who are fighting for the Social Revolution.

"We invite the Left Socialist Revolutionaries to enter that coalition, insisting, however, that they cease looking backward, and that they break with the 'conciliators' of their party....

"As far as the Constituent Assembly is concerned, it is true, as the preceding speaker has said, that the work of the Constituent will depend on the revolutionary determination of the masses. I say, 'Count on that revolutionary determination, but don't forget your gun!'"

Lenin then read the Bolshevik resolution:

The Peasants' Congress, fully supporting the Land decree of November 8th... approves of the Provisional Workers' and Peasants' Government of the Russian Republic, established by the second All-Russian Congress of Soviets of Workers' and Soldiers' Deputies.

The Peasants' Congress... invites all peasants unanimously to sustain that law, and to apply it immediately themselves; and at the same time invites the peasants to appoint to posts and positions of responsibility only persons who have proved, not by words but by acts, their entire devotion to the interests of the exploited peasant-workers, their desire and their ability to defend these interests against all resistance on the part of the great land-owners, the capitalists, their partisans and accomplices....

The Peasants' Congress, at the same time, expresses its conviction that the complete realisation of all the measures which make up the Land decree can only be successful through the triumph of the Workers' Social Revolution, which began November 7th, 1917; for only the Social Revolution can accomplish the definite transfer, without possibility of return, of the land to the peasant-workers, the confiscation of model farms and their surrender to the peasant communes, the confiscation of agricultural machinery belonging to the great land-owners, the safe-guarding of the interests of the agricultural workers by the complete abolition of wage-slavery, the regular and methodical distribution among all regions of Russia of the products of agriculture and industry, and the seizure of the banks (without which the possession of land by the whole people would be impossible, after the abolition of private property), and all sorts of assistance by the State to the workers....

For these reasons the Peasants' Congress sustains entirely the Revolution of November 7th... as a social revolution, and expresses its unalterable will to put into operation, with whatever modifications are necessary, but without any hesitation, the social transformation of the Russian Republic.

The indispensable conditions of the victory of the Social Revolution, which alone will secure the lasting success and the complete realisation of the Land decree, is the close union of the peasant-workers with the industrial working-class, with the proletariat of all advanced countries. From now on, in the Russian Republic, all the organisation and administration of the State, from top to bottom, must rest on that union. That union, crushing all attempts, direct or indirect, open or dissimulated, to return to the policy of conciliation with the bourgeoisie-conciliation, damned by experience, with the chiefs of bourgeois politics-can alone insure the victory of Socialism throughout the world....

The reactionaries of the Executive Committee no longer dared openly to appear. Tchernov, however, spoke several times, with a modest and winning impartiality. He was invited to sit on the platform.... On the second night of the Congress an anonymous note was handed up to the chairman, requesting that Tchernov be made honorary President. Ustinov read the note aloud, and immediately Zinoviev was on his feet, screaming that this was a trick of the old Executive Committee to capture the convention; in a moment the hall was one bellowing mass of waving arms and angry faces, on both sides.... Nevertheless, Tchernov remained very popular.

In the stormy debates on the Land question and the Lenin resolution, the Bolsheviki were twice on the point of quitting the assembly, both times restrained by their leaders.... It seemed to me as if the Congress were hopelessly deadlocked.

But none of us knew that a series of secret conferences were already going on between the Left Socialist Revolutionaries and the Bolsheviki at Smolny. At first the Left Socialist Revolutionaries had demanded that there be a Government composed of all the Socialist parties in and out of the Soviets, to be responsible to a People's Council, composed of an equal number of delegates from the Workers' and Soldiers' organisation, and that of the Peasants, and completed by representatives of the City Dumas and the Zemstvos; Lenin and Trotzky were to be eliminated, and the Military Revolutionary Committee and other repressive organs dissolved.

Wednesday morning, November 28th, after a terrible all-night struggle, an agreement was reached. The _Tsay-ee-kah,_composed of 108 members, was to be augumented by 108 members elected proportionally from the Peasants' Congress; by 100 delegates elected directly from the Army and the Fleet; and by 50 representatives of the Trade Unions (35 from the general Unions, 10 Railway Workers, and 5 from the Post and Telegraph Workers). The Dumas and Zemstvos were dropped. Lenin and Trotzky remained in the Government, and the Military Revolutionary Committee continued to function.

The sessions of the Congress had now been removed to the Imperial Law School building, Fontanka 6, headquarters of the Peasants' Soviets. There in the great meeting-hall the delegates gathered on Wednesday afternoon. The old Executive Committee had withdrawn, and was holding a rump convention of its own in another room of the same building, made up of bolting delegates and representatives of the Army Committees.

Tchernov went from one meeting to the other, keeping a watchful eye on the proceedings. He knew that an agreement with the Bolsheviki was being discussed, but he did not know that it had been concluded.

He spoke to the rump convention. "At present, when everybody is in favour of forming an all-Socialist Government, many people forget the first Ministry, which was *not* a coalition Government, and in which there was only one Socialist-Kerensky; a Government which, in its time, was very popular. Now people accuse Kerensky; they forget that he was raised to power, not only by the Soviets, but also by the popular masses....

"Why did public opinion change toward Kerensky? The savages set up gods to which they pray, and which they punish if one of their prayers is not answered.... That is what is happening at this moment.... Yesterday Kerensky; today Lenin and Trotzky; another to-morrow....

"We have proposed to both Kerensky and the Bolsheviki to retire from the power. Kerensky has accepted-to-day he announced from his hiding-place that he has resigned as Premier; but the Bolsheviki wish to retain the power, and they do not know how to use it...."

"If the Bolsheviki succeed, or if they fail, the fate of Russia will not be changed. The Russian villages understand perfectly what they want, and they are now carrying out their own measures.... The villages will save us in the end...."

In the meanwhile, in the great hall Ustinov had announced the agreement between the Peasants' Congress and Smolny, received by the delegates with the wildest joy. Suddenly Tchernov appeared, and demanded the floor.

"I understand," he began, "that an agreement is being concluded between the Peasants' Congress and Smolny. Such an agreement would be illegal, seeing that the true Congress of Peasants' Soviets does not meet until next week...."

"Moreover, I want to warn you now that the Bolsheviki will never accept your demands...."

He was interrupted by a great burst of laughter; and realising the situation, he left the platform and the room, taking his popularity with him....

Late in the afternoon of Thursday, November 16th, the Congress met in extraordinary session. There was a holiday feeling in the air; on every face was a smile.... The remainder of the business before the assembly was hurried through, and then old Nathanson, the white-bearded dean of the left wing of the Socialist Revolutionaries, his voice trembling and tears in his eyes, read the report of the "wedding" of the Peasants' Soviets with the Workers' and Soldiers' Soviets. At every mention of the word "union" there was ecstatic applause.... At the end Ustinov announced the arrival rival of a delegation from Smolny, accompanied by representatives of the Red Army, greeted with a rising ovation. One after another a workman, a soldier and a sailor took the floor, hailing them.

Then Boris Reinstein, delegate of the American Socialist Labor Party: "The day of the union of the Congress of Peasants and the Soviets of Workers' and Soldiers' Deputies is one of the great days of the Revolution. The sound of it will ring with resounding echoes throughout the whole world-in Paris, in London, and across the ocean-in New York. This union will fill with happiness the hearts of all toilers.

"A great idea has triumphed. The West, and America, expected from Russia, from the Russian proletariat, something tremendous.... The proletariat of the world is waiting for the Russian Revolution, waiting for the great things that it is accomplishing...."

Sverdlov, president of the *Tsay-ee-kah,* greeted them. And with the shout, "Long live the end of civil war! Long live the United Democracy!" the peasants poured out of the building.

It was already dark, and on the ice-covered snow glittered the pale light of moon and star. Along the bank of the canal were drawn up in full marching order the soldiers of the Pavlovsky Regiment, with their band, which broke into the *Marseillaise.* Amid the crashing full-throated shouts of the soldiers, the peasants formed in line, unfurling the great red banner of the Executive Committee of the All-Russian Peasants' Soviets, embroidered newly in gold, "Long live the union of the revolutionary and toiling masses!" Following were other banners; of the District Soviets-of Putilov Factory, which read, "We bow to this flag in order to create the brotherhood of all people!"

From somewhere torches appeared, blazing orange in the night, a thousand times reflected in the facets of the ice, streaming out smokily over the throng as it moved down the bank of the Fontanka singing, between crowds that stood in astonished silence.

"Long live the Revolutionary Army! Long live the Red Guard! Long live the Peasants!"

So the great procession wound through the city, growing and unfurling ever new red banners lettered in gold. Two old peasants, bowed with toil, were walking hand in hand, their faces illumined with child-like bliss.

"Well," said one, "I'd like to see them take away our land again, *now!*

Near Smolny the Red Guard was lined up on both sides of the street, wild with delight. The other old peasant spoke to his comrade, "I am not tired," he said. "I walked on air all the way!"

On the steps of Smolny about a hundred Workers' and Soldiers' Deputies were massed, with their banner, dark against the blaze of light streaming out between the arches. Like a wave they rushed down, clasping the peasants in their arms and kissing them; and the procession poured in through the great door and up the stairs, with a noise like thunder....

In the immense white meeting-room the *Tsay-ee-kah* was waiting, with the whole Petrograd Soviet and a thousand spectators beside, with that solemnity which attends great conscious moments in history.

Zinoviev announced the agreement with the Peasants' Congress, to a shaking roar which rose and burst into storm as the sound of music blared down the corridor, and the head of the procession came in. On the platform the presidium rose and made place for the Peasants' presidium, the two embracing; behind them the two banners were intertwined against the white wall, over the empty frame from which the Tsar's picture had been torn....

Then opened the "triumphal session." After a few words of welcome from Sverdlov, Maria Spiridonova, slight, pale, with spectacles and hair drawn flatly down, and the air of a New England school-teacher, took the tribune-the most loved and the most powerful woman in all Russia.

"... Before the workers of Russia open now horizons which history has never known.... All workers' movements in the past have been defeated. But the present movement is international, and that is why it is invincible. There is no force in the world which can put out the fire of the Revolution! The old world crumbles down, the new world begins...."

Then Trotzky, full of fire: "I wish you welcome, comrades peasants! You come here not as guests, but as masters of this house, which holds the heart of the Russian Revolution. The will of millions of workers is now concentrated in this hall.... There is now only one master of the Russian land: the union of the workers, soldiers and peasants...."

With biting sarcasm he went on to speak of the Allied diplomats, till then contemptuous of Russia's invitation to an armistice, which had been accepted by the Central Powers.

"A new humanity will be born of this war.... In this hall we swear to workers of all lands to remain at our revolutionary post. If we are broken, then it will be in defending our flag...."

Krylenko followed him, explaining the situation at the front, where
Dukhonin was preparing to resist the Council of People's Commissars.
"Let Dukhonin and those with him understand well that we shall not
deal gently with those who bar the road to peace!"

Dybenko saluted the assembly in the name of the Fleet, and Krushinsky, member of the *Vikzhel,* said, "From this moment, when the union of all true Socialists is realised, the whole army of railway workers places itself absolutely at the disposition of the revolutionary democracy!" And Lunatcharsky, almost weeping, and Proshian, for the Left Socialist Revolutionaries, and finally Saharashvili, for the United Social Democrats Internationalists, composed of members of the Martov's and of Gorky's groups, who declared:

"We left the *Tsay-ee-kah* because of the uncompromising policy of the Bolsheviki, and to force them to make concessions in order to realise the union of all the revolutionary democracy. Now that that union is brought about, we consider it a sacred duty to take our places once more in the *Tsay-ee-kah*.... We declare that all those who have withdrawn from the *Tsay-ee-kah* should now return."

Stachkov, a dignified old peasant of the presidium of the Peasants' Congress, bowed to the four corners of the room. "I greet you with the christening of a new Russian life and freedom!"

Gronsky, in the name of the Polish Social Democracy; Skripnik, for the Factory-Shop Committees; Tifonov, for the Russian soldiers at Salonika; and others, interminably, speaking out of full hearts, with the happy eloquence of hopes fulfilled.... It was late in the night when the following resolution was put and passed unanimously:

"The *Tsay-ee-kah,* united in extraordinary session with the Petrograd Soviet and the Peasants' Congress, confirms the Land and Peace decrees adopted by the second Congress of Soviets of Workers' and Soldiers' Deputies, and also the decree on Workers' Control adopted by the *Tsay-ee-kah.*

"The joint session of the *Tsay-ee-kah* and the Peasants' Congress expresses its firm conviction that the union of workers, soldiers and peasants, this fraternal union of all the workers and all exploited, will consolidate the power conquered by them, that it will take all revolutionary measures to hasten the passing of the power into the hands of the working-class in other countries, and that it will assure in this manner the lasting accomplishment of a just peace and the victory of Socialism."

Notes and Explanations

To the average reader the multiplicity of Russian organisations-political groups, Committees and Central Committees, Soviets, Dumas and Unions-will prove extremely confusing. For this reason I am giving here a few brief definitions and explanations.

Political Parties

In the elections to the Constituent Assembly, there were seventeen tickets in Petrograd, and in some of the provincial towns as many as forty; but the following summary of the aims and composition of political parties is limited to the groups and factions mentioned in this book. Only the essence of their programmes and the general character of their constituencies can be noticed....

1. *Monarchists,* of various shades, *Octobrists,* etc. These once-powerful factions no longer existed openly; they either worked underground, or their members joined the *Cadets,* as the *Cadets* came by degrees to stand for their political programme. Representatives in this book, Rodzianko, Shulgin.

2. *Cadets.* So-called from the initials of its name, Constitutional Democrats. Its official name is "Party of the People's Freedom." Under the Tsar composed of Liberals from the propertied classes, the *Cadets* were the great party of *political* reform, roughly corresponding to the Progressive Party in America. When the Revolution broke out in March, 1917, the *Cadets* formed the first Provisional Government. The *Cadet* Ministry was overthrown in April because it declared itself in favour of Allied imperialistic aims, including the imperialistic aims of the Tsar's Government. As the Revolution became more and more a *social economic* Revolution, the *Cadets* grew more and more conservative. Its representatives in this book are: Miliukov, Vinaver, Shatsky.

2a. *Group of Public Men.* After the *Cadets* had become unpopular through their relations with the Kornilov counter-revolution, the *Group of Public Men* was formed in Moscow. Delegates from the *Group of Public Men* were given portfolios in the last Kerensky Cabinet. The *Group* declared itself non-partisan, although its intellectual leaders were men like Rodzianko and Shulgin. It was composed of the more "modern" bankers, merchants and manufacturers, who were intelligent enough to realise that the Soviets must be fought by their own weapon-economic organisation. Typical of the *Group:* Lianozov, Konovalov.

3. *Populist Socialists,* or *Trudoviki* (Labour Group). Numerically a small party, composed of cautious intellectuals, the leaders of the Cooperative societies, and conservative peasants. Professing to be Socialists, the *Populists* really supported the interests of the petty bourgeoisie-clerks, shopkeepers, etc. By direct descent, inheritors of the compromising tradition of the Labour Group in the Fourth Imperial Duma, which was composed largely of peasant representatives. Kerensky was the leader of the *Trudoviki* in the Imperial Duma when the Revolution of March, 1917, broke out. The *Populist Socialists* are a nationalistic party. Their representatives in this book are: Peshekhanov, Tchaikovsky.

4. *Russian Social Democratic Labour Party.* Originally Marxian Socialists. At a party congress held in 1903, the party split, on the question of tactics, into two factions-the Majority (Bolshinstvo), and the Minority (Menshinstvo). From this sprang the names "Bolsheviki" and "Mensheviki"-"members of the majority" and "members of the minority." These two wings became two separate parties, both calling themselves "Russian Social Democratic Labour Party," and both professing to be Marxians. Since the Revolution of 1905 the Bolsheviki were really the minority, becoming again the majority in September, 1917.

a. *Mensheviki.* This party includes all shades of Socialists who believe that society must progress by natural evolution toward Socialism, and that the working-class must conquer political power first. Also a nationalistic party. This was the party of the Socialist intellectuals, which means: all the means of education having been in the hands of the propertied classes, the intellectuals instinctively reacted to their training, and took the side of the propertied classes. Among their representatives in this book are: Dan, Lieber, Tseretelli.

b. *Mensheviki Internationalists.* The radical wing of the *Mensheviki,* internationalists and opposed to all coalition with the propertied classes; yet unwilling to break loose from the conservative Mensheviki, and opposed to the dictatorship of the working-class advocated by the Bolsheviki. Trotzky was long a member of this group. Among their leaders: Martov, Martinov.

c. *Bolsheviki.* Now call themselves the *Communist Party,* in order to emphasise their complete separation from the tradition of "moderate" or "parliamentary" Socialism, which dominates the Mensheviki and the so-called Majority Socialists in all countries. The *Bolsheviki* proposed immediate proletarian insurrection, and seizure of the reins of Government, in order to hasten the coming of Socialism by forcibly taking over industry, land, natural resources and financial institutions. This party expresses the desires chiefly of the factory workers, but also of a large section of the poor peasants. The name "Bolshevik" can *not* be translated by "Maximalist." The Maximalists are a separate group. (See paragraph 5b). Among the leaders: Lenin, Trotzky, Lunatcharsky.

d. *United Social Democrats Internationalists.* Also called the *Novaya Zhizn* (New Life) group, from the name of the very influential newspaper which was its organ. A little group of intellectuals with a very small following among the working-class, except the personal following of Maxim Gorky, its leader. Intellectuals, with almost the same programme as the *Mensheviki Internationalists,* except that the *Novaya Zhizn* group refused to be tied to either of the two great factions. Opposed the Bolshevik tactics, but remained in the Soviet Government. Other representatives in this book: Avilov, Kramarov.

e. *Yedinstvo.* A very small and dwindling group, composed almost entirely of the personal following of Plekhanov, one of the pioneers of the Russian Social Democratic movement in the 80's, and its greatest theoretician. Now an old man, Plekhanov was extremely patriotic, too conservative even for the Mensheviki. After the Bolshevik *coup d'etat, Yedinstvo* disappeared.

5. *Socialist Revolutionary party.* Called *Essaires* from the initials of their name. Originally the revolutionary party of the peasants, the party of the Fighting Organisations-the Terrorists. After the March Revolution, it was joined by many who had never been Socialists. At that time it stood for the abolition of private property in land only, the owners to be compensated in some fashion. Finally the increasing revolutionary feeling of peasants forced the *Essaires* to abandon the "compensation" clause, and led to the younger and more fiery intellectuals breaking off from the main party in the fall of 1917 and forming a new party, the *Left Socialist Revolutionary party.* The *Essaires,* who were afterward always called by the radical groups *"Right Socialist Revolutionaries,"* adopted the political attitude of the Mensheviki, and worked together with them. They finally came to represent the wealthier peasants, the intellectuals, and the politically uneducated populations of remote rural districts. Among them there was, however, a wider difference of shades of political and economic opinion than among the Mensheviki. Among their leaders mentioned in these pages: Avksentiev, Gotz, Kerensky, Tchernov, "Babuschka" Breshkovskaya.

a. *Left Socialist Revolutionaries.* Although theoretically sharing the Bolshevik programme of dictatorship of the working-class, at first were reluctant to follow the ruthless Bolshevik tactics. However, the *Left Socialist Revolutionaries* remained in the Soviet Government, sharing the Cabinet portfolios, especially that of Agriculture. They withdrew from the Government several times, but always returned. As the peasants left the ranks of the *Essaires* in increasing numbers, they joined the *Left Socialist Revolutionary party,* which became the great peasant party supporting the Soviet Government, standing for confiscation without compensation of the great landed estates, and their disposition by the peasants themselves. Among the leaders: Spiridonova, Karelin, Kamkov, Kalagayev.

b. *Maximalists.* An off-shoot of the *Socialist Revolutionary party* in the Revolution of 1905, when it was a powerful peasant movement, demanding the immediate application of the maximum Socialist programme. Now an insignificant group of peasant anarchists.

Parliamentary Procedure

Russian meetings and conventions are organised after the continental model rather than our own. The first action is usually the election of officers and the *presidium.*

The *presidium* is a presiding committee, composed of representatives of the groups and political factions represented in the assembly, in proportion to their numbers. The *presidium* arranges the Order of Business, and its members can be called upon by the President to take the chair *pro tem.*

Each question (*vopros*) is stated in a general way and then debated, and at the close of the debate resolutions are submitted by the different factions, and each one voted on separately. The Order of Business can be, and usually is, smashed to pieces in the first half hour. On the plea of "emergency," which the crowd almost always grants, anybody from the floor can get up and say anything on any subject. The crowd controls the meeting, practically the only functions of the speaker being to keep order by ringing a little bell, and to recognise speakers. Almost all the real work of the session is done in caucuses of the different groups and political factions, which almost always cast their votes in a body and are represented by floor-leaders. The result is, however, that at every important new point, or vote, the session takes a recess to enable the different groups and political factions to hold a caucus.

The crowd is extremely noisy, cheering or heckling speakers, over-riding the plans of the *presidium.* Among the customary cries are: *"Prosim!* Please! Go on!" *"Pravilno!"* or *"Eto vierno!* That's true! Right!" *"Do volno!* Enough!" *"Doloi!* Down with him!" *"Posor!* Shame!" and *"Teesche!* Silence! Not so noisy!"

Popular Organisations

1. *Soviet.* The word *soviet* means "council." Under the Tsar the Imperial Council of State was called *Gosudarstvennyi Soviet.* Since the Revolution, however, the term *Soviet* has come to be associated with a certain type of parliament elected by members of working-class economic organisations-the Soviet of Workers', of Soldiers', or of Peasants' Deputies. I have therefore limited the word to these bodies, and wherever else it occurs I have translated it "Council."

Besides the local *Soviets,* elected in every city, town and village of Russia-and in large cities, also Ward *(Raionny) Soviets*-there are also the *oblastne* or *gubiernsky* (district or provincial) *Soviets,* and the Central Executive Committee of the All-Russian *Soviets* in the capital, called from its initials *Tsay-ee-kah.* (See below, "Central Committees").

Almost everywhere the *Soviets* of Workers' and of Soldiers' Deputies combined very soon after the March Revolution. In special matters concerning their peculiar interests, however, the Workers' and the Soldiers' Sections continued to meet separately. The *Soviets* of Peasants' Deputies did not join the other two until after the Bolshevik *coup d'etat.* They, too, were organised like the workers and soldiers, with an Executive Committee of the All-Russian Peasants' *Soviets* in the capital.

2. *Trade Unions.* Although mostly industrial in form, the Russian labour unions were still called Trade Unions, and at the time of the Bolshevik Revolution had from three to four million members. These Unions were also organised in an All-Russian body, a sort of Russian Federation of Labour, which had its Central Executive Committee in the capital.

3. *Factory-Shop Committees.* These were spontaneous organisations created in the factories by the workers in their attempt to control industry, taking advantage of the administrative break-down incident upon the Revolution. Their function was by revolutionary action to take over and run the factories. The *Factory-Shop Committees* also had their All-Russian organisation, with a Central Committee at Petrograd, which co-operated with the Trade Unions.

217

4. *Dumas.* The word *duma* means roughly "deliberative body." The old Imperial Duma, which persisted six months after the Revolution, in a democratised form, died a natural death in September, 1917. The *City Duma* referred to in this book was the reorganised Municipal Council, often called "Municipal Self-Government." It was elected by direct and secret ballot, and its only reason for failure to hold the masses during the Bolshevik Revolution was the general decline in influence of all purely *political* representation in the fact of the growing power of organisations based on *economic* groups.

5. *Zemstvos.* May be roughly translated "county councils." Under the Tsar semi-political, semi-social bodies with very little administrative power, developed and controlled largely by intellectual Liberals among the land-owning classes. Their most important function was education and social service among the peasants. During the war the *Zemstvos* gradually took over the entire feeding and clothing of the Russian Army, as well as the buying from foreign countries, and work among the soldiers generally corresponding to the work of the American Y. M. C. A. at the Front. After the March Revolution the *Zemstvos* were democratized, with a view to making them the organs of local government in the rural districts. But like the *City Dumas,* they could not compete with the *Soviets.*

6. *Cooperatives.* These were the workers' and peasants' Consumers' Cooperative societies, which had several million members all over Russia before the Revolution. Founded by Liberals and "moderate" Socialists, the Cooperative movement was not supported by the revolutionary Socialist groups, because it was a substitute for the complete transference of means of production and distribution into the hands of the workers. After the March Revolution the *Cooperatives* spread rapidly, and were dominated by Populist Socialists, Mensheviki and Socialist Revolutionaries, and acted as a conservative political force until the Bolshevik Revolution. However, it was the *Cooperatives* which fed Russia when the old structure of commerce and transportation collapsed.

7. *Army Committees.* The *Army Committees* were formed by the soldiers at the front to combat the reactionary influence of the old regime officers. Every company, regiment, brigade, division and corps had its committee, over all of which was elected the *Army Committee.* The *Central Army Committee* cooperated with the General Staff. The administrative break-down in the army incident upon the Revolution threw upon the shoulders of the *Army Committees* most of the work of the Quartermaster's Department, and in some cases, even the command of troops.

8. *Fleet Committees.* The corresponding organisations in the Navy.

Central Committees

In the spring and summer of 1917, All-Russian conventions of every sort of organisation were held at Petrograd. There were national congresses of Workers', Soldiers' and Peasants' Soviets, Trade Unions, Factory-Shop Committees, Army and Fleet Committees-besides every branch of the military and naval service, Cooperatives, Nationalities, etc. Each of these conventions elected a Central Committee, or a Central Executive Committee, to guard its particular interests at the seat of Government. As the Provisional Government grew weaker, these Central Committees were forced to assume more and more administrative powers.

The most important Central Committees mentioned in this book are:

Union of Unions. During the Revolution of 1905, Professor Miliukov and other Liberals established unions of professional men-doctors, lawyers, physicians, etc. These were united under one central organisation, the *Union of Unions.* In 1905 the *Union of Unions* acted with the revolutionary democracy; in 1917, however, the *Union of Unions* opposed the Bolshevik uprising, and united the Government employees who went on strike against the authority of the Soviets.

Tsay-ee-kah. All-Russian Central Executive Committee of the Soviets of Workers' and Soldiers' Deputies. So called from the initials of its name.

Tsentroflot. "Centre-Fleet"-the Central Fleet Committee.

Vikzhel. All-Russian Central Committee of the Railway Workers' Union. So called from the initials of its name.

Other Organisations

Red Guards. The armed factory workers of Russia. The *Red Guards* were first formed during the Revolution of 1905, and sprang into existence again in the days of March, 1917, when a force was needed to keep order in the city. At that time they were armed, and all efforts of the Provisional Government to disarm them were more or less unsuccessful. At every great crisis in the Revolution the *Red Guards* appeared on the streets, untrained and undisciplined, but full of Revolutionary zeal.

White Guards. Bourgeois volunteers, who emerged in the last stages of the Revolution, to defend private property from the Bolshevik attempt to abolish it. A great many of them were University students.

Tekhintsi. The so-called "Savage Division" in the army, made up of Mohametan tribesmen from Central Asia, and personally devoted to General Kornilov. The *Tekhintsi* were noted for their blind obedience and their savage cruelty in warfare.

Death Battalions. Or *Shock Battalions.* The Women's Battalion is known to the world as the *Death Battalion,* but there were many *Death Battalions* composed of men. These were formed in the summer of 1917 by Kerensky, for the purpose of strengthening the discipline and combative fire of the army by heroic example. The *Death Battalions* were composed mostly of intense young patriots. These came for the most part from among the sons of the propertied classes.

Union of Officers. An organisation formed among the reactionary officers in the army to combat politically the growing power of the Army Committees.

Knights of St. George. The Cross of St. George was awarded for distinguished action in battle. Its holder automatically became a *"Knight of St. George."* The predominant influence in the organisation was that of the supporters of the military idea.

Peasants' Union. In 1905, the *Peasants' Union* was a revolutionary peasants' organisation. In 1917, however, it had become the political expression of the more prosperous peasants, to fight the growing power and revolutionary aims of the Soviets of Peasants' Deputies.

Chronology and Spelling

I have adopted in this book our Calendar throughout, instead of the former Russian Calendar, which was thirteen days earlier.

In the spelling of Russian names and words, I have made no attempt to follow any scientific rules for transliteration, but have tried to give the spelling which would lead the English-speaking reader to the simplest approximation of their pronunciation.

Sources

Much of the material in this book is from my own notes. I have also relied, however, upon a heterogeneous file of several hundred assorted Russian newspapers, covering almost every day of the time described, of files of the English paper, the *Russian Daily News,* and of the two French papers, *Journal de Russie* and *Entente.* But far more valuable than these is the *Bulletin de la Presse* issued daily by the French Information Bureau in Petrograd, which reports all important happenings, speeches and the comment of the Russian press. Of this I have an almost complete file from the spring of 1917 to the end of January, 1918.

Besides the foregoing, I have in my possession almost every proclamation, decree and announcement posted on the walls of Petrograd from the middle of September, 1917, to the end of January, 1918. Also the official publication of all Government decrees and orders, and the official Government publication of the secret treaties and other documents discovered in the Ministry of Foreign Affairs when the Bolsheviki took it over.

Made in the USA
Lexington, KY
22 August 2012